MW00773289

ADVANCE REVIEW OF THE UNSUSPECTED HEROES

A doorway into the sacred mysteries and magic of autism opens when one hears the call and steps into a new soul journey, hand in hand with us. For years, Alex has been deep in that journey with me, listening with her heart, and helping me to build my bridge of truth and move it out into the world. Out of our sacred journey together arises *The Unsuspected Heroes*.

I LOVE this book! Why? In this epic fairy tale, Alex reveals a true-to-life side of autism that few have ever been privileged to experience. Through Alex's genius as a master storyteller, readers will be able to hear and feel into "this side" within the comfort and safety of a make-believe experience.

They may even dare to wonder could this actually be true? Only when hearts open, can minds follow! On behalf of all my soul brothers and sisters, we thank you, Alex, for this gift to us, to your readers, and to the planet!

Lyrica Marquez
Nonspeaking Autistic Mystic
Co-Author of *Autism to Ascension* and *AWEtizm: A Hidden Key to Our Spiritual Magnificence*

Copyright © 2020 Alex Marcoux

All rights reserved. No part of this book may be reproduced or stored in a retrieval system, or transmitted in any form or by any means, mechanical, recording or otherwise, without the prior written permission of the copyright owner, except for the use of brief quotations in a book review.

To request permission, contact the publisher at jenness333@gmail.com.

Paperback: 978-1-7352611-3-3

Library of Congress Number: 2020912626

First paperback edition September 2020

Edited by Rae Bryant
Cover art, layout and copy edit by Smythtype Design

Printed in the USA.

616 Editions, an Imprint of Jenness Ltd.
P.O Box 620681
Littleton, CO 80162

A JOURNEY TO THE NEW EARTH

VOLUME 1

THE

UNSUSPECTED

HEROES

A VISIONARY FICTION NOVEL

ALEX MARCOUX

616 Editions

OTHER BOOKS BY ALEX MARCOUX

Novels
A Matter of Degrees
Back to Salem
Facades

Nonfiction
Lifesigns: Tapping the Power of Synchronicity, Serendipity and Miracles

Contributing Author
50 Great Writers You Should be Reading
Awakening and Applying Intuition and Psychic Ability

I dedicate this book to all autistics,
the selfless heroes doing the work,
whether knowingly or unknowingly.

CONTENTS

FROM THE AUTHOR

Dear Seeker of Truth,

Many years ago, two exceptional people came into my life, a mother-daughter team. The daughter has severe autism. She is nonspeaking, considered low functioning, severely impaired. At the same time, the mother has Asperger's syndrome, is high functioning, in many ways brilliant, yet considered to be on the low-end of the Autism Spectrum Disorder.

Shortly after we met, they introduced me to two other nonverbal autistics and their families. My friendship with all of them grew, and they permitted me into their world. Without getting into specifics, I learned how gifted these autists are and genuinely pondered if they are angels here to help humanity. Then I discovered that the autistics' parents are also extraordinary people, perhaps angels themselves. Within a couple of years, the autistics asked that I write their journey and share autism from a unique perspective, one that reflects many of their gifts and why they are here at this critical time in humanity's evolution.

We live in an unprecedented time: a rise in the autism rates, an astrological rotation occurring every 26,000 years, and a shift in the collective consciousness. It is no coincidence that all of this is happening together, and *it is no coincidence that you are reading this.*

Within this novel, inspired by real events, I delve into the crystalline grid, the ascension, the New Earth, the Great White Brotherhood, the Anunnaki, Archangels, Ascended Masters, and much more. If you're not familiar with these terms and concepts, I encourage you to refer to my **biography** of the Ascended Masters and Archangels and the **glossary** in the back of this book. I have also published similar material on my website at https://alexmarcoux.com/ascension-glossary/.

I call my autistic friends "Autistic Avatars," and I've learned that much of what they share is mythology. Not that the myth is a lie because it isn't, it is a metaphor to convey profound concepts to explain things where no words exist to do so.

My life changed after meeting these people. I have spent years researching, experiencing, and learning. I approach this book series with the same spirit; there are many Truths in this tale thinly disguised as fiction.

Not all superheroes wear capes and have their stories told on the big screen. Some heroes wear masks to hide who they are. Lyrica Marquez, a nonspeaking autistic, writes, "WE agreed to sit in harsh suits of AUTISM until WE are freed to share our purpose for being here. Our suits of AUTISM are like Halloween masks."

It is time to remove the heroes' masks. I am honored to tell their tale and reveal why they are here. These heroes deserve our honor.

If you're up for a journey into a hidden world, and ready to learn the *truth about who you are*, and why you are here, I invite you into my world and the world of superheroes who are working selflessly behind the scenes to assist humanity in its spiritual evolution and to save the planet.

It is my wish that you awaken and remember because the world needs you.

With Love and Light,
Alex Marcoux

Inspired by Real Events

Prologue:
Project Last-Ditch Effort to Save Earth

Sometime in Earth's Near Future, and yet, Time Is an Illusion

One may think of it as twilight, that soft, glowing diffused light, but that is not quite right. It is the space between nothingness and Oneness, where it appears that there is nothing except the promise of the coming day or night. That is where the Ascended Masters and Archangels of the Cosmic Council meet to discuss the destruction of Earth in the early twenty-first century.

The Divine Father, Master Melchizedek, steps toward the center of the heavenly landscape. "We know the implications of the other failures. This disaster will impede the involved souls even further. It'll take many, many millennia for the soul scars to heal, if ever."

From the outside circle, Archangel Mikael emerges, bowing his head, his sword by his side. His enormous white wings now folded in defeat, and his voice low. "With Gaia gone, the universe is out of balance. Earth was the Divine Feminine. This entire universe and all of its parallel existences are on a course of self-destruction."

Archangel Metatron moves forward, sacred geometric patterns illuminating his being. He adds, "Yes, we have seen failures in thirteen parallel expressions of Earth already. All will go soon, and we are starting to see the collapse of Earth-616, the New Earth."

Her Grace, Lady Anna, steps forward with vibrant red robes fluttering out at her feet. She looks around, seeing silhouettes of the council members. "What are we going to do about it? Do we give up on this universe and these souls? This was their chance to ascend."

A Galactic Being of Light, a master from another universe, steps forward, "This is the fourth planetary destruction in this universe. Avyon, Avalon, Maldek, now Earth. These souls will not recover from this."

A female voice reverberates from the outside circle. "We can't fix this. Only humanity can." The others step back, permitting the Divine Feminine, Master Magdalene, space. She moves slowly from the crowd; a scent of roses lingers as she passes.

A multidimensional embodiment of Magdalene is Mother Gaia. Magdalene's every step is with pain, from echoes of losing Earth, and the failures in parallel worlds. Those near her form a ring around her. As she moves, they respond, as if an orbit pulled by Mother Gaia.

"Humanity will always destroy Earth until it awakens." Magdalene waves a hand, and a holographic map forms around and above the group.

The Light Beings respond by falling into a large full circle, eyeing the multidimensional schematic of the moment. One can see all in the moment as it's connected to every life, every timeline, every parallel existence, every aspect of themselves, including the Source, the most powerful Energy. In the moment, one connects to their Godself.

Standing in the center, Magdalene closes her eyes, pauses, and sets an intention. With a wave of her hand, the holographic map responds. Three specks light up in the projection, revealing a glimmer of hope.

Jesus, the Cosmic Christ, steps forward, his cascading robe illuminated with star systems. He studies the work of his beloved, Magdalene, and raises a finger toward one of the three specks. As if he has a lasso, he harnesses one bit and hurls it above their heads. Holographic cinematic images stream various tweaks to the timeline, revealing possibilities to averting Earth's destruction.

Similarly, Jesus facilitates the second and third simulation of changes to the timeline. It is the third recreation that piques the Cosmic Council's interest.

Mother Ray, Mother Mary steps into the inner circle, a blue cape covering her robe. "This is it!" She points to the third simulation. "This is the one point in time, and one parallel reality that offers the most opportunity to correct the course of history and avert Earth's destruction."

There is immediate consensus among the Masters, the inner and outer rings. One Mind. They will plant seeds throughout history. Some of them will embody and walk among humanity before the great cataclysm and plant the seeds that will give humanity a chance to choose differently and save Earth.

The Gatekeeper steps from the outer circle and into the inner ring. This androgynous Light Being had watched the events with great interest, knowing that her time would come. It was her job to identify which Light Beings would return to Earth.

Much like an orchestral conductor, determining the proper balance of trombones to violins to bases, the Gatekeeper sets the intention to identify the precise vibrational patterns needed to achieve the desired results. She works swiftly, using ritualistic hand gestures, though the real magic is in mind. She re-verifies the results, assuring that her feelings weren't impacting the information. After all, in one of her bodily incarnations, she had turned her back on *him*.

When confident, she speaks, "The Blue Ray vibrational pattern will be the inner circle. It will be the pebble that drops in the pond, reverberating concentric waves. The other teams will modulate the waves. This plan will only work, however, if Hakathriel joins us. The Dark and the Light must work together."

To the Gatekeeper, it seems only fitting that the Blue Ray Alliance is on the front line, the pebble in the pond, given that they were indirectly involved in the fall of Atlantis, humanity's fall in consciousness shortly after its creation. The team had been back to modulate these actions numerous times in ancient Egypt, ancient Greece, the time of Merlin, but the time humanity seems to remember the most, though not accurately, is the time of Jesus.

The Gatekeeper calls out the individual teams in her mind, and correspondingly, each squad takes its position, forming a series of large concentric rings that look much like a bullseye from above.

At the center of the group's configuration, is the Blue Ray Alliance, where the Gatekeeper looks at her colleagues. She knows this team very well. The last time they had all been together in a timeline, they were all Essenes. The Gatekeeper nods at Lady Anna, Mother Mary, Jesus, Magdalene, Archangel Mikael, and a Galactic Being.

"I told you that this would only work if Hakathriel joins us," the Gatekeeper says to the Blue Ray Alliance.

The team knows that working with Hakathriel, the fallen archangel would place the project in a bit of uncertainty. But they know it is the only way. Intuitively the group works together. Simultaneously they all back up, creating a larger circle with ample space at its center.

In an instant, the Gatekeeper telepathically summons Hakathriel from beyond the Cosmic Council. She knows he gets the message instantly and yet is not surprised by his delay. She waits, eyes closed with hand stretching upwards, knowing that he will not resist her invitation to talk.

She jolts backward from the sudden rush of air caused by Hakathriel's magnificent wings. Standing before her is the dark archangel, wings fully expanded, almost touching members of the inner circle.

Mikael responds spontaneously, his wings now enlarged, with his sword in hand, while the other members of the group stand by on alert.

Hakathriel looks around the circle at each of his adversaries. For thousands of years, these beings had been his opponent in the game, including his brother. He looks beyond the initial inner circle and sees the countless Light Beings.

Hakathriel's wings contract and he steps toward the Gatekeeper. "What is this all about?" his voice echoes.

"The future of Earth," the Gatekeeper says.

"It does not look very promising," he glares.

Magdalene steps closer to him. "We're resetting the timeline to save Gaia."

Jesus moves forward also. "We want to give humanity a chance to choose differently."

"You mean, not side with me?" Hakathriel asks with a smile on his face.

Lady Anna moves closer. "Your side's success ends with planetary collapse. This loop has to stop."

Mikael contracts his wings and sets down his sword. He approaches. "Let's give them a chance to ascend. Brother, without it, we both lose."

To Hakathriel, there may have been logic in that they'd both lose. Maybe it was time to end the match and take the game to a new level. He was tired of being viewed as Satan, Lucifer, and the Devil. He remembered when he was the hero in the game, not the villain. Humanity changed everything for him.

"The dark and the Light working together?" Hakathriel softens. "What do you have in mind?" he asks, though he knows because there is One Mind.

Chapter 1:
A Rocky Start

April 26, 1978

Rebecca Griffin sits in the waiting area of the doctor's office. She pulls her long brown hair away from her face and glances at her watch; it is 11:11 a.m. George is late. Married six years, and he still apologizes for his tardiness. The physician will call for Ami soon. Ami lies in the car carrier perched on the end table.

She is expressionless and stares at the ceiling with eyes wide open, appearing to look at nothing. She makes no sound.

Rebecca glances at her daughter's medical records stuffed into the two-inch file in her hands. The last eighteen months have been a blur.

They had dreams of building their family.

Rebecca glances at her tiny, eighteen-month-old child with big brown eyes and wavy brown hair. She picks up the baby carrier and places it on the chair beside her, positioning her daughter in such a way that her eyes gaze out. As expected, without expression, the child diverts her gaze.

"What are you thinking, little one? What do you see?" she whispers. She reaches for the little arm and gently strokes it. The child gives no acknowledgment. Still.

The door opens, and George rushes in.

"Sorry I'm late. My meeting ran long." He leans over and kisses his wife lightly on her lips. Then he turns to their child. "How's my little girl this morning?" He waits for some response, and when there is none, he parks on the other side of the carrier, sandwiching Ami between them.

"Which doctor is this?" he asks.

"Hawkins."

"What does he specialize in?"

"Cerebral palsy."

"Do you think that's what's wrong with her?"

"That's why we're here, for a second opinion." She pauses. "I'd like to think there's nothing wrong with her, and she's perfect the way she is."

"We're past that, Rebecca. Perhaps we need to start exploring whether it's genetic. We *are* planning for two."

She shakes her head. "I can't think about having another child without understanding Ami and getting her the help she needs."

Another door opens, and a nurse emerges. She smiles at Rebecca and George and leans over the carrier. "Is this Ami? The doctor is ready to see her."

Dr. Hawkins silently reviews Ami's file in his office, while Rebecca and George sit across from him at his desk. He doesn't say much, from time to time, looks at Ami, who is in the bulky car seat on top of his desk. At some point, he stands, picks up the carrier, and explains that he is taking Ami to the examination room to evaluate her. "Why don't you remain here, this shouldn't take too long."

"Can't we come along?" She asks.

"I'd prefer not. I'd like to see how your daughter responds to the separation."

To George and Rebecca, it feels like their daughter is gone forever. When they finally return, the doctor places the infant carrier on top of his desk and watches the parents reunite with their child. While Ami shows no reaction to seeing her parents, Rebecca lights up, smiling at her child.

"Doctor, do you think it's CP?" George asks.

"Likely. While Ami doesn't seem to be a *classic* case, she indeed appears to be more symptomatic than not. If I were a gambling man, I'd bet it was spastic cerebral palsy.

"CP affects Ami's ability to control her muscles, which explain her stiffness and the occasional fluttering. She may or may not ever walk. She may be destined for a wheelchair.

"We don't know how much of her brain is impacted. Let me ask you, Mrs. Griffin, in the medical file it suggests that you had a healthy pregnancy and delivery. Is that accurate?"

"Yes."

"No accidents or illnesses while you were pregnant?"

Rebecca shakes her head, "No."

"No complications in childbirth?"

"No. It was a textbook pregnancy and delivery."

"Any trauma or infections when Ami was a newborn?"

"No," Rebecca answers, looking at George, and he nods. "Except she had jaundice when she was a couple-days-old."

"Ami is still young for a CP diagnosis. But I think you may need to brace yourself for the probability that it *is* cerebral palsy combined with mental retardation. This will not get any easier," Dr. Hawkins says, a bit detached.

"Meaning?" Rebecca asks.

"Meaning...the decisions you make about Ami's care will impact not only her life but also *your* lives."

"We understand that," Rebecca says, glancing at George.

"As harsh as this may sound, you may want to consider institutionalizing Ami."

"Are you serious?" Rebecca stares at the doctor in disbelief. "Ami is our daughter. We aren't going to institutionalize her!"

"Mrs. Griffin, do you have any idea of the difficulty it will be to keep her safe? You'll need to modify your home for special needs, which will be expensive and burdensome. It will impact your life and your family."

"Ami *is* our family." She glances at George, who is looking at the floor. "Ami is only eighteen-months old. Maybe the medical community has given up on her," she squeaks out the words, "I *never* will."

Outside the Children's Hospital, the couple is silent. They migrate toward the parking lot.

George, carrying Ami in the car seat, spots Rebecca's Pinto and walks toward it. Rebecca keys the passenger-side door and opens it. It is a mild April, in the sixties, the car is warm from the sun. George secures the infant carrier to the passenger seat then rolls down the window. Rebecca opens the window on the driver's side to cool the car.

"Do you have time for lunch before heading back to work?"

"I really shouldn't. I have a full afternoon of appointments." He avoids eye contact. He is a tall man at 6'2", and many would describe him as attractive and charismatic with deep brown eyes and a dark mustache. His mother was Latina.

"We really should talk about this...about Ami."

"What's to talk about?"

"Am I shortsighted to think we can do this?"

"I don't know. I just know that since Ami's come along, we haven't had a life. We're almost thirty, Rebecca. That's not old! When was the last time we had friends visit? Or went on a vacation? Or simply went on a bike ride or hike?"

"Are you serious?"

"Forget I said anything."

"No! You can't put the toothpaste back in the tube. Tell me what's on your mind. You've been so distant lately."

"I've had a lot of pressure at work. That's all. But how do we know Ami should be with us? She has needs that we haven't even figured out, and how are we going to pay for all this?"

"Is *that* what this is about, the money?"

"The expenses are pretty staggering!"

"Money is the least of our worries, George." Rebecca points toward Ami in the car, "That's our daughter. We're not abandoning her. We love her. We'll figure out what help is available." She walks around the car to meet him. At 5'9", she is tall and slim, fit from carrying Ami and choosing to walk most everywhere since she hadn't been able to hike since Ami's birth. "We can do this, George. I'll figure it out. I promise."

A sudden gust of wind blows Rebecca's long hair in her face.

George pushes the hair away so he can see her eyes.

"I will figure everything out," she says. "I'll learn to navigate the system and understand what we can get to pay for these expenditures. I'll manage our expenses better. I promise."

He pulls her to him.

In the safety of his arms, she affirms, "No institution will ever give Ami the love she needs."

Minutes later, Rebecca is behind the wheel, and George is gone, off to sell a copier or two. Ami is beside her. As usual, the toddler stares at seemingly nothing.

What Rebecca does not see is the scaled-down archangel perched on top of the dashboard. She is blind to the sacred geometry in the ethers, and the being's pink and green aura.

Metatron's voice is deep. "Ami, you got this!"

Ami stares at him.

Rebecca starts the car and is ready to back up when she sniffs. "Gosh, Ami, do you smell the chilis?" Certainly not expecting her to answer, she looks in the backseat. Nothing is there.

Metatron smiles. Rebecca senses him.

Chapter 2:
A Glimmer of Hope

September 23, 1980

One in 5000 children has autism.

Today is like every other day; it is four o'clock, and Rebecca is at the Sewall Child Development Center to pick up Ami from school. Every day she watches the other children reunite with their parents. The children, once eyeing their loved ones, would light up. Big smiles and shouts of excitement would ensue. Those who could do so would run to their parents. Others, on crutches or leg braces, would eagerly plod toward their mother or father and throw themselves into their arms.

Day after day, Rebecca hopes that Ami acknowledges her in some small way. Today, she walks into the classroom, and the remaining children glance at the door, hoping to see their parents.

"Ami, it's your mother!" One of the kids eagerly calls out.

Ami is in her wheelchair in the corner of the room. She makes no effort to look at her mother. One of the staff approaches. "Ami had a little incident with lunch." Rebecca sees sauce splattered over Ami's shirt.

"Looks like spaghetti to me!" Rebecca smiles.

"Yes. Ami didn't care for it," the attendant says.

Rebecca approaches Ami. She reaches to embrace her, but Ami's back stiffens with her contact, and she screams. Rebecca patiently lets go of her daughter. Every day she'd tell Ami the same thing, hoping and trusting that one day she'd respond with less disdain.

"Mommy is so happy to see you, Ami. I missed you today! I love you."

Then, ceremoniously, she rises and wheels Ami out of the classroom, with tears streaming down her cheeks. Today is like every other day until she passes the office on the way out.

"Mrs. Griffin?"

Rebecca wipes the tears from her eyes, collects herself, and turns to greet the principal coming toward her. "Mrs. Jacobs, how are you?"

"Busy as usual," she says with a slight smile. "I was wondering if Ami had ever seen Dr. Remington over at Children's Hospital. He seems to be one of the area's leading experts in children's special needs."

"Yes, Scott Remington?"

"That's him."

"He has evaluated Ami, and we have our follow-up visit this Thursday."

"Excellent. I hope the doctor can help. I've heard good things about him from other programs in the area. Gotta run," Mrs. Jacobs says, then ducks into a nearby class.

It had become a full-time job for Rebecca over the years to manage Ami's care. It never seemed to end, between coordinating doctor's appointments, researching programs, filling out applications, writing letters. That was her job, and she took it seriously, while George sold photocopiers, and was quite good at it.

The entire experience of caring for Ami was an inward journey for Rebecca. Their lives had been going to plan until Ami was born, then all their dreams came to a screeching halt. There were times when she missed being a science teacher, her colleagues, and friends. Rebecca missed the dinners, the gatherings, the weekend getaways. When she heard that their friends had planned the annual ski trip without even mentioning it to her and George, she spiraled into depression, self-pity, and anger. She crumbled. Ami was such a mystery to them and the medical community. Like hitting a lightbulb switch, though, a squeal from her daughter would bring her back.

It wasn't the financial burden that haunted Rebecca; it was the loneliness, even though she wasn't alone. She was Ami's full-time caregiver, but there was no communication between them. Ami never showed any sign that she knew or appreciated what she did for her. It was as if Ami had an impenetrable protective barrier, and no matter what she said or did, Ami never acknowledged her. She might as well have been a piece of furniture. The only time Ami responded to her was one that brought her to tears.

★★★

It was like every day. Rebecca was in the kitchen preparing their lunches, and Ami in her wheelchair by the table. "What do you want to do today, dear one?"

Rebecca dressed the table setting in front of her daughter, who stared at the ceiling. She moved into Ami's line of sight, and her daughter looked away. She began humming the tune she had sung to Ami since she was an infant, then followed with singing. "Twinkle, twinkle, little star. How I wonder what you are. Up above the world so high. Like a diamond in the sky." She hummed.

'Certainly one day, Ami will remember the melody with fondness.'

That day, however, Ami didn't even register her voice. When Jordan, their cat, sauntered into the room, intrigued by what Rebecca set on the table, the calico tested her patience. Jordan jumped on the table, and she was there to swiftly sweep her away, but not without lightly brushing against Ami.

It was her daughter's scream that threw her off. How

could it be that the only response she got from her daughter, ever, was screeching out of pain?

That realization brought the tears, and they didn't stop for some time.

★★★

Later that week, Rebecca is sitting across the desk from Dr. Remington. A glance around his spacious office boasts degrees from universities, including the University of Colorado School of Medicine.

She is not exactly sure what to expect from this doctor who had come highly recommended by Ami's primary physician three months earlier. It took *way* too much time to get in to see him. The initial meeting was simply a handshake, and Rebecca hopes today's meeting is worth the two months' wait.

"Well, it's so sweet to see you today, Mrs. Griffin," the physician says. "Mr. Griffin was unable to make it?"

"Nice to see you too, Dr. Remington—"

"Scott, you can call me Dr. Scott."

"Certainly, please call me Rebecca, and George is traveling, so he can't make it today."

"And I see Ami is doing well!" He says, looking directly at her.

As usual, Ami acts as if he isn't in the room.

"How are you feeling today, Ami?" He moves to a chair beside her wheelchair. "Don't you think it's time to start walking?" He moves so that he is in Ami's line of vision, and she diverts her eyes quickly.

"Walking?" Rebecca asks with more hope than she prefers.

"I don't think Ami has CP," Dr. Scott says unexpectedly. He turns to Rebecca. "Have you heard of autism?"

"Autism? No, can't say I have."

"Autism is a bit of a mystery," he says, still observing Ami.

"And you think Ami has it?" Rebecca retrieves a small pad and pen from her purse and begins writing. "How do you spell it?"

"A–U–T–I–S–M."

"I don't know anything about autism."

"It's a developmental disorder that impairs a person's ability to communicate. It impacts the nervous system. Unfortunately, it's chronic, it's manageable, though, and there are some treatments."

Rebecca feels her heart skip a beat. "Are you telling me that she will improve with treatment?"

"With treatment, her symptoms can be *managed*."

"You mean, we may be able to communicate with each other?"

"There aren't many treatments, Rebecca. Autism is not common, so there hasn't been as much research as other disorders. CP, for example, affects one in every 325 children, but only one in every 5000 kids has autism.

"What are the treatments?"

"Unfortunately, the treatments sound barbaric. Institutionalized children have received electroconvulsive therapy, behavioral therapy using punishment, and even LSD."

"Are you serious?"

"Regrettably, yes, the treatments are indeed archaic, but things may be changing a bit. There's some discussion that the next Diagnostic and Statistical Manual will include autism. That will encourage the research community to seek more treatments. Until then, there are some communication tools, cue cards that may prove helpful. But first, I think we need to do some physical therapy to help Ami walk and be more mobile."

"You think she can?"

"Yes, I do." Dr. Scott pulls a paper from his desk. "I have a list of books that may be helpful to understand autism."

Referring to some paperwork, "Also, I see that Ami attends the Sewell school?"

"Yes."

"How is it going there?"

"I'm not sure what to say. It feels like a daycare center."

He hands Rebecca a large envelope. "I believe when the school knows what they are dealing with, things will improve. Lastly, I want Ami to be evaluated by our Physical Therapy Department so we can put together a program to get her mobile."

Rebecca leaves her appointment feeling something she hasn't felt in years. She can't put her finger on it, and then it hits her, 'It's hope.' She excitedly brings Ami to her class at the school, but before she leaves, she goes to the principal's office, and the door is open. She knocks gently, announcing herself.

"Come on in," Mrs. Jacobs says.

Rebecca can't hold back, "Ami and I met with Dr. Scott this morning."

"Dr. Scott?"

Rebecca smiles. "Dr. Scott Remington."

"Oh, and how did it go?"

"He thinks Ami has autism. I'm heading out to the library now to pick up some books on it. Are you familiar with it?"

"I can't say I've had anyone in my school that was autistic, but I am aware that some schools have used picture cards for communication. That is encouraging. I'll talk to Ms. Stephens about introducing cards in the classroom."

"Thank you.

When George returns from his business trip to Connecticut later that week, Rebecca greets him at the backdoor of their Denver Park Hill home. She hugs him. "I have encouraging news about Ami."

George sets down his briefcase, eyeing Ami in the nearby wheelchair. He also sees a stack of books on the kitchen table.

"What is it?"

"Ami had her follow up with Dr. Scott Remington today. He doesn't think Ami has CP. He thinks it's autism."

After a welcomed discussion about Ami, George is grinning from ear to ear. "This is excellent news. He thinks she'll even be able to walk?"

"Yes! PT begins next week."

"Wow! What a switch." Excitedly he pulls Rebecca to him, and they kiss. "I know this gives us some hope for Ami. Do you think we can consider having another child? Ami is now four."

Rebecca knows that was their initial dream. They wanted at least two children, two years apart; then, she would return to teaching when both children were in school.

'How can I think of having another child, when there's so much uncertainty with Ami?' Rebecca ponders. She knew so little about autism, and apparently, the medical community was also ignorant of it.

Rebecca looks over at her daughter, who is now drooling on her shirt. She moves to her, and with the bandana tied loosely around Ami's neck, she gently wipes the dribble from her face and clothing.

But, Rebecca can't imagine taking her energy away from her daughter at this point. "I don't think it'd be fair to Ami. We may be able to communicate with her! Don't you believe that we should devote our energy to her?"

She sees the disappointment in her husband's eyes. How can she explain that she's Ami's advocate? She needs to be her daughter's voice. After four years of being in the darkness, there appears to be a glimmer of hope.

"George, let's see how she responds to physical therapy and school. Then we can revisit this."

CHAPTER 3:
CARE FOR MILK OR JUICE?

February 25, 1984

George is on his knees on the hardwood floors of the spare bedroom directly across from Ami's bedroom. There are large corrugated boxes scattered around the small room, and as he opens each and removes the content, he becomes more excited. "This is going to be an excellent opportunity for us," he shouts to Rebecca, who is with Ami in the kitchen.

He knows she can hear him, as the two main-floor bedrooms feed into the dining room, which is next to the kitchen. "It means that rather than going to the office to schedule my appointments on Mondays, I can do it here, from home!" He picks up a clunky monitor and sets it on a desk.

"That's great, George!" She calls out from the kitchen.

"It's all part of a study the company is conducting on telecommuting. The only thing is, I need to do my reports. No more secretary."

Rebecca doesn't sound so sincere, "Poor baby," she smiles and winks at Ami, who is sitting at the kitchen table.

"This machine costs $4,000! It's an IBM personal computer." George places the keyboard and mouse in front of the monitor. "It has two gigabytes of storage and includes 256 kB of RAM." He then feeds the cords behind the furniture and connects them to the PC beneath the desk.

When he's satisfied that everything is correct, he begins tidying the area. He combines a couple of cartons and picks up another in the dining room. With the boxes in hand, he goes into the kitchen where Rebecca prepares lunch, and Ami sits at the table playing with her favorite saltshaker.

"And," he continues as he approaches the back door to dispose of the trash, "we get to write off the expense of a home office!"

"Daddy is very excited," she says to Ami.

Ami gets up from the table and waddles slowly to the back window. She turns and shuffles to the dining room entry, where the floor changes from tile to hardwood. Here, she turns around and walks back to the window, bumping into one of the chairs.

Her walking improved over the years, although her gait was unusual. She was unsteady on her feet, and at times, she walked on her toes. She would repeat her footpath, sometimes for an hour.

George comes back inside, "Hello princess," he says as he squeezes by Ami to return to his new office. Here he picks up another load.

"I almost have lunch ready."

"I'll grab something later!" he says as he passes through the kitchen with more boxes.

"You will not. We need to demonstrate consistent meal patterns for Ami. Please sit with us for at least fifteen minutes."

Ami is a very picky eater and objects to specific colors, smells, textures, and temperatures. There seems to be no rhyme or reason for what she likes, and meals had become a dreaded time to him.

"Okay!" He complies. "Do you have a minute to see the office?"

She stirs the contents of a pot on the stove, lowers the temperature, and turns, "Sure."

George leads Rebecca out of the kitchen, and she notices that Ami is following them. Rebecca slows at the threshold to the dining room, where the floor transitions from tile to hardwood. She knows Ami will struggle here and waits for her. When Ami reaches her, she takes her daughter's forearm and leads her around the dining table, then into an alcove where she lets go, and Ami follows George into the small room.

The spare bedroom is no longer a guestroom. There is a desk, file cabinet, and futon.

"Isn't it cool?" George says as he approaches the computer. He pushes a button and waits for it to turn on.

To Rebecca, it looks clunky. Having a computer in their home is unusual. "You know how to work this thing?"

"The company is arranging classes for the program's participants. I know how to turn it on and get past the DOS prompt."

"The what?"

"DOS is the operating system." At that moment, the computer monitor comes alive with a black screen and white letters ending with $C:\_$. He tries to impress his wife, types something, and the display changes colors, and moments later, a white screen appears. "This is a new word processing program called Microsoft Word."

A clicking noise comes from Ami's throat. She had seemed disinterested in what they were doing until the monitor displays colors. Now she approaches looking at the screen.

"Want to see the computer, Ami?" George asks. He guides her to the machine. With his index finger, he presses the keys.

"It's like a word processor?" Rebecca asks.

"Yes, but much more powerful. Have you used a word processor before?"

"Of course! All the time, when I was a teacher."

"Maybe you can teach me a thing or two," he suggests.

"You know, it would be beneficial for writing my correspondences about Ami with it. That way, I don't have to type all the letters from the beginning each time."

"I don't see any reason why you couldn't do that," he offers. "The printer should be in next week. Let me get trained on it, and I'll teach you."

Moments later, the family is in the kitchen, and Ami sits at the table, moving her fingers in front of her eyes. She seems intrigued by the motion of her hands dangling and fixated on the repetitive movements of her fingers.

Rebecca brings a large picture card to the table and sets it by Ami. There is a grid with images of different food and beverages on the cardstock.

"What would you like to drink?" she asks Ami. "Milk or juice?" She gestures toward the card and repeats the question while pointing to the corresponding pictures. "Milk or Juice?"

Ami's hands awkwardly try to aim at an image, but she points to a picture of pizza instead.

Rebecca takes Ami's right forearm to steady it. Patiently, she asks again. "Milk or Juice?"

This time, while Rebecca stabilizes Ami's arm, she points to a picture of juice.

George watches amusingly. "We don't have much juice left. There's plenty of milk, though."

Rebecca goes to the fridge and removes a bottle of orange juice and empties it into a glass. "But she wants juice."

"Rebecca, you guided her hand to the picture."

"I did not! I keep telling you this," she says a bit miffed. "When are you going to listen to me? I don't guide her. I provide resistance. I've been trying to show you this for a week now. Do you think you can get over your bad self and just listen to me for a moment?"

"You have my attention," he says.

Rebecca positions herself beside Ami, who seems disinterested in what her parents are discussing. "Ami, Mommy wants to show Daddy that you understand the cards—and that

I am not guiding you." She places another card beside Ami. "Can you tell me what you want for dessert?"

Ami's hand moves uncontrollably and clumsily slams down on the visual cue card.

Rebecca places her left hand on Ami's right shoulder. "I see that you want something, for sure," she says calmly to Ami while looking at George. "I take Ami's arm in my hand," she explains, "I can feel her movements now, and I'm not holding her back or guiding her. I am just feeling her motion. Much of her movement is spastic and seems to have no intention. That's the only way I can explain it. So, I feel her natural movements that seem uncontrollable."

"Kind of like monitoring?" He asks.

"I guess so. Then, I pose a question and *feel* a difference in Ami's motions, but if I allow her strength to move without providing resistance, she will lunge uncontrollably. It's as if her motor skills are off, and there's only one speed, fast. So, I slow her hand down by applying ever so slight resistance, *not guidance.*"

Rebecca asks, "What do you want for dessert?"

Immediately, Rebecca feels the forward motion of Ami's hand. She applies slight resistance against the forward movement, which changes Ami's hand from oscillating back and forth to an intentional calm and pointing motion. Ami's index finger moves to an image of pudding.

George watches amused, yet still in disbelief. "Repeat that, without looking, and you'll have my attention."

"Why are you such a doubting Thomas?" Rebecca places her left hand back on Ami's shoulder and retakes her arm. She looks at Ami. "Sweetheart, can you point to the pudding again?"

Ami doesn't make a move. George waits, impatiently.

Rebecca realizes that she had not asked the right question. Of course, Ami can point to the pudding. Still looking at Ami, she says, "What would you like for dessert?"

Rebecca stares at her husband. She senses a movement of Ami's arm and provides slight resistance, resulting in Ami pointing at the pudding while she facilitates blindly.

"My God!" George whispers. "She did it!" He says excitedly. "Why didn't you tell me?"

Rebecca faces her husband, "Are you kidding? I've been trying to tell you this for a week!"

"You know what this means?" he asks.

"What?"

"This is the first time we are communicating with her."

The parents look at Ami, who is babbling and repeating gibberish, nothing that makes any sense. As usual, Ami expresses no emotion nor interest in her parents.

Rebecca smiles at her daughter. Somehow, she feels they are on the precipice of something much bigger than communicating with picture cards. This journey with Ami had been a lesson in unconditional love. After Ami's diagnosis with autism, it hit her that her daughter was alone. It was her job to protect her, and something changed over the years. She went from feeling obligated to care for her, to loving to care for her. When it hit her that it didn't matter to her if Ami even knew she existed, she knew it was unconditional love.

Rebecca knew there was something inside Ami that ran deep, though she couldn't explain it. Most of the time, Ami wouldn't make eye contact with anyone, but from time-to-time, Rebecca had held the gaze of her child, and she saw something that she couldn't explain. While the doctors had ruled out the CP diagnosis four years earlier, they never eliminated the diagnosis of mental retardation. But, she sensed there was awareness. Could it be that Ami wasn't retarded, yet lived in a body that just didn't cooperate? Could it be that Ami was captive because her brain wasn't communicating with her body? Or, was Ami wired differently?

Those early years were the most challenging, yet she vowed, early on, to be an advocate for her daughter because Ami had no voice of her own.

George, on the other hand, has more challenges seeing hope for his daughter. He, of course, loves her, but he loathes the situation. George feels the weight of the world on his shoulders. Where his wife sees promise, he worries about making them comfortable. He knows his daughter will require assistance for the rest of her life and knows she will never live on her own. His deepest fear, though, is that Rebecca will not want more children.

Consequently, George had thrown himself into his work. He knew his outgoing personality, resilient nature, and tenacity was the perfect combination to excel at Xerox.

Now, as he sees his daughter's finger point at the picture of pudding, he must do whatever he can do to support her growth. 'But what? What can I do?'

"This is encouraging news," he says. "I have a couple of proposals to write." And, he retreats to his new office, where he sets out to help where he can, selling photocopiers.

Chapter 4:
My Journey Begins

Reflections

Ami

As I look at mom, clearly annoyed because dad has not been listening to her about the picture cards, I consider for a moment how difficult things have been for them since my arrival. I know things are going to get even bumpier. If they only knew that they chose this. Would it matter?

'I remember deciding to be here. It was my choice. I also remember before I was Ami, and the moment I chose to return,' Ami begins.

★★★

There is only light, peace, harmony, and balance. It is ideal. I am in that perfect place, a place of unconditional love and connection with Source, yes, God, that's what I mean by Source. It is a place I know as Oneness, where there is no duality, no separation between anything, including Source energy. It is a place where there is only love because that is what God is.

I call Source Energy "God," mostly because there is a bit of a translation issue here. I am speaking in simple terms so that you can understand me and understand the journey I am about to undertake. There is no translation for the higher-dimensional insights that I want to convey and the complexity of this Truth. How can I explain concepts that you have no language to describe? Keep it simple; less is more. That's my plan.

I know I need to go, and it is time. I cannot wait any longer. I have a great journey ahead of me, I don't want it to begin, but I must go, and today I start this passage.

★★★

That feeling and memory of being with Source, as Source, is still strong, and I hope it remains with me.

I want you to know that I love you. That's why I've incarnated because I love you, and I want to reveal how magnificent *you* are. I will, in time. My truth is that I chose to experience life with a condition called autism. It's my choice, no one else's. There is no one or nothing to blame.

While many don't see it, I am perfect the way I am, and I choose to wear my autism suit because it is my protection. Would you ever suspect autistics to be the catalyst to change the world?

Not everyone desires to have a favorable endgame for humanity. Some yearn for the end of days, and they cannot know what we will do. What better place to hide than in our autism suits? That's why we are here. I say *we* because I am not the only one, and there will be an increase in the autism rate in the years to come. While everyone will try to explain it, and even blame it on something, understand that there is a reason we are here. I'll share later, just know that our autism suits protect us from those who want to stop us.

For now, remember, I love you, every one of you. I see each of you as perfect, whole, and complete. Unfortunately, *you* don't see yourself this way, and because of that, you and your planet will face tremendous challenges in the days to come. I am here to show you that there is another way.

My mom and dad believe my journey is just beginning at eight years old, but my wisdom is beyond humanity's comprehension, and I am ageless.

Chapter 5:
"I Am Not Retarded..."

April 17, 1984

"I'll be right there, Mrs. Jacobs!" Rebecca tells the principal of Ami's school. She hangs up the phone, grabs her purse, and bolts out of the house, into her car and speeds toward Ami's school. It wasn't pick-up time, so parking is painless this time of day. She rolls into a spot in front of the school. Once in the building, she hurries to Ami's class.

She slips into the back of the classroom but doesn't see Ami. The teacher sounds out the letter B and writes it on the chalkboard. When Ms. Stevens turns around and spots Rebecca, she hands the session over to her assistant and approaches Rebecca.

"Mrs. Griffin, thank you for coming right away, but Ami isn't here, she's at the nurse's office."

"Yes, I figured. I just wanted to hear firsthand what happened."

"Oh, I understand!" Ms. Stevens says in almost a whisper. She leads Rebecca to her desk at the back of the class. "I'm not sure what happened, to be honest. We started working on the alphabet, and Ami was sitting at her desk, and all the students were tracing their letters when she just had a tantrum."

"What did she do?"

"She screamed and pushed her chalkboard off her desk. She wouldn't stop yelling. They were guttural sounds. They're a cry for attention, of course, but that wasn't what was so upsetting. She kept biting her hand."

"I haven't seen her, how bad is it? Did she break the skin?"

"Oh, yes, I don't think she needs stitches, but she was bleeding for sure."

"Well, I'm sorry for the commotion. I want to go see Ami now."

Moments later, Rebecca arrives at the nurse's office, where she finds Ami sitting in the waiting area. She is staring into space, seemingly intrigued by something, but there is nothing there. "Ami?" She goes to her daughter, sits beside her, and pulls at her left hand, where there is a large bandage.

"It's not as bad as the Band-Aid makes it look," says a voice from behind her.

Rebecca turns and sees a woman approach. She sits in a chair adjacent to Ami.

"I'm Mrs. Archuleta," the nurse introduces herself. "But, please, call me Betty."

"Nice to meet you, Betty. I'm Rebecca, Ami's mother. Is she okay?"

"She had a tantrum but seems to be alright now. When she bit herself, she did break the skin, it's not deep, though. I applied some antibiotic ointment. You should do the same. If it gets infected, check in with her doctor."

"Any ideas what could have caused the tantrum?"

"Your guess is as good as mine. Most of the time, we never know with these special ones. Does Ami have meltdowns regularly?"

"No, not too often. I think Ami gets frustrated with herself at times. That's when she acts out."

"How about the biting?"

"This is a new one for me."

"Well, it's not uncommon for autistic children to bite or hit themselves. We just need to keep them safe."

"Of course. Don't you think it would be helpful to pinpoint what upset her?"

"Absolutely! I just don't see that happening, unless, of course, she decides to speak. Without that, it's like putting a puzzle together; only the pieces don't fit." She smiles kindly, "How has she been sleeping?"

"Not good. Ami always has difficulty falling asleep, and then she gets up early and turns on the lights. We seem to have coped with this, but she doesn't get a lot of quality sleep. It isn't any different than usual, though, she's always been like that."

"Yes, that's pretty common with autistic kids. Any mealtime issues?"

"Oh, yes! She's always been a picky eater and gets upset if I give her anything new. I've learned to introduce new foods gradually."

"Good, how do you do that?"

"When I cook something that she's never seen before, I never put it on her plate. I just place it on the table. The next time I make it, I may put it near her on the table, and the third time I may place a small amount on her dish."

"That's an excellent approach. Any food sensitivities?"

"Yes. Ami has her fair share of GI issues. We've been working with her pediatrician to figure out her allergies. What seems to work for her is scrambled eggs with sausage, meatballs, roasted chicken, and steamed vegetables, nothing from a can, of course! When she deviates from her diet, she always seems to get a bellyache."

"I have a theory on these peculiar children," Betty says. "Are you interested in hearing it?"

"Of course."

"I think these kids are special in ways we don't understand. When I see these autistic's parents, I often find that they are amazing people, too. Patient, kind, they are pure angels themselves. I believe that the autistics choose their parents and likewise, their parents pick the situation too. Perhaps these are life lessons."

"Well, that's an interesting way of looking at it," Rebecca says. She wasn't exactly sure why, but she wants to share more with this stranger, maybe because she longs for an adult conversation. She and George hardly talk anymore, mostly because he is always traveling.

"I blamed myself for Ami's autism forever. I kept wondering if I caused it," Rebecca looks at her daughter, who is now busy with a ball in her hand. She is rolling it back and forth. She marvels that Ami rarely drops it. "I've learned humility for sure! I was one of those people who believed that things like this happen to other people, never me," she laughs.

Becky smiles kindly and listens.

"Today, I can't imagine Ami any other way. I'm no longer ashamed. I know I'm stronger for the experience. I am so grateful to her; she has taught me patience and so many other things, like being able to give love without receiving it in return," she chokes back the words.

"I can well imagine," Betty says.

"Well, I'm sure I've taken up enough of your time," she turns to Ami, "Ready to go home, sweetheart?" Without expectation, she offers Ami, her hand. While Ami has never reached back, it had become recognized as a gesture to leave.

As expected, Ami stands. "Thank you, Betty, I appreciate the kind words."

The mother and daughter turn and exit the school.

Later that evening, Rebecca notices that Ami is more agitated than usual. She paces in the front room for nearly an hour. Then Ami walks from their family room through the dining room ending in the office near George's desk. She knows it is unusual that Ami walks without assistance on the dining room hardwood floor.

She follows her into the office, where Ami stops by the desk. Her daughter begins hitting the desktop, near the keyboard.

"Ami, what's wrong?"

Ami strikes the desktop, even harder.

"Sweetheart, I don't want you to hurt yourself."

Ami pauses as if she is responding to her request.

"Help me understand what you want." With that, Ami begins slamming the desktop again.

"Do you want me to turn on the computer?"

Ami stops.

'Could it be?' she wonders.

Rebecca goes to the desk and turns on the PC. It takes a few minutes for the monitor to reveal the DOS prompt, but during that time, Ami stands calmly beside her. Rebecca had become familiar with the computer since she had been using it to correspond regarding Ami's condition. She quickly starts the Word program.

"Your teacher was discussing the alphabet in class today," Rebecca begins. "That was when you got upset. Wasn't it? Do you want to learn it on the computer?"

Ami nears the keyboard and raises her hand. With a stiff pointed index finger, she repeatedly slams the keyboard, displaying nothing but nonsense on the monitor.

She guides Ami's hand away from the keys, and with all the gentleness yet firmness she can muster up, she says, "I am thrilled you want to play with the computer, Ami. It is very fragile—"

Ami strikes out again on the keyboard, and Rebecca takes her hand.

"You know the way we use the picture cards?"

Ami stops.

"I help you control your strength," she smiles. "Do you want to try that here?"

Ami does not respond.

"I can teach you the A B Cs." Rebecca stands and positions her daughter in front of the keyboard. She then takes her index finger and strikes a key, while simultaneously sounding out the letter and pointing to it on the monitor. "Here is "A," "B," and "C," she says.

"Do you want to try it with me?"

A shriek of excitement escapes from Ami's lips. Her hands are flailing.

As if working with the picture boards, Rebecca rests her left hand on Ami's right shoulder then takes Ami's right forearm with her right hand. "Want to try A-B-C?"

With that, Rebecca feels an intentional surge as Ami tries to rapidly type, again, revealing only nonsense on the screen.

"You're too fast for me!" She laughs. Rebecca deletes the text displayed on the monitor and starts with a blank screen. "Can we go slowly?"

Again, she takes Ami's forearm. "Try to type the letters as I say them."

"Type A."

With that, Rebecca feels Ami's hand moves to the left side of the keyboard and hover over the A. She types A.

"That's incredible!" Rebecca encourages her.

Without missing a beat, Ami goes to the center and strikes B and immediately follows with a C."

Rebecca did not tell Ami what to type, but she must have remembered the sequence. In awe of what is happening, she glances at the monitor where she sees letter after letter appearing on the monitor, "D E F G H I J K L M N O—"

"You know the alphabet?" She mutters.

With that, Ami points her finger at the keyboard, and Rebecca supports her hand, as Ami types.

Rebecca voices each letter as Ami types. "I, spacebar, A, M, spacebar, N, O, T, spacebar, R, E, T, A, R, D, E, D, period, I, spacebar, A, M." The rest of Ami's message is a blur to her as emotion overcomes her. Tears well in her eyes, clouding her vision. She feels her daughter continuing typing, but she closes her eyes and prays, 'God, please don't let this be a dream.'

When Ami stops typing, Rebecca opens her eyes and brushes away the tears. She looks at the monitor. It says, "I am not retarded. I am intelligent."

CHAPTER 6:
I'M DIFFERENT TOO!

October 20, 1984

Elisha (AKA Levi)

My name is Elisha, but that name doesn't feel right. I'm sixteen years old. Most kids my age talk about their new CD player, blast their boomboxes, sport their stone-washed jeans, or chat about Michael Jackson's hair catching fire during that Pepsi commercial. Someone assassinated Gandhi, and doctors finally figured out why those gay men are dying from the AIDS virus, and you'd think my friends would be interested. Hardly.

I know I'm different than most. I can't explain how, but I just feel it.

There was this one time when I was three or four years old. We were at a family gathering, and I looked around the yard and watched my parents, brothers, grandparents, aunts, uncles, and cousins. Oddly, an overwhelming sadness over-came me. It was one of my earliest memories, indeed. Tears filled my eyes, and I found myself retreating to an area of my uncle's yard where I was alone and fell into uncontrollable sobs as I watched everyone from afar.

I knew at that moment that one day, all *this* would come to an end.

You may wonder what I mean by *this.*

I meant life, and at the time, I thought of life as *my* movie. It was all my creation. I knew that when my life was over, everything would come to an end. Everything would stop. I knew that all life was playing out, like a movie, for *my* benefit. I was so sad. I wanted to change it. I wanted to give everyone a chance to continue to live, but I didn't know how to do so, and this left me in deep sorrow.

Did I believe that the world was an illusion, and all life was playing out for me? Did I think that when I died, it'd all come to a screaming halt? I have no idea. I have never been able to shake that memory, though, at the time, it all felt so real to me.

Then there was that time in the fourth grade when I was with my friends at St. Anne's. Three friends and I were hanging out at the church after school. The church was old and drafty, with tall cathedral ceilings. We were by the statue of Mother Mary in the front of the north transept. One by one, all three of my friends moved toward the Virgin Mary behind me. I'm not sure what got their attention, but they all stared at the statue with eyes wide open and mouths ajar.

I turned around toward the figure. The holy Mother stood tall with arms open, adorning a bluish robe. It all looked the way it always had, from her sacred heart to the snake by her feet. I didn't understand what my friends found interesting. No one else was around.

From behind me, I heard startled gasps escape my friends' lips, and when I turned, I saw them all backing away from me, and then one by one, they each turned and hightailed it out of the church, screaming at the top of their lungs.

I didn't know what to do. Nothing seemed wrong. I ran after my friends until I was outside of the church, where the three of them huddled. Tears ran down their faces.

"What happened?" I asked them.

One of them looked at me and said. "What are you, blind?"

"What do you mean?" I asked.

"Didn't you see all that light?" another asked.

I hadn't seen any light. I didn't understand why the three saw something while I hadn't. Somehow, I felt *less than* my friends because I missed what they had seen.

That was about six years ago.

Tonight, it's a fall evening, and my friends are all hanging out at the pier, drinking, I'm sure, and I am walking peacefully under the stars. The street lamps are few and far between in my parents' neighborhood, so I always find that peaceful place away from the lights, and that's when I get a better glimpse of the stars. I locate the North Star and quickly note the different constellations. That's when I feel the most centered.

I feel a bit lost. I'm not entirely clear about anything in life. I mean, I am fortunate for sure. I love my family, which is dysfunctional as just about any other family, but they are my family. I don't think I'm like my brothers. I do pretty well in school, though I haven't figured out what I am to be when I grow up. When I was younger, I wanted to be an astronaut; I'd look up at the sky and imagine what it was like to journey to distant worlds and meet other civilizations. I often wonder if Sally Ride, the first American woman in space, last year, had similar thoughts when she was young. Is it just me who wants to learn how other aliens handle the threats we currently face? Like hunger, our environment, the arms race, nuclear threats, or disease? How about religion and philosophy? We sure seem to have made a mess of things. Don't you think?

I mentioned my desire to explore other extraterrestrial civilizations to my friends after we watched *ET* a couple of years ago. I became the laughingstock of the party. They all believed we were alone in this galaxy and all the many galaxies out there. How can that be? It's 1984, how can we be so ignorant?

I go to church because my parents expect it. They are Catholic, but, I mean, are you serious? They think God is some bearded guy in the sky who sits in judgment of us! They believe that when we die we go to heaven, hell, or a way station called purgatory! All I know is that when I ask questions of the nuns or the priests, they don't answer them and look at me as if I'm the anti-Christ. My poor parents, I guess I have given them some different lessons over the years. While my brothers engaged with alcohol, marijuana, and violence, my parents had some interesting conversations with Mother Superior when I challenged authority, questioned the interpretation of the Bible, and debated the meaning of the Holy Spirit. Then I wore my blue corduroy pants to school that, in *their* opinion, looked too much like jeans.

That was last year. I had words with the principal, Sister Clara, and remember it like yesterday. I was rushing to my next class, minding my own business when I entered the stairwell and heard Sister Clara's voice from behind me.

★★★

"Elisha! You know we have a strict dress code, and there are no jeans permitted, only navy blue *dress* pants."

I looked at my new pants. They were navy blue corduroy slacks. Certainly, dressier than *my* jeans, though admittedly, maybe I was pushing it.

"You have a chip on your shoulder," the nun continued, "A complete disregard for rules and authority. You don't seem happy here."

"You're right," I agreed. I knew my parents were spending a lot of money to send me to my mother's alma mater, which was forty minutes by bus from home. I lost all my friends from middle school and felt like a fish out of water there. "I'm not happy," I admitted to her in the stairwell. Other students walked around us as we talked on the landing.

"Follow me," the sister ordered. The nun climbed the stairs, and when she reached the next floor, we exited into the hallway. The hall was almost empty as most of the students had made it to their classes.

I glanced at my watch. I had, maybe, a minute before I was late for my class. 'If I'm going to get a tardy slip,' I thought, 'I'm going to make sure it's worth it!'

I took a deep breath and said, "I ask questions, but get no answers. You tell me that I'm not a good Catholic because I must accept your doctrine on blind faith. Maybe I'm not a good Catholic, but I'm a good person. I'm kind, I'm generous, and I'm honest. Isn't that what matters?"

"St. Thomas says, 'Obedience unites us so closely to God that in a way transforms us into Him so that we have no other will but His. If obedience is lacking, even prayer cannot be pleasing to God.'"

I couldn't resist. "Albert Einstein said, 'It is a miracle that curiosity survives formal education.' I can quote people too!"

Sister Clara's eyes clouded, and her lips pressed together, amplifying the creases around her mouth. She had been a smoker. "Detention for a week," she said.

"What? All this because you don't like my pants?"

"No, because I don't like your mouth."

"You know that detention will not punish *me*; it *will* be a hardship for my parents, though. If I don't make the city bus, my mom will need to get off work to come get me."

"That is not my problem," the nun turned and stormed away.

I went home that day and told my mom that I wasn't going back. She never asked why or said anything. The next morning, she took me to the local high school and enrolled me. I often wondered if she ever heard from Sister Clara.

I had a couple of years left of high school and needed to

figure out what I should study, where I wanted to go to college, and where to live after I graduated. No one in my family had been to college. I knew I must do it, not sure why. Maybe it was just a logical step in life. Perhaps it was my ticket to move away. It didn't feel like I belonged there. Don't get me wrong. I love my family, but I felt alone there. I didn't think I felt like them. Then again, I wondered, 'How is it that I know how they feel?'

★★★

I know I have been sheltered in life, living only in Founders, which is a small town about an hour outside of San Francisco in the Central Valley. Perhaps when I leave the nest, things will become more apparent about what I should do. In the interim, I just keep doing what I'm doing. I blend in. I don't make waves anymore. I'll wait until I can get out in the world and find people that feel like I do.

CHAPTER 7:
"NEED MORE TEACHING."

Rebecca is mystified. For eight years, there was no communication with Ami, and suddenly there is a conduit into her thoughts. She is confused and very emotional. Her daughter is not mentally disabled, perhaps physically, but not mentally challenged. For an hour, Ami types with Rebecca's assistance.

Rebecca, not knowing when to stop, "Ami, I could talk with you forever!"

Ami yawns broadly. She is tired, and her hands are now flapping in the air.

It hits Rebecca, "It's time to call it an evening."

Overjoyed with the events, Rebecca wants to call George and share the news. 'Where is he tonight?' She knows that he stays at different hotels most nights when traveling. He's the one who would call, and this was one night he didn't.

The following morning, Rebecca wakes, today she will show Ms. Stephens that Ami can communicate with them. Until then, she powers up the computer then returns to Ami in the kitchen. Her face is in a bowl of oatmeal.

"Would you like to talk before we go to school?"

Ami looks up, with cereal on her chin she rises from the table and walks toward the dining room. She hesitates at the threshold, as she does every day. Rebecca is there to ease her through the doorway. Once Ami passes, she makes her way to the computer.

Rebecca positions herself to chat with her daughter. "I can't tell you how meaningful this is to me. To be able to talk to you is so important to me. Sweetheart, why did you bite yourself yesterday?"

"I angry," she types.

"What are you mad at?"

"Me. People. World."

"You're angry at yourself, people, and the world?"

"Yes."

"Why?"

"Wasting gifts."

"Are you saying we're wasting a gift? And that's what is making you angry?

"Yes. And angry can't reach."

"You're mad that you can't reach what? Communicating with people?"

"YES."

Rebecca notices the capped letters. Could it be that she was trying to stress this? "What gift are we wasting?"

"Life."

This conversation is not what Rebecca expected, but after so much silence, any communication is perfect.

Rebecca and Ami enter the classroom. Ms. Stephens is talking to another parent. She patiently waits until she sees an opening and then eagerly jumps into a conversation with her. "Ami had a breakthrough last night! I'd love to share it with you and Mrs. Jacobs."

Within minutes, the teacher's assistant is given instructions from Ms. Stephens, and Rebecca, Ami, and Ms. Stephens make their way to the principal's office.

Rebecca explains to Mrs. Jacobs, "I need a computer or word processor for a demonstration."

Moments later, Ami is typing with Rebecca's assistance at the secretary's computer in the reception area. Both Mrs. Jacobs and Ms. Stephens watch a bit skeptically. It is Ms. Stephens, who points out, "Mrs. Griffin, it looks like you are guiding Ami."

"Not necessarily guiding her, Ms. Stephens. I *am* providing a small amount of resistance to her, though. It's very similar to the way I have been communicating using the picture cards."

The principal reads the passage Ami had typed aloud, "Here to learn more." She pauses. "It is a bit unbelievable that she comprehends how to put words together," Mrs. Jacobs points out.

"We haven't covered putting words together and sentence structure yet," says Ms. Stephens.

Ami points downward with a finger.

"This is new. I think Ami wants to say something." Rebecca takes her arm.

"Need more teaching."

"What does that mean?" Ms. Stephens asks.

Ami points and Rebecca assists her in typing out her next message.

"Too easy."

"Ami, are you saying the curriculum is too easy?" Rebecca asks.

"YES," she types.

"Well, Mrs. Griffin, of course, we'll have to explore this further," Mrs. Jacobs states. "I've never in my life seen a nonverbal autistic communicate with this type of assisted typing. I'm sure you can understand our skepticism here."

Rebecca is surprised. "Ah, no! I can't say I understand it at all! I thought you'd be thrilled to see her communicate."

"This will have to be verified by someone else typing with her," says Mrs. Jacobs.

"Who can do it? Who has the time?" Ms. Stephens asks. "We don't have enough time to devote to the students' classroom needs as it is."

"I'll work with Ami," a woman's voice comes from behind them.

The group turns to Mrs. Archuleta, the school nurse, in the doorway. Rebecca doesn't know how long she had been standing there.

"When will you have time to do this?" the principal asks.

"Are you serious? I'll make time. This method may be a breakthrough in communicating with a nonverbal. We not only owe it to Ami and her family, but we owe it to *all* nonverbal autistics." Betty approaches Ami. "Ami, would you like to work with me and show me how you talk?"

Ami points down.

"Why don't you begin right now?" Rebecca says, showing Betty how to hold Ami's forearm with her right hand. "I always put my other arm on her shoulder, like this." She places her left hand on Ami's shoulder.

Betty follows Rebecca's prompts. She feels Ami's fluctuating hand. "Remember, you provide resistance, and she will type."

At that moment, Betty senses Ami's motion. When she applies some opposition to Ami's movement, it becomes pinpointed and intentional, though slower. By placing less resistance to Ami, her responses are quicker; however, not as precise.

After a few minutes of practice, Ami types, "Yes, want help."

Betty laughs out loud. "Excellent!"

"Did you see that?" Ms. Stephens says.

"See what?" Rebecca asks.

"Ami didn't even look at the keyboard. How can she be communicating if she isn't watching what she is typing?"

"I noticed that too," Mrs. Jacobs says.

Ami lifts her index finger, and Betty moves back to the position.

Ami types, "I saw it once with eyes."

The women look at each other. They don't understand.

Rebecca asks for clarification, "We don't get it, Ami."

Knowing that Ami wants to say something else, Betty takes her arm, and the message that comes through is, "I see letters in mind."

"This is incredible!" Betty is excited.

While the teacher and principal do not share Betty's enthusiasm, Rebecca is comforted that Betty is on her side.

"I promise to work with Ami a few hours each week, and if that interferes with my work, I'll do it after hours."

CHAPTER 8:
REFUSAL OF THE CALL

Reflections

Ami

Where did I leave off? Oh, yes, I had decided to be here. It was not the most pleasant experience.

I remember it as if it was yesterday.

★★★

My peace and perfection come to a screeching halt as my awareness drifts from nirvana to the womb. I am in utero. My harmony is now gone; instead, there are recurring whooshing sounds, the absence of light which I hadn't been accustomed to and a soggy mess. There is darkness, and I am alone, though I know that is not the case.

I sense a presence, and amid the rhythmic whoosh, there is a voice. It is indeed foreign to me, though I know this is my mother, and another distant sound tells me my father is also close.

I don't know how long I have been this way, but I don't like it. My body is undeveloped. It will in time, except it can't grow correctly. I need to orchestrate the perfect storm, the conditions to create autism.

Over this thing you call time, I am increasingly more comforted by my mom's presence, her heart beating, her voice, I particularly like it when she plays something called music. Not all tunes, but much of it is comforting. My dad sometimes reads to me, and I can feel the pressure of his hand massaging my mom's belly. I hope one day I can tell him that I like his touch and his voice.

Time passes.

Time is strange to me, and I will explain it later.

One day there is pressure and panic. While I'm not thrilled about the next step in this journey, I know there is no way to avoid it. I have died many times, but birth is always more challenging and more fearful than death. Does that surprise you?

Mom's rhythmic heart thumps are louder and faster; there is pressure all around me, my head hurts; it feels crushed. I sense Mom's panic, her pain, and I want it to be over, but it goes on for what you call hours. With each passing minute, the intensity is more and more powerful. I hear a strange voice urging Mom to push, and the pain in my head gets worse before it gets better. Then, like floodgates opening, I rush through, and the pressure on my head is gone, and there is light. This light, though, is not the Light I am accustomed to. I close my eyes, shielding them, and hear wailing escape my mouth.

I am cleaned and swaddled, and everything that touches my skin feels like shards of glass. That light still hurts my eyes, so I keep them closed. The noise hurts my ears. There is so much noise I can't stand it. Innately, I turn inward and find what is familiar. Peace. I find stillness and know I will need this secret place to help me manage being human.

As the months go by, the inner journey becomes my life. It is easier for me to stay inside, in my different dimensional home, than it is to be present in my poorly formed body. I call this place Homeland and remain there in peace and harmony and sense my closeness to Source.

While I know my parents tend to my needs as a baby, I

ignore those moments when they cheer me on to meet certain developmental milestones. I can't hold up my head well, can't roll over, and cannot take my first steps when I should. So, in my parent's eyes, I fail. In my doctor's eyes, I fail. According to the system's standards, I fail.

It is easier for me to escape to my Homeland, where I remain for many years because it hurts too much to process life in my autism suit.

How can I explain this better?

When most of you were born, you fully embodied into your physical body. Me? At best, I am 30 percent in this physical body.

Where does the rest of me reside?

I live in the higher realms, with the angels, archangels, and higher Light Beings. It is easier for me there.

When I was about three years old, my doctor forced me to look into his eyes. All I saw, felt, and knew, was his experiences. I saw his troubled relationship with his parents and his addiction to alcohol. I felt his pain and sobs when he lost his wife to cancer and watched her casket lower into the ground. There was so much agony. I avoid people's gazes because when my eyes meet another's, I experience their life, and some are full of trauma, pain, and hatred.

I can look into the eyes, from the side, though. There's safety there, as that way, I don't perceive your heaviness. You may feel my gaze from time to time when you're not looking because I do care for you.

You wonder why I have my ears covered at times. Everything is energy and vibrates at a frequency. *Everything*! Even atoms that consist of rapidly moving particles called electrons create vibration and noise. Everything vibrates, and I hear it all. If you had any idea what my ears hear, you might be gentler with me.

When I was four, I couldn't handle the noise. If you were there, you'd remember my tantrum. Covering my ears, I screamed at the top of my lungs, and all eyes were on me in horror. I'm not sure what set me off. Perhaps the refrigerator's groan, the TV motor buzzing (even though it was off), the siren blaring in the distance, or the voices of all those people at my birthday party. It may have been the blood pumping through my heart. Does it matter?

The noise is why I tap the table. It distracts me from the other sounds. I like my earphones and listen to my music because it helps drown out those other noises. Most of the time, I prefer that television has no sound. There is one sound I especially love, though, I love the sound of drums!

There are good and bad food choices too. The crunch of a hard cookie may throw me over the edge, that's why I choose ice cream or pudding. I can't explain texture or smell right now because thinking about it makes me sick!

Let me tell you what I see, too. I guarantee you; it is nothing like what you observe. I perceive the energy and the movement of atoms, even electrons. Everything is composed of energy, some very dense, and some wispy. What I discern with my eyes is the differences in particles. I see everything at once, rarely one thing at a time. I have trouble moving from one place to another when the materials and textures around me change because of the energy changes, and I see it. While this will ease in time, I rely on Mom and Dad to help me through some doorways, like the one in our dining room.

I like watching my fingers dancing in front of me because I see the light particles moving around. It is so fascinating. I love rolling something in my hand for similar reasons. My favorite thing is a ball, but an empty bottle works well too. I enjoy watching the light dancing and moving around it as I roll it in my hand.

There are times I get so angry with myself. I want to do

things, but my poorly wired body just doesn't cooperate. It makes me mad. Those are the times that Mom may find me chewing on my hand or hitting myself. The pain calms me, because I remember, of course, that I chose this. I opted to be here at this point with autism.

The truth is, without autism, I wouldn't be able to do what I have come here to accomplish. I am here to achieve a grand purpose. Do you believe me? I see the way you look at me. I sense your pity. I see you turn the other way and avoid my family and me when I approach. If someone told you I was intelligent, would you believe it, or would you laugh?

So, I stay incognito, in the body of someone who one day will have an IQ of twenty-three. That's our suit of armor, no one will suspect that we autists will gather, bond, and organize as a human force field to do *our thing*.

My life will not be easy, but don't feel sorry for me; it is the path that I chose and the path of many others that are coming. Like every person born, we each have a mission, a purpose, a reason for coming here. My aim, while grand, is no more important than your own.

What if I told you that significant changes are coming to the planet and that I and others will work behind the scenes to help humankind find other ways to get around these challenges? I know what I am supposed to do. It is hard, though.

It is easier for me to stay in my Homeland, where I feel my connection to Source, rather than be here. When I am there, I forget why I have come to the planet, and since it is so much more comfortable there, I regress. I stay in my Homeland and forget who I am, why I'm here, and what I am supposed to do until Mom wakes me up.

How? Mom looks at me in a way that tells me she loves me the way I am. That look shows me that no matter how much I ignore her, how much I lash out at her, how much she thinks I hate her, that she loves me unconditionally. In that moment of realization, I see in Mom, that Divine flicker of Light, and I realize it's a reflection of *me.* That's what lights me up. That's what lights up *all* autistics. And once we light up, watch out world!

I bet you wonder if all autistic people have a Divine purpose.

Yes, we do. The autists will help whether they know it or not. But their lives will be so much more enjoyable, purposeful, and meaningful if they remember how important they are. It is my wish, hope, and prayer that all autistics are loved by their family or caregiver to awaken to their magnificence because humanity needs our help!

★★★

The assisted typing method that everyone seems to be treading cautiously about will be introduced in the United States soon. It began in Denmark, where it failed to test scientifically, but Australia is using it today with more and more acceptance. It is called facilitated communication, and one day it will be dubbed FC.

I like Mrs. Archuleta. She was kind to me when I was sent to her office last week. She spoke to me like I was intelligent. That rarely happens. She spent a lot of time talking with Mom, explaining that she thinks we autistics are unique people here for a particular purpose. She is right.

So, I'm thrilled she watches as I type with Mom in front of Ms. Stephens and Mrs. Jacobs. When she offers to help with my assisted typing, my heart leaps with joy. I want to reach out and hug her. It takes all my control to point my index finger down.

"Why don't you begin right now?" Mom tells Betty Archuleta. She shows her how to hold my forearm and gently rests her other hand on my right shoulder.

I sense her excitement, and Mrs. Archuleta has good energy. I feel it.

"Remember, you provide resistance, and she will type," Mom instructs.

'Yes, yeah, yeah! I want to work with someone to help me communicate. I need someone with a kind heart and no tragic stories that can pull my energy spiraling down,' I think. What I type is, "Yes, want help."

Betty laughs out loud. "Excellent!"

"Did you see that?" Ms. Stephens says.

"See what?" Mom asks.

"Ami didn't even look at the keyboard. How can she be communicating if she isn't watching what she is typing?"

"I noticed that too," Mrs. Jacobs says.

I lift my finger again, and Betty resumes her position.

How can I explain that once I've seen the keyboard, I see it in my head? That I don't need to look at it, and if I do, I prefer to look at it sideways?

Betty takes my hand, and I type, "I saw it once with eyes."

The women look around at each other perplexed.

Mom says, "We don't understand, Ami."

As if reading my mind, Betty takes my arm and waits for me to type again.

I wonder if they can handle the truth. 'Probably not, given that there are no words in this world to explain the way I know where the keys are without looking at them.'

I type, "I see letters in mind."

CHAPTER 9:
"IT WILL BE A LONG BATTLE."

April 20, 1984

Rebecca can't wait. It is finally Friday, and George is returning home soon. At the sink, she rinses romaine lettuce and vegetables for their dinner salad.

It had been a long week. Rebecca had wanted to share the excitement of Ami's breakthrough, and her high hopes for their daughter's future the night of the discovery. When he called the following night, it hit her that it'd be challenging to explain what happened without demonstrating, so she didn't tell him. She'd wait and see his excitement firsthand.

Rebecca slices a cucumber. "We're having pizza tonight!" She says to Ami, who sits at the table, wiggling her fingers in front of her. "Daddy should be home any minute."

Ami rises and waddles to the kitchen window overlooking the back alley.

"Looking for Daddy?"

Ami gazes out the window and begins to hum a low, steady, monotonous tone.

This humming is new for her. Rebecca goes to the window. "Are you trying to say something, Ami?" At that moment, Rebecca follows her gaze and sees George's car come from the back alleyway and pull into the detached garage.

Moments later, George opens the back door carrying his briefcase and suitcase. Ami dawdles near him.

He sets down the luggage and approaches Ami, and gently and carefully kisses the top of her head, wary not to touch other parts of her body. He had learned the hard way when, years earlier, he hugged her, and she lashed out with a tantrum.

After his peck on her head, Ami presses into George gently, surprising him. He glances at Rebecca then lightly rests one of his hands against his daughter's back. This gesture is as big of a hug he has ever received from her.

Rebecca approaches smiling and kisses him. "We've had a breakthrough this week."

"I can see that," he says.

The pizza arrives, and the family sits down to dinner. Rebecca can't wait to share about Ami's typing but is enjoying the subtle changes she sees in her. Could it be that Ami is more still than usual and even listening to what George is saying?

George rambles on about his workweek, "We're burying Kodak's photocopiers. They can't compete. After all, the industry calls it xeroxing, not kodaking." He laughs and realizes that he's monopolized the dinner conversation.

At the end of their dinner, George looks at Ami then back to Rebecca, "You said Ami had a breakthrough this week. Are you going to share?"

'I thought you'd never ask,' Rebecca thinks. "Yes, of course! To do this, though, I need to use your computer."

"My computer?"

"Yes. You don't mind, do you?"

Rebecca doesn't give him a chance to object. She's on her feet and makes her way to the office. Ami follows, and as she hesitates at the dining room entry, George takes her arm, permitting her to pass quickly.

The three wait for George's computer to boot up. George sees a notebook and empty glass near the keyboard. Signs that they had been in his office. "The computer *is* business property. It isn't a toy," he says a bit sternly.

"We know that," Rebecca says.

"What are you doing?"

"We want to show you something." When Microsoft Word loads, Ami approaches the computer.

"Remember our breakthrough with picture cards?" Rebecca asks.

"Of course, I do." How could he forget? It was the first time in eight years he saw his daughter communicate.

"That was the tip of the iceberg," Rebecca says. She takes Ami's hand, and Ami types a message to George.

"I missed Dad."

George is skeptical. As the principal and teacher had earlier in the week, he voiced his observations. "Rebecca, you're typing, not Ami. She's not even looking at the keyboard!"

Rebecca patiently walks through the process with him, and after a convincing performance, George utters under his breath. "My God! She's talking!"

Ding-dong, the doorbell sounds promptly at ten o'clock the next morning. Rebecca opens the front door, and Betty is on the front stoop, holding a large package.

"Come in, Betty," Rebecca permits her to enter their living room. "Any problems with the directions?"

"No, not at all. I'm on this side of Denver often. My sister has a house in Park Hill.

George enters, "Hi, I'm George, Ami's father," he shakes her hand. "I understand you've volunteered to work with Ami."

"Yes. Happy to do so."

"We are very grateful."

"Indeed, we are. I've set Ami up in the kitchen," Rebecca gestures toward the dining room.

Moments later, Betty sets her large box on the table. "Good morning, Miss Ami."

Ami glances at Betty and looks away.

"What do you have there?" Rebecca asks.

65

"I borrowed this from the school district. I was hoping we could see if this works for Ami," she says as she opens the box.

"What is it?"

"It's called a Canon Communicator," she removes it from the carton and sets it on the table. "It's a battery-operated portable keyboard and typically used by students with speech impediments. They've been around for about ten years." Betty demonstrates the device and explains that it has a built-in paper printout. "It's a bit more sensitive than the computer keyboard we've been working with, so, there may be a learning curve."

Within no time, Betty sets up the device and turns to Ami. "Want to take a spin?"

Ami moves away from the table and proceeds to flap her hands, turning in circles. One of her favorite pastimes.

Betty turns to Ami's parents, "That's my fault. I'm sorry." To Ami, "My apologies. I mean, would you like to try the new keyboard?"

Reluctantly, Ami stops and approaches the table. She sits where she usually does.

"Autistic people do not understand our idioms or our figurative speech," Betty says.

Rebecca ponders about the events of the past. "You're right! I hadn't thought about it before, but that makes perfect sense."

Betty and Ami settle in and soon type using the new device with George and Rebecca at the counter, awkwardly looking for something to do with themselves while watching.

Betty and Ami work for some time before stopping. Then, Betty tears the printout from the device and hands it to Rebecca. It reads,

```
    I  liike  the  other  keyboard
 beetter. Will adjust.
```

```
    Message for Mom and Dad. I love
you very much. Broken me can't show
you. Love that you love the broken
me besides. Please don't give up. It
will be a long battle, I will win.
That is why I have come. To win.
Love, Ami.
```

Tears well in Rebecca's eyes as she reads the teeny print. She wants to run to her daughter and sweep her in her arms, hug her, kiss her and squeeze her, but she knows better. Instead, she moves to her daughter and looks at her.

For the first time, ever, Ami holds her stare.

"I will never give up on you, Ami. If there is one thing I know for sure," tears roll down her cheeks, "I swear that I am here to be your voice until you can speak on your own." She wipes her face. "Then, I will listen to your words. I will *never* give up on you."

George also caught up in the emotion, nears the table. "We love you very much, Ami."

"I'm going to leave CC with you for the week," Betty says.

"CC?"

"That's what I've nicknamed her, CC, the Canon Communicator. Take it with you and see if it works. If you like it, they run about $400. I just thought it'd be fun to try it out before you make such an investment."

Rebecca looks at the printout in her hand. It is priceless.

Chapter 10:
Accepting the Call

Reflections

Ami

Maybe I haven't been entirely honest with you. I don't want to scare you, though.

There's this thing called time, and it doesn't exist. You believe that time is linear and two dimensional, that there is the past, present, and future. At your soul level, however, there is no such thing as time. Like me, you are a multidimensional being. The only difference, well, one of the differences is, I am consciously aware of this, and you are not. Not yet, anyway.

You have other incarnations, other lives, *at the same time.* You live in different dimensions *at the same time.* You, however, are only aware of this life, and you think that this life is real. Would I surprise you if I told you that your life is an illusion? Think of your life as a hologram, though that is not wholly correct, either.

From time to time, you may have a sense of a past life, even a parallel life, perhaps from dreams, maybe a vision, or you may hear things, feel things, see things, or just know things. You may be somewhere and experience déjà vu. You may think of it as a past life, but there is no past, only the now. There are other timelines, but they all happen now. It is also probable that you are tapping into one of your multidimensional lives.

I am getting off track here.

While my body has been on this planet for eight years, I

am—timeless? Ageless? What is the term? I have been around since before the beginning of your universe. I have resisted staying in my small autistic body as my consciousness has spent much of this life in other dimensions. One dimension, I have shared with you is *Homeland*. I prefer it there because there is only peace, joy, and love. There, I am with others, and we are One. Some may call them angels, light beings, guides, even animals. My point is that there I am in joy; here, I am in pain and have so much suffering.

I can't describe how uncomfortable and even painful my life is. I can't speak my truth, and I get angry. Anger does some unfortunate things to my body, and I am getting ulcers in my stomach and intestines. Eating is always a balance of sustenance and pain.

Then, I see the way people look at me. There's no judgment; after all, they don't know how painful life is for me. If they could walk my path for one day, I think they'd understand my sensitivities.

The hum of a refrigerator is piercing to my ears.

Contact on my skin can be electrocuting.

The odor of some foods is overpowering and makes me nauseous.

When I have sensory overload, I erupt, much like a volcano, and there is no stopping me. You call them tantrums, but they are releases.

So, I resist staying in my body and frequently retreat to my Homeland, and I don't communicate.

Not too long ago, I was at school, and my teacher seemed to have given up reaching me. It wasn't a good day for her, or me, so I went to my Homeland. There I wondered about my teacher, and because there is no time, I perceived what you call the future.

I was startled, and my body trembled in my chair as I witnessed devastation and destruction. I saw a societal collapse. I felt how sad Mother Earth was because of the way people have treated her. Then, I watched how Earth responds to her pain, with constant natural disasters, tornadoes, hurricanes, floods, and droughts. I saw the misuse of Ramsgate off-world technology by humans, creating earthquakes, landslides, fires, tsunamis, extreme cold and scorching weather. I even saw erupting volcanoes.

That wasn't the worst thing, though. I saw the way people treated each other: riots, guns, missiles, biological and chemical warfare, human-made viruses, and guerrilla warfare. I saw brothers killing sisters, children killing parents, it was horrifying. Then, I saw a series of nuclear detonations, and then nothing.

I had known that I have come here to help, to show there is another way, but I was in denial. I hadn't committed thoroughly to the mission. I had not woken to my calling. However, that harsh glimpse of where humankind is heading was my wake-up call! I now know there is not much time.

Like a repressed memory from past trauma, suddenly, it all came flooding back. I know that I must begin communicating. I must stay more in this uncomfortable place of the third dimension rather than escaping to those higher realms, with the angels. I know that while I am here, I must team up with others like me, my comrades. There is no turning back anymore. No matter how painful it is for me to be in my body, I must be here, I choose to be here, and I am here to help.

Why? Because I love you. You deserve another chance.

Chapter 11:
"Testing Only Serves the Ego."

May 6, 1985

The day Rebecca received her first transcript from CC, the Canon Communicator, she taped it to her mirror above her sink. Each morning, as she got ready for her day, she read it. Today is like every day.

Rebecca reads the transcript aloud, "Message for Mom and Dad. I love you very much. Broken me can't show you. Love that you love the broken me besides. Please don't give up. It will be a long battle, I will win. That is why I have come. To win. Love, Ami."

Life changed for all of them the day Ami shared her feelings on the Canon Communicator, but what changed for Rebecca wasn't tangible. She was more committed. For the first time in her life, she knew her purpose. Her purpose was to reach her daughter and be her daughter's voice. She had more energy, a drive she had never felt before. She also sensed that Ami was special. While every parent feels the same about their child, to Rebecca, it went deeper than that. When she looked into her daughter's eyes that day, and Ami held her stare, something within her shifted. They had connected on a level she didn't understand.

For George, he realized he needed to devote himself to Ami and abandon the idea of having other children, at least temporarily. Somehow, he knew that Ami's care was more important, and he was here to protect her. He would do so the only way he knew—by providing the income needed for Ami's help.

Rebecca had set up a time after dinner to type with Ami every night. The two would first chat about their day; then, the conversation usually morphed into unexpected subjects that always blew Rebecca away. She'd often wonder how Ami knew about world events. They rarely had the TV on in Ami's presence. She didn't understand how Ami knew topics not covered in school. How did a nine-year-old know algebra? Or chemistry?

Tonight, Rebecca is stunned by her conversation with Ami.

"Why don't you like Jell-O? Most kids love it!" Rebecca asks Ami after dinner.

Ami types, "Great green globs of greasy grimy gopher guts."

Rebecca laughs. She never knew her daughter to have a sense of humor. She wonders where she had picked up the playground song.

"Slimy," Ami types.

"Jell-O is slimy?"

"Yes."

"How was school today?"

"Need harder learning," Ami types.

"Your work isn't challenging enough?"

"Too EZ."

"Maybe we can ask Betty if she has any pull with the curriculum."

"New books in your bookcase?"

"My bookcase?"

Ami stands away from the kitchen table and moves toward the dining room. Rebecca follows with the Canon Communicator in hand. While Ami hesitates at the doorway, she pushes through and makes her way to a small bookcase in the living room.

Rebecca smiles. More and more, Ami can make it through the dining room entrance without assistance. She follows her to the bookshelf, which houses her books from college and some novels. "I'm sure these aren't interesting books for you. What kind would you like me to get?" She places CC on the coffee table near the bookcase.

"Studied chemistry and algebra."

Rebecca looks at the bookshelf and sees that her chemistry and algebra books are upside-down. "Are you saying you have studied these?" She points at the two.

She types "Y."

"You typed Y. Is that for yes?"

"Yes."

"Cool, we're developing shorthand?"

"Y."

Rebecca pulls her algebra book out and opens it. 'Surely, Ami couldn't comprehend college-level algebra,' she thinks. "If you studied this, would you be willing to take a test?"

"Y."

"How many chapters did you look at?"

"All."

"All? Let's go back to the kitchen table."

Ten minutes later, Rebecca has the algebra book open to a sample quiz at the end of a session in the middle of the book. She wonders how her daughter could work through any of the problems without using paper and a pencil to "show the work."

Without asking Ami a thing, her daughter looks at the textbook and points down.

Rebecca facilitates her typing but hasn't a clue what Ami is doing. She stops typing. The CC printout shows,

$$"(a^b)c$$
$$y = ax - b$$

9
$-4 < b < 4$
$(1 + i) (1 - i)$"

"What is this?"

"Answers."

Rebecca looks at the problems, and it has been years since she studied the material. She opens the back of the book to see the answers to the five-question quiz.

"They're correct!" Rebecca says in disbelief. 'But how can that be?' She wonders.

She asks, "Ami, would you take the test at the back of the book? The final?"

Twenty minutes later, Rebecca reviews the answers Ami had typed. "You got an 85!" She says a bit incredulous. 'How can this be?' She takes the textbook back to the bookshelf and retrieves her college chemistry book.

"Up for another test?" Rebecca tests Ami, and she scores 88 percent on the final chemistry exam.

Ami types, "Need harder learning."

A week later, Betty, Rebecca, and Ami are in the kitchen at the table. Canon Communicator printed transcripts lay on top of the table with glasses sitting on top of them to prevent the paper from curling. The five texts have scores ranging from 81 to 92 percent.

"Let me get this straight," Betty points to a stack of five college textbooks. "Are you saying that Ami studied these and took the test in the back of the book? And these are her results?"

"Yes!"

"Algebra, chemistry, biology, social studies, history?"

"Exactly!"

"Ami, what was your least favorite subject?"

Rebecca puts CC in front of Ami and helps her type.

"History."

"How come?

"It is HIS-story. Not the truth. Here to write HER-story."

Betty laughs out loud, "His-story? I love it. I have to say this is amazing!" She has another thought, "I'm not getting a lot of support from the school on Ami's assisted typing. Everyone believes we're guiding her. What if Ami studies a topic that the typing assistant doesn't know, and then Ami is tested?"

"Kind of like a blind test?"

"Yes. Only let's do it in front of an audience, so we clearly show that Ami is intelligent. I think she may be what the French call an idiot savant. What do you think, Ami?"

Ami grunts and points down, and Rebecca assists her typing.

"Testing would be for ego. No test."

"You don't want to be tested, Ami?"

"Not important what others think NOW."

Rebecca knows Ami's perspective is a mature way of looking at it. She wonders if it is her ego that had created the desire to test Ami in the first place. "You want to learn more, right? What if you give me the subjects you're interested in learning, Ami, and I'll look for new books and put them in our small library?"

Ami stares off into space, smacks her lips together with arms and hands fluttering.

"Ami, are you okay?" Rebecca, a bit alarmed, "This isn't the first time this has happened."

Ami continues to stare into space, lip-smacking getting louder. Her long dark hair falls on her face, and saliva dribbles from her mouth. While it is only, perhaps, fifteen seconds, it feels like minutes to Rebecca before Ami comes back. Her arms stop flailing, her lips part, and she looks at Rebecca.

"Are you okay, sweetheart?"

Ami sits quietly, looking around the room for some time before she lifts her hand. Rebecca takes her arm to the keyboard, and Ami types, "Controller botch up."

A couple of days later, Rebecca and Ami sit with Ami's neurologist. The doctor reviews her EEG and MRI results. "Ami is experiencing petit mal seizures or what you may have heard as absence seizures. They're common for children with autism. Hopefully, it's temporary." He pulls out a pad of paper and jots down something illegible. "Let's try a low dose of anti-seizure medication." He hands Rebecca the script.

CHAPTER 12:
ELISHA DOESN'T FEEL RIGHT.

1988

Elisha (AKA Levi)

Iinitially thought that after I left Founders and arrived at UCSB, I'd have a chance to chat with others about their experiences and find people who felt like me. I just wanted a place to fit in.

After I arrived, I started going to parties and did the club thing; I even scored a fake ID at one point. I have to say that initially, there was something fun about having a drink or two and feeling a little more comfortable about meeting others.

I met a guy named Mike, who I dated a little more than a semester. We ended our relationship a while ago. I think sex complicates matters, now every time I see him on campus, he ignores me. I don't get that, once you care for someone, how can you pretend it never happened?

One of the other things I noticed was that when I am in a large crowd, particularly in a club, I eventually get sick. Sometimes I get a headache, other times I feel anxious, often nauseous, and frequently I get a bellyache. It isn't just the clubs; it happened at the Thunderdome while I was at a basketball game, then at an outdoor concert at the Santa Barbara Bowl. So, I started experimenting and realized the common denominator was being around large groups of people. It got to the point that I didn't want to go to group functions anymore. Then when I heard that my favorite vocalist was going to perform at the Bowl, I became determined to figure it out.

★

I am at the Student Health Service building with a physician and his grad student, a woman perhaps four years or so older than I. I just finished explaining what had been going on. I say *explaining,* but it was more like rambling on and on, and I have to say I'm quite embarrassed even to be here.

"I just seem to get sick in different ways, whenever I'm around a lot of people," I summarize my symptoms.

"And you grew up in a small town, right?" Dr. Mike says.

"Relatively speaking," I say.

"I wish I could give you better news. I believe it's enochlophobia."

"Which is?"

"The fear of crowds." Now it's his turn. He's babbling on and says something about there is no "cure," something about modifying my diet, taking supplements, and considering hydrotherapy.

I am not exactly the best patient because my mind is all over the place. He can't be right, can he?

"I'm going to pull some information on this, and I'll have Lisa bring it to you in the lobby."

I gather that Lisa is the grad student who had been sitting quietly in the corner, and that is my cue to leave the examination room.

I wait in the lobby for about ten minutes. During this time, I keep thinking, 'The fear of crowds? That can't be right! Can it?'

I'm getting ready to leave when the grad student emerges with a stack of paper.

"Sorry, it took so long. There was a paper jam," Lisa smiles and hands me the material.

"Thank you," I say, not entirely sincere.

I turn to leave, and she follows me, she has her book bag with her, so I figure she is also going. When we get outside, she says from behind me, "It could be something else."

I turn.

"You don't believe that fear of crowds is the cause, do you?" she says.

I nod in agreement. "It doesn't feel right."

"Do you have time for a cup of tea or coffee?"

I glance at my watch. I have an hour before my next class. "Sure."

In no time, we make our way to a nearby coffee shop and find a bench outside.

"I could be wrong," Lisa begins, "but I think it may be something worth considering."

"What's that?" I sip my strong coffee.

"Have you ever heard of something called clairsentience?" She asks.

"No, can't say I have."

"Clairsentience is the psychic ability of clear-feeling. It's more commonly associated with gut feelings and sometimes empathy. How are your gut feelings?"

"I never really thought about it. There are times when I have hunches about some things. Or, I just know things for no reason."

"The knowing is intuition. Clairsentience is feeling energy. Everyone and everything consists of energy, and when you're around many people, that's a lot of energy. People with clairsentience have good hunches and are often empathic."

"Meaning?"

"They often tune into other people's emotions and physical feelings. In other words, if an empath is in a crowd and they tune into someone who is grieving, they may become incredibly sad and not understand why. On the other hand, if an empath encounters someone with a headache, they'll likely get a headache."

This description made more sense to me than the fear of

crowds. "Are you empathic?"

"I am a bit clairsentient," she admits. "I want you to know because without understanding what could be happening, it can lead to anxiety, depression, physical pain, and even addictive behaviors. Without understanding it, and shielding yourself in crowded situations, you can take on too much energy and feel things that aren't yours."

"I can see how that'd be confusing. How do I shield myself?"

"You build a protective cloak around you with your imagination."

"Are you serious?"

"Yes, very. When you wake up each morning, use your imagination to create a robe or cloak. Imagine putting the cloak on and pulling the hood up over your head. Then set the intention that this is your psychic protection."

"You imagine your protection?"

"Yes. You can also work with different colors. If you're going into a huge crowd, visualize the cloak as white or rose. If you're working on psychic skills, imagine it's purple. There are reasons for the different colors depending on your needs. Other people carry stones or gems or crystals."

I look down at the stack of papers on enochlophobia. "I guess there are no instructions for clairsentience in this," I smile.

Lisa smiles and glances at her watch. "I hate to cut this short, but I have a class I need to get to." She pulls out a scratch pad and jots down something. "We have a small group of like-minded students on campus; if you would like to meet others. Or if you have any questions," she hands me a piece of paper, "My number."

"Thank you. I appreciate that."

Lisa stares at me for a moment. "I have to say that I have a block with your name. I know you said it is Elisha, but it doesn't feel right."

"I know. My name has never felt right."

In the months to come, Lisa and I become friends, and she introduces me to a handful of others who feel a bit like me. They feel different, misunderstood, and want to fit in, and just don't get many of humankind's actions.

CHAPTER 13:
"HORSE FOOD HIT THE CAR."

March 13, 1990

Rebecca heads down the hallway to her classroom and glances at her watch. 1:11 p.m. She has nine minutes before the next period begins. She opens the door to her class. No one is there yet, a moment of quiet before the middle schoolers arrive.

At her desk, she sits and pulls her planner from the top drawer, and as she opens to the day, she notices the blinking light on the answering machine. It is Betty's voice, "Rebecca, if you can, stop by after school today. I'd like to share something with you." Betty rarely calls her at work, so she knows it must be important.

Rebecca had returned to teaching a couple of years earlier. Ami, now a teenager, had educated herself over the years with books that she had placed in their bookshelf. Rebecca never lost hope that Ami would one day move into a regular classroom to have the same opportunities as the other students. She and Betty had tried to get the school to accept Ami's assisted typing. Betty had encouraged her to file requests to have the typing method evaluated by an educator. In the end, though, they were met with resistance and rejection. Betty remains an advocate and assists her daughter with typing outside the class. Still, the school has not permitted supported typing for Ami's classwork, and she remains in special education.

Ami was the one who put it in perspective, "Is it more important that I be educated? Or is it important that I tell people I'm educated?"

82

Comments like these Ami had made over the years, made Rebecca realize that her daughter, in many ways, was becoming her teacher, not the other way around. Ami's responses always seem mature for her age and often were filled with wisdom and understanding.

Later that afternoon, Rebecca walks into Betty's office, and Betty smiles when she sees her, "I have some exciting news!"

"Great, what is it?"

Betty pulls out a document that looks like it was xeroxed a dozen times; its title is *"Crossley's Facilitated Communication."* She says, "You need to read this. I made you a copy."

"And..."

"They've been communicating with nonverbal autistics in Australia for years using the assisted typing that we use with Ami."

"What?" Rebecca is baffled.

"And it's made its way to the United States through an educator named Biklen, who studied Rosemary Crossley's work in Australia."

"What does this mean?"

"It means that Ami has been communicating with us for six years using a method that is being introduced in the United States *now*."

"How can that be?"

"That's not what's important. With it now in the US, there may be some support for what we've been doing."

"Do you think we can get her out of a special needs class? Or have her IQ re-tested with typing?" Rebecca is sick that Ami's latest IQ test placed her at twenty-three and labeled her with "severe mental retardation."

"It may take us a school year or two to make tracks. We should, at least, petition for reconsideration, and if that's unsuccessful, perhaps a complaint against the school system may move the process along," Betty replies.

Later in the evening, Ami and Rebecca are talking as they usually do. They had just finished dinner, and Rebecca set aside a plate for George, who would be in shortly.

"Betty learned something exciting today," Rebecca begins. "I know that getting a regular education has not been that important to you, but there may be a good reason to include typing with your schoolwork."

Ami does not register an emotion. She is indifferent.

"Don't you think it'd be fun to be able to go to school and make friends your age? Maybe go to a dance? Take regular tests? Perhaps even go to college?"

Ami points down, and Rebecca fetches her keyboard. She types, "I AM SORRY."

Rebecca knows that capital letters mean she is emphasizing something. "What are you sorry about, Ami?"

"If I knew how hard autism was for you, may not have caused."

Rebecca doesn't know how to respond. "Baby, are you suggesting that you *caused* your autism?"

"Y."

"How did you do that?"

"Starved me."

"You starved yourself? When?"

"In the womb."

"Why on earth would you do that?"

"To hide."

This comment confuses Rebecca, 'I must have missed something,' she wonders. "Why would you want to hide, Ami?"

"Avoid annihilation."

"Are you saying to protect yourself?"

"Here for an important role. Not everyone wants what we bring. Autism suit is a disguise."

"Who are *we*?"

"Autistics."

"What significant role do autistics serve?"

"Here to show the way."

"You're here to show the way to where?"

"To God."

"To God?" Rebecca has never spoken with Ami about God before. She hadn't thought about it, mostly because she considers herself agnostic. It's not that she doesn't believe in the possibility of God; she doesn't believe in religion.

"And some people don't want you to do this?" Rebecca asks.

"Autism is a perfect cloak."

"Are all autistics here with this role?"

"N."

"No?"

"No. Many tho. Many more coming soon."

"Many more with autism are going to be born?"

"Y." Ami has a distant look in her eyes. She stares into space.

"Ami?"

Ami is somewhere else. Rebecca has learned that it is best to let her daughter return without jarring her back. She waits.

"Dad is okay. He will be late," Ami types.

"What's going on?"

"Accident with the car. He's okay."

Rebecca is hesitant. "He's had a car accident?"

"Y."

"How do you know this?"

"Saw on my head TV."

"Head TV? You see the images in your head?"

"Y. Horse food hit the car."

Of course, Rebecca is alarmed. She doesn't understand the horse reference. "How long has this head TV been going on?"

"Always."

Rebecca looks at her daughter and wonders what else she has missed. 'Could Ami be delusional?' She wonders at that moment. 'Autistics are here to help people find God? They are hiding? From who or what? More are coming?'

At that moment, the phone rings. The last thing Rebecca wants is to leave the conversation, but she picks up the handset. "Hello."

"Rebecca, I've had an accident," George says. "I'm OK, though."

'How did she know?' Rebecca turns and stares at Ami. "What happened?" she asks George.

"I was on 25, heading back from the Springs, and I was behind a truck hauling hay bales. A deer ran in front of the semi; the driver swerved to avoid it. The next thing I knew, I had hay bales hitting the car."

"Oh, my God! Hay?"

"I know! Of all things."

Rebecca looks at Ami, she recalls her message, *"Horse food hit the car."*

"I'm calling from an officer's cell phone. A police car just happened to be behind me. I think the car is drivable, banged up for sure. I'm just waiting for the mess to get cleaned up and settle my nerves; then, I'll be on the road again."

"Okay, sweetheart. Thank you for calling. Please drive safely, and I love you."

"Love you too."

Rebecca hangs up. Ami isn't delusional—she is an enigma.

Chapter 14:
"I Am Not Human."

One in 2500 children has autism.

Rebecca is in the living room watching TV. She hears the backdoor open. It must be George. She powers off the television with the remote and heads into the dining room, where she detours to Ami's bedroom. She peeks in. Asleep. She closes the door and heads to the kitchen, where George has his head in the refrigerator.

He pulls a beer from the fridge.

Rebecca hugs him. "I wrapped a plate for you."

"Thanks. I grabbed something in Castle Rock." He gulps the beer.

"Are you okay?"

"Yeah, nerves are just a bit shot!"

"Take a seat," Rebecca begins. "I have some news."

She wastes no time and tells George about her meeting with Betty. "George, there *is* a supported typing method called facilitated communication. It's been used in Australia and has made its way to the United States."

"Get out of town!"

"I'm serious. But George, there's something else. Ami told me you had an accident *before* you called."

"What did she say?" he asks.

"She told me you got hit by *horse food*."

George pauses on this one. "She *predicted* it?"

"I don't think so. I believe Ami told me as it happened. How long did it take for you to call?"

"Oh, it was only a few minutes. I used the cop's brick cell

phone, who was traveling right behind me."

"I think she saw it as it happened."

"So, she's psychic?"

"Perhaps. Ami called it her mind TV. But that isn't what has me churning inside."

"What is it?"

Rebecca takes a deep breath and spits it out, "Ami said she's here to show the *way to God*. She also said she *caused* her autism to protect herself from annihilation."

"Annihilation?"

"She says that not everyone wants her to be successful. But she also said that more children with autism would 'come in,' Rebecca says.

"What does that mean?"

"It sounded as if she was saying that they were being born for this particular reason. And more autistics were going to be born."

George is thoughtful. "When first diagnosed with autism, what did the doctor say the rate was? Do you remember?"

Rebecca recalls, "Yes, in 1980, there was 1 in 5000 children born with autism."

George leaves the kitchen where they had been talking and returns with a file folder labeled, "The Autism Society." He opens the file and retrieves their latest newsletter. He searches the text and points at a number, "2500. It suggests here that five years ago in 1985 that one in 2500 kids is autistic.

"That was five years ago, and the rate doubled!" Rebecca is deep in thought.

"What are you thinking?"

Rebecca knows that George is an atheist. "George, where did Ami get her concept of God?"

"Certainly not from me."

Religion is a sensitive subject for Rebecca. As a preacher's kid or PK, she had a strict upbringing in the Baptist faith, raised under a magnifying glass, and lived under the scrutiny of her father and his congregation. As soon as she went off to college, she looked at life with eyes wide open, and shortly after, walked away from her faith. Deep down, she knew there is a higher power, though she did not believe it is the judgmental, patriarchal God depicted in the doctrine. She left the church and never looked back, creating a wedge between her parents and herself.

After meeting George, her relationship with her parents became even more strained when they learned that he was an atheist. Then, when Rebecca refused to get married in the church, she was given an ultimatum, George, or her family. She has remained estranged from them ever since.

'Where on Earth did Ami come up with her impressions of God?' Rebecca ponders. 'From school? Betty?' The following evening, after their dinner, Ami and Rebecca retire to their living room. The Canon Communicator is on the coffee table, and they sit side-by-side on the sofa.

"Ami, you mentioned last night that you were here to show the way to God," Rebecca begins. "Do you mean those with disabilities challenge us in ways that can create spiritual breakthroughs if we overcome them?" She retrieves the communication board.

Ami repeats her statement from the previous evening, "Here to show the way to God."

"What is God?"

"Love."

"God is *not* a higher power?"

"Y. Love."

Rebecca did not expect that. "Where did you learn about God?"

"Know God from the soul."

"At your soul level, you know of God?"

"N. Know God from the soul."

Rebecca doesn't understand the difference. "When did you learn about God?"

"There is no WHEN where I come from."

"How are you to show the way to God?"

"Need to be more in the body."

"What do you mean?"

"Need to be more human."

"You are human. Sweetheart, just because you have a disability doesn't make you any less human than me!"

"I am not human."

This comment scares Rebecca. She doesn't know what to ask. "If you are not human, what are you?

"Not fully here, but here to help save the world."

"And how are you going to do that?

"Show the way to God."

"If you don't succeed, what will happen?"

"End of days, with no one moving forward."

"The world will end?"

"Will end as we know it if I succeed or not."

"I don't understand. It's going to end, no matter what?"

"Y. In joy or destruction."

"Am I to help you succeed?"

"Y."

"How?"

"Find God inside."

This conversation is not making any sense to Rebecca. In her wildest imagination, she could never have conjured up a story like this even if she tried. Once again, she wonders if her daughter is delusional. 'Where could she have come up with this? Should I get her some help?' As she looks at her daughter, a cloud comes over Ami's deep brown eyes.

"You don't believe me."

'Can Ami read my mind?' It hadn't been the first time Ami had reverberated her thoughts. "Sweetheart, you're sharing some concepts I don't understand. I don't know *what* to think. Please don't be hurt."

Chapter 15:
There Are No Shortcuts in This Thing Called Life.

March 21, 1990

Elisha (AKA Levi)

It's a bit before 9:00 a.m., and I expect a call at ten o'clock from Mr. Samson from Oracle. It is a beautiful spring morning in Santa Barbara. I'm only five minutes from my favorite spot on campus, a peaceful hideaway I found my freshman year. I go there whenever I need to think, pray, or just be alone with nature. It's a quiet space sandwiched between the lagoon and the ocean and has an incredible view of the Pacific and some beautiful vegetation.

I interviewed with Oracle a couple of weeks ago. They have an opening at their Redwood facility, which by most standards, would be a desirable position to attain right out of school. I wish I could say that I always wanted to work for them, but the truth is, I just fell into it, much like how I came to UCSB and decided to study computer science. I was guided, for lack of a better word, by what I call the Universe.

I think it was the name *Oracle*, that initially drew me to the job posting at the student center. Standing there, as I started to read the post, I noticed more light coming from it than other postings. This occurrence of seeing objects glow happens to me occasionally. Whether a person, place, or thing, for some reason, some things hold more energy or light than other things. I rationalize that there is a reason it is happening, and sometimes I figure it out, and other times, not.

There were times over the years when I did not follow this energy, and as if it were fate, I got led back to that choice through coincidences or accidents. One time, after being guided back to something trying to get my attention, I still chose to go in another direction, and my world suddenly became chaotic. I came down with a cold, I got into an argument with a friend, someone stole my credit card, and I had an accident with my bicycle. Since then, I have learned without question; when I experience this energy, I pay attention.

This morning as I approach my favorite meditation spot, I glance at my watch. I have almost forty-five minutes before my call with Oracle. I know I can center myself, leave in thirty minutes, and be back to my apartment to take the call.

I arrive at my spot. I sit and quiet my mind and find the stillness.

My body tingles as I sense the subtle energies, and I know all is well at this moment, and this moment is the only thing that matters. It is here, in nature and stillness, I feel most at peace. I say a silent prayer, which resembles more of an affirmation than a plea to a patriarchal God. I affirm that the meeting with Mr. Samson is fruitful, and only the highest and best prevail for all parties involved. I pray for guidance and purpose, and invite all-loving and wise, spirit guides, angels and Ascended Masters of the highest vibration to be with me.

After a moment of silence and profound peace, there are flashes of brilliant light in my head. There is an emergence of a presence, merely a shadow. I don't see him, and this is the second time this being has come to me. I have a conversation, which resembles more of an inner dialog.

'Thank you for your presence,' I think.

"Is it a big day for you?"

'I have a call with Oracle about a job. There is a part of me that wants it, but I don't feel this work is my purpose or passion. More like a means to an end.'

"You must find some joy in whatever you do, or it will not thrive."

'What if I cannot? Would it be bad to take on a job to pay the bills?'

"You are talented and can excel at anything if you can find a place of joy with it."

'Won't I be wasting my time working on something not aligned with my higher calling?'

"Everyone has an inward and outward purpose. Think of your inner purpose as your spiritual goal while you are here. It is your soul's purpose. Your outer purpose is to experience what it is like to be human. To pursue only the inward journey or outward journey by themselves would leave you unfulfilled. You need to learn balance."

'An occupation is part of the human experience?'

"Yes, it is part of a three-dimensional experience."

'This is confusing.'

"When you get to the end of your human life, you do not want to regret that you didn't experience what it is to be human. Your life is to learn lessons. There are no mistakes; your growth or demise is related to how you live as a human being. There are no failures."

'I sense I am here to do something and don't want to be distracted by all the other stuff.'

"You are *here to do something. You will need to hone your skills and your inner knowing to recognize the guideposts along your journey. But you will also need to experience life; your life isn't a distraction.*

"You will need to experience different types of love.

"And understand what it feels like to fail, even though there is no failure.

"You will need to learn what inspires and motivates you.

"You will need to be hurt by someone so that you can learn the power of forgiveness.

"You will need to learn sacrifice and loss and need to find your missing heart piece.

"You have much to learn, and there are no shortcuts in this thing

called life."

It's clear—I have much to learn. 'You mention guide-posts. These signs led me to this company.'

"Then you should feel good about your conversation this morning, knowing that you have been supported to at least have this conversation with them. See how you feel after the interview. The only certain thing is that the Universe supports this discussion. It doesn't mean that you have the position, nor does it mean that it is the highest and best. Perhaps, what is best is to have the experience of the interview, not the job. See what your heart tells you and follow it."

'How will I know?'

"The best path holds a higher frequency. You will learn to discern the difference. Until then, remember there is no right or wrong; it is the experience. You are here to experience, remember that!"

'Thank you for your guidance. I am so grateful to have you in my life.'

"I am in everyone's life, as long as they desire it, and ask."

As abruptly as the presence joins me, he is gone. I say he, but I didn't see him. His energy feels masculine, fatherly. His voice wasn't a voice—the words were my thoughts in my head. I come out of my meditation and look at my watch. It is 9:39 a.m. I stand.

'Time to talk to Oracle.'

Chapter 16:
I Choose to Stay.
Humankind Needs Us.

Reflections

Ami

Iknow you look at me and wonder if I'm home at times. I may have a distant stare or be nonresponsive to voices or what's happening around me. My eyes may roll back, and my demeanor may change or slow down. Look all you want, it doesn't bother me.

When this happens, I am not here. I go to a place where there is love, joy, peace, and something you may know little about, bliss. A place where there is no negativity, not in thought or action. A place where you can see yourself in anyone and everyone, and everything, because here you recognize the truth about all that is: that we are One.

You live in something referred to as the third dimension or third density. Here, time is linear, past, present, and future, and there is space. Where you go when you die, or transition is the fourth dimension. Where I go, often is the sixth-dimension and beyond. These other dimensions are higher in consciousness, frequency, and vibration.

I've already told you, everything is energy and vibrates at a frequency. The third dimension is very dense and has a lower vibration. The third density is a condensed form of pure consciousness. While I am here in this body, more of me remains in a higher realm. I exist in more than one place, like you. Only, unlike you, I know it.

I am unable to embody here wholly. So, while a small fraction of me is here, much of me is with the Angels, Archangels, and other beings.

My vibration is very high compared to your own, so much so, that I am unable to control the third-dimensional body, I hold on Earth. This is why I need someone to grip my arm when I type. It grounds me; the assistor is my ground wire, and I am the antenna.

The higher dimensions are mental and spiritual realities. In these realms live misinterpreted entities. Call these beings whatever your mind can accept—Angels, Archangels, Beings of Light, the Ascended Masters, Cosmic existences, entities of Light, some even say aliens.

When I'm in the higher realms, there is only *one* energy. This energy comprises everything, and it connects to Source or God. Your higher consciousness lives in a higher field, and it is your job, while you are here on Earth, to get its attention. Many of you try to get the attention of God, Archangels, Angels, Ascended Masters, and Light entities through prayer and meditation. You seek them in need. While they are here for you and love you more than you know and will answer your prayers if you listen, you don't realize that the entity that you should call upon first, before anyone, is your Higher Self.

It is in this dimension that the collective consciousness begins, and it is here that the Christ Consciousness exists. Here we are *One* with each other. When in this place, you recognize and know this about yourself and each other. You know how powerful you are. There is nothing you cannot do. You manifest the perfect world. By understanding your truth, that you are a Divine emanation of Source Energy, you have the treasures of the Universe before you, and you manifest the ideal world quickly. This dimension is the realm of sacred geometry.

I have shared that life is all an illusion. It is, only it's hard to swallow, knowing that your experience is not reality. You see, you are capable of great things in the third dimension, but you are distracted by the ego. Your concerns are a bit... what's the proper term, swacked? Maybe that isn't a word, it seems fitting, though. Yes, your priorities are swacked!

The ego wants to think it's in control. Your ego wants to believe that you, as a human being, are of supreme intelligence on Earth. How can I explain that this is *not* true? It is your ego that keeps you tethered to the third dimension. It is your ego that keeps you separate and keeps you from manifesting your perfect world. Your 3D world *is* the illusion, and your real life is in higher dimensions with me.

Your presence on Earth reflects your inner thoughts and actions. Whatever experience you have in life, you have created it. That may sound a bit harsh, but it is the truth. The good news is if you don't like what your life's experience is—you can change it.

While I'm in my higher-dimensional escape, my mind is quiet, and time slows down. Here I only experience the moment. I am not in my past, and I don't ponder my future, I am in the moment. After all, this moment reflects peace, joy, love, and bliss. We can experience this in the third dimension if we tame the ego. That's the key. If we tame the ego, the third dimension can morph to a higher realm.

When I am in my Homeland, there are no voices. I communicate with others by blending my energy field and consciousness with them. You may relate to it as inner know-ing, intuition, and psychic awareness but without effort. Here is a state of existence without restrictions and a life free of dissonance. Here, people know me for who I am; I am not someone with a disability.

I wish I had the language to explain life better. There is this translation issue. There are no words for the images in my mind. Our communication is visual, not literal, so I do my best to boil things down to simple terms while I am in this body.

That is why my language may seem staccato or even anastrophe.

There are beings in the fourth, fifth, and higher dimensions that make their way to us to communicate and guide us. I effortlessly talk with them on these higher realms, which is why I escape. Here I speak with the Ascended Masters, and they remind me of the journey I am on. Today I will meet with Melchizedek, you know him as the king of righteousness and the priest of the highest God.

★★★

Lights and vibrant colors fill the sky. Geometric symbols and patterns illuminate the horizon, and before me, there is a purple ocean with gentle waves cascading on the shores. The sounds are soft on my ears, unlike those I hear with my earth ears, which can be very harsh.

The sand beneath my feet is warm and pleasing, and I sit to be in the moment. At the heart of the geometric symbols of circles, triangles, and other shapes in the sky, there is a gathering of intense light and warmth. It is just above the heavens on the horizon. The sun here is different from the one in the third dimension. I have missed the beauty and harmony that Homeland offers.

I am at peace and in awe of this moment and don't want it to end. There is a presence here, and I am honored and grateful for his visit. It is Melchizedek, the cosmic being, and holder of the secrets of God, the Universe, and the planet Earth.

Before I can rise to greet him, he sits beside me; our energy fields approach each other. We both enjoy the view before us and each other's presence. I feel his love, and I know he feels mine. My heart warms, and our conversation occurs with no words to be heard, only mind speaking and reading.

"I miss you and miss home," I tell Melchizedek.

"You are missed and dearly loved, dear Shawnami Kaliyuga. Is

it bearable? The pain?"

"Perfect, everything is," I convey.

"You do not have to continue. It is your choice. You can come home, and the pain will end," Melchizedek suggests.

Since he sits beside me, I don't have eyes on him, yet I see him in my mind. He has long white hair and a long white beard, kind eyes, and there is a great light all around him.

"How much time do I have?" I ask.

"Changes are coming soon. There will be much work to do. There is still time, though, if this camouflage is too painful. There is time to incarnate in another form," Melchizedek suggests.

"No, I chose this path. I will continue."

"There is much tension brewing; wars will begin soon."

"My comrades are coming?"

"Yes, some have already incarnated. Many more soon, as long as you feel this is the right vehicle to do this work."

"Yes. I feel it is. It will not be easy for those coming in. I hope one day, people view autistics differently. I don't like that my brothers and sisters will endure the difficulties I have experienced."

"They are ready and willing."

I feel their love in my heart, and in my mind's eye, the beautiful horizon is replaced with the image of beings of Light, surrounding me, hand-in-hand. There are no words to convey the message they send me, yet, what I feel is unconditional love.

I return my adoration and admiration for their selflessness and willingness to accept this journey.

"You may not remember who you are and why you have come once you've incarnated," I broadcast to them. *"I hope we meet. If we do not, just know how much you are loved and how important your role is."*

I turn to Melchizedek; there are rays of light surrounding him. We both stand and face each other.

"I choose to stay. Humankind needs us," I send my message.

"Never forget that you are the flame of eternal life. It will always protect you and guide you home."

He smiles and suddenly disappears.

CHAPTER 17:
JAMES THE MYSTERY MAN

February 3, 1987

James enters the control room with a short glass of scotch in hand. He sips, then sets it on a small table beside his favorite Georgian diamond-tufted leather chair. From his inside jacket pocket, James removes four envelopes and places them beside the glass. He removes his jacket and hangs it on the mahogany coat rack near the entrance of the windowless room.

One would never know that the control room is in the heart of a luxury apartment in Manhattan. A large conference table centers the area with a sculpture of an equilateral triangle. There is an all-seeing eye inside the polygon and a circle crowning the triangle.

On one wall, multiple televisions from floor to ceiling broadcast various channels. No sound. Then there are TVs picturing people's lives. They are all on, but at this moment, James is more interested in those envelopes awaiting him.

On two walls of the large room are mahogany built-in bookshelves. In one section, there are sacred texts, one would expect to be in a museum, but the world doesn't even know they exist. Then there is a collection of editions that would bring tears to any book collector's eyes. Another area contains photo albums, while some are recent, others date back to the early 1800s.

At that bookshelf, James pulls the newest photo album and sits in his favorite chair with it on his lap. He turns to the stack of envelopes and fans them on the small table, revealing unique wedge-shaped symbols on the outside of each.

James sips the whiskey, then opens each envelope, showing four sets of pictures. Each set includes four images of the same person. He picks up one batch and thoughtfully studies each photo, then methodically places them in the album. On one of the photos, he smiles and caresses it as if the person was there.

The first set contains four shots of a young teenage girl with dark curly hair, possibly of Mexican American descent. The images are from a birthday party. He affectionately smiles at each picture and places them in the album on a page with the label "Little Sister."

The second assortment contains photos of a young woman, perhaps in her late teens with Asian features. She has beautiful long dark hair. James ceremoniously studies the images and places each on a page prelabeled "Eternal Love." He turns back a couple of pages, seeing the same girl, a year younger.

He has four images for each year of her life, the same for the other subjects. None of the photographs include James. At the time, the subjects were unaware of the camera capturing their essence.

James is a mystery. To his neighbors, he is a hermit living on the upper east side. He owns the building, or one of his companies does. His neighbors have no clue about who he is, and if they knew, they'd hightail it out of the building or even the city. Having the penthouse, and a private elevator, he is rarely seen coming or going. When he does leave, bodyguards escort him into his private limo.

Two men continually stand guard outside the penthouse, in the hallway where the elevator door is. Occasionally, the elevator opens, and often it is a political leader from DC who regularly visits him behind closed doors. Sometimes it's a delivery person with a package, and the security person signs for it and then gives it to James. Other times it's his female friend.

The apartment is the entire floor and has windows from floor to ceiling on all four sides, offering incredible views from all directions, including Central Park.

By looking at James, you'd think he'd be in his early forties, but he is much older than he seems. He is an attractive man, tall, athletic build, and unquestionably charming. The type of man that when he walks into a room, all eyes are upon him, no matter what the gender, as he has a magnetism that is rare and misunderstood.

James has it all. One would think he has everything to live for, but the truth is—he is tired. With all his wealth and power, he has lost his interest in it. Things seem to have gotten out of control over the years. He believes he started his quest with good intentions, but it became compromised over time. When alienated by his family, he was so angry with them, particularly his brother. He vowed to survive and prosper and teach the truth. That is what he has done precisely, to a select group.

His secret group grew over time. While it was fulfilling at one time, it no longer fuels him. He is tired and really, just wants to go home. His brother, however, made sure that he wasn't ever able to return. Today, his group, or groups, all seem to be out of control.

James is the top of it all. He is the leader of the most influential secret societies in the world, which all report to him. Of course, only a select few know who James is. He knows the world is heading for dark times and knows there must be a balance, or life will all come to a screeching halt. He's a bit at a loss as to how to get it all back under control. Without having his heart and soul invested in controlling it all, the situation is getting worse by the minute.

Buzzing from an alarm brings James out of his head and

into the moment. He is in his control room with the photo album on his lap. The televisions flash in front of him. He eyes the live camera feed to the entry to his apartment. His guest has arrived. He sighs. He closes the album, returns it to the bookshelf, and disposes of the envelopes. James picks up the remaining two sets of photos, thinking, 'You will have to wait as I need to get my head back into the game.'

From out of the control room, he emerges into his apartment, where he closes the doors to control central. The lock clicks automatically. He proceeds to his front door where he opens it and says, "Mr. Vice President, come in."

CHAPTER 18:
"YOU CAN MIND READ?"

May 23, 1996

Ami shrieks with excitement; it is the morning of her high school graduation. It is hard to believe that only four years earlier, she had been in the autism Special-Ed class, and today she is accepted among her peers and thriving.

For Rebecca and George, the journey was a challenge at every turn. Even after facilitated communication came to the United States, it took a year before they could get an audience with the school board to review Ami for regular classroom consideration. Then the board declined Ami for no good reason. At that point, Betty had moved out of the Denver area, so they lost Ami's cheerleader.

It took Rebecca and George to file a complaint against the school district to get any traction. The proceedings were financially and emotionally exhausting for both Rebecca and George. During the proceedings, a psychologist testified that Ami was evaluated and tested at the fifth-grade level, conflicting with the school system's reported IQ of twenty-three. Then, an independent assessor of the typing process, which had become known as FC, concluded that there was a significant portion of the time Ami had typed a letter without the assistance of Rebecca's hand.

Once Ami transferred into a standard class, there was the challenge of finding a school facilitator who could successfully work with Ami. Ami was unsuccessful with two assistants before finding a third person, Cheryl, who stayed with her through her senior year. The only thing Ami repeated was that she needed an assistant with "proper frequency." This statement, of course, threw the school board, but once Cheryl was found, Ami was assessed for her grade level and excelled academically.

Rebecca chokes back her tears as she brushes Ami's hair before graduation. It has been a long journey for them all. Four years earlier, she would not have seen this day coming. Today, she can't imagine their lives without the ability to communicate with Ami. In some ways, Ami's graduation is a point of transition for Ami, Rebecca, and George.

Ami wants interaction with other autistics. She expressed interest in going into a supported living situation after graduation. Rebecca searched exhaustedly for an arrangement in the Denver metro area, but none seemed to please Ami. She kept typing, "Not the place."

★★★

Three months earlier.

While picking up Ami from school, Cheryl shares with Rebecca, "Ami says she wants to go to Cheyenne Village."

"Where is Cheyenne Village?"

"I haven't a clue. Ami just keeps saying it is a program for adult autistics. I called around, but nobody has heard of the program. I checked the Cheyenne, Wyoming, area and didn't find anything either."

That night when Ami and Rebecca connect after dinner, Rebecca broaches the subject. "What is Cheyenne Village?"

"Need to go there to live."

"Where is it?"

"In Springs."

"In . . . Idaho Springs? Glenwood Springs? Colorado Springs? Pagosa Springs?"

"Manitou."

"Cheyenne Village is in Manitou Springs?"

"Y."

"Why do you need to go there?"

"To meet comrade."

"I don't understand. You're to go to Cheyenne Village to make friends?"

"N. To meet an old friend."

"Did someone from your other school move there."

"N."

"Who is there?"

"Another like me."

"Sweetheart, why do you want to move away?"

"Time, it is."

Rebecca hadn't talked with Ami about God since that time many years earlier. It was uncomfortable for her to do so, but for some reason, it had been on her mind, and she couldn't shake it. "You told me many years ago that you came here to show people the way to God."

"Y. You are to help me."

"Me?" This wasn't what Rebecca expected. "Why do you say that?"

"Your soul purpose," Ami types quicker than usual.

"It's my soul purpose to help you?"

"Y. Need to find God 1st."

"To help you, I need to go to church?"

"N. Look inside."

"I need to work on my spirituality?"

"Y."

"Then what?"

"Then, you help me show the way to God."

Rebecca is confused by this conversation.

"You don't understand."

"Ami, can you read my mind?"

"Y."

Rebecca looks at Ami. While she suspected it, she has never imagined this response. "You can read my mind? For how long?"

"4ever."

"You've *always* been able to read my mind?"

"Everyone."

"You can read *everyone's* mind?"

"Y."

The following day Rebecca and Ami go to Lakewood, a city west of Denver, to the Autism Society of Colorado to do some research.

The receptionist greets Rebecca while smiling at Ami. "Hi, I'm Julie. How can I help you?"

"I'm looking for information on a place called Cheyenne Village, perhaps an assisted living facility for autistics?"

Ami's hand bobs up and down, indicating she wants to say something.

Rebecca has a letterboard draped over her shoulder. Over the years, Amy and Rebecca have adapted to using a light-weight board with a QWERTY keyboard layout. It is much simpler and lighter to use over the Canon Communicator. Rebecca takes Ami's arm and positions the board for Ami to speak.

"Ma—" Ami begins messaging.

Rebecca somehow knows what Ami is going to say and speaks before Ami finishes her typing. Rebecca says, "Manitou Springs, Cheyenne Village is in Manitou Springs." She feels Ami's arm ease and notes that Ami did not object to being interrupted.

"Yes, I think that's close. It is in Colorado Springs. Man-itou Springs is about six miles from Colorado Springs," Julie goes to a file cabinet and opens it. Within minutes, she returns with a brochure from Cheyenne Village. Rebecca browses through the booklet, which states, "Cheyenne Village helps people with disabilities lead happy, healthy, and fulfilling lives."

"I don't see where they provide assisted living, Ami," Rebecca says.

"You may want to call them," the receptionist says. "These brochures don't always explain all their programs."

"Thank you. I'll do that."

Rebecca and Ami return to the car, and as soon as they get in it, Ami's index finger points downward. "You want to say something?" Rebecca asks. She positions herself so that she can facilitate the message while in the car.

"You can mind-read."

"I can mind-read? You mean I can be telepathic?"

"U R. You guessed Manitou Springs."

"That was only logical, Ami. Earlier, you told me Manitou Springs."

"We can practice."

"We can practice telepathy?"

"I type a letter. You say the word aloud. If right, I move on."

"Are you saying, you'll begin to type a word and want me to guess what I *think* you are saying? If I'm right, you'll move onto the next word. If I am wrong, you'll keep typing?"

"Y."

"Yes," Rebecca repeated and smiled.

Ami types, "Let us pr—"

"Let us practice?"

"Y."

"Okay," Rebecca looks around. She knows there is a park not too far from their location, as they met some of George's friends there years ago for a gathering.

Within twenty minutes, Rebecca and Ami sit beside each other at a picnic table beneath a shelter. It is a pleasant spring day. Rebecca places the letterboard on the table. It takes some time for her to guess the words that Ami is trying to say, then as she builds more confidence, she becomes bolder. Soon Rebecca realizes that it is okay to incorrectly speculate because Ami keeps spelling out the word until she guesses correctly. To Rebecca, it starts as a game, but the more they play, the more joy she feels each time she guesses correctly.

"Soo—"

"Soon," Rebecca deducts.

"Y—"

"You."

"W—"

"Will?"

"Rea—"

"Soon, you will *realize?*"

"Y—"

"You?"

"A—"

"Are?"

"No—"

"Not?"

"G—"

"Soon, you will realize you are not *guessing!*"

When Rebecca finishes, she smiles. She still doesn't believe in any way that she is telepathic but realizes she has speeded up communication with her daughter.

Ami types, and Rebecca sounds out the message. "Can we go to Cheyenne Village?"

Rebecca hides her sadness behind a painted-on smile. "I'm just getting to know my daughter, and you want to leave me?"

When they finish typing using "mind-reading," the

message is, "I need to move to the next phase of the journey. You visit me."

"I'll make you a deal. Let's get through graduation, and I'll make an appointment right after. Okay?"

It is a beautiful sunny morning at Red Rocks Amphitheatre, the perfect place for high school graduation. Family and friends of the 1996 graduating class fill the stadium. Rebecca and George sit hand-in-hand, center stage, waiting for the principal to call Ami's name. With each name announced, an outburst of cheers erupts from different sections of the stadium where family members and friends gather. Then the applause stops, and the cycle repeats.

With only George and Rebecca there to celebrate Ami's accomplishment, Rebecca is committed to being the loudest one in the stadium to cheer Ami on. But when she hears "Ami Griffin" on the PA system, something unexpected occurs. As Ami, escorted by Cheryl, walks across the stage, the entire class of 1996 stands and cheers her on.

George and Rebecca jump to their feet clapping, with tears rolling down Rebecca's face, she realizes everyone around her is also on their feet celebrating Ami's big moment. Overcome with emotion, Rebecca finds herself sobbing like a child, and seeks comfort in George's arms.

George chokes back his tears as he holds Rebecca and looks around. Everyone in the stadium is applauding.

Ami had touched everyone in one way or another.

CHAPTER 19:
"MUST BE LEYLA'S HOUSE."

June 19, 1996

"We should have left a little earlier," Rebecca says as they merge onto I-25 heading south toward Colorado Springs.

Ami is in the passenger seat, with her new portable CD player playing music through its headphones. Her music selection of Mozart, Rossini, Tchaikovsky, Grieg, Bizet, and Offenbach always amuse Rebecca. She prefers either classical music or Native American drums.

"Our appointment is at ten o'clock. I didn't factor in rush hour traffic."

Ami is not concerned.

Rebecca knows it'll be close. They have a ten o'clock appointment with the director of Cheyenne Village in the Pikes Peak Region of Colorado Springs.

Ami is content, strapped into the passenger seat. Being in the car is one of her favorite places. In fact, at times, the mother and daughter had their best conversations parked on the side of a road, under trees, with the windows open. Today, because of traffic, they won't have time to stop and chat on the way to Cheyenne Village.

Rebecca recalls her telephone conversation with the director from the previous week.

***

"A group of parents started Cheyenne Village in the early 70s," the director started. "Each parent had a child with disabilities and wanted more than traditional programs. Cheyenne Village initially started with twelve individuals instructed in self-care, basic living, and job skills, which was entirely new at the time. Today, the program has a couple hundred participants and accommodates adults with disabilities, including autism."

"And the supported living program?" Rebecca asked.

"That program provides supported living assistance for each of its participants, but the services provided will depend on the needs of the resident. Come down and take a tour of the facility. I'm confident you'll be impressed."

It all sounded dreamlike to Rebecca. She can't imagine being away from Ami. For twenty years, Ami had been her life. How could she adjust? What would life be like for her without Ami?

★★★

It's precisely ten o'clock when Rebecca and Ami walk into the administrative office.

"I'm so sorry to tell you that the director has been called away on an emergency. I'm Mary, her assistant, and I am happy to give you our tour."

During a forty-five minute presentation, Mary discusses the supervised homes. The facilities provide care twenty-four hours a day, 365 days a year. They have a few group homes, and each accommodates four to seven people. Each participant has a private bedroom but shares common areas of the house. They receive support for nutrition and meal preparation, personal care, home maintenance, transportation, financial management, and healthcare coordination.

"We currently have openings at two homes—" Mary begins.

A loud grunt comes from Ami.

"Do you have something you wish to share, Ami?" Rebecca places the board in front of her.

"Must be Leyla's house."

Rebecca vocalizes what Ami types for Mary's benefit.

"Well, we don't have a house in the name of Leyla," she says thoughtfully. "But...one of the resident's name is Leilah, its spelled a little differently, L–E–I–L–A–H."

"Which home?"

"One of the Joslyn and Marshall group homes, in Manitou Springs."

Ami excitedly types. "That's it."

Within a half-hour, Mary escorts Rebecca and Ami to Manitou Springs. The campus is on multiple acres and includes apartments along with a group home. Gambel Oak trees and shrubs surround the house, and while the household itself seems unremarkable, the setting is quite picturesque.

They tour the four-bedroom house, and while there are signs that the house is full of life, there is no one inside. No clutter. Everything is tidy and well organized. Each bedroom reveals an entirely different decorating taste and personality.

"Here is the vacant room we currently have," Mary says as she opens the door revealing a simple room with a twin bed, a dresser, a chair, and a nightstand beside the bed. It is a monastic–like setting, void of a cross on the wall. A window overlooks the backyard, and Rebecca sees people gathering outside.

"We keep it simple, and each resident transforms their room into their home. The new occupant will share the bathroom with one other, and the bathroom is across the hall," Mary shows them the bathroom. "Let's go outside to meet the attendant on duty."

Rebecca, Ami, and Mary migrate to the rear of the property where they meet Sarah, one of four full-time aides who supervises the home. There are three residents outside, all women, two are older, perhaps in their 40s while one is around Ami's age, maybe even younger. The older ladies are engaged in a board game on the patio while the third young woman is rocking in a patio rocker beneath a large cotton-wood tree away from the group.

Sarah, the attendant, introduces Rebecca and Ami to two women playing the Game of Life. Then she asks Rebecca, "Would you like to meet the other resident living here?"

"Yes, that'd be great."

The small group walks toward a large cottonwood where a young woman with long golden hair rocks in the glider.

"This is Leilah, she's relatively new, been here, about six months," Sarah explains. "She is nonverbal," Sarah says, seeming to want to explain Leilah's behavior.

"So is Ami," Rebecca shares. "But she does communicate through FC, facilitated communication."

Sarah is a bit intrigued, "I've never seen FC, but I've read about it. Does Ami type with everyone?"

"Ami, would you like to share something about who you type with?" Rebecca asks.

As they are standing there, Rebecca swoops up Ami's arm. "Easier to type with a person without heart scars."

"Heart scars? What does that mean?" Sarah asks.

"Ami is empathic," Rebecca explains. "She picks up on the feelings of the facilitator. I think what she means is, it helps if the person doesn't harbor emotional injuries."

Mary, who had been listening, chimes in, "But everyone has emotional wounds!"

"True, being human is about experiencing life, and life doesn't come without bumps, but there are healthier ways to cope with emotional pain," Sarah says. She turns to Ami and asks, "Is that what you mean, Ami?"

Ami types, "Need a person who goes over the bumps."

Sarah smiles, "I like that. I would love the opportunity to type with you someday, Ami." From behind them, the voices of the two ladies playing on the deck escalate, and gameboard pieces are flying. "I think that's my call! I'm needed elsewhere at the moment." She smiles and leaves to tend to the others.

Ami moves closer to Leilah and sits beside her in the gliding rocker.

"Look at that," Mary says. "Maybe they've met before?"

"Where is Leilah from?" Rebecca asks.

"I think here. Somewhere in El Paso County."

Rebecca shakes her head. "I can't see how they would have ever met."

"Leilah's mother comes to visit every Saturday and occasionally weekdays at dinner time."

'Could it be that Ami knew Leilah was here?' Rebecca is a bit bewildered.

"What else can I help you with today? Do you have any other questions?" Mary asks.

Rebecca watches her daughter sit beside Leilah. She knows what Ami has to say about this place. "I guess I need to look into the expense, see what financial assistance is available and if we can swing it."

Chapter 20:
There Is Bliss When Merging with Nonhuman Life!

Ami

It is so good to see Leilah, who I have known in my Homeland as Korkle. My heart warms being near her on the glider. We sit and rhythmically push the ground with our legs, and the swing moves back and forth gently beneath the large tree.

As we glide, I try to mind-talk to Leilah, *"Korkle, it is me, Shawnami,"* I tell her.

Leilah does not respond. She continues to kick the ground to move the swing, maybe even with more thrust.

"Korkle, don't you remember?" I ask.

Leilah's kick increases.

I know she is resisting me. She is pushing back. In time, I will reach her. I need her.

I sense the tree's energy. It is almost instantly that my Light Body, my higher-energy-self, envelopes the giant tree. We merge, the tree and me, and I am one with the tree. In moments like this, I do not know where I begin and where I end. I only feel one energy. I sense the tree's life force as mine, and there is peace here. There is bliss when merging with nonhuman life. It is in this way I know that God, Spirit, Source, lives in everything. It is through this experience that I discern Oneness; that we are all one with everything. I feel the tree's energy from its deep roots anchored in the earth, seeking water, to its high branches reaching for the sky and sensing the sun on its leaves. I feel the complexity of photosynthesis, and how carbon dioxide transforms through a chemical reaction and how its byproduct benefits our air.

At some point, my apparition shifts from seeing crisp details and outlines of objects to watery-flow-like images, where the colors are more vibrant and exude energy. Objects bleed into each other, somehow explaining how I don't know where I am, and where the tree is. I smell the sweet essence of life itself. It is clean and fragrant. I hear the leaves gently quaking, providing music to my ears. I am at peace. I am at One.

My bliss is severed when I hear Mom getting ready to leave with Mary, and I know I will need to go back to my physical body. I love the tree and feel its strength and love. My attention returns to my physical body, beside Leilah.

"I will be back," I tell Leilah.

Leilah stops pushing the ground with her leg and permits me to get off the swing safely.

"You hear me, after all."

She ignores my comment, and as soon as I move away from the glider, she resumes thrusting her feet at the ground.

I feel Mom's hand take my arm, and we turn to leave.

"It was nice to meet you, Leilah," Mom says. "I hope to see you again."

I am going to miss Mom. Her journey, though, is significant. It is essential to her path, and it is central to our mission-mission. She needs to grow, and when I'm around, I know she won't. So, as I begin my work away from home, she will start her spiritual deepening. We need her.

CHAPTER 21:
I LOVE NEW BEGINNINGS.

June 1996

Elisha (AKA Levi)

I love new beginnings. There's something about a fresh slate that warms my heart; a chance to start anew. It's exciting, in a way, an opportunity to recreate myself. I closed on my new house in the foothills of Colorado. The ink is barely dry on the documents. I just left the title company and merged onto the highway, heading west toward the mountains. I have a clear shot of the Front Range and see the Dakota Hogback, and the rolling green mountains to the snow-tipped continental divide. Breathtaking. How cool that I will enjoy this drive returning home from work every day.

It's late in the afternoon, so I drop the visor to shield my eyes from the sun's rays. The sunlight hits the quartz crystal hanging from my rearview mirror and reflects into my eyes. I remember when I bought the stone in California. That was before Oracle transferred me to Denver. At the time, I was learning about how crystals can protect me when entering places with lots of people. That was when I was still called Elisha. I changed my name to Levi when I moved to Denver four years earlier. There is a story about how I came up with the name too.

★★★

It was happy hour, and I was meeting friends from work at a busy hotel bar in Redwood City. I entered the lounge, and through thick pheromone air from the roomful of yuppies, I considered leaving. I felt my skin crawl from all the energy. I reached into the pocket of my tailored suit jacket for the labradorite stone. 'Keep me at peace as I ride out others' pain,' becomes my mantra. Between my pocket stone and the rose quartz pendant hanging around my neck, I trusted that I was protected.

My coworker, Maurine, wore a vibrant red suit that day, so I searched for her. Bingo! Corner of the room. She was at a raised-top table with a bunch of guys from a local software company.

I joined them. These guys talked shop trying to impress my two friends. They were doing a good job, too. Then one of them started hitting on me. I wasn't interested, but I didn't want to be rude. What to do?

"So, what's your name?" he asked, leaning toward me.

It was weird. It was an automatic response. "I'm Levi," I said. 'Where did that name come from?' It had just popped into my head. I wasn't even sure if Levi was a girl's name. 'Did it matter?'

★★★

I don't remember what happened to the guy at the bar, but the name stuck. My friends that evening started calling me Levi. The odd thing is, the name just fits, and when I moved to Denver, I legally changed my name from Elisha to Levi.

When Oracle asked me to transfer a few years ago, I asked them to give me a week to consider the relocation. The following morning, while in meditation, I set the intention to understand if relocating to Colorado was the highest and best good. I didn't get anything in the reflection, but I started to watch for signs in my walking life. The signposts came. Like, sitting in a restaurant, the people at the table next to me begin chatting about Denver. Passing a kid on the street with a Denver Bronco shirt. Then a car passed me with a Colorado license plate as John Denver belts out "Rocky Mountain High" on our car stereo.

I was to come to Denver. It's so cool that the Universe does this. I keep telling my friends about these synchronicities, and they think I've got a screw loose. Maybe I do.

I work over in DTC, which is the Denver Tech Center. After being in the metro area, I am moving to the foothills, which has breathtaking red rock formations, rolling hills, and rising mountain peaks. It gives me the sense that I'm residing in the mountains, but I still have access to DTC and downtown.

I love being in the mountains and open space. I'm good at my job, but it doesn't make my heart sing. I honor my employer, though, and do well for them, and they reciprocate with a generous salary and benefits.

I pass through an opening on a short mountainous ridge into a residential community nestled in a valley between the mountains. As I approach my new house heading toward the end of a cul-de-sac, I see the tall ponderosa pines in front of my home. Behind the house rises an open space hill. It's a quiet neighborhood, and I feel so blessed to have some property between the houses, a novelty in the Denver area for sure. The for-sale sign that says "Sold" is still prominently displayed in front of the house. I drive up a terracotta-style driveway that matches the house's stucco color.

I click the garage door opener given to me at the closing, and one of the doors opens to a clean, empty, three-car garage. I pull in and park. I don't go into the house. Instead, I exit the back door of the garage to the backyard. There is a patio area with a view of the rising open space and mountain, indeed a peaceful and serene setting. The property was the selling point for me. Don't get me wrong, the house is beautiful, but the quiet, private setting sealed the deal. To my left is a massive red rock formation, and to my right are towering blue spruce. I sit on a sizable landscape rock and feel the sun beat down and warm my body. For the first time in a long time, I feel like I am home.

A couple of weeks pass, and I have made great strides getting settled in my new house. I bought some new patio furniture because I know I will spend a lot of time here.

Today my friend Nina, one of the other software developers at Oracle, asked if she can swing by and see my house. She lives on the east side of what the locals call the hogback, which is a narrow ridge of steep rock bands that are the first peaks seen from Denver. Out of all my coworkers, Nina and I hit it off. The more I got to know her, I learned we had similar spiritual interests, and now we live on the same side of town.

The doorbell rings, and I know it is Nina. I open the door, and she has a plant in her hand. "Happy housewarming," she says and hands me a rather large arrangement.

"Thank you, come on in." I admire the plant, "It is beautiful. You didn't have to do this."

"I wanted to," she smiles.

"It is lovely, and I do love plants."

After the requested tour of my new place, we migrate to the backyard, my sanctuary, where I've set up some bird feeders, and there are beautiful plants with a fountain and my statue of Buddha. We sit with our iced teas.

"Your home is beautiful and so peaceful," she cocks her head toward my Buddha, "Now that you're on this side of the metro area, you should come to a service with me at my church."

"I'm not an organized religion person," I smile.

"And you think I am?"

"No, I didn't believe you were."

"I'm not. I go to connect with like-minded souls. I also

enjoy some of the classes. Come with me this Sunday."

I try to come up with an excuse not to go, but I know I have no conflict. "I don't like going into crowds," I say honestly.

"That's what crystals are for," Nina calls me on it. "I'll pick you up just after nine, and we can have lunch after."

CHAPTER 22:
YOU'RE NOT READY FOR THE CHANGES COMING!

May 1997

Rebecca returns home from school. George is on the road this week, and since she expects some company, she quickly feather-dusts and vacumes their home. Cleaning is somewhat cathartic to her—a time of reflection. 'So many changes over the year,' she ponders. 'Ami moved to Cheyenne Village, George's promotion, my spiritual deepening.'

Everything seemed to be part of a plan and fell into place. A timely promotion for George, qualifying for financial assistance, and the vacancy at the Leilah house stayed open until Ami took it.

That first month had been challenging for Rebecca. After being Ami's fulltime caregiver, what would she do? She recalls a conversation with Ami, shortly after she had moved in, then considers the changes over the year.

***

"What am I to do with all my free time since I won't be looking after you?" she asked.

"Time to do the work. Go inside."

This comment was not the first time Ami had suggested that Rebecca work on her spirituality. "I'll go back to church."

"Don't go to church. Go inside."

Rebecca knew she needed more structure, though.

When a coworker at school mentioned she was taking a spiritual growth class at a New Thought church in Lakewood, she looked into it. The church was non-denominational and regularly taught classes that offered practical tools to live a more spiritual life. Rebecca had a traditional Christian upbringing, and she wasn't familiar with its teachings. When she saw the foundation class taught meditation, affirmations, affirmative prayer, and the power of thoughts, in the fall, she enrolled in the thirteen-week course.

At the heart of the church's teachings was Oneness. The church suggested that there is one energy, and that energy is God, and everything is a unique expression of God.

Rebecca jumped into the institution's teachings and learned about a form of prayer where the individual acknowledges that God is all, and each individual is an expression of God, worthy of claiming whatever they desire. What troubled her was that all the examples of such prayers suggested that God was ideals of love, light, wisdom, joy.

'If God is all there is, wouldn't God be both the Light and the Dark? Wouldn't God also be hatred, darkness, ignorance, and misery?'

Rebecca considered approaching the minister and asking about it, but when she mentioned the paradox to Ami, her daughter said, "Minister won't answer. Answers come with discernment and experience."

This response was an invitation for Rebecca to throw herself into the teachings. She read the course books, and then others. She meditated daily and attended other workshops at the church. She noticed a subtle shift in her life that was hard to describe, but she knew it was positive. Her intuition, that inner knowing, grew. She saw an interconnectedness of life that she hadn't noticed before. Small miracles of serendipities and synchronicities became meaningful to her. All seemingly positive changes, but as she went deeper into the fundamental teachings, she didn't find an answer to the paradox.

Every Sunday, Rebecca, and occasionally George, jour-
neyed to see Ami. When George wasn't there, she would share
what she learned in her classes and books. Many compelling
discussions took place. This one discussion confirmed that Ami
was the mentor, and she, the student.

"You must go deeper and deeper," Ami typed
on the letterboard.

"I must continue my spiritual growth? Why?" Rebecca
asked.

"You're not ready."

"I'm not ready for what, Ami?"

"The changes that are coming."

"I need to spiritually grow because I'm not ready for the
changes that are coming?"

"Yes. You're not ready. Not much time to
prepare."

"Ami, what happens to those not prepared."

"As of right now, they will be left to a
painful existence and eventually perish."

Rebecca stared at her daughter. What was Ami telling
her? That she needed to continue her spiritual work because
her life depended on it? 'How can that be?'

Rebecca did not doubt her daughter and trusted she needed to continue her work. She threw herself into more classes
and workshops throughout the Front Range. She noticed that
her circle of friends changed. She had less in common with
her peers at the school, who seemed stuck in the gossip mill,
and gravitated toward new people who were committed to an
inward path.

She marveled at how deeply her new friends were committed to their spiritual work; after all, they didn't have a
daughter telling them to go deeper because they would have a

painful life and perish if they weren't ready. 'Ready for what?'

★★★

Rebecca's cleaning supplies are back in the cabinet. Her home is tidy for her small gathering, and she is ready for her company.

Nina, one of Rebecca's new friends from a course at the church, asked Rebecca to join a small meditation group. Each Tuesday night, the small cluster gathers and tries different meditation techniques. There are five women in the group, and they always begin with a sharing time over dessert, then there is meditation time. They rotate homes, and it is Rebecca's turn to host the gathering.

Rebecca sets out bite-size gourmet treats she picked up after school from the bakery. She pulls the blinds in her living room so that the summer evening light doesn't distract the meditators. It is the first time the ladies will gather at her house, and there is just enough room for five people after pulling a dining room chair into the living room. She is excited about this evening. She isn't sure why it just feels like something big is brewing.

Chapter 23:
She Is a Being of Light

May 1997

Levi

I'm not entirely clear why I am in this meditation group. When Nina asked me to join it, I began to conjure up a lame excuse, but the frequency shifted. My hands and face began to tingle. Over the years, I have learned this is a sign-post for me.

'Am I supposed to join this meditation group?' I wondered, and instantly my heart chakra opened, and chest flooded with warmth. I had my answer.

I've meditated with these ladies for a couple of months now, and this evening I'm heading to Rebecca's house, in Park Hill. It hasn't come to light why I am to be with the group. Maybe I'll learn tonight. My Jeep veers onto the Interstate 70 exit, and I head down Monaco scanning the street signs.

As I drive into the South Park Hill neighborhood, I begin searching the house numbers. I know I'm getting close, so when an open parking spot appears, I take it. I look at the number on the house I've parked in front of and realize this is it.

Moments later, Rebecca greets me at her front door.

"Levi, welcome. Come on in."

I don't know much about her, but she is eager to learn about spiritual practices and new philosophies. Rebecca is about twenty years older than me. I'd place her in her late forties. She has long brown hair that is showing a bit of gray.

She is slim and has a kind smile. A couple of members of the group are here also, but we're waiting for Nina to arrive before we begin.

As soon as I enter Rebecca's home, my bells and whistles start to go off. My hands start tingling, then my face, and as I approach a wall decorated with photographs, my heart warms.

An image of Rebecca with a young woman draws me to it. It isn't Rebecca who catches my eye; it is the younger woman in her late teens or early twenties. She has long dark hair and is short next to Rebecca. When I look full-on at the image, I don't see it, but when I relax my eyes and glance away from the picture, the younger lady in the photo lights up. I've never seen this before, its an aura in an image, so I am curious. I experiment with this phenomenon enough until I'm sure the light is coming from the young woman in the snapshot.

I feel a presence. It is then I realize that Rebecca is standing beside me. She is slightly shorter than me. "Is this your daughter?" I ask.

"Yes," she answers.

"She is special," I whisper.

"Yes. Ami is autistic," Rebecca says.

"That's not what I mean," I say.

"What is it then?"

I reach for the photo and look at Rebecca. "May I remove it?"

She nods, and I take the photo from the wall and hold it, feeling the energy of the picture. It is compelling. I know the power is coming from her daughter. As I embrace the image, I feel compelled to walk. I migrate away from the living room where the others gather and into the dining room. I know if I continue walking, I'll enter the kitchen, but a cubbyhole calls to me. I stand in the small hallway outside two rooms; a bedroom, and what appears to be an office. There is more light coming from the bedroom.

"This is her room," I say.

"Yes. Ami is living at an assisted living home for a bit, but this is her room."

I move into the room, cradling the picture in my hands and sit on the bed. Out of nowhere, intense feelings begin percolating within me. I begin to speak, not clear where the information is coming from, and yet, I know it is accurate.

"Your daughter has had many lives in the physical," I close my eyes. "Through these lives and her free will and hard work, she has raised her vibration in such a way that she has mastered herself and the elements through matter, time, and space."

I am sure Rebecca hasn't a clue what I just said, but she is listening. "Your daughter, you said her name was?"

"Ami."

"No, that's not it. It's close, though."

"Excuse me?"

"She is a Being of Light...she is a Master."

"Levi, I'm sorry, I don't know what any of this means."

I'm not exactly sure where this is coming from. I just know it and repeat what arises within me. "Your daughter has incarnated in human form to help with the ascension of humankind."

As I look at Rebecca, I know she does not know what I'm saying.

"I'm sorry, Levi. This information is all new to me. I don't understand it."

I smile. "You will. I'm glad you are in our small group. You are very special, Rebecca."

"Just because my daughter may be unique doesn't make me *special*."

I look deep into Rebecca's eyes and hold her stare. "Your daughter, Ami..." I pause, "She chose you to be her mother. That makes you extraordinary."

"I feel like I'm very... oblivious! Yes, ignorant about all this stuff."

"If I remember correctly, you are Christian?" I say.

"Yes, I was, I'm a PK."

"Many people aren't being satisfied by dogmatic faiths any longer and are looking elsewhere. Is that how you found the church?"

Rebecca shakes her head, "No. My daughter told me I am not ready for changes that are coming. She said I need to keep going deeper. Do you know what she means by changes?"

At that moment, Nina bolts into the room. "Oh, there you are!" She looks at me and must have sensed that she was interrupting. "I'm sorry, I didn't mean to interrupt. Is everything okay?"

"Absolutely," Rebecca says. "I apologize. I didn't mean to be rude."

"Let's get together to continue our conversation another time," I say.

"Certainly, let's join the group," Rebecca suggests.

When I leave the meditation group that evening, I can't forget the photo of Ami. I cannot get her out of my head. I don't know much about Rebecca, except she's a new member of the church and classes, and her husband works at Xerox. Ami is in an assisted living facility. I wonder, 'Where?'

I now know why my inner bells and whistles went off when Nina asked me to join her meditation group, but I'm not clear what to do about it. I am to meet Ami, though I am not sure if I am to learn from her, or help her. I have a sense that my spiritual purpose somehow connects to Ami.

I have so many questions. As I get ready for bed that night, I decide to sleep on it. I ask for a dream about it.

I crawl into bed and bring the image of Ami to mind. I lay still and silently ask to remember a dream that'd give me clarity. I repeat the request, in my head, over and over, until it becomes meditative and I slip into sleep. 'I will remember a dream that'd give clarity to what I am to do with Ami.'

★★★

I am pleasantly warm, not hot, nor cold. It isn't dark, though it isn't bright either, it's balanced. Every color I am aware of, and then some, are visible in an almost complete spectrum. The colors are vivid and vibrant. Aside from the various shades, there is nothing for me to see. I lift my hand before my eyes, and it isn't my hand. Or is it?

Before me, there is a hand with long slender fingers that emanate white light. It isn't like the glow I see surrounding people from time to time. It isn't similar to the aura. It is different; it is brighter, whiter, and more transparent. The light I see around people is often cloudy and has stuff in it. I extend my arm and see the white light radiating from my forearms and upper arms too.

I look down, and I have an androgynous torso with long slender legs. My flesh is gone, my entire being radiates light.

'This is a dream!' I think. 'It's a lucid dream at that! What could it mean?'

As if answering my question, a vision emerges before me. I see the butterfly life cycle, starting with round eggs clumped together on a leaf. Then, there is one egg, the others disappear. The egg hatches into a caterpillar. The caterpillar eats the foliage on which it had been born. It quickly grows, molts, and sheds its outgrown skin.

Somehow, I know I am witnessing my journey. I understand the egg hatching is symbolic of my desire to grow spiritually. I also realize the caterpillar is where I am today. I need to shed my outgrown skin many times before I can enter the

133

cocoon. That cocoon is the chrysalis. Intuitively, I know that while I am in the chrysalis, there will be enormous changes in my life. That will be when I will have real metamorphosis and spiritual transformation.

'That is when I am to meet Ami,' I think, 'I am not ready.' I know I am dreaming, and for one second, I question my thoughts. 'Is this my imagination? A meaningless dream?'

I know that what I am dreaming of isn't pointless. It is my destiny to meet Ami. Her name is not Ami, like I am not Elisha. She is Shawnami, denoting *I am a gift from God.* I know her. I am here to help her, though I cannot until I advance in my spiritual growth.

'So, what am I to learn from this?'

With that thought came the answer, a reverberating voice in my head, "Ages ago you were given an assignment. You are a protector guide for spirit communicators such as Shawnami. You only permit higher vibrational energies and spirits to work with these communicators. Many extraordinary beings are incarnating in this lifetime, as well as others. Your role continues in the physical. Go within, study the signs, and you will understand how you can assist Shawnami and others."

★★★

Abruptly, I wake. I sit up in bed and raise my hands to my face, assuring I am back. I glance at the digital display on the clock; it is 3:33.

I get out of bed and go to another bedroom. My cat, Ralph, follows me and jumps on my lap as I sit at a desk in the corner. I turn on my computer and wait for it to boot up. I am a bit shaken. That is the oddest dream I've ever had. While I gather that I am not ready to meet Ami, I am confused by the visual that my appearance was anything but human. 'What on earth does that mean?' I wonder.

I'm twenty-nine years old, and I have moments of clarity and use those moments to steer my course. That is how I have guided my life. I have been led away from the Central Valley, into UC Santa Barbara to study computer science, to work for Oracle, to transfer to Denver, and now to meet Ami when I am ready. This visual of me with an odd body rattles me. I try to rationalize and whisper aloud, "It was a dream."

There is a part of me that wants an ordinary life. Most people my age are either married or in a relationship. I haven't had a successful relationship. I look down at my cat, curled on my lap. I scratch Ralph's neck, and he responds by purring. I've met a couple of great guys, one I even lived with, but it didn't work. I keep telling myself that I just haven't met the right guy. But, something tells me that I don't need anyone to complete me, and a relationship may even take me off course.

My mind wanders back to my dream. I am different, and I've known that. How different am I, though? I sense the vision is a metaphor, a riddle perhaps to tell me that it is okay to feel differently than others. Maybe even everyone thinks like this. Could that be? How would I know what others think?

"Let it go, Levi," I whisper aloud.

CHAPTER 24:
I LIT NOW. I REMEMBER WHY HERE.

July 12, 1997

Rebecca pulls into a parking spot at Ami's assisted living home beside a gray Camry. Over the year, she became familiar with the attendants and most family members of the residents, but she doesn't recognize the Toyota. 'I wonder who's here?' She retrieves the key from the ignition, opens the car door, and instantly feels the summer heat.

Voices and laughter tell Rebecca everyone is in the backyard. She heads there and finds the group engaged in an art project at the picnic table.

"Hi, Mrs. Griffin," Sarah says as she helps one of the older residents with a paintbrush.

"Good morning!" Rebecca approaches the table where Ami strokes a canvas. She kisses the top of her head, then glances at the painting. Before her is an abstract watercolor with colorful vertical strokes.

"Don't you just love her art?" Sarah says as she stands behind Ami's other shoulder.

To Rebecca, it didn't look like anything particular, very abstract. "I'm not an art expert, but to me, it's beautiful because Ami did it. I do like the selection of colors. They all oddly seem to work well together."

"Oh, I think Ami has some real talent. Can't you feel it?"

"Feel it?"

"Yes, it's very energizing."

'Energizing?' Rebecca studies the piece with a different eye. She looks at the paintings of the other two residents. After seeing them, she agrees, 'There is something unique about Ami's work.'

It is then Rebecca realizes that Leilah isn't at the table. She looks around and sees her at the glider beneath the large cottonwood. There is a woman with Leilah now waving at her.

Rebecca waves back. "Is that Leilah's mother?"

"Sure is. Haven't you met Crystal yet? She's here every Saturday."

"That explains it! I'm usually here Sundays."

She migrates toward Leilah and her mother, a tall, attractive woman in her late forties with long chocolate-blond hair with a tinge of gray. She extends her hand. "Hi, I'm Rebecca, Ami's mom."

"It's so sweet to meet you finally! I'm Crystal, Leilah's mother."

Rebecca turns to greet Leilah. "Good morning, Leilah."

Leilah continues kicking the ground with her leg while holding an empty cup in her hand. She glides the chair forward and backward.

"Yes, I've heard all about you," Crystal says, "About the facilitated communication. I've wanted to meet you to chat about it."

"Has Leilah tried it?"

"No. I've seen Sarah type with Ami, and I understand that you taught Sarah."

"Yes, I did."

"I was wondering if you'd be willing to try with Leilah, too."

"I'd be happy to try!" She turns to Leilah, "Leilah, would you like to type with me?" Not expecting anything in return. A non-response would be the best indicator that she didn't object.

Leilah ignores her.

Rebecca smiles. "I'll get the Canon Communicator. It's

in the car. I'll see if Ami is interested in joining us too."

Sometime later, the small group gathers beneath the cottonwood. Rebecca and Leilah are sitting on the glider, now still, while Ami and Crystal are in lawn chairs nearby. Sarah stands, mindful of the other residents playing cards on the deck with a visitor.

"These days, Ami and I speak mostly with the letterboard, mainly because it's easier to carry around. But, first words must be recorded!" Rebecca smiles and picks up the keyboard. "Here is her Canon Communicator, which is very similar to the first one we used when she first began typing."

Rebecca reviews some basic instructions with Leilah and asks if she could take her arm. She does, and Leilah does not object. Within a couple of minutes, the two are practicing typing. After a period of typing gibberish, Leilah settles down, and she better regulates her stroke. Leilah begins to type.

Rebecca smiles when Leilah finishes her first sentence. She looks at Leilah's mother, prints the message, tears off the paper, and hands it to Crystal.

Crystal reads the message to the group aloud, "Want to tell Mom I love her very much." Tears pool in Crystal's eyes. "I love you too, sweetheart, very much!" She tells her daughter.

Rebecca senses Leilah wants to keep talking, and types again. Rather than printing the message, Rebecca reads it aloud. "Leilah says, 'I miss Dad. See him often tho.'"

Tears run down Crystal's face. "He passed a couple of years ago," she explains. "What do you mean that you *see* him, Leilah?" She moves to her daughter so that she can read firsthand what Leilah types.

"Soul doesn't die. Lives in another dimension," Leilah types.

Crystal doesn't know what to say to that. Ami stands and

begins pacing. She walks past the group, turns and returns to where she starts, then repeats the path.

Leilah continues typing, "Did not like Ami mind talking at first."

"What does that mean?" Crystal asks while looking at Rebecca, then Ami.

"Loner, I wanted to be. Mad that Ami got in my mind."

"Leilah, are you telling me you and Ami talk telepathically?"

"Yes."

Rebecca is intrigued, "What do you talk about?"

"Everything."

Crystal is more interested in learning practical things about her daughter since she has never had a conversation with her. "Sweetheart, is there anything you need at your home here?"

"Library, like Ami's at home, I want."

"What does that mean?" Crystal looks at Rebecca.

"We have a bookcase in our living room, and I originally had college textbooks there," Rebecca begins. "Ami would take the textbooks and read them. I used to test her. I would replenish the books with new subject matters when she finished. But—how would she know about it, unless they *are* communicating telepathically?"

"Leilah," Crystal begins. "I can bring you as many books as you like. What would you like to read?"

"College math, sciences, history, Bible."

The request for the Bible, surprises them, especially Crystal. "Which version of the Bible?" Crystal feels silly right after asking her. Thinking, 'Duh! How would Leilah know about Bible versions?'

Leilah surprises her with, "King James is okay. The truth, I know."

Crystal doesn't know how to respond to that, and her mind races until Rebecca speaks.

"I have a question," Rebecca says. "If you don't mind?" she looks at Crystal.

Crystal nods.

"Leilah, Ami had been adamant about coming here to Cheyenne Village. She even went so far as saying she wanted to live in the "Leyla's" house. Did she come here to connect with you?"

"Yes. To light me up. Now, I lit. Why here, I remember."

Crystal and Rebecca glance at each other, trying to understand the meaning of the message. "Leilah, what do you mean by *Now, I lit*? Crystal asks.

"Put a person of God near us, and we light up."

"What does that mean? That you light up?" Rebecca asks.

"Remember who we are and why here."

"You remember who you are? Why are you here, Leilah?" Crystal asks.

"Here to open hearts."

"And how will you do that?"

"By loving them."

Leilah stops typing. She stands and begins to pace also, beneath the tree.

Sarah, who had witnessed the messages, "This is incredible, ladies!"

Ami, who had been pacing, lies down in the grass, and soon Leilah does the same.

When Crystal saw Rebecca, only an hour earlier, she had hoped to have a conversation with her daughter and learn things like, does she like potatoes? Or what is her favorite music? Or pastime? This discussion, however, left her wanting to know much, much more.

Chapter 25:
Leilah Awakens

Reflections

Ami

Leilah fought me. The last thing she wanted was to leave her safety cocoon. She had been there for so long, and when I spoke to her with mind talking, she closed up. No matter what I did or how I tried, Leilah ignored me.

I'd say, *"Leilah, it is our time."*

She'd snub me.

"Leilah, you are needed," I'd tell her.

She'd turn away and go deeper into her inner world. I'm sure the drugs don't help. She's on something to control her behavior, and it makes her sleepy. Oh, the pharmaceutical companies think they are helping—or do they? They are numbing many of us and causing cognitive decline, not incline. Many with autism will sleep their lives away, not realizing how important they are to our world. We need to let them know.

I didn't give up. Day after day, I'd mind-talk to Leilah, and for months, she'd shut me out. She'd ignored me; she'd turn her back to me. One day I had pushed her too far, and she had a tantrum. The caregivers didn't know what to do.

Then I tried even harder.

"Leilah, you are loved. You are needed. You matter. I can't do this alone. It is time. You need to come out of your cocoon. This is why you are here. I love you, Leilah. You are important. You can do this. You don't want to live your life, not being part of this. This is

why you are here! Don't you remember?"

Repeatedly, for 48 hours, every waking moment, no matter where I was, I broadcasted the message at the top of my mind until there was a crack in her shield.

★★★

We are in the dining room at the dinner table, and I am shouting, if there is such a thing in mind talking, *"Wake up, Leilah! I need you! We need you! They need you! Melchizedek needs you. Metatron—"*

"LEAVE ME ALONE!" I hear with my inner ears, and it is not such a kind volume, I must say.

"I can't, Leilah," I try to convey in a kind tone.

"GET OUT OF MY HEAD!" She yells.

"My friend and comrade, I cannot."

"You are NOT my friend," in a bit less hostile tone.

"You and I have known each other for many, many lifetimes. Don't you remember me?"

Leilah remains quiet, staring at her dinner plate.

"We are here together in density again."

Leilah still ignores me.

"Don't you remember why you are here? I cannot do this alone. I need you. I miss you—I love you."

There is a long pause.

"Shawnami?"

That did it. After months of trying to reach Leilah, I got through.

"Yes. It is me, Korkle."

Leilah goes silent; her mind must have been working overtime and in overdrive. She must have been assessing the situation. Where she was, what she was doing here, and recalling her purpose while she walked this planet as Leilah.

"Where do we begin?" She asks me.

"We have much to do. We need help from others with voices, our moms, until we get our own," I tell her. "The others have started to come in."

"They are autistic too?"

"Many are autistic."

"We are hidden? Hakathriel doesn't know who we are?"

"They do not suspect the autistics of our generation as being Masters. Unfortunately, they learned that a powerful force was coming in and became nervous."

"What have they done?"

"They have been poisoning a particular demographic of babies through vaccinations which are causing autism."

"Has Quasar been tainted?"

"Yes."

"Will this stop him from doing his thing?"

"No. Quasar and others will be misunderstood, as we are. The Dark Brotherhood does not suspect we are here. We are safe for now."

"Eventually, they'll learn it's us, though."

"If we do our jobs correctly, it shouldn't matter at that point. The stronger the Light, the dimly lit souls, will have less power," I say.

"But they are powerful now?" Leilah asks.

"Very. The dark team's power will continue to grow. Hatred and fear will become second nature. Horrid acts of terror will occur, and systems will crumble."

"What is our next step?" Leilah asks.

"We need to get Rebecca and Crystal onboard. Jerhesa is here, not ready yet. Levi is here too, though she doesn't know. Until then, we need to encourage our mothers to go deeper, by doing so, the negative entities will not attach, and they will be protected, and our jobs will be easier."

"How will you lead anyone?" Leilah asks. "We can't speak. People think we are mentally retarded. How will you ever direct anyone?"

"We will," I tell her. "We will need to embody fully. This is life work for us. We need to take one step at a time."

CHAPTER 26:
THE PEARL HARBOR EFFECT

April 29, 1996

James is in the back of his limo with his special lady friend he took to the Nederlander Theatre for the premiere of *Rent*. He has so much on his mind that he hadn't enjoyed the musical. He keeps thinking about *his plan*. The plan seems to be getting a bit out of control, in his opinion. Perhaps it isn't the plan but the identified deliverables to achieve the goal that is bothering him. He knows if things progress the way they are, there won't be a world left for him to rule. 'What good is it to be top dog if there are no puppies left to control?'

His date, an attractive brunette dressed to kill, sits silently beside him. She senses that small talk is not what James wants now, so she waits for him to say something, anything, but the silence thickens.

His cell phone rings. James answers. He speaks cryptically to whoever is on the other end and hangs up. The limo pulls to the side of Broadway. One of the two men in the front seat gets out of the car. He hails a taxi.

"I'm afraid our evening must come to an end," James says with an indistinguishable accent. "Something has come up." His intensely dark blue eyes stand out from his black hair and sparkle in the light. "My man got you a taxi," he smiles.

"Should I come by later?" she asks.

"No. Not tonight."

He takes her hand in his own, kisses it, and the door of the limo opens, and one of his guys, swiftly escorts her into a cab.

That man hands the taxi driver a couple C-notes. "Take her wherever she wants to go." The driver grins.

Moments later, the vehicle pulls into the street, and the window between James and the two men in the front seat opens. The man in the passenger seat hands James an envelope. "This came today, special delivery."

"Thank you." He takes it, "We need to go to Brooklyn."

"I understand," the bodyguard says, and the glass pane closes.

James has a thick envelope. He knows what it is and has been waiting for it. He turns on the overhead light, and tears open the packet removing photographs. The first set of images is of an Asian woman in her twenties, beaming at whoever is snapping the picture. He smiles while looking at the subject. In one photo, the woman, surrounded by friends, is laughing with her head thrown back. James sees something and looks closely at the picture. From a nearby compartment, he retrieves a magnifying glass and eyes the photograph carefully, focusing on one spot beneath her chin, which is only visible because her head angles back.

"Could it be?" James whispers. He pulls the magnifying glass away from the picture, closer to his eye, and the image enlarges. A smile emerges as he compares the mark on the woman's chin to the gold signet ring on his finger. They match. "She has the mark."

Beneath the woman's neck is a birthmark, and yet it looks like the symbol of James' father or the sign of the deities. He hadn't seen this birthmark in the other pictures of his eternal love.

He continues looking through the other images in the envelope until he reaches a photo of a young Hispanic or Mexican woman with a toddler boy.

He marvels at how much she has changed in a year and wonders if she will be ready to assume her role in the events to come. There is not much time before she'll need to do *her thing*. His gaze diverts to the young boy. 'A minor complication,' he thinks. 'Nothing that I can't fix if needed.' Then he reconsiders, 'Will she forgive me? She always has.'

It seems to James that his only joy in life these days is watching these young women grow. If they only knew how important they are to him or his *plan*. Of course, they have no idea, but will in time. That's the plan at the moment.

The sound of rubber hitting the bridge draws James back to the present situation. They have reached the Brooklyn Bridge, and he knows he will have the task of tearing his subordinate a new asshole. Ever since he read the preliminary plan of attack to justify war on terror in the Middle East, he had been outraged. He's horrified that they would ever consider taking out such a large-scale terrorist attack on U.S. soil, where thousands would undoubtedly die. 'My god, of all places, the World Trade Center.'

James is beginning to wonder if he's losing control of some of his minions. He taught them all too well and needs to put them in their place. He understands the Pearl Harbor effect, to get the American people behind the justification of war in the Middle East, attack the heart of America and Americans will rise, unknowingly to be soldiers and members of *his* team.

Undoubtedly, he can achieve his plan without attacking the heart of New York City! He can get the central banks, and the thirteen families inline without this act. He can create a police state in the U.S. another way. He can gain control of oil and gas in the Middle East without taking down the heart of the financial district, right?

James knows the leaders of his secret groups are smart, but he realizes this is entirely wrong and could lead to the destruction of everything. 'But how can I get my message across to these idiots?'

Control used to be fun for James, but all this seems to be getting old. It has been years since he has had real joy in his life. He needs to find a way back to it. With all his power, in many ways, he feels like a prisoner.

All he wants is to go home.

Chapter 27:
Detours Orchestrated by a Higher Intelligence

July 13, 1997

Levi

A warm summer's breeze rustles my journal's paper. My hand stops the pages from turning prematurely. It is night-time, and I am at my patio table, lit by a string of patio lights and Tiki Torches. It is peaceful, and I am content. I sip my cabernet and set the glass down. I am writing my daily entry.

I started this journal a few months back right after I was told in that lucent dream to study the signs to learn what I am to do to assist Ami. The same dream that suggested I am a protector guide. I don't understand any of it, but I am intrigued by watching the Universe; I always have been.

When I was younger, particularly in my teenage years, I rarely shared my thoughts and feelings with others. Why? I'm not quite sure, except it just felt like it would be an unnecessary exchange. So, I wouldn't share my insights, and when someone asked what I thought or felt, it became an uncomfortable place for me. Had I been in therapy, a psychologist might have suggested low self-esteem. I can see how I was wrong back then, but now I wonder if it has to do with my role here. I believe I am here to observe, witness, and record. It's just a feeling.

I have a theory. I believe there is intelligence that governs everything. There's an interconnectedness with all. I think we get so busy with life that we fail to see it. I call this intelligence the Universe, though you may call it God or Spirit. I believe the Universe guides us, or it can if we open to it.

When the dream suggested that I watch the signs, the first thing I thought of was the experiences I had at UCSB. At the beginning of the second semester of my freshman year, I dropped a class because it was at the butt crack of dawn, then I had no courses until one o'clock in the afternoon. I figured I'd make it up another year, but a couple of days later, I experienced conflict. I couldn't get a refund on the books from the dropped class, I lost the keys to my dorm, and there was a screw up with my meal plan. I also felt guilty about dumping the course, and intuitively sensed the conflict was because of it. After missing a week of lectures, I resumed the early period, and the discord resolved. It ended up being a remarkable course confirming my interest in computer science; the professor was excellent, and he retired the following year.

I find it interesting that we remember events in hindsight when things rock our world. We don't usually remember them as well when the events flow with ease and grace. Today, I watch the Universe and notice its rhythm. I record my observations and how they relate to things transpiring in my life. It is a tedious process.

When things go smooth and effortless, I don't take it for granted anymore; I express gratitude for it. On days when things go awry, I sort through what has changed, and express thanks for the lesson, even though I may be clueless what it is. I wonder, 'What have I changed?' I consider the possibility that the Universe disagreed with it. Or perhaps I was heading in the wrong direction.

I started psychic development classes shortly after that dream about having an alien-like body. It has increased my awareness of what is happening around me. I have learned that when I quiet my mind and pay attention to what is going on, I become aware of the Universe's rhythm. It was then that I began noticing coincidences. I started journaling them and soon realized that the more attention I give to looking for them, the more they occur.

It hit me that these coincidences were giving me messages. I turn my journal to an entry a couple of months earlier.

> *While at work, I was talking with a couple of colleagues outside the conference room. One of them mentions her husband, Frances. A couple of minutes later, in the meeting, I am introduced to Frances from the home office. Then the presenter refers to an article in a journal published by the Francis Group. I think, 'My brother, Dennis's middle name is Francis.' I wondered how he was doing. I hadn't spoken to him in months.*
>
> *I leave the meeting; I call Dennis. He was in the emergency room, with Joshua struggling with pneumonia.*

As I read my journal entry, I remember how scared Dennis was. It was the second time my toddler nephew, Josh, had pneumonia. I wouldn't have known if I hadn't called Dennis, and I wouldn't have called if I hadn't experienced the synchronicities.

They were, without a doubt, meaningful coincidences. Could it be that the Universe guides us through synchronicity? Or could it be that when we are more spiritually engaged, synchronicity is a side effect? Or perhaps both?

Then there is this other thing that happens called serendipity. I turn the pages to another journal entry.

> *I was heading home from work on C-470 and got stuck in traffic because of construction. I decided to get off the highway and take the frontage road. As I pass a gas station, I figured I'd fill up.*

> *While doing so, a car pulls into the next bay, and a woman steps from the vehicle. I looked at her—do a double-take—it was Lisa, from UCSB. We had lost touch with each other. We went to dinner and talked about the forces at play. After all, I was in traffic and took a detour. Lisa was lost and stopped for directions. It was such a serendipitous reunion.*

As I read my words, I am so much more convinced that the universe sends us messages in serendipity. We don't meet people of like minds often, so when we do, we owe it to ourselves to remain in contact with each other. That was my message.

I'm convinced that a higher intelligence orchestrates these detours in life. I believe that these coincidences are messages from the Universe and that the Universe's pulse can provide insight into whether we are heading in the right direction, or not!

I take a sip of my wine, then continue writing today's journal entry. I realize this is all my experience of the way the Universe seems to work with me. I have much to learn and know that it will take years to understand all this thoroughly.

CHAPTER 28:
"NEED TO LIGHT UP AUTISTICS COMING IN."

July 19, 1997

Sunny, warm and dry, another beautiful summer day in Colorado. Rebecca arrives at Ami's home and finds the gang in the backyard, including Crystal and Leilah.

"Would you and Ami be interested in joining Leilah and me for a picnic at a nearby park?" Crystal asks Rebecca.

"That sounds like a lot of fun."

In no time, the four of them are in Crystal's car and begin to leave when Sarah emerges from the house and flags them down.

Crystal lowers the window to talk to the attendant, "Is everything alright?"

"It's fine. I forgot to give you Leilah's medicine. She takes it at meals," she explains and hands her a small zippered plastic pouch.

"Thank you." Crystal takes the bag and drives away.

"I hope you don't mind me asking, what does she take?" Rebecca asks.

"Haloperidol...for behavioral issues."

Rebecca is grateful that Ami has not needed medication. She had been weaned off the seizure meds after the episodes stopped, and Ami assured her, she did not need it.

"I called Leilah's doctor this week and shared her FC breakthrough," Crystal says.

"What did he or she say?"

"He wasn't as thrilled about it as I would have expected.

It was odd. I asked if we could lower Leilah's meds, and he was not happy with the idea at all."

Rebecca has to bite her tongue. She wants to share her experience regarding Ami, but she knows how vital medication management is for autistics, and she hasn't known Crystal and Leilah very long.

Sometime later, they arrive at Palmer Park. They had picked up lunches from a nearby deli and bottles of water. Once in the park, they see a cluster of picnic tables beneath large trees that provide the needed shade from the warm Colorado sun. Crystal and Rebecca approach the tables, each holding their daughter's hand. There are three tables, one has a group of young adults, another has an older woman sitting alone, and the third table is empty.

The older woman smiles at them as they park themselves at the table. Rebecca smiles back, noting the woman's arthritic hands. They are similar to her grandmother's, who had rheumatoid arthritis. Then she sees the cane leaning against the picnic table near the woman.

Crystal and Rebecca set up their daughter's lunches and then prepare their own. They sit across from each other.

"This is a pleasant break from the group home," Rebecca says as she assists Ami with a plastic utensil.

"It is. I thought it'd be nice for the girls. I have to say that this has been such a long week. After the excitement last weekend, I've been looking forward to getting together again," Crystal pulls her long hair away from her face.

"Yes, I remember when Ami started writing, I couldn't wait each night to talk to her."

"Would you be able to teach me to facilitate? I would love to chat with Leilah independently." Crystal wipes Leilah's mouth with a paper napkin.

"Absolutely. Before we leave, I'll show you."

"There's so much controversy with FC. I started research-ing it this week."

"There is. It took years to get the school system to accept that Ami had been communicating with us and that her mes-sages were hers, not my own. It was bizarre." Rebecca looks at Ami. "I don't want to sound all conspiracy-like, but, at one point, I challenged the school board by asking, 'What are you afraid that the autistics will tell us?'"

The women fall into a pregnant pause. Then Crystal asks, "Don't you think it's strange what Leilah typed?"

"Which part? That Ami and Leilah talk telepathically?"

"Yes, that's strange, but I was thinking more about why she is here."

Rebecca searches her memory and repeats what Leilah had told them, "She is here to open hearts."

"Yes, don't you find that odd?"

"Much of what Ami has shared over the years is strange. Sometimes I even wondered if she was delusional." Rebecca is acutely aware that Ami sits beside her and knows she is listen-ing. "But, after all this time, I have to say that I believe her."

"Do you think they are talking telepathically?" Crystal asks.

"Ami has shared with me that she is telepathic. It is not surprising to me that Leilah is also."

"Do you think all autistics are telepathic?"

"I don't know. I believe that autistics all have gifts, like all of us, only they're harder to recognize. Perhaps, because they are so different, we don't give them a chance to express these gifts fully."

The girls finish their lunch, and Ami and Leilah rise. They awkwardly walk away from the picnic area, with some young adults at a nearby table staring at them.

Both Crystal and Rebecca are accustomed to the stares of bystanders and continue their conversation while watching their daughters.

"Leilah said she is here to open hearts...has Ami shared anything like that?"

Rebecca nods, "Ami has shared some pretty outrageous things." Rebecca pauses. She knows she hasn't spoken about much of what Ami has said. Not even with George. She hardly knows Crystal, but somehow she trusts her.

"Ami told me that..." she wonders where to begin. "God is love and that she is here to show people the way to God."

Crystal stares at her, not knowing what to say.

"Ami even stated that she's here to help save the world from the end of days." As soon as she says it, though, she wonders if she has made a mistake.

Crystal stares at her with eyes wide open. She doesn't say a thing.

Rebecca continues, "She said more autistic people are coming in, and they have chosen autism intentionally because it protects them from annihilation."

There—she said it and got it off her chest. For years she has kept this secret, and hadn't shared it with anyone, except George. Oddly, she and George had never spoken of it since then, and she never broached the subject with Ami.

"I don't know what to say," Crystal finally breaks the silence.

"She also has encouraged that I must grow inwardly, something about needing to be more spiritual to live through the changes that are coming, and that I am to assist her in her journey."

"Of saving the world?" Crystal says with a smile.

"I know this all sounds crazy."

Crystal nods in agreement. "A bit!"

Rebecca wonders if she had made a mistake sharing with Crystal.

At that moment, the girls return to the table. This time, Leilah sits beside Rebecca. She is much more flexible than Ami and effortlessly hops onto the picnic table bench. Ami approaches Crystal, who assists her with negotiating the seat.

"Did you want to talk, Leilah?" Rebecca asks as she takes her hand and proceeds to type.

"True, what Rebecca says," Leilah types.

"Of course, it is," Crystal says politely.

"Don't believe her, we know."

"My feelings aren't hurt," Rebecca says, smiling at Crystal. "It *is* outrageous."

"Need U to believe," Leilah types.

As Leilah finishes typing, though, Rebecca knows that Crystal finds all this to be unbelievable. She suspects that Crystal is beginning to doubt the FC messages. Perhaps even, Crystal believes that she is the delusional one.

"I think, maybe, you should type something only your mom and you know, Leilah, so that she believes the messages are from you. Not from me," she suggests.

Leilah is quiet for a moment. Then she begins typing, "A green man, when you first met Daddy, he was."

While Rebecca hasn't a clue about what the message means, she knows it is meaningful to Crystal.

"How would you even know that?" Crystal asks her daughter.

"Daddy."

"When did he tell you?"

"Now."

There is a long pause as Crystal gathers her thoughts. 'My husband is here? At the park? And Leilah can see him?' Her voice is shaky. "Daddy is here?"

"Yes. Macho Man and Boogie Oogie Oogie, fondly, he remembers."

Tears fill Crystal's eyes. She remains still and tries to pull

157

herself together before speaking. "I met my husband at a party in 1978, at the height of the disco era. He always thought he was such a dancing stud," she laughs. "We danced to those songs the night we met."

"I don't understand the green-man comment," Rebecca says.

A smile emerges from Crystal's lips. "It was a Halloween party, and he was Lou Ferrigno's Hulk."

Leilah types, "What Rebecca says, true. Need U."

Almost simultaneously, the girls stand and swap places so that the mothers and daughters are sitting beside each other, and Ami begins typing.

"Need to light up autistics coming in."

"We need to light up autistics? What exactly does that mean?" Rebecca asks.

"They need to awaken to who they are and why here. Autistics need to be Activated."

"Help us understand. How does that happen?" Rebecca asks.

"Lit when honored."

"Didn't Leilah say something about putting a person of God near her woke her up?" Crystal adds.

"Yes, I think that is what she said."

Ami types, "Need a parent to recognize the truth about who they are, and they wake."

"What is the truth?"

"Divine. Perfect as-is. Don't need to be fixed."

The young adults near them get up from their table. They take a frisbee and move into the nearby field where they begin playing frisbee football. The older woman nearby remains at the other table reading.

"I don't understand," Crystal says.

"Is it as simple as honoring them by recognizing that they're not broke? They are just different?" Rebecca asks.

"Begins there. Unlit autism has no joy. Once lit, we love life. We have a purpose. We remember."

"You remember what?"

"Have a significant role to play. Planetary healers, we are."

The older woman who had been sitting at the nearby table stands. She is smiling and humming. She picks up her book and proceeds to depart, leaving behind a cane leaning on the picnic table's edge.

It is Crystal who notices the cane. "Excuse me, ma'am?" she says.

The older woman turns, smiling, "Yes?"

"Your cane?" Crystal points.

She looks at it and smiles. "Do you believe in miracles?"

Crystal, looking at her daughter, nods. "Yes, I do."

"I no longer need it. My prayers have been answered. But I have a feeling that someone in the park will find a better use for it." She smiles again and looks at Ami and Leilah. "You have a blessed day."

The woman walks confidently toward the parking lot.

Crystal returns to the subject at hand. It is a lot to take in for her. And yet, is it? 'Isn't this what leaps of faith are about?' She looks at her daughter, then Ami. "Okay, I get it. FC is for real, and," looking at Rebecca, "our daughters are here to change the world. What can I do to help?"

Ami types, "Need to turn inward. Need voices to educate how exceptional autistics are so they can be lit."

"I need to turn inward?" Crystal asks.

"Ami has told me the same, that I need to be more spiritual," Rebecca offers.

All this is a lot to take in for Crystal. She's not sure how to begin, then she asks, "Can I learn how to facilitate?"

For forty-five minutes, Rebecca schools Crystal on facilitating first with Ami then follows with her daughter. She is getting comfortable with it when there is a blood-curdling scream from the field.

Both Rebecca and Crystal turn to the field where the young adults were playing football frisbee. The young men and women now huddle around two men on the ground where they had collided.

Slowly they stand. One has a bloody nose, and the other rises more slowly, hopping on one leg, trouble putting weight on one ankle. The man with the bloody nose supports his friend, and they both make their way back to the picnic area. The others follow and quickly gather their belongings.

The injured man sits at a nearby table, and Rebecca sees his swollen ankle. The man with the bloody nose presses a tissue to it. "Do you think it's broken?" he asks his friend.

"I don't know."

"Let's get you to the ER," someone in the group says.

Rebecca sees the cane leaning on the other table. 'How did she know?' she wonders. She retrieves the walking stick and hands it to the young man.

"Whose is this?" he asks.

"I believe it is for you.

CHAPTER 29:
EVERYONE NEEDS TO RECOGNIZE THEIR GIFTS

Ami

I love the park. It is calming to my soul, and I feel the energy from the trees and plants. I need to let Mom know that she should bring us here more often; it is so peaceful. As we approach a cluster of picnic tables, I see a group of people having their lunch. They are young and vibrant and are enjoying their day. Most of them have only a few emotional scars at this point, if any. Their energy flows together, and there are few holes.

The lady that sits alone at one picnic table reading has many scars and many energy holes. Remember? I see energy. Where there are holes, there is no movement, no light, only darkness. She is sad and alone and has little joy in her life. She has had a falling out with her daughter and is searching. As she holds her book in her hands, she appears to be reading, but she is praying. I hear her prayers. I see that she is sick, and slowly becoming crippled, which is why she has a cane.

Mom and Crystal are talking, and Leilah and I don't need to be part of this discussion. *"Leilah, let's do some healing,"* I tell her.

I rise, and Leilah follows my lead. Slowly, I walk past the table where the woman who has many energy holes sits. She looks up from her book at me. I permit our eyes to meet. It does not take very long. With my mind, I tap into God's resonance and draw down the Light. I cast the beam of white Light upon her. The Light shifts the woman's awareness of God, and her soul wakes up to her higher Godself.

After the Light reaches her, we have a conversation. I telepathically talk to the woman's higher Godself as I continue my way to the grass where I lay down, and she basks in the Light.

Did you know that everyone has a Godself and that It recognizes the Truth? Did you know that the Higher Self can talk with us?

I say, *"You are a blessing, and you are blessed."*

She tells me, *"I am so in awe of all that you are and all that you are doing. Thank you for being here on this planet."*

I see her beauty. *"I understand you are in pain. I hear your lower-self prayers. Does your Godself desire to heal?"* I ask her.

I feel Leilah quietly stir near me on the grass. I know she is watching and learning how to heal. Leilah can do this too. She has done it, without knowing what she has done.

"I would very much like to be healed. My daughter is expecting her first child. I want to be around to see him grow and to love him. I need to mend fences with my daughter, who has become estranged to me." The woman pauses. *"I have forgotten who I am. I am stuck in a faith that demands obedience to some far-reaching, judgmental God. I live in fear and don't think I can heal myself with my current frame of mind."*

"Very well," I tell her.

When I look at a person in my mind, I see their energy. The human energy field is a combination of overlapping energy patterns that express an individual's mind, body, and soul make up. It should be no surprise that people's energy is different. Inside the frame of a person, I see energy meridians. These are energetic pathways throughout the person's physical body that connect organs and subsystems like digestion, circulation, and so on. Then I perceive what you perhaps refer to as chakras, spinning wheels, or if I am looking from the side, I see little tornadoes. That is if they are open. Then there are the five energy bodies that resonate outward from the physical body.

When someone is not healthy, the energy has holes or dark spots within the meridians and energy bodies. The chakras' spinning wheels can be distorted with an elliptical turn, or even become severely flattened on its sides. The woman's energy pattern has many holes and jagged lines that don't flow together.

Now that the kind woman's Godself is awake and has asked for healing, I can work, but it isn't me that does the healing, it is Source energy or God.

With my mind, I send my Light, which is God's Light, to the woman and see her energy respond. Those blocked energy areas instantly begin flowing, and her energy patterns change, the voids are now full, and the jagged edges are now smooth. I see her heart lit with God's Love and Light.

I sense the woman's unconditional love. I say, "*You are Love, and you are loved.*" I leave her in her glory to be with the Divine and return to myself, laying in the grass.

Leilah watches intently and sees the energy vehicles of Light awaken God within the woman. She sees the shift in her energy and healing.

Leilah talks to me. "*I can heal people too?*"

"*Yes, Leilah. It is one of our gifts. Once lit, an autist treats consciously. Even unlit, unconscious autistics have a healing presence that is not recognized.*"

"*I saw that you didn't touch her hurt. You touched her when she awoke to her Higher Self.*"

"*Yes, that is right.*"

"*Does she know?*"

"*Her Godself does. If It did not, it would not be right to help. The person treated needs to permit the healing because you never know if the High-Self desires to transition. Most people do not remember when they return to their lower selves. Their low vibration energy scars become healed. They get a fresh start. They are stirred to find healthier ways of life to maintain their higher vibration, or they will slip into old ways and relapse. But they have a chance to shift their lives for the better."*

"So, the woman is healed temporarily?"

"At this moment, the woman is healed and has been seeded with a deep yearning for love and life. If her lower self can anchor in that love, she will let go of the fear, and she will remain healed."

Leilah and I return to the picnic table and have a conversation with Crystal and Mom. It is essential to get Crystal onboard. She is vital to our journey, and we need her, yet her path is uncertain, and if she is hesitant, Leilah's role in the events to come become questionable.

I watch the healed woman become aware that she is whole. Some don't always embrace their healing. They may feel better, but they look for the aches and pains, and rather than rejoicing that they are whole and perfect, they chalk it up to having a good day. Then, when any discomfort emerges, they give it attention and relapse.

Did you know that the symptom only has power through the attention you grant it? The human body has everything it needs to heal itself and can do so spontaneously. But, when we give any symptoms, any discomfort, any pain, any negative thoughts, our energy, we nurture it, and it grows.

What I did with the kind woman at the park was a spiritual reset or reboot of her energetic system. I got the energy to flow. It is she who will keep it flowing, or she may fall into the falsehood of life.

The lie of our existence is that we are separate from God. We are not separate at all. That is part of the illusion. To think that God is some distant entity that sits in judgment is an illusion. The truth is that you are just as all-powerful. You need to awaken to this Truth. It is time. There is no gift that any one person has that another doesn't have. Every one of you has it. It was Jesus who told us that someday people would do what he did and so much more. It is that day, but you have to awaken to it.

I say this not to boost your ego because it is the ego that keeps you small and from recognizing how powerful you indeed are. I say this because everyone is needed and has a role to play in the events to come. Everyone needs to get on board and recognize their gifts because the world needs them. I hope that you uncover your role, and soon.

Some time passes, then the kind woman rises from the bench, picks up her book, and starts to leave. She is feeling awe and wonder and gratitude for her life and healing. She looks at her hands and sees her previously curled-under fingers straighter than she had seen them in years. She smiles and begins humming.

"Excuse me, ma'am?" Crystal says.

"Yes?" the woman asks, smiling.

"Your cane?" Crystal points.

"Do you believe in miracles?" the healed woman asks.

Crystal looks at her daughter. I hear her mind chatting, *"My daughter is talking to me—that is a miracle!"* Crystal nods, "Yes, I do."

"I no longer need it. My prayers have been answered. But I have a feeling that someone in the park will find a better use for it." She smiles again and looks kindly at me, then Leilah. "You have a blessed day."

If my heart had lips, it would smile when I see the young man limping toward the picnic area. Of course, I am not happy because he is injured. I am pleased that the kind lady tapped into one of *her* gifts, whether it was intuition, clairsentience, or clairvoyance. The woman knew that someone would have a use for the cane. I had nothing to do with it.

CHAPTER 30:
I TOOK THE CUP OF BLOOD.
I DISCIPLE JOHN.

July 30, 1997

The scent of pork fried rice fills Crystal's car as she arrives at the Cheyenne Village home. She had picked up take-out while passing through Manitou Springs. 'Leilah's favorite.'

It is Wednesday evening, and Crystal typically visits after dinner. She's excited, though. After nearly twenty years of silence and not being able to communicate with her daughter, she is determined to make up for the lost time. 'We can test drive my new letterboard!' She grabs it along with the bag of takeout and heads to the house.

Crystal is an accountant for a local engineering company and has been loyal to the firm for nearly twenty years. In return, she's earned flexible hours, which helps manage the challenges of having a special-needs child.

When she lost her husband only a couple of years earlier, her life changed dramatically. Jason had been a technical writer and worked out of their home. Without him to help with Leilah's programs, doctor's visits, maintaining the house, Crystal could not manage her daughter, the household, and her career. She needed a solution, and a full-time caregiver wasn't affordable. Someone at work encouraged her to look into Cheyenne Village. Leilah was just shy of eighteen years at the time. Crystal hated the idea at first, but as it turned out, by going to Cheyenne Village, the quality of their time together improved. Her visits were no longer about being a caregiver. They were about *being* a mother visiting her daughter. She didn't have to worry about feeding her, administering her meds, changing her if she had an accident, or clothing her. All those things that seemed to be chores were no longer her responsibility, and she could love her daughter and enjoy helping the attendants with her care when needed.

When Leilah first moved in, Crystal's time with her daughter was challenging as the two of them needed to find their way. After Ami moved in, Leilah changed in subtle ways that she couldn't put her finger on.

Now that Leilah was communicating with FC, their conversations were deep and meaningful. These days, Crystal looks forward to seeing Leilah just about every night, and most evenings, they share dinner. She even takes Leilah out to a restaurant at times, a feat she had never attempted by herself before.

She arrives at the home in time to see the other residents and Leilah finishing their dinners and clearing their plates.

"Hi, Crystal," Sarah says, eyeing the bag of Chinese food, "She's had dinner. We ate a bit early tonight."

Crystal hides the bag from Leilah. She can always have some later and doesn't want her daughter to know she had brought her favorite if she's already eaten.

Shortly after, Crystal and Leilah are in the sunroom, away from evening activities and the other residents. A letterboard is on the table between them.

"What would you like to speak about this evening?" Crystal asks.

Before she finishes the sentence, Crystal feels Leilah's hand move to the keys. "Life," she types.

"That's a big topic! What do you think life is all about?"

"A freewill game. A chance to uncover the truth."

"Life is a freewill game and a chance to uncover the truth? What truth?"

"God creators, we are."

"Chance to learn that God creates us?"

"NO. GOD creators, WE are."

"We are God creators?"

"Yes."

"How do you know this?"

"Master of many lives."

"You've had other lives?"

"Yes."

"Do you remember any?"

"Most."

"You remember *most* of your lives?"

"Yes."

"How many?"

"Many."

"Well, I have many questions, but is there anything you want to share about your past lives?"

"Was expecting Jesus to be here."

"Jesus? You mean Jesus Christ?"

"Yes. Jesus is supposed to be here."

"And he is not?"

"No."

"How do you know Jesus?"

"Him, I followed."

"Leilah, this is a past life you're talking about?"

"Yes."

"Were you a priest or minister? And that is what you mean by following him?"

"No. I followed."

Crystal looks at her daughter. 'Could it be?' She feels pressure from Leilah's hand. She wants to say more.

"The cup of blood I took. I disciple John. Expecting him here, lonely without him."

"You were the apostle, John?"

"YES."

Crystal doesn't know how to respond to this. How could Leilah come up with these thoughts? She changes the subject intentionally. "Why are you here?"

"Don't believe me, I know. I here to ensure way. To show the will of God."

"What is the will of God?"

"To save the planet."

Crystal still doesn't know what to say. She stares at her daughter.

"For you, too much. You don't believe it."

"I need to think about this, Leilah. It is a lot to absorb. Let's chat more tomorrow night. Would you like me to bring some dinner?

"No. Fried rice you brought tonight, let's have."

It's hard for Crystal to keep her mind on her work the following day. After an early afternoon staff meeting, her boss asks if she'd mind picking up supplies from the local office supply store. Crystal agrees and leaves, but finds herself heading west instead, back to Leilah's Cheyenne Village home. She knows the office supply store is open until nine o'clock, and it is a beautiful day. Crystal can always work on the monthly P&L from her home computer too. Perhaps she and Leilah can enjoy their afternoon together.

Within a half-hour, Crystal picked up Leilah and the two head east. Within ten minutes, they are at the Garden of the Gods, perfect for a short hike and place to connect. Crystal puts on her hiking sandals she has in the trunk and grabs a fanny pack with some water, a snack, and hangs her letterboard from her shoulder.

She takes Leilah's hand, and they head toward the Perkins Central Garden Trail. It is an effortless mile and a half trek, but given that it was late in the afternoon, it seems to be a perfect way to end any workday. She knows the challenge will be to find a quiet place to chat with Leilah because of all the tourists. She never worries much about Leilah's athletic ability. Her daughter always loves being outside, and hiking is their favorite way to connect.

It is warm and pleasant in the mid-eighties. While there are tourists along their way snapping photos of the unusual sandstone rock formations and dramatic views, Crystal and Leilah are in their own world. They are about a mile into the walk when Leilah releases Crystal's hand and heads away from the paved path into the natural dirt and brush.

Crystal permits Leilah to lead the way, and as expected, as soon as they are away from the beaten path, Leilah sits in the dirt. With knees bent to her chest and arms down by her sides, she feels the earth beneath her hands. Leilah rests her head on her knees, picks up a pile of dirt, and runs it through her fingers.

After a few minutes, she lays down on her side, curls her knees forward, and rests her head on one of her hands. She sifts through the dirt, seemingly fascinated with it. She giggles and looks around at what would seem to be nothing.

Crystal sits not far from Leilah and patiently waits. After about ten minutes, Leilah sits up and looks near her.

"Would you like to talk, Leilah?" She scoots over to her daughter and retrieves a letterboard from her bag and takes her daughter's hand.

"Yes," Leilah types.

"Yesterday, you shared with me that you were Apostle John."

"Yes."

"You had expected Jesus to be here. And he is not."

"Yes."

"From what I remember of my Christian studies, Jesus is to return for the end of days."

170

"Yes."

"You expect the world is coming to an end this lifetime?"

"YES."

Crystal doesn't know what to say. She stares at her daughter, 'Surely, she could be wrong or delusional.'

"You don't believe me."

Crystal doesn't know what to tell her daughter. She doesn't want to believe her. "If Jesus isn't here, maybe this isn't the life for the end of the world." She could have presented it as a question though Crystal wasn't sure she wanted to learn more. "Why are *you* here? What is *your* purpose?" Crystal asks.

"Show will of God and save the planet."

"That seems to be such a massive undertaking. How are you going to do this?"

"Open hearts will show the way to God."

"So, you will open people's hearts?"

"Yes."

"And *that* will save the planet?"

"Yes."

"How will you open hearts?"

"Love them, I will."

Crystal can't imagine how her daughter's love would be the answer to saving the planet. She changes the questions. "Are you here to learn something?"

"Yes. Everyone is here to learn something."

"You want to share more?"

"Here to learn humility. Here to teach you patience."

The mother and daughter chat for another hour. Before that day, Crystal could never have imagined such deep philosophical conversations with her. That afternoon they exchange thoughts about God, purpose, and other things she could never have imagined possible.

Crystal is in awe of all that is transpiring between the two. A shadow is cast upon the letterboard, revealing the sun is sinking behind the mountains to the west. "I think that's our cue." Crystal puts the letterboard back in her bag and stands. She places her hand on Leilah's shoulder. "Let's head back. We have some fried rice waiting for us."

When Crystal returns home that night, she wants to share her conversations about Leilah with someone, and the first person that comes to mind is Rebecca. She knows she'll see her the following night as Friday nights had become a bonding time for the women.

Crystal had offered Rebecca her guest room anytime she visited Ami, and Rebecca had started coming down on Friday afternoons after classes. It had become customary for Rebecca, Crystal, and the girls to have dinner together. The women often would find themselves back at Crystal's house, enjoying a glass of wine while sharing their experiences that week.

The following evening, Crystal and Rebecca are on the deck. Crystal stuffs her chiminea with pinon branches, and with a flick of the lighter, a flame ignites the fire stick and slowly burns the branches. Soon the air has a sweet aromatic piney scent.

Crystal hands a glass of wine to Rebecca and settles in a chair beside her. "The information our daughters are telling us...where do you think the information is coming from?"

"Doubting it?" Rebecca asks.

"Questioning. Testing. Wondering about it. This week Leilah shared some unique information about her past lives."

"Leilah's previous lives? Wow! I can't say Ami has done that," Rebecca says, "What did she say?"

"Leilah claims to be here to learn humility and teach me patience."

"Seems very fitting to me," Rebecca chuckles.

"She says that she is here to share her Light with the world. Her purpose, she said, is to show the will of God, which is to save the planet."

Crystal waits for what she told Rebecca to sink in, then, "She said that she's almost finished with her Earth incarnations and that the soul begins with God and always ends with God."

"The soul begins and ends with God! Wow! You had an insightful week with her."

"In a past life, she was a high priest in ancient Egypt. She said something odd. She said, 'I was way.' She believed that 'the way' should be shared with all, not just the privileged. She was a man in that lifetime and set out to teach those deemed unworthy. The pharaoh cursed and murdered her. She thinks she's still cursed."

"Interesting, in the Bible, 'the way' means an understanding of Truth itself."

"She told me that Xerxes and Cleopatra were ones that cursed her. And it prevents her from, and I quote her, 'seeing everything.'"

"Xerxes and Cleopatra lived in different centuries. From what I remember, they both were pharaohs of Egypt, though, and both were tyrants and ruthless."

"Leilah said it was in Egypt around 38 BC."

"That would be Cleopatra's life. Xerxes ruled in the 400s BC. He was the king of Persia."

"Perhaps someone else had the same name during the Cleopatra reign?"

"Could be, or maybe Cleopatra was the reincarnation of Xerxes?"

"Now we're letting our imagination soar!" Crystal chuckles.

"True, but such a thought-provoking life," Rebecca says. "About spreading Truth, and yet ending with a cruel demise."

"Rebecca, the first life she told me about, I can't shake."

Rebecca senses Crystal's unease. "What was it?"

"She claims she had been one of Jesus' apostles."

"Really? Who?"

"John."

Rebecca leans forward, considering what Crystal had told her. She grabs a log and places it in the chiminea.

"There's more. Leilah says she was expecting to see Jesus here because the end of days is near."

"My gosh! That *is* fascinating."

"You call that fascinating? Is it bad that it alarms me?"

"What's fascinating is that she claims to be *John* and here to reveal God's will to save the planet."

Rebecca seems a little too excited for Crystal. "Thrilled that you think this is good stuff!"

"Crystal, do you know *what* John wrote?"

"The Gospel of John would be my guess."

"That's correct. Also, First, Second, and Third John, but more importantly, John wrote The Book of Revelation."

"The gloom and doom book that prophesied the end of the world?"

"Yeah!"

"Why are you so fascinated by this?"

"Well, it is interesting that John wrote the end of days prophecies, and is here claiming that it's God's *will* to save the planet, and she's here to show the *way*. I think that would be good news—that God wants to save the world. Don't you?"

"You believe her?"

"Much of what Ami has told me over the years is unbelievable, yet, I do believe it. I have no reason to doubt what Leilah has said also. Why would she fabricate something like that?"

The women fall into silence.

"Have you thought about what *we* should be doing to

support our daughters with their purpose?" Rebecca breaks the quiet.

"Leilah said that she's here to open hearts by loving people, and that will save the planet."

"And Ami told me years ago she is here to help people find God. How are we to support them? Or, if they are here to help autistics get, what was the term? Lit? How do we help parents or caregivers recognize that their autistic children are perfect and Divine the way they are? How can we spread this info?"

"Good questions," Crystal ponders.

"Ami somehow knew where to connect with Leilah."

"I know, how odd!"

"Maybe they need to connect with others. Or, perhaps we should try to reach out to other autistics and see if they also have the ability to wake up and communicate."

"And if they wake up?" Crystal asks.

"If they *do*, and they express similar insights, don't we owe it to the world to let people know that their autistic loved ones have a purposeful life waiting for them?"

"I think there is another autistic man at Cheyenne Village."

"What if we reach out to the autism centers in the Springs and Denver and say we're looking for nonverbal autistics to communicate using FC?"

"I think that's a start."

"I can reach out to the Denver metro area. You take on Colorado Springs. Perhaps if we can find a few others that demonstrate similar insights, we may have something worthy to share with the world."

"Don't you think we have something worthy now?"

"Facilitated communication is not widely respected and has such a controversial history. If we could teach other nonverbals and their parents or caregivers how it works, *and* if they

'Light' up, we'll have more to share."

"Then what?"

"If we can get some momentum and a reputation, we can reach out to organizations across the country," Rebecca said. "Maybe even write a book and spread the good word."

CHAPTER 31:
TELL MOM TO LET DAD GO!

August 2, 1997

George had been supportive of Ami's life in Manitou Springs and encouraged Rebecca to visit most weekends. When Ami first moved to the supported living house, he'd visit her once a month, but over the last few months, he had become so busy at work that his Cheyenne Village visits took a backseat.

A couple of years earlier, he was promoted to district manager. He excelled rapidly. The previous district manager had been enjoying a smooth ride into retirement, and made no significant changes, even when he had pointed out some new ways of doing things. It was probably his manager's inactiveness that forced him to retire, and George moved into his position.

For years, his suggestions went unheard. Once given the opportunity, he made quick changes to policies, goals, expenditures, and upgraded technologies for the staff. These moves got the attention of upper management, and they watched what he was doing like a hawk.

After the first year was over, his district had met its quota for the first time in years and paid for all their technology upgrades by cutting unnecessary expenses. Office morale had significantly improved, and turnover dropped. After two years, his district's sales were up almost 30 percent, and he was beckoned to headquarters to share what he was doing to manage his office.

His meeting with senior management went fantastic, at

least that was his take on it.

When Rebecca returns home the following evening, she is excited to share with George their plan to get Ami and Leilah's messages out into the world.

George had been traveling all week and came home earlier that day. While he's sitting there looking at her, Rebecca knows he isn't listening.

"Where are you?" she asks. "You're not here."

"That obvious?"

"Yes."

George takes a deep breath, "I don't know where to begin."

"Tell me what's so important that you're elsewhere."

"My boss asked me to take on a new position, one not in Denver," he says, eyeing her.

Rebecca knew this day might come but somehow just didn't see it happening this soon. "Where do they want you to relocate?"

"Headquarters, in Norwalk."

"Are you serious?"

"They want me to work with the district offices that are struggling and turn them around. I'd be traveling from an office in Connecticut to Boston, Chicago, and Phoenix to start."

Rebecca doesn't know what to say. "Do you have to take it?"

He's shocked. "Yeah, I do. It'd send the wrong message if I didn't. It's a promotion. A big one at that!"

"So, you'd be traveling all over the country."

"Pretty much. The company wants me to recreate what I've been doing in Denver at a handful of locations."

"So, you'd be absent the majority of the time?"

"Yes."

"Why do you have to relocate then?"

"It's considered a promotion. I'd be vice president of some long title." He smiles. "All senior-level managers work out of headquarters."

"I don't want to go. Why would I relocate just to be alone in a strange house?"

"I'm sorry, sweetheart, you'll learn to like it."

Rebecca is surprised at how quickly the words come out. "I'm not going."

"Sweetheart, you—"

"It doesn't make any sense for us to uproot Ami and relocate to the east coast just so that you travel all over the country, with me being there, not knowing anyone."

"I don't think we should take Ami out of Cheyenne Village. She seems to be doing well there, and with all my frequent flyer miles, we can get you to the Springs every few months."

Rebecca does not believe what she is hearing. Did he expect her to drop her life in Denver to go to Norwalk? Did he expect her to leave her daughter? Her job? Her friends? Her community?

Rebecca's head is pounding. She cannot think. "George, I love you, and I don't want to lose you, but given the choice of visiting every few months, I'd prefer to stay here in our home and visit you every other month."

"You'd prefer to stay here with Ami than to be with me?"

George is hurt, and Rebecca knows it. "I'm sorry, I don't mean to hurt you, George. I just feel Ami needs—"

"You win," George's voice rises. "You stay with Ami. Don't visit, though."

"George, what are you saying?"

"We're done."

"Just like that?"

"Rebecca, it's been over for some time now. Let's both..." George pauses to compose himself and gather his thoughts. "Let's both move on while we're still young enough to start over, and we still respect each other enough not to turn on each other."

Rebecca did not see this coming. Her mind is racing. While she and George have not been the closest couple, she still cares and loves him very much. They had gotten into a rhythm of life that was comfortable to her. He was away much of the time, which gave her the freedom to do what she wanted. She could attend spirituality workshops, visit Ami, join her meditation group, or be more involved at her school. She hadn't even considered that he might want something else.

"You want to separate?"

"No. I think we need to divorce."

Rebecca's stomach drops. Her face pales. It isn't that she fears to move on without him because he left some time ago. It is more about failure. She hates to fail. The intimacy of marriage was long gone, but there had been a mutual respect between the two. They had become the best of friends. 'Isn't what we have something worth fighting to keep?' She wonders.

"We're always going to have Ami, and we'll always be a part of each other's life. We're almost fifty, Rebecca, I just want the opportunity to have an ordinary family. Is that so bad?"

"I guess I just don't know what to say, George. I assumed this was working for you. I didn't realize you were unhappy."

"It is no secret, Rebecca. I've always wanted other children, but my desires always took a backseat. It's time I start taking care of me," he lets the words sink in. "I will always take care of Ami. You know that, don't you?"

"Yes, I don't doubt that."

"We'll need to liquidate and split everything."

The telephone rings.

"Let the answering machine get it," George says. "We're not finished."

Rebecca moves to the phone, and because of a new caller ID feature, she sees it is Ami's Cheyenne Village house calling. She picks up the phone and looks back at George. "Apparently, we are." She holds the phone to her ear. "Hello?"

Crystal's voice reveals concern. "Rebecca, I'm at the house with Ami, and she keeps typing the same message. She asked me to call you and tell you."

"What is it?"

"Tell Mom to let Dad go," Crystal says. "She keeps typing it over and over again. Does it mean anything to you?"

Rebecca turns and looks at George. "Oh, yes."

CHAPTER 32:
I AM CERIAN

Freedom is a privilege. You chose to participate in an experiment; only you do not remember. You knew you wouldn't be able to recall any of this, but it was such a unique game and test, and everyone wanted to join in. You are a participant in the Humanoid Experiment.

The humanoid DNA was manipulated on more than one occasion. On Earth, many blame the Anunnaki for this, and they did re-engineer it. However, the DNA manipulation began before even Tiamat, all the way back to the beginning of your universe's creation.

While this may sound harsh, this dismantling of the DNA was intentional; to make the ascension of humanity *nearly* unachievable.

This *was* the Divine Plan.

This *was* part of the Master Blueprint of the Humanoid Expression in your universe.

This *is* the foundation for the human story—the greatest experiment in all worlds.

What I ask at this moment is that you absorb this and know this in your being. You signed up and chose this. There is no one to blame. Here are fundamental Truths you have failed to remember.

Source, or what you would call God, created every soul as a step-down version of Itself so that It could experience more of Itself, and every soul is Divine. Source created darkness so that It could truly discern Light by experiencing its polarity. Each human soul is pure Christ Consciousness, is perfect, Divine, and whole in every way, only it does not remember.

What is the Humanoid Experiment?

What if Pure Consciousness, that God-awareness was separated from matter intentionally, from Its being, but It remains intact, complete with the remembrance of its Pure Consciousness at Its Higher Soul or Higher Self?

What if the lower self, the lower consciousness, had a veil obscuring that It is Divine and given free will to choose whether it would follow a Light path or a dark path?

How would the existence now manifest? How would it create? Because all souls are creators, and they are here to create. Would the consciousness seek its Higher Self, it's Pure Consciousness? Would it seek out its stabilization, its polarity integration, or would it pursue power? Would it strive for control? Manipulation? Or beauty, love, and harmony?

Is it not a grander story to have consciousness awaken itself and realize Itself and Its capabilities, again? Isn't that a more meaningful story? That was always the hypothesis, and humankind is an experiment.

The game moderators, beings from different galaxies, and universes were involved in the development and implementation of the Master Blueprint of the universe. They were invited to participate in the game throughout time. They are the Cosmic Council, though you, at times, refer to some of its members as the Great White Brotherhood. These members were invited to fully participate and incarnate throughout time with one caveat, like you, they needed to forget who they are, and they needed to play on both sides of the spectrum, the Light, and the dark. Most of these Ascended Masters found their way back to their Higher Selves, and their mission remains to assist in the spiritual evolution of the planet's occupants. Other game moderators never made it back to the Light, however, and became lost in power and control and remain a threat to humankind and a menace to the game.

Remember that freedom is a privilege, this is an

experiment, and *the time has come to awaken to the truth about who you are.*

I am Cerian

CHAPTER 33:
ALIENS WALK AMONG US

March 2000

Levi

There is a part of me called to write. Of all things, writing! I was never good at it in school, nor did I have an interest. But lately, I keep thinking that I need to write something. I'm not sure what. I've regurgitated an idea in my head about what it's like to feel different, but somehow that falls flat. Maybe I am supposed to write about my observations of the signs, about how the Universe guides me.

I guess it comes down to purpose. *Why* do I want to write? I haven't a clue. The Universe keeps nudging me in this direction, even in my dreams. I went to a conference called "Finding Your Mission in Life." While I wasn't entirely successful pinpointing what my purpose is, the exercises and revelations suggested that I use writing as a tool to fulfill my reason for being here.

I set out to search for a local writers' group in the Denver area. On Google, I saw there is a Denver writers' conference for writing fiction, but I'm not sure if I am to write a novel. Then I saw the Pike's Peak Writers Conference, which seems broader and caters to both fiction and nonfiction. It's at the Broadmoor Hotel, which was the deciding factor. I have never been to the Broadmoor, but I've seen many pictures. I figure if the conference doesn't appeal to me, I can spend the weekend pampering myself at the resort.

I'm heading to the Springs now, and it's an early spring

day in late March. We had one of those spring snowstorms earlier, and I just white-knuckled it over Monument Hill. Now, as I enter Colorado Springs, the snow stopped, and the roads cleared.

Hours later, I register for the conference and go to the first session, which is running over its allotted time. When the meeting dismisses, I glance at my watch and see that I only have a minute to get to the next session.

Everyone bolts out, and I head toward another conference room around the corner, but by the time I get to it, it is full. People line the back of the wall. I walk down the center of the room, searching for an empty chair. There is one sandwiched between an older man and a woman. A glance around tells me I better take it, so I squeeze by people to reach the vacant chair. As I brush by a brunette beside the untaken seat, I lock eyes with her for an instant. She smiles at me, pauses for a bit, then bends her knees, permitting me to pass.

After what I would describe as a tedious session covering writing from multiple points of view, I look at the schedule to see what interests me in the next period.

Most everyone else around me is exiting the conference room when the woman beside me says, "Nothing appeals to me for the next session."

"Nothing looks interesting to me either," I say.

"Any interest in grabbing a cup of coffee?"

"That sounds good about now," I say.

The two of us make our way to a ballroom, which had coffee set up earlier, but the brewer is empty. "Let's go to the restaurant. My treat," the stranger offers. "I'm Angela, by the way."

"Levi," I say. "Nice to meet you."

Moments later, we have coffee to go and find a quiet spot in the lobby to sit. "I feel a little like a fish out of water here," I admit.

"Why?"

"I'm not really a writer. I've been toying with the idea."

"What do you mean?" she asks.

I'm not exactly sure how much I should share with this stranger. She seems very friendly, and I feel like I can say just about anything to her, but I'm not sure why. "I have this...inner guidance system, for lack of a better word. Lately, everything seems to lead me to believe I am to write something, but I haven't a clue what. So, I thought I'd come to a writers' conference and be inspired by all the creative energy and hope to gain some clarity."

The woman smiles. Angela has the most mesmerizing chestnut eyes and the longest eyelashes I have ever seen. She is dressed a bit eccentrically, with a black leather jacket, a vibrant red scarf to match her lipstick, designer jeans, and tall boots. She has beautiful long dark hair, and her makeup is flawless, unlike my own. For a moment, I wonder if she is a famous author. I wouldn't know; I especially don't read commercial fiction.

"What a perfect place to come for inspiration. Mingling among creative-likes should give you some ideas," Angela says.

"How about you? What do you write?" I ask.

"It depends on the day," she says vaguely. "You know, I want to share something with you. I'm told I should."

I wonder, 'Who told her?'

"I too, have a...what did you call it? An inner guidance system?" She smiles. "Something happened to me when you brushed by me in the conference room. Right before you sat beside me."

"What happened?"

"I glanced at the crystal around your neck, and spiraled to another time and place," she says.

"What do you mean?"

"One minute, I was in the conference room, and the

next I was in another time, in Europe walking on cobblestone streets during a period reminiscent of the Elizabethan era."

She says it so matter-of-factly that it makes me wonder if she is okay. I look at her, waiting for her to crack a smile and say, "Gotcha!" But, she doesn't, she just keeps staring at me.

"Are you serious?" I ask.

"Very. I wouldn't have said anything, but somehow, I think it's important for you to know. One minute I was here, then the next minute I was somewhere else...with you."

"With me?" There have been times in my life when I've had unique and bizarre experiences. But this one seems to have taken the cake. "What were we doing?"

"That isn't what is important," she says with a straight face. "I think, somehow, it's important that you know it *can* happen."

"Are you referring to previous lives?"

"I'm not certain it's about *past* lives. Because all time is one, and I could have gone to a place perceived as the future, but, in reality, it all happens concurrently."

"What do you mean?"

"Our many lives happen at the same time. Time isn't linear. It is more circular, and I could have gone to what our intellect would suggest is the future instead of the past because it's just as close. Time is unique for humanity or this dimension. Time, as we know it here, is simply for our brains to process experiences, but everything happens concurrently."

I don't know what to say. I stare at Angela. "What do you think I am to learn from this?" I ask without emotion.

She smiles. "There is one other thing I am to tell you though this isn't as easy. I'm not sure why, but apparently, it is also important for you to know, perhaps even the reason you have come here today."

Now I'm intrigued. "What is it?" I ask.

The woman looks at me and is silent. It seems like Angela

is trying to gather her thoughts, perhaps attempting to find a way to break it to me.

"What is it?" I ask. "Just spit it out!"

"On our planet, people are not always what they seem."

"I agree with that, for sure!"

"Some people that walk among us are not of this world."

"What do you mean?"

"Many people that live among us are from other worlds."

"Are you saying, aliens?"

"I guess you can call it that, but they blend in among us, and we wouldn't know they are ... alien."

"Why are you telling me this?"

"I am told it is something you need to know."

"Who told you?"

"Everyone has spirit guides. My guide tells me things to help me all the time. It is a bit unusual for it to share information about others. Given that you triggered a glimpse into one of my other lifetimes, it is evident we are connected, and there is a higher purpose at play here."

"So, your guide thinks I need to know that *aliens walk among us?*"

"Yes, and some are in very high places, places of power, and authority. My guide wants you to know that we don't recognize them as alien because they seem, in most ways, human. Another thing is the aliens, most of the time, haven't a clue who they are."

"I don't understand."

"While some are in positions of power, and may know who they are, most of these *beings* think they are human because of a veil. They have no reference to believing otherwise. They live ordinary lives, they work among us, go to our churches, get married, have children. They can spend an entire life unaware of who or what they are."

"Are you telling me this because it is to inspire me to

write about it?'"

"Perhaps. I don't know the reason. My guide told me it is important that you be aware of it at this point in your life."

Now my head is starting to hurt. I look at Angela and say, "I'm not sure what to do with this information or what to think."

"Don't worry about it! The reason it is coming to you will come to light at the perfect time. There is one other message for you."

"What is that?"

"Your nephew will be coming to stay with you soon."

This message doesn't give me warm fuzzies. Josh is my godson; he's my brother Dennis' child. He's five or six. Why would he come for a visit without his parents?

The sudden flurry of other conference attendees in the lobby signals that the next session is going to start soon. I politely thank Angela for the cup of coffee and head to my next class, very confused, and my head spinning.

When I leave the conference the following day, flashbacks of my conversation with Angela rerun in my head as if they're on "replay." My discussion with her was the oddest experience of my life, and I am convinced that it happened to me to direct me to do something. When I get home later that evening, I sit at my desk and go online to the search engine prompt and type in "aliens among us."

Using Google's endless listings and my inner guidance, I surf to sites that relay information on things that one would only believe was from a sci-fi novel. I read about secret societies, like the Bilderbergers, Freemasons, Skull and Bones, Illuminati, and about world control by these groups and that at the origin of these clandestine organizations is a demon-like being who is alien. According to these sites, this alien ruled these societies since their beginning, and remains in power today, controlling the world. The information reads like a novel, fiction I mean, only conspiracy-theory readers and writers believe it to be true.

'Do I believe it?' I ponder for a moment. "Hardly," I laugh out loud. "It would make a good story, though."

I light a candle and set an intention. I open a Word document and type,

> *Could it be that the father of humankind is not only an alien but also has come to be known as Beelzebub and the prince of demons?*

CHAPTER 34:
THE ALLIANCE BETWEEN THE LIGHT AND THE DARK

A Timeline Tweak–Return to March 1994

Mikael is to meet with an aspect or embodiment of his long-time nemesis, Hakathriel. The Dark Team leader has many guises to humankind. To some, he is a great man, a leader, perhaps even the most powerful man on the planet at this time, and worthy of being worshipped. To others, he is Lucifer, or Satan himself. The name he uses to walk among humanity in the twenty-first century is James.

Just as Archangel Mikael can walk among Earth's people and blend in as one of them, James can do the same and has, for eons. The only difference is that Mikael chose to play the game on the Light Team, and James picked the Dark Team long ago. What most don't realize is that there can't be one without the other. There can't be light without darkness, and Source created it to know light. Source or God indeed created polarity to experience more of Itself.

Mikael knows that while James is a fierce opponent on one level, he knows he is just like him and that they are connected and are one and the same. At times, Mikael feels sorry for him, as history has not been kind to the father of humankind. Sure, James made some self-centered choices throughout time, but he also knows it's a game. They were all asked to play on both the Light Team and Dark Team for the experience. Everyone had to play on both sides. Is it wrong that James is a master of the game and chose to play his role so well?

Unfortunately, like some others, James got caught up

with power and control. He couldn't let it go. He has chosen to stay in this role though he has had some aspects of himself play on the Light Team throughout humankind's various timelines.

Mikael hopes that the Gatekeeper is right and that James is ready to switch teams. There is some logic; one would think that if the most powerful dark power and the Light Team joined forces, Mother Earth would stand a fighting chance. Mikael's task now would be to convince James to switch teams to correct the course of history, and avoid the destruction of the planet—again.

James and Mikael meet in a private room of a small Italian restaurant on the Upper East Side. Elio, the manager of the restaurant, waits on the two men. He hasn't a clue who Mikael is but is very familiar with James, the most powerful man in New York City, perhaps even the country. So, when the reservation comes in, Elio takes it upon himself to assure that everything is perfect, and the men have the privacy James has requested.

It doesn't take long for Mikael to get down to business. "Brother, we need you to come back to the Light Team," he says, looking into his eyes. "If you continue on your current path, Gaia will end in destruction in the early twenty-first century."

James is curious and smiles. "Is the Light Side losing steam?"

"We all lose steam, James. I can tell you that if you continue this course of action, your team destroys Earth."

"Speculating?"

Mikael shakes his head. "I wish I were, but I'm disappointed to say that your team won, again, and again and again, each time ending with Earth's destruction. I've met with your Higher Aspect, Hakathriel. He agrees. We're not going to keep this going; the loop needs to end. Let's end the game on a high note."

Now for Mikael to come to him and admit this, something went wrong.

It is not the objective of the Dark Team to destroy the planet. The Dark Team aims to remain in service to the self rather than others. The group seeks material growth and controls others through power, hierarchy, and competition, and James has been on top of the food chain forever. But, without a planet, James knows that the Dark Team would fail also.

"When does it happen?" James asks.

Elio brings in a bottle of wine, opens it, offers a taste to James, who samples it. He nods, and the men remain silent as the restaurant manager pours two glasses, sets the bottle on the table, and leaves the room.

"You and I both know that the less you know, the better it will be. What you do need to know is that you should not pull *her* into your life this time."

"Who?" James is curious.

"You know, your sister."

"Why?"

"Because it ends badly."

"I've always pulled all of them in."

"Yes, sometimes they join you, and other times not. But, you need to let it go this time. This *must* change. While she is clueless right now, she is way too powerful this lifetime."

"And that will be enough to stop Armageddon?"

"No. You need to come home."

"Last I checked that is not a place where I am welcome."

"You and I know that every game comes to an end. For the sake of the souls playing, let's call a truce and stop the chain of events that ends Mother Gaia badly. She is too young to go, and many of these souls have not healed from what happened on Avyon, Avalon, and Maldek. Let her go and come back to the Light."

"How? Last I checked I've been banished here."

"Your immortality will end if you pledge allegiance to the Light."

"Are you telling me I can die?"

"The Cosmic Council pledges to work with you."

"The Great White Brotherhood wants to work with the Great Dark Brotherhood?" An eyebrow raises.

When the Gatekeeper contacted James to set up this meet, he had never expected this turn of events. There's a part of him that wants to know how things got out of hand so badly. Then again, understanding is the booby prize. Humanity has misunderstood him over many eras, and the thought that he could go home is so tempting to him.

"James, get your affairs in order," Mikael says. "We can discuss your exit strategy later, but just know that the Galactic Suns are coming in as part of this one last chance for planetary ascension, rather than the apocalypse. It would be nice to have you back on the team."

Mikael offers his hand to shake, and James stares at it.

'Could this be true? Could I once and for all leave this existence and go home?' he wonders.

"Yes, brother," Mikael responds. "It is time to come home."

James had forgotten what it was like to talk with his peers, who are telepathic. He takes Mikael's hand, and the two men shake.

CHAPTER 35:
"QUESTIONS STUPID."

George and Rebecca divorce, the house sells, their assets divvy up. Rebecca settles just outside of Denver in a patio home near her school, where she teaches.

Following up on her and Crystal's desire to seek out other nonverbal autistics, Rebecca posted an ad online at a Denver metro autism group. The ad read,

> *I am seeking nonverbal autistics to participate in a facilitated communication study.*

Right away, she received a handful of inquiries that led to interviewing the parents and caregivers, then meeting the autistics. She selected three and committed to working with them one evening each week.

Over time, all three demonstrated some unique gift or gifts, whether it was writing prose, music, telepathy, or philosophical insight, and they all morphed during a process of self-exploration. They all appeared grateful in some way to awaken to a higher realization. Rebecca took meticulous notes, thinking that one day they'd be used in a book or research paper.

One participant was a teenage girl named Holly. She has long, dirty-blond hair and rather large brown eyes and a curiosity about everything. Over time she communicated with Rebecca on philosophical subjects. She always claimed to be living in another place, one she called her starship, and her life here was her holographic role play. She wrote,

```
While I am in my Galactic
```

```
Sun chair, I am in control of
everything. From this place, I am
connected with the Creator, and
we are on equal ground.
```

Holly picked up communicating with Rebecca quickly, yet her parents never seemed to get the knack for it.

Another participant was a young man named Colin, who was quite prolific with his responses to Rebecca. His parents were just as excited as Rebecca was when Ami began to communicate. Shortly after Colin started talking with his parents through FC, something changed. Rebecca had worked with him for nearly a year, and one evening, Colin's father told her that the sessions would have to end. Apparently, Colin stopped talking to his parents, and his dad wanted their meetings to conclude.

His parents permitted Rebecca a final meeting with him.

★★★

When Rebecca arrives at Colin's home, the first thing she notices is damaged paint and drywall on one of their kitchen walls. There is also one less chair at the kitchen table. It must have been Rebecca's inquisitive facial expression because Colin's mother responds, "Colin did not take kindly to stopping your meetings."

"What happened?"

"He threw a chair."

Rebecca is grateful that Ami had never demonstrated such destructive behavior. Moments later, she greets Colin in the family room. After an awkward acknowledgment, with Colin's mom watching, Rebecca inquires, "Why have you stopped typing with your parents, Colin?"

Colin types, "Questions stupid."

Rebecca inquires further and learns that his parents had been asking questions that most parents ask their children, like, what would you like for dinner? Do you like that TV show? Are you thirsty?

Colin expands, "You ask important questions. You honor me. I only want to answer these types of questions."

Rebecca is taken back by Colin's comment. Then she feels Colin's hand with more potent energy and determination. He keys out another message. "Bring a picture of Daddy and me this weekend."

Rebecca is confused by the message. She holds Colin's hand, not knowing what to ask. "Colin?"

"No, Ami. The picture of us at the zoo. In my new room."

Rebecca looks at Colin and tries to understand what happened. There was a difference in the energy of the typing. Ami has never been to her new home, but Rebecca does have a picture of Ami and George while at the Denver Zoo in Ami's room at her new patio home.

When Rebecca senses that Colin is back, she explains to him that sometimes everyday life questions need to be answered, and it helps to establish a dialog with a parent. She tells him that, in time, those other inquiries will organically emerge from his parents.

Before Rebecca leaves, she talks to Colin's parents. She explains that their son has a much higher expanded awareness and prefers the challenge of asking questions about life, rather than trivial everyday matters.

In the days to come, Colin's parents discover that he shares insights on topics they had no idea he knew about, and they were clueless how he knew. The week after that meeting, they call Rebecca excitedly. The mother shares that he sat down at their piano, which hadn't been played in years and began playing a tune flawlessly after hearing it on their stereo.

★★★

Rebecca had similar experiences working with the third autistic. All three autists were more interested in talking about more profound insights, and less about the day-to-day activities. By teaching the parents that their child was intelligent and deserved the honor and respect that any of their other children merit, the child-parent relationships grew.

Crystal had similar, yet not as significant experiences with the two autistics she worked with over the year. Her participants were taking the same drug Leilah had taken. It took Crystal a year to convince Leilah's physician to wean her off the medication, which numbed Leilah.

She began researching medications commonly prescribed for autistics. The medicines were to treat anxiety and depression, behavioral problems, seizures, and inattention and hyperactivity. To Crystal, it seemed like the doctors were more interested in chemically restraining the autistics to the point where many were unable to feel or experience life. While she understood that the medications gave the parents or caregivers a bit of a respite, it seemed that they were creating problems. Aside from being unable to reach the autists, obesity was fast becoming an issue from one of the drugs.

Crystal began digging deeper. She started asking questions about the medicines and the industry. She learned that pharmaceutical companies hugely influence doctors. The drug companies spend millions developing products for a disease. After approval, they set out to recoup the investment by promoting the new drug as the best option for an ailment, even though that may not be the case.

Each pharmaceutical company would direct its sales reps to wine and dine the doctors. They'd exaggerate the benefits of the new medicine while downplaying side effects. It hit Crystal that the physician's recommendations were not for the best intentions of the patient.

All this was sobering to Crystal. If pharmaceutical companies influenced doctors on what to prescribe to treat autism, and health and healing weren't the primary motives, what better group to medicate into a stupor than nonverbal autistics?

'Certainly, there has to be a watchdog over the drug industry. Isn't that what the FDA does?' she pondered.

Over the years, both Rebecca and Crystal continued meeting most weekends and worked with their daughters. They'd compare notes about the other autistics they were working with and strategize about how to reach others. They knew they had challenges before them. How will people ever take autistics seriously? According to one study, nearly 80 percent of autists were on medication, with over half on behavior-modification drugs. How will the world ever look at autistics, most in a chemically induced slumber, some even wearing diapers, in a different light? How will they be able to reach autistics all over the world? The challenge was beginning to seem bigger than life to them.

CHAPTER 36:
"I DIED TO GIVE YOU LIFE!"

June 15, 2001

The late spring air flirts with all that summer brings—including flies.

Rebecca eyes the inebriated fly, clearly enjoying her wine more than she. With a tissue, she sends it a lifeline, but it doesn't seem to want rescue. Lit only by the chiminea flame and moonlight, her salvage mission is becoming hopeless.

"What on earth are you doing?" Crystal asks.

"Trying to extract an unwanted fly. I give up!" Rebecca sets the wine down.

"I'll get you another glass," Crystal offers.

"No, don't bother. It seems to be my luck lately."

The women had dinner with "the girls" that evening and were back at Crystal's chatting about their projects. They are both in a funk. Their end goal of getting the message out that autistics are more than what they seem is becoming more of a challenge for them to see.

Everything seems too big, and each had started questioning what they were doing. Thoughts like, 'Am I wasting my life?' had popped into their heads. Both women had devoted their weeknights to working with other autistics and their weekends to connecting with their daughters. They never take care of themselves, and both had fallen into a bit of depression. They were both lonely.

This last year had been challenging for Crystal. The closer she got to Leilah, the more she missed her husband.

Rebecca also missed George, who had been her best

friend for a couple of decades. Now he was gone. At first, it wasn't difficult because she was used to him being absent. He was gone because of work all the time. But this was different; he wasn't coming back. Earlier in the month, she learned from one of the attendants at Cheyenne Village that he had swung by to visit Ami, and had a girlfriend with him. It was the first time he neglected to let her know he was in town.

The following morning Rebecca and Crystal pick up their daughters. They are still preoccupied. They take the girls to their favorite park with a picnic lunch. There is a full parking lot, so they have to park further away than usual. At the picnic tables, the mothers begin to unpack their lunches when the daughters get up and start walking. Ami is on one side of the table and Leilah the other.

Each pace back and forth behind their parent, Leilah is speedy while Ami is slower. Rebecca and Crystal are used to self-stimulatory behavior. Rolling a ball, spinning a bottle, or brushing against a makeup brush are everyday occurrences to the women. The professionals tell them that stimming, or repetitive motion, comforts autistics by helping them cope with excitement, boredom, anxiety, or fear.

"I wonder what this is all about," Rebecca says.

"Perhaps they'll tell us."

"Perhaps." Rebecca waves a fly from the lunches on the picnic table, accidentally hitting her water bottle. It falls and spills. "Crap! What's with the flies?" she quickly moves the wrapped sandwiches away from the puddle.

"Maybe we should put the lunches away until they're ready," Crystal says.

Rebecca looks at Ami, who has stopped and is standing away from them. She notices that Leilah is also still. "Yeah, you're right." They pick up the sandwiches and return them to the bag.

The women remain sitting, both a bit agitated that their daughters are elsewhere while a couple from a nearby table gawk at Leilah's and Ami's odd behavior. Both Rebecca and Crystal have much on their mind and are getting more and more restless with each passing moment.

"I think I'll head back home after lunch," Rebecca says.

"Not staying tonight?"

"No. I'm feeling a bit out of sorts, I think I should leave."

"We didn't chat about your work with Colin and Holly this week. What's the third one's name?"

"Matt. Not much to say this week."

Silence falls between the woman, and the loud babbling from their daughters is becoming more annoying to both.

Crystal expresses her irritation first. "Ladies, are we going to sit here all afternoon?"

The autists ignore her, which amplifies her frustration. "You know I have been very impatient lately," she admits. "I haven't felt like myself."

Something about this resonates with Rebecca. "Me, too! I've been short, abrupt, and agitated with everything," Rebecca confides.

"Yeah. Same here," Crystal begins. "I feel like I hit resistance with everything I do. It seems like conflict is everywhere."

"And, I've been so depressed," Rebecca admits. "I think that's it. I typically see the joy in everything and lately—not so much!"

"And I've been so tired. I feel like I need to sleep all the time," Crystal shares.

"I've had the oddest dreams," Rebecca says. "I wake up after them and can't get back to sleep. Then, I have these thoughts once in a while that come out of nowhere. They're *so* negative. They just don't feel like me."

"I know what you mean," Crystal says. "Once those

thoughts begin, it's hard not to engage them."

The two women look at each other. They each know something is going on and gaze over each other's shoulders. Rebecca sees Leilah behind Crystal, and Crystal observes Ami behind Rebecca.

"What do you think this is all about?" Rebecca nods toward Leilah.

The women know to be silent. Crystal closes her eyes, Rebecca follows the lead, and both find stillness. Both innately struggle to find joy at that moment.

Crystal is self-conscious that she's in a park, eyes closed with her daughter out of sight. Rebecca struggles also. The women open their eyes at the same time. They weakly smile at each other and close their eyelids, back into unsettledness. Minutes pass. The feeling of gratitude emerges, quenching all anxiety. Then, the heaviness lifts. Peace comes over both. They feel more like themselves.

Within a couple of minutes, Rebecca and Crystal feel the presence of their daughters sitting beside them.

Rebecca opens her eyes and meets Ami's gaze. She smiles at her. She doesn't say a word but opens the insulated bag and removes everyone's lunches. In silence, they have lunch, enjoy the afternoon, and being in the moment.

After their meal, Rebecca asks Ami, "What did you and Leilah do?" She sets the letterboard in front of her and takes her hand.

"You needed an energy lift."

"I needed something for sure. I feel more like myself."

"I feel better, too, yet—" Crystal begins.

"What is it?" Rebecca asks.

"Odd, I feel lighter like a weight has lifted. Yet, it's like something is missing. Does that make sense?"

"Sometimes things that are not good grow on you," Ami types.

Leilah sits quietly, not engaging anyone.

"Need to go inside more," Ami keys.

Rebecca thinks about her conversation with Ami years earlier when she told her she needed to turn inward and deepen her spirituality. She had become so busy with life that she had abbreviated her spiritual practice. Some days she had even cut it out entirely.

"You're right, Ami. I've been so busy I had cut down my meditation time."

"Need to be strong. Inside is your Hercules. Great storm brewing."

There is something ominous about what Ami shares. Rebecca and Crystal's eyes meet from across the picnic table.

Abruptly the autists rise, both walk around the table, and Ami sits beside Crystal and Leilah beside Rebecca. The women glance at each other, wondering what their daughters are up to now.

Leilah gestures an interest in typing. "Would you like to say something to me, Leilah?" Rebecca takes her hand.

"Sisters, we are."

"We're sisters? Is that what you are saying?"

"Yes."

"You mean we were sisters in a past life?" Rebecca asks, glancing at Crystal.

"My past, your present."

"Leilah, honey, are you saying that you are Rebecca's sister *this* lifetime?" Crystal tries to clarify.

"Yes."

"Well, I don't know how that could be," Rebecca ponders. "My mother and father never had other children. Unless—. No, that can't be." For a fleeting moment, she considers the possibility that her father, a minister, had another child with another woman.

Leilah read her mind, "Your mom and dad, are mine."

"Sweetheart, I never had siblings."

"I am your twin."

"Oh, my God!" Rebecca remembers she had a twin who died in utero. Her parents always claimed that she was a miracle child because she had survived. "Could it be?" She looks at Crystal and back at Leilah, "It is true. I had a twin who died before birth."

Leilah types, "To give you life, I died."

CHAPTER 37:
SHE HAD AN EARTHBOUND SPIRIT ATTACHED TO HER!

Ami

If you knew how common it was, you would freak out. It happens to almost everyone. It isn't right, but it happens, and most of the time, you haven't a clue. To the outsider, most of the time, it plays out like the person just doesn't seem to be themselves. To the insider, however, it can be very confusing and depressing, and you certainly don't feel like yourself. Attachments are what I am referring to, spiritual attachments.

Attachments are when the energy or spirit of a deceased person connects to a living person. They are unwelcomed guests. You can think of them as a hitchhiker without an invite.

When Leilah and I arrive at the park, it is evident that Mom and Crystal have uninvited companions. They are not alone, and they don't know it. Perhaps if they knew about attachments, they would suspect something is amiss, but most people aren't familiar with them, and they chalk it up to something else.

If you had my eyes, you would see that most people aren't alone. Most people have earthbound spirits attached to them. Some even have two to three specters. These ghosts are usually individuals who have crossed over and, for whatever reason, have refused to go to the Light. Yes, when the body transitions, there *is* Light, it isn't a metaphor, and you should go to it. For whatever reason, some spirits don't, and there are many reasons. Perhaps they have unfinished business, or they can't let go of their loved ones while they are grieving their loss. Maybe their death was unexpected, and they may not even realize they are dead. Or, perhaps they have a fear of being judged on the other side. Maybe they believe in heaven and hell and don't think they are one of the few good souls worthy of spending the rest of their days at the throne of God. So, they don't go. For whatever reason, some souls stay, and the longer they remain here, the more challenging it is to cross over.

There is a lesson here. Be careful what you believe about the afterlife because whatever you think will determine your experience. You are a creator, and you will manifest your afterlife experience. Yes, the illusion will continue. If you believe in heaven, hell, or purgatory, you may just end up there, but it is an illusion.

I shared earlier about the human energy field that emanates from your body. Most spirits, or earthbound ghosts, will attach where there is a weakness in the energy field or aura. Throughout life, your energy field can have temporary or permanent holes, cuts, or distortions. These flaws occur when experiencing weak emotions or a loss of personal power. The temporary holes can be created by soul loss from experiencing fear, anger, hatred, surrendering yourself to others, even substance abuse.

The reason a spirit may attach will vary. Some may connect because they love the person, and the person's grief keeps them here, and they live their life through them. Others need life force to feed off of or a body to occupy. I am referring to earthbound spirits here, not dark entities, that's *another* subject.

In my mom's case, after Dad left, she didn't talk about it. She has pent-up anger, which has festered. I think learning that dad has a meaningful girlfriend recently may have made Mom susceptible. Then, when she visited her coworker, at Swedish Medical Center last week, she picked up a hitchhiker named Henry. Spirits commonly hang in hospitals.

For Crystal, it's an entirely different story. Her spirit has been with her for some time.

As soon as we get out of the car, I go to work. Leilah is a bit more hesitant, and I understand why.

Mom takes my hand and leads me toward our favorite picnic area, and Crystal does the same with Leilah. I keep looking back at Henry attached to Mom's back; he is jubilant in his new home, in Mom's energy. He isn't a dark entity, but he sure doesn't belong on Mom.

"Leilah, I need to show Henry the Light. Can you help your mom's guest too?" I ask Leilah.

Leilah looks at the spirit attached to her mother, the man says, *"Hi, sweetheart, how are you today?"*

"You know he has to go, Leilah," I tell her. *"You don't want your father stuck here forever."*

"I know," she says sadly. *"I will miss Dad so much, though."*

I know that since Leilah's dad passed, they have been able to communicate, and while he was alive, they couldn't. The thought of losing her father again must be particularly challenging for her, but the longer he is here, the harder it will become for him to cross over.

When we arrive at the picnic table, we get to work. While Leilah spends time chatting with her dad, saying good-bye, I work on Henry. I intentionally walk a distinct pattern on the ground.

Henry tells me that he likes his new host. He says Mom has good energy. Henry has been earthbound for nearly 100 years and has had many hosts during that time. He doesn't understand that his negative thoughts and beliefs impact the people he attaches too. He doesn't know that he was to go to the Light. Perhaps he hasn't been given an opportunity over the last century.

As I pace, I feel his racy hot energy. It is very low vibration and pulls Mom down in many ways. He corrupts her thoughts and confuses her. He lowers her frequency.

In my mind, I pray. *'I invite my Higher Soul Self to merge with me now. I welcome Divine Light into my heart and my entire being on all levels. I ask for the assistance of my friends, the Watchers, the Divine Light Guardians, to work with me now.'*

I know that help is on its way, *'All for the highest good and fully aligned with all parties, their Divine soul essence, and purpose. I ask that this area, the space we all occupy, be filled and surrounded with Divine Light and Love.'*

Within me, a new language emerges, it is an ancient sacred code known as Light Language, and I feel the words chant and reverberate my soul,

> *'Weassawea–Rawedabefun–Feswator–*
> *Weassawea–Liesasuroesa–Sawaseaesa–*
> *Weassawea–Asducaasa–Ifespleeda–Bapoprures.'*

I feel help arrive; in seconds, Archangel Metatron is with us. His aura is deep pink and green, and his high Light is warm and hugs me. I called upon Metatron regularly when I was younger, so I am familiar with his work. Metatron is here to support us with working with the lower energies. He will escort the spirits to the other side.

I feel the magnanimous Light energy flowing through my body, from high above, into my head, my torso, down both arms, down both legs and deep into the earth. I feel Its energy flowing through every cell of my being and oozing out of my pores so that I know I stand tall as a pole of Light—my body pulses with high Light energy.

I stay here, and I'm not aware of how much time it takes, but the Light heals Henry, and I know that his past life traumas are being treated and dissolved. When I feel Henry's peace, I know it is time to call for his loved ones.

"I invite all of Henry's loved ones, his family, and friends, to welcome him so that his recovered soul can continue his journey and transition into the next world, into the Light."

I feel Henry leave Mom's energy, and just before he departs this world, I sense his overwhelming gratitude for finding his way to the Light. Then he is gone, his hurt, intense energy is gone. He has peace.

Before the Light ceases to stop running through me, I check in with Leilah. She has said goodbye, and her father is aware of the Light. At that moment, I invite all of his departed loved ones to help him transition. In no time, he goes to deceased family and friends. He does look back for a moment, first at his wife, Crystal, who is unaware of what is going on. He looks at Leilah, and they have a love exchange, and then he crosses over.

I sense Mom and Crystal and send them Light, healing any wounds or voids they may have experienced from the attachments. When there is only peace, I feel the energy current going through me dissipate, and I return to my mother's side, and Leilah returns to Crystal at the picnic table.

Mom and Crystal are curious about what happened. How can I tell Mom that she had an earthbound spirit attached to her that has wandered this planet for a century? How can I inform Crystal that Leilah and I helped her husband cross-over? That it was her tremendous grief of losing him that kept him here. That he was loyal to her and would be by her side until she passed away, only then, he would wander the planet as Henry did.

I don't tell them, and it will remain Leilah's and my secret for now. I will share it with them when the time is right. Unfortunately, it will be a long time because the collapse has begun.

CHAPTER 38:
"IT'S BEGUN."

September 11, 2001

It's an ordinary day for Rebecca. Buzz! Her alarm sounds at 5:00 a.m. She dismisses it with a gentle touch. A cup of tea in hand, she sits quietly, sips, rests the mug on her end table. She sets her watch to buzz at 5:30 and enters meditation.

At 6:31, she fires up the car and heads to school.

Everything is normal until—in the teacher's lounge, she pours a cup of coffee and stirs in sugar. The math teacher, Mr. Young, enters in a hurry.

"Have you heard?" he asks excitedly.

"Heard what?" she asks.

"A plane just hit the World Trade Center!"

"What?"

Rebecca takes her coffee and makes her way to the central office, where a few teachers gather. A television broadcasts a smoking north tower beside its twin. The voice of a news anchor speaks with another person who must be near the World Trade Center. Suddenly, an explosion on the south tower erupts, and the talking intensifies.

A second plane hit the other tower.

"Oh, my God!" Rebecca whispers.

Reporters talk intensely over each other, and then one voice. "This is no accident—the United States is under attack."

To Rebecca, it is numbing. In some ways, surreal. 'It couldn't be happening to us, the United States?'

Around 7:30, the TV broadcast switches to a new location, a Florida elementary school. President Bush addresses the nation and says, "two airplanes have crashed into the World Trade Center in an apparent terrorist attack on our country."

Rebecca is like everyone. All eyes glued to the television, she cannot stop watching. The small group has grown as more teachers and staff look on in horror. She knows George lives fifty miles or so from New York City. She just wants to hear his voice and know he is okay.

It takes all of her willpower to break away from the TV. At a nearby desk, she picks up a telephone handset and punches in George's cell phone number. No ring. No busy signal. It won't connect.

"Do we know where those planes were coming from?" she asks.

"They haven't said," someone answers.

Rebecca tries again—and again—and again.

A teacher shrieks, "Oh my God!"

She turns back to the small television where there is a live announcement. Gasps escape the lips of her coworkers. Smoke and destruction all over the TV. A reporter, saying, "A third plane hit the Pentagon."

Her heart skips a beat. Torn between calling George and watching the coverage, she notices Marcie. The social studies teacher is at another desk, desperately punching keys on the phone, listening, hanging up, and starting over.

Rebecca knows Marcie is from the east coast. She tries to recall, 'New Jersey?' She goes to her. "Is everything okay, Marcie?"

"I'm trying to reach my family."

"They are in New Jersey?" Rebecca asks.

"That's where they live. Yes," Marcie pauses. "My father and two brothers are traders—they work on the trading floor."

Horrified at the implication, "At the World Trade Center?" Rebecca asks.

Marcie nods. Her eyes are wide with fear. They both

213

glance at the television, now showing two smoking towers.

Rebecca looks at the twin towers; she knows things are going to change. Life as she knew it was over.

The phone rings. Marcie grabs it, "Hello?"

She looks up at Rebecca. "Yes, she's right here." She hands Rebecca the phone. "It's for you."

"For me?" She takes the handset. "Hello?"

"Rebecca, it's Sarah," a voice comes from the phone.

"Is everything okay?"

"Ami had a seizure, and the ambulance is taking her to Penrose."

"I'm on my way. Do you have my cell number?"

"Yes, of course. You didn't answer it."

Rebecca pulls it from her purse and sees the missed calls. With all the excitement, she hadn't heard it. "I'm on my way." She hangs up and looks for the principal to make arrangements.

"This is going to be a *really* long day," she whispers.

Within a couple of hours, Rebecca arrives at the hospital, where a television continues coverage of the terrorist events. Déja vù? She notices people passing her. Some eyes are red from tears. More than a few look mad as hell. Others walk dazed with fear.

She needs to get to Ami. When she can, she'll reach out to George and make sure he is okay.

Rebecca sees Sarah's head popping out of a curtain. When their eyes meet, Sarah emerges from the examination room. "Rebecca, I'm so relieved you're here!"

"How is she?"

"She's sedated. She stopped seizing."

Rebecca moves the privacy curtain and peeks inside. Ami lies still on a hospital bed, her eyes closed. An IV bag hangs near her.

"Odd thing, though," Sarah says, "before she started

seizing, she was crying—with *real* tears."

"She had tears?" Rebecca has never seen tears in her daughter's eyes.

"Yes, tears. That wasn't what was odd, though."

"What is it?"

"We didn't have the TV on, nor radio. There was no way she could have known about the World Trade Center."

"Okay."

"She had tears running down her face, and she wouldn't respond to me. For about ten minutes, no matter what I said, it was as if I wasn't there. Then, she started seizing. The phone rings, thank God the handset was right there. It was my sister calling to tell me it just had happened."

"What are you suggesting?"

"I don't know," Sarah says. "It was just an observation. I'm sure it's just a coincidence."

Rebecca isn't so sure, as odder things have happened with her daughter. She moves the curtain open and goes to Ami.

"Hi, baby. How are you?"

It is rare, but occasionally Ami's eyes meet her gaze dead-on, and this is one of those times. Rebecca notes the incredible sadness in the moist eyes.

"Do you want to say something?" She takes the letter-board that is draped over a shoulder and places it in front of Ami.

Ami's arm is cumbersome and sluggish to Rebecca as she types. "`It's begun.`"

"Sweetheart, what has begun?"

"`Collapse.`" Ami closes her eyes.

Rebecca isn't sure if Ami fell asleep from the exhaustion of the seizures or the drugs.

CHAPTER 39:
"HOLY MOLY, I'M NOT READY!"

Ami

I am incredibly sad. I have seen this day coming, and no matter how prepared I thought I was, nothing could prepare me for this act of terror. One day, September 11, 2001, will be recognized as the day things went wrong. Not only from the horrific act, and the loss of lives but the United States' response to it. All of this will cripple the world on different levels.

These acts of terror will lead to years, then decades of war, the collapse of many systems, like the financial, health, and societal systems. Before that, however, we will experience the loss of individual liberties. Many people at the World Trade Center and Pentagon will become mysteriously ill, both physically and psychologically. The U.S. government will perform racial profiling at a level that will boggle your mind. People will be searched, beaten, and imprisoned all because they are immigrants or Muslims. The United States will devolve from being recognized as the most civilized country and the guardians of human rights to barbaric persecutors and torturers.

What no one knows, except for those involved in the events of today, is that the happenings are all part of a plan. It is part of *the plan* devised by dimly lit souls to control the world; only it isn't who you think they are! It is from whom the autistics hide.

Most people are not aware that energetically, today, is a victorious day for the dimly lit souls or the Dark Team. Some people thrive on positive things in life, while others thrive on the negative. Then, there is a vast population that swings both ways. Today, everyone got caught up in the drama. All over the world, eyes glued to their televisions, ears to radios; no one can get enough of the events of 9/11 coverage. With each person witnessing the proceedings, feelings of hatred, despair, anger, horror, and fear swell.

Negative emotions hurt the body physically, and if they are not released, they harm the body in ways you may not be aware of for a long time after the event. Then one day, cancer will emerge, the heart may fail, the blood will be imbalanced. There is something else, though. Once a person suffers such feelings of fear, anger, hurt, despair, and hate, so intensely, they become nourished by them. They are fed by them and begin craving more negative emotions. Indeed, it doesn't happen overnight or after one bad feeling, but an event like today will have an impact on the entire planet. Energetically, the vibration of Earth lowered today as we all fell into horror and fear.

As I lay here in this hospital bed, I feel the heaviness of the drugs pumped into my body. The medications bring me back down and pull me to this earth. They bring me back here to deal with the sadness.

When my brain misfires, and I seize, I usually know when it is coming. I have a chance to prepare myself so that I don't fall or do something that will hurt me. My eyes become glassy-eyed, I only can stare at a fixed point, and the colors begin to change. My heartbeat is so loud. I wonder why the people around me aren't holding their ears. The side of my face burns. I feel the multiple levels of my body, from my very dense physical body to the higher subtle layers of the etheric body. I am deep in threads of bright shining gold. I float and undergo reflections of my soul's experience, sometimes this life, often others. I travel home, to the place I often refer to as Homeland.

Seizures are not the way I like to come here. I know the seizure has a toll on my physical body. I much prefer to go to Homeland on my terms. Once I am here, though, I bask in the comfort of where I am and where I will return. I am in a place where there is only God. It is true that we come from and always go back to God. Even the dimly lit souls who masterminded today's horrific events come from God, and there they will return.

Some may refer to these men as evil or darkness. They may appear to be dark, but at the core of their being, there is an ember of Light. With all the pain and suffering they have caused, it is hard to see this, but they have a role to play in this collapse of humanity, and there is a spark of Light within them even if it is minuscule. For their journey, the challenge is to claim that Light. In the end, they are just as loved by God or Source as anyone. Like you, they are a fractal of Source—a difficult concept for most to understand.

Remember that this is all a game, and this life is about ending cycles. Everyone should do their best to complete unfinished business because the slate will be wiped clean, and there will be no more karma moving to the New Earth. When working out karma, one learns a vital lesson. When leaving karma unexplored, there is a lost opportunity to grow.

Today's seizures are different. They are more intense than others. Sometimes people don't even know I have them. Sometimes insight comes in, and I think "Holy Moly, I'm not ready," but the download happens anyway, and perhaps it triggers the seizure.

Other times, I know that Light—whether you call it Source, God, or insight, it's all the same—hits my crown chakra, a doorway, and my brain mechanics trigger the seizure to facilitate the download of information. A download is a direct communication from God. You may have experienced downloads at times yet interpret them as an epiphany. These epiphanies or sudden realizations are downloads.

Today, as usual, I knew the seizure was occurring before it happened. It was incredible sadness and feeling the fear of those who died that triggered it.

It is evident to me that we need to act. We need to attract autistics, remind them who they are. We can no longer wait. It is time. Autistics have an essential role in the shift that is coming. If not awakened, the world will end badly.

CHAPTER 40:
"BOOK IS A LOVE LETTER TO THE WORLD."

One in 150 children has autism.

Ami spends most of 9/11 in the ER until they admit her for observation, but she doesn't get a room until six o'clock that evening. Rebecca juggles conversations with doctors, nurses, and hospital staff while continuing to reach out to George. She has little success until around seven o'clock when she can leave him a voicemail.

Crystal shows up shortly after and brings her some food. She had learned about Ami's episode when visiting Leilah for dinner. Rebecca is in Ami's new hospital room when Crystal arrives.

"I just heard what happened!" Crystal rushes into the room with a bag in hand. She hugs her and then turns to Ami. Sleeping. "How is she?"

"They have her drugged. She's been asleep for over an hour." She glances at her watch. "I haven't been able to reach George all day."

"Where does he live? Connecticut?"

"Yes, Norwalk—but he travels all over the place."

Crystal senses that Rebecca is contemplating worst-case scenarios. "I'm sure he's okay. If he was in the air, all planes were grounded."

"Why wouldn't he call, though?"

"If he's in the New York area, there's limited service."

At that moment, a man comes into the room. He removes a clipboard from the wall, glances at it, jots something down.

"Hello, I'm Doctor Stanton."

"I'm Rebecca Griffin, Ami's mother."

"I take it that Ami is sleeping peacefully."

"She has been. It's the drugs?"

"Yes. We sedated Ami to stop the seizures," he refers to his clipboard. "Diazepam. I understand she does *not* regularly take anticonvulsants?"

"No. Ami had absence seizures as a child, but she was weaned off the drug and has been seizure-free for years—or at least I thought so."

"She's a nonverbal autistic?"

"Yes."

Referring to the clipboard, "It says here that she doesn't take any medications. Nothing for behavior? Mood stabilizers? Antidepressants?"

She shakes her head, "No."

"This is a bit unusual," he says.

"Doctor?" Crystal jumps into the conversation, "Who regulates drugs for autistics?"

The physician looks at her. "Well, the FDA."

"I read an article recently that the pharmaceutical industry controls the FDA, and there is a *wink-nod* relationship between the two."

Rebecca interrupts. "Dr. Stanton, this is Crystal, a close family friend, who also has a nonverbal autistic daughter."

"A pleasure," he says though it sounds a bit insincere. "I am unfamiliar with—what did you call it? A wink-nod relationship?"

"Yes. The article implied that the FDA is privy to clinical trial test results, and the pharmaceutical company doesn't have to report the *bad* results and can cherry-pick what to say to the public. For an exchange, the government looks the other way."

"An exchange?"

"Money."

The doctor laughs. "I don't know where that was published." He smiles and changes the subject by turning to Rebecca. "Ami should be awake soon. She will need ongoing medication to control these seizures. The seizures, if untreated, can take a toll on her body and her brain, which certainly can shorten her life." He removes a pamphlet from the clipboard and hands it to Rebecca. "In case you're interested in learning more about some of the drugs used to treat autism." His exit is much swifter than his entrance.

"I think he was a bit agitated with me," Crystal says.

"You think?" she says, sarcastically.

"Oh, come on! You know, the more the industry sedates autistics, the more challenging our work becomes to reach them!"

The last thing Rebecca wants to hear now is a "big pharma" conspiracy. She looks at the brochure the doctor had handed her. It is from Marquette, a large pharmaceutical company, and lists their drugs by classification. She is ready to toss it in the trash when something catches her eye.

"This can't be right!" She says.

"What is it?"

"This says that the autism prevalence is about one in every 150 kids during the surveillance year of 2000."

"That sounds high!" Crystal agrees.

"When they diagnosed Ami, it was one in every 5000 kids. Now it's one in 150?"

"That's an enormous shift."

Rebecca remembers a conversation. "Ami once said that more would be coming."

"More autistics?"

"Yes. Ami said it so long ago I hadn't thought about it."

A grunt. Ami stirs. Rebecca pushes her dark hair from her face. Ami's brown eyes are wide and sad. "How do you feel, sweetheart?"

Ami stares ahead. Unresponsive.

"Sweetheart, can you hear me?"

She keeps staring, not acknowledging them.

"Baby, are you in pain? You had terrible seizures. You're in the hospital. Do you remember any of it?"

With all her effort, Ami taps her fingers into the bed. She has something to say.

Rebecca scrambles, looking around the room for the letterboard, she sees it. She brings it to her and lifts the lethargic arm.

"Need to write a book."

"You want to write a book?"

"Y. We write."

"You want *us* to write a book?"

"You, me, other autistics you work with."

"What will the book be about? What is its purpose?"

"Time to let people know about autism Truth."

"You want people to know why you're here."

"Need to wake autistics. Need parents to help."

"You think a book can help autistics remember why they're here?"

"Book is love letter to the world. Parents need—" Ami's typing slows to a turtle's pace, "to honor autistic kids."

"By honoring the autistics, you wake them up?"

"Y."

Rebecca looks at the brochure that suggests that one in 150 kids born in 2000 is autistic. "Ami, you once said that more autistics were coming. Are they here?"

"Many here. More coming."

"There is an extreme increase in autism—are they all people like you?"

"Not all. Dimly lit souls had been causing autism now."

"They are causing it? Why?"

"To stop incarnation of blessed great Light being. Holy one already here tho."

Rebecca doesn't know how to respond to this. After all, how could anyone cause autism?

Ami wants to type more. "Need to light autistics up all around the planet."

"Sweetheart, I'm not a writer. I know nothing about getting a book published."

"We publish. 10 years."

"We'll self-publish the book? It'll take ten years?"

"Y." Ami closes her eyes, and in seconds she's out.

Rebecca doesn't know what to think. She glances at Crystal, who is standing on the opposite side of the bed. Her cell phone chimes.

She grabs it from her purse. Sees the phone number. "It's George!" she says excitedly. "Hello?"

She is relieved beyond words to hear his voice. Tears well in her eyes as she listens to his great tale. He was in the air during the event. The plane, forced to land in Kentucky, left him seeking ground transportation. As she hangs up the phone, grateful that he is safe, she glances back at Ami, then Crystal.

"Our journey is just beginning," Rebecca whispers to Crystal.

Chapter 41:
Star People and Starseeds

November 14, 2001

Levi

I empty my mailbox at the cluster box unit, just down the street from my house. I see the self-addressed and stamped envelope with my custom return address label. I want to tear it open but resist. I had submitted a query to a literary agent and know this is the answer to my first book submission.

I finished my manuscript, "Among Us," about a month ago and sent a query and a sample chapter to a couple of agents in New York. It is my first response, and I can't wait to get home and tear it open.

Writing this book was indeed a rollercoaster ride. I can't explain precisely how the story developed in my head and managed to get on the pages. It just happened. Every day for a year, I'd rise early and write for a couple of hours before I'd head off to work. Every spare moment I'd spend at my computer researching or writing this conspiracy novel, which seemed to have a life of its own.

How the story came together is bizarre. I'd watch events in my own life, and they'd direct me to something that'd inspire parts of my novel. I didn't realize what was happening for the first few months, and then it hit me. The Universe was telling me the story, much like how it would guide me. I'd follow synchronicities, serendipities, and especially strange events. I would just know it was for the story. Once I realized what was happening, I started to trust it, and within a short year, I had a multi-layered novel written. Then I outlined the next two books because my tale is a trilogy.

The first book is a conspiracy story revealing that secret societies control the world, and the leader is a Lucifer-like character who is a mysterious being, an alien who looks human and has led these secret groups forever. This Lucifer, which I've dubbed Beelzebub, though in the story is called James, is a badass who runs the world and doesn't age as we do. I've started the second book in which the protagonist learns some good aliens walk among us, too, and she eventually discovers that she is one of them. Yes, I am sharing this tongue-in-cheek and laughing a lot because the Universe has an incredible sense of humor and is quite the storyteller!

I know the book is a bit over the top, and the Roman Catholic Church, as well as any Protestant churches, won't be thrilled with it, but it is fiction. I made it up—with the help, of course, of the Universe's orchestration, and I must say that *It* has a sense of adventure!

Moments later, I am at home and drop my purse and attaché case on my kitchen table. I set down the mail, too, except for *the* envelope. I tear it open and read. My heart swiftly plunges into disappointment.

> *Dear Levi Hendricks,*
> *Thank you for allowing us to consider your manuscript.*
>
> *Your novel's premise is interesting, but all I can say is, WTF? Do you think a publisher will ever take on a story about secret societies and corruption at the highest level, including the government, the media, and the Catholic Church? Your writing is good, clean up the premise, and you may have*

something. Aliens? Are you serious?

I flick on the gas fireplace and slump into the loveseat in my family room. 'That's only one opinion!' I tell myself, but as I sit there, I feel myself spiraling into a funk. Maybe *I am* crazy to think someone would publish this story.

After a few minutes of feeling sorry for myself, I glance at my watch. It's just before six o'clock. I need to be at Rachel Kelly's at 8:00 p.m. for a reading.

Kelly is an upcoming Denver area psychic. She is a medium. She communicates with spirits, and for the last six months, I have heard rave reviews from people at work, both believers and non-believers. It took me six weeks to get this appointment, so I don't want to miss it. I have enough time to get a bite to eat and will need to head out soon.

It's just before eight o'clock. I'm at the luxury loft apartment building on Market Street, near Union Station and Coors Field. My instructions were to call Ms. Kelly with the intercom system when I get to the lobby.

I press the button and wait.

"Hello?" A woman's voice comes over the speaker.

"Hi, it's Levi Hendricks. I have an eight o'clock appointment."

"Yes, I'll be right there."

A couple of minutes later, the elevator door in the lobby opens, and I recognize Kelly from her pictures. She's about my age, looks perfectly normal with long dark hair, and is professionally dressed. I was half expecting that she'd dress like a gypsy. You know, with dangling jewelry, a colorful scarf around her forehead, a wrap as a belt, and boots up to her knees. Not at all. Instead, she wears dress pants and a conservative silk blouse.

Rachel Kelly shakes my hand. She seems to be sizing

me up then says, "Nice to meet you, Levi. Let's go up to my apartment."

Perhaps she does some sort of check–in with her spirit guides to see if her client is safe to take to her home. 'Good to know I passed!'

Within a couple of minutes, I am in her apartment. A man is sitting in front of a laptop in the dining area. He waves at us. 'Her husband? Or security?' She leads me to a private room set up for the reading. There is a small table in the center with two chairs. An altar is in the corner with candles ablaze. The rest of the room is minimal, a couple of paintings on the wall, an area rug, not what I was expecting. 'No crystal balls?' I smile at the thought.

She sits in one chair and welcomes me to take the other. "This is your first time with me?" she asks.

"Yes. Some friends recommended you."

"Great! Let me share how I work and give you a chance to tell me which way you'd like me to proceed."

I nod, "Okay."

"I am a medium. I communicate with spirits that may be around you or departed souls that may be interested in talking with you. I'm not what people know as a trance medium, like Whoopi Goldberg in *Ghost*. In that case, the psychic goes into a trance, and their body is a conduit. That type of medium hasn't a clue what happened to them after they come out. Instead, I retain that knowledge.

"All the information is received mentally. I may have a vision in my third eye," Rachel Kelly rubs the center of her forehead. "I may hear voices; I may just know things. For example, if you want to speak with your departed aunt, it won't be as if I see her beside you. It'll be in my head."

"Okay," I say.

"Many people come to me with a list of questions for deceased loved ones, and I answer them. Others are more interested in learning if there is something that is screaming to be told by the Universe or a spirit guide, or a departed loved one. In this case, I tune into whatever wants to come through and share those messages. If I do this, there is usually a time in the end if you have a question or two. Do you have a preference?"

Aside from my grandparents, I don't have any departed loved ones. "I do have a question, but I think I'd prefer to experience your second way and hope there is time for questions," I say.

"Great," she smiles. "I'm going to be quiet and still myself. I will close my eyes, and at some point, I will speak. I will tell you anything that wants to come through. Sometimes, I'll even answer questions the client intends to ask." She presses a button on a cassette player beside her and closes her eyes.

Rachel is quiet and still for quite some time. After a bit, I wonder if she has even fallen asleep. She begins to speak at first slowly, then very fast, and I am grateful she is recording the reading.

"Much wants to come through here—it is a bit overwhelming. So many voices and beings here. They all want to get a message through...I am asking for one at a time and telling them they should be patient...I will give everyone a turn."

She is quiet as if listening, then she speaks, "You are a scientist with an artist's heart. You've recently begun a new hobby—writing. You need to know that while society will not support your work at this time, you must continue. Your new manuscript will get published after a famous author publishes a book, which is similar in concept, with a different, more conservative spin. His book will have a more commercial appeal than your own. His success will be what opens the door for you. Without it, it will take a long time to get your work published. If you can, wait...2003 is when his book will be released."

All I can think is, *"Wow!"* I hadn't told her about my writing project, and it was the one question I was going to ask.

"He, this author, is working on his book now. His book will be *hugely* popular. Yet, it also will lead to much litigation with other writers and many conflicts with the Roman Catholic Church. Your book will go under the radar, and that's okay, it won't be hugely successful in the early years. The world isn't ready for its messages today. It will be one day, though."

'Messages?' I'm confused. 'There are no *messages*. It's fiction,' I tell myself.

"You will be tempted to stop writing and give up. But you will come back to it. When you have left this world, this book will get the credit it deserves, not until then, though."

Okay, so I am a wee bit disappointed that I won't become a famous author.

"Next," she says, and waits. She seems to be listening.

"Another being wants you to know that you are very psychic and intuitive. You know this about yourself, but you need confirmation and don't always trust things that come through. You must trust your inner guidance; it will lead you to where you need to go. Without trust, you could miss the mark."

There is a pause as if she is waiting for another person. She smiles and continues. "You are so loved by someone here. It is...if you believe in soulmates, it would be your soulmate. This being cannot be in this incarnation with you and wants you to know how deeply loved and missed you are. This presence is with you in spirit and will be with you again, just not in this lifetime. He, or she, it's so androgynous, I can't tell. It cannot be in this life here." She shakes her head. "I don't understand," she whispers.

I wonder, 'Is that why I struggle with relationships? Is that why I feel so unsettled when I am with others?'

Rachel continues. "Another one here wants you to know that you are different than others here. Different in many ways.

You are here with an important purpose. You are here to serve humanity's future. However, you are not—"

She stops. She seems to be struggling a bit with the information. She opens her eyes and searches my own. "I want to share with you what I see," she says. "You may find this upsetting, though. So, I will ask you to check in with your intuition, check in with your gut feelings too. Once I tell you, I can't take it back. It will stay with you until your dying day." She waits for my answer.

There's a part of me that's intrigued by what she has said. There's another part of me that is a bit troubled. I take her advice seriously, quiet my mind, and turn inward. I ask my Higher Self if I am ready to hear what she must tell me. The thought comes to me, 'You will need to know soon. You will not like it, but you will need to know.'

I open my eyes and nod at Rachel.

"I see others around you," she continues. "These others have been with you before in many other lifetimes. Do you believe in reincarnation?"

I look at her and nod, *yes*. It isn't a topic discussed while growing up, but it is something I have come to believe in over the last decade or so.

"These others that you have been with are very tall and androgynous. They have long heads and long fingers. They are luminescent, they're—"

"Are you telling me that they're alien-like?" I can't resist it. I know I am not supposed to talk, but I had to ask.

"Yes—you are just like them, only you incarnated in human form."

I'm shocked, and yet not. How could this be? I think about my manuscript and the second book that I'm currently writing. The protagonist learns she is a *good* alien. Perhaps Rachel has this all wrong. Could she be tapping into my stories? Or, am I connecting with my past-life stuff and writing it?

"You have many of them around you now," she continues. "You are the only one here of your kind from this world—and a different universe. That's what they tell me." She is quiet, then, "Except...no. That can't be." She sighs and remains silent as if listening. "I am not even sure I believe in this concept, but it is what they tell me to tell you, so... You are here with a twin soul. One is the Yin and the other the Yang. I'm not sure I even believe in twin souls or twin flames, but that is what they tell me."

I don't know what to say. When the woman I met a year ago at a writers' conference told me that aliens walked among us, and many do not know this about themselves, I hadn't even considered she could have been referring to me. How could that be? How could I be an alien when I feel human? Or, do I? 'How would I know what it is like to feel human or alien when the only experience I have is my own?'

"You have come here to help humanity. You will connect with others who also are here to help humankind ascend. There are many people like you, from *other* worlds that have incarnated to help, except you and this twin soul are from a different world altogether.

"There are others who work with darkness here. Your book is about dark ones. The darkworkers feed off fear. You think it is fiction, but it's not."

My head hurts. There is so much here that I need to process, and I'm not sure how much more I can hear. How could this woman be so dead-on about a manuscript I have recently written? How could she know about the plot of future books I've outlined?

"Your antagonist in your book is real—" She stops. "*Was* real. He's on the other side now. He was here...this info is a bit confusing. He was here for a long time. He died about a handful of years ago."

My antagonist is fiction. His name is James, and he's an

alien. He came to this planet before the ancient civilizations of Egypt, Greece, and Babylon. He is from Nibiru, an Anunna-ki, and ages differently because, like the Ascended Masters, he is a higher dimensional being and can live hundreds of years. He has been called many things over the centuries, including Lucifer and the Devil. He is the power at the top of all secret societies. I created this character after the Universe took me to various websites and inspired the story.

"My story is fiction," I say. 'Could it be real?' I wonder at that moment, yet, I can't hear another word. I stand. I retrieve my wallet from my purse.

"You're upset," Rachel says.

"You've thrown me," I admit. I count the cash to the agreed amount and set it on the table.

"We have more time," she says.

"I'm done," I say. I have a splitting headache and need to get out of here.

"Look, I hate to have you run out of here like this. You wanted a reading for something. Did you have any questions?"

I shake my head. "You broached the subject. I wanted to know about the manuscript. I've put so much time into writing it, and I've begun the next in the series. I don't want to waste my life on it, but—it *is* fiction."

"I don't know about your book. The words I spoke were from one of your guardians. I sense that whatever you are writing will help spread Truth in a safe, unthreatening way. You will one day tell a different grand tale that will publish as fiction, only it will be the truth. It has nothing to do with this project you are working on, though they connect in some crazy way.

"Like you," Rachel continues, "I have a purpose here, too. I am to help people who are here for the shift to find their way to fulfill their mission."

"The shift?"

"You will learn more about that in the years to come," she tells me. "You should know that you are not the first person I've done a reading for where the subject learned they incarnated from another planet. I understand there is a word for it. It is star people or starseed, and there are a lot more of them than we know."

CHAPTER 42:
THE SINKING OF POSEIDA AND THE THIRTEENTH SKULL

New Year's Eve, 2001

Rebecca watches Rudy Giuliani on TV push the button as his last official act as Mayor. The ball begins its one-minute descent to ring in the New Year. The 2002 New Year's Eve ceremony was unlike any other year. Usually, a couple of million people venture out for such a celebration but only a half-million tonight under heightened security. The world is seeing how resilient New Yorkers are after September 11, through the lens of *Dick Clark's Rockin Eve* broadcast.

Rebecca can't imagine what it is like to be there. Everyone just wanted 2001 to be over and three—two—one. There is an eruption of cheer and jubilee as people sing, kiss, toast, and cheer the arrival of 2002. With tears in her eyes, she presses the remote, and the television turns black—an emotional end to 2001.

Minutes later, she's in bed. Much of the evening's celebration tonight was about America prevailing after the events of September 11. She can't help but think about that day. It was when Ami asked that they write a book together. She recalls her message. "Book is love letter to the world. Parents need to honor autistic kids."

Writing a book is such a daunting task for Rebecca. Ami told her they'd publish in ten years. 'That's plenty of time,' she tries to convince herself as she falls into a deep sleep.

***

From the steps of the Temple of Poseida, Ishkamet, the Atlantean high priestess, looks through rain-obscured eyes at the rising waters surrounding them. There is not much time before the water buries the island. The neighboring islands, Og and Aryan, are gone, and most of their treasured island, Poseida, is also buried. She and her peers, three priests, and three priestesses need to hide the sacred piece.

It is not the first time she has risked her life to keep the sacred piece from getting into the wrong hands. In the wrong hands, the crystal could bring the experiment to a cataclysmic end. Once a guardian of a crystal skull, that responsibility follows to other lifetimes. It is up to the seven of them to protect humanity by hiding the crystal. It must remain concealed until the time of humanity's ascension. She knows that one day, she will return, albeit in another life, during the time of humanity's awakening to participate in the recovery of this crystal. This responsibility she accepted eons ago will always follow her.

A sudden and forceful tremor beneath their feet jars the seven. "It's time," Ishkamet yells out in howling wind. It was time to send the thirteenth crystal skull to its hiding place. The other priests and priestesses follow her into the temple.

Alta-Ra scientist priests had pledged their lives to preserve and illuminate the knowledge contained within thirteen crystal skulls. Twelve had already been sent away and hidden. The last crystal is Ishkamet's responsibility.

She often considers how all this occurred. There was a failed experiment by their neighbors to the north. On that day, a call broadcasted to all negative entities in the universe and other dimensions to seek refuge here. Darkness came—dozens of negative beings attached to those susceptible. The fall began.

Over time, the consciousness of the people plummeted. Rather than living in unconditional love, with high-frequency light and psychic and spiritual gifts, humankind began desiring power and became greedy. They no longer valued goodness but endeavored for material wealth.

The failed experiment that drew negative entities occurred less than two hundred years earlier. That was when earth changes began. People became fearful, and most left the islands and sought refuge to the land's due east. The ascended ones led by Master Thoth had rushed away in the great starship to distant lands and resettled in three areas of the world.

Except for the seven Atla-Ra priests, all had left the islands. Those attempting to confiscate their skull had perished in the cataclysm. It was just the seven of them now. Their job was almost finished. Ishkamet was responsible for leading the seven in a ceremony to hide the thirteenth crystal until Mother Earth was ready to ascend.

Within minutes, the priests and priestesses gather in a sacred chamber. They all sit around the altar in a meditative state. At the center of their small circle, sitting above them on the high platform, is a reddish-purple skull, *the* thirteenth crystal.

Ishkamet knows it isn't enough to hide the skull at the bottom of the ocean with their remains for someone to steal one day. This precious stone knows all. Its secrets must remain hidden for humankind's sake. For this reason, Ishkamet and the other six will send the crystal skull to someplace secure. They will teleport the piece where no one will ever find it.

The chanting is melodic. "Weassawea, rawedabefun, feswator. Weassawea, liesasuroesa, sawaseaesa. Weassawea, asducaasa, ifespleeda, bapoprures."

The Light Language not only supports the ceremony to transport the skull but also to release fear, as the seven Atla-Ra priests would soon face their deaths in this realm.

Ishkamet's eyes close. Her third eye sees all. Just before the sacred chamber doors burst open from flooding waters, she visualizes the crystal skull clearly in mind. It slowly fades away, vanishing as it teleports to its resting place. Where it will remain until the time is right—the Halls of Amenti.

The roar of water crashes upon her body. She opens her eyes in time to confirm—the thirteenth crystal skull is no longer on the altar. The water overtakes them all, and the Temple of Light entombs the seven.

★★★

Rebecca jars awake, gasping for air. Her heart races. She looks around. 'I'm home. My God, it was a nightmare!' She says, "It was so real!"

Rebecca recalls how the water swept her away to her demise. She can't shake the dream and reaches for the journal in her nightstand. She can't shake the image of the skull. It was a transparent crystal skull.

"How creepy," she whispers.

Rebecca begins to journal the experience. Usually, she journals fast before the memories of the dream slip away, but this dream is different. She didn't think she'd ever fail to recall this one, so she writes very slowly, in great detail.

CHAPTER 43:
JOSH

February 2005

Levi

Some events happen in our lives that change who we are and change the path we are on. Sometimes we welcome incidents like a breath of fresh air, while others are more reminiscent of nightmares. Often, we snap to judgment and suggest those situations that cause pain and hardship are wrong turns in life and setbacks. There was one event in 2002 that rocked many, including me, my family, and a seven-year-old boy.

***

It is a Wednesday evening in early February, and I am just getting ready to head into meditation when my phone rings. A glance at my caller ID tells me it is one of my parents. I immediately sense that something is wrong. I had just spoken with them on Sunday, and know it is unusual for them to call midweek.

"Hello?" I answer. "Is everything okay?"

While I hear breathing, indicating someone is on the other end of the phone, I can tell something is dreadfully off. "Mom? Dad? Who's there? What's wrong?"

It was barely audible, "Oh God . . ." my mother sobs. "I can't do this." A thud.

"Mom!?" There is no sound, 'She must have dropped the phone.'

I hear crackling from the handset. "Elisha?" My father says.

"Yes, Dad? What's going on?"

"There's been a car accident." My father solemnly squeaks out the words, trying his best to remain composed, "Dennis and Monica are gone."

After a long pause permitting me to digest what my father had said, that my brother and sister-in-law were dead, I ask, "What about Joshua?"

"He's in the hospital. In a coma. He was in the backseat of the car."

"Is he going to make it?" I ask.

"They don't know. You better come home. The funerals are Saturday."

Minutes later, I hang up the phone just in time to run to the bathroom, where I become sick to my stomach. As my head hangs over the toilet, I recall the conversation I had with Angela at the writers' conference a couple of years earlier, as if it happened yesterday.

"Your nephew will be coming to stay with you soon," echoes in my head.

The next few days are a blur to me. As soon as I get to Founders, I head to the hospital where I see my nephew in the ICU. He is still in a coma. I speak with the doctors, and they aren't sure what his prognosis is, they say something about brain swelling and hopeful he will wake up on his own, but it could be hours, days or weeks.

Then my older brother and I take the lead on working with the funeral home director, along with my sister-in-law's family to coordinate the wakes and funerals together. Coffin selections, obituary information relayed, arrangements for memorial services, then we order gravestones. Everything is logistically and emotionally challenging, and I see my parents age overnight.

Saturday, after the service at the gravesite, after I set

a rose on the coffins and escort my parents to their car, the phone vibrates.

It is the hospital calling. Three days after the accident, Josh had awakened, reminding me that we need to make other pressing decisions.

My brother and I go to the hospital, not quite sure what to expect with Josh. Perhaps it is a blessing, but my nephew has transient global amnesia. He lost his memory of the accident, and many of his other memories were fuzzy.

My deceased sister-in-law's only sibling is her brother, who is a hotshot corporate executive at a tech company and is living in Tokyo. He couldn't make it back for the service. He is Josh's godfather, and I am the godmother.

I know the family expects that I take in Josh, and I wouldn't have it any other way.

Overnight, my life changes. I gladly back-burner much of my spiritual work while I take in, care for, and raise my nephew. I adore him, and he becomes my priority and the center of my world. Thrown into the deep end—parent-teacher meets, volunteering at school, soccer, baseball, basketball, then, the talent shows and science fairs. In truth, I did not know what I had been missing.

My nephew adapts well. His memories before the accident are vague from traumatic brain injury. While he remembers his life, he oddly is unattached to it. He knows he should miss his parents, but one time, Josh admitted that it is like all his memories of his parents are censored. They were like a download of information, with no emotions attached.

This part is baffling because my nephew is one of the most sensitive and emotional beings I know. The more I watch him grow, the more I realized that he is part of a new generation of children coming to the planet. I had known about the Indigo Children, but he was part of a later group coming in during the nineties known as Crystal Children.

Perhaps his failure to remember his parents with the appropriate emotions was some sort of protection or coping mechanism.

It did not take him long to start introducing me as "Mom" to his friends. When I asked him about it, because I did not want him ever to forget his parents, he said, "When kids lose their parents and get adopted, they get a new mom and dad. Why can't I?"

★★★

That request was last year, and I had to think about it. It's going on three years since Josh came to live with me, and both our lives are different from those first fragile days that fate put us together.

Today is Valentine's Day, and with the anniversary of Josh's parents passing last week, I wanted to give something special to him. As he gets ready to head out the door for school, I hand him an extra-large envelope.

"Happy Valentine's Day!" I say.

"What's this?" He smiles.

"Open it and see!"

The ten-year-old tears open the envelope, and inside there is a certificate of adoption.

"What is this?" he asks with a confused look on his face. "Is this...are we...are you, my mom?"

I smile. "It's official, dear one, we are officially parent and child."

Josh throws his arms around me and hugs me. "This is the best gift ever!"

It hits me at that moment that all events, even those tragic ones, have a silver lining if you look for it.

Chapter 44:
Gridding the Christ
Consciousness Grid

June 13, 2006

Ami

It has been five years since the day darkness prevailed. Existence for all has changed. People began living in fear, which fed and strengthened dimly lit souls while Light hearts faltered. For five years, mom and I have been on a journey. Mom has been writing our book in Denver while I worked with a facilitator in Manitou Springs to write at Cheyenne Village. Our progress has been at a turtle's pace, yet steady.

I was hoping that Leilah would help with the book, too, but her mom is planning to relocate soon and didn't want Leilah to participate. Three other nonverbal autistics are writing with us. I have never met them in the physical, but we telepathically-talk all the time. I like Colin and hope one day we can meet physically.

Mom still visits every weekend. I don't see Dad much anymore since he got remarried. I was sad that he didn't invite me to his wedding. I understand his reluctance, though; after all, I would need a caregiver to take me to Connecticut and travel with me. He didn't want Mom there. I understand, but I hope he knows how much I love and miss him.

Today I am outside with Leilah in the back of our home. She is running back and forth, and I am a bit envious that she moves so swiftly. Her body type is thin and lean, and she is athletic, while I am shorter and what's the word, wider? I am laughing inside. I am heavier and do not move swiftly at all. My body just does not move like others. I have shorter limbs than most, I am blocky, and my hips are fuller than my clavicles. Doctors tell Mom it is because of my body type. I know, though, that the energy I receive to sustain life goes to more critical areas, leaving my body as my Achilles' heel. My body will one day give out because of the seizures. I only hope and pray I accomplish everything before I transition.

I walk toward the cottonwood tree in the back of my Cheyenne Village home. I have come to love this tree. The tree is old and wise, and being with it always brings joy. I see the tree's subtle vibration that many may refer to as the aura, but I call it energy. Like me, and like anyone, the tree is a grid of energy, mass, and space-time.

There are many energy matrixes in many dimensions. I see these lattices both altogether and separately, depending on my intention. When I was younger, it was challenging to separate the energy networks, and I would become unsettled with changes in energy, like the floor from the kitchen to the dining room in our old house. Mom and Dad helped me negotiate that doorway all the time. Now I understand it better and don't get bogged down with sudden energy changes.

Not only do living species have energy, but they have energy grids or electromagnetic fields. Each species, all thirty-million of them, though just fourteen-million remain today, has a unique template around the planet, without their matrix, they would not exist. A planetary grid is an etheric crystalline structure that covers the earth and holds consciousness for a species. It is no wonder that Mother Earth herself has a network, given that Earth is the living Gaia and has a unique awareness.

On our planet, there are five levels of consciousness for humanity. Two are beyond humanity's capability at this time. There are three different kinds of human beings on Earth today, and each type has a unique electromagnetic field. These electromagnetic fields are the primal grid, our existing aware-ness grid, and the Unity or Christ Consciousness Grid. These matrixes are templates, and the Christ Consciousness Grid permits life to accelerate through ascension.

My eyes dart to the ground beneath my feet, where my x-ray vision sees a crystalline network, a long chain of twelve-sided balls with pentagram faces. I sit, both knees facing forward, my calves on the earth's surface, and I am closer to the primal grid beneath me. This grid is the crystalline structure that holds the consciousness of the original people on Earth, like the Aboriginals.

Those studying sacred geometry may call this crystalline matrix the dodecahedron, which has twenty faces of penta-grams. Pythagoras knew of its importance as a form of Divine thought. It is beautiful. You would be in awe if your eyes could see its magnificence. It is the first grid, some refer to it as the gravity grid, but I know the Truth. It is anchored deep within the core of the Earth and on the surface of the planet too. This primal or Aboriginal Grid is embedded in the first dimension, to just below the third, and currently functions as the planet's gravitational field. What most do not know is that it was the primary consciousness of our Earth until the flood of Atlantis.

There *was* an Atlantis, and it sank about eleven thou-sand years ago. The awareness at that time was unity or col-lective consciousness. If one person experienced something, everyone in the mass would have that memory. At that time, there was no need for written communication, for we knew all. Atlantis fell, and with the fall, we forgot who we are. We became separated and cut off, and our consciousness became disharmonic.

A second grid emerged. It is visible in the lower dimensions also. When I shift my focus, I see it. It is also beautiful with chains of icosahedron balls. These geometric shapes have twenty-sided balls with equilateral triangular faces. It is the electromagnetic grid and runs from the earth's surface, extending upward for almost six miles. With my eyes, I follow the pattern up in the sky until I lose it in the distance. It is the existing human grid which regulates electromagnetic systems, such as vortexes and ley lines, and fluctuates from the first and second dimension to just below the fourth. It is currently the central consciousness grid of most of humanity.

Would you believe the governments of Russia and America know about these electromagnetic fields? The information, though, is withheld from the people. It is no coincidence that military installations between the United States and Russia happen to fall on nodal points on this human consciousness grid. Could it be that the governments believed there was an opportunity to control the population if they could control the network? Is it being used to manipulate people to instill fear? I am not paranoid.

There is sacred geometry associated with these consciousness grids. The Aboriginal Grid has a relationship closer to Phi or the Golden Mean ratio and links to patterns in nature. Humankind's existing consciousness grid does not relate to Phi, perhaps explaining why humanity is not in tune with nature and killing our mother, Gaia. This current humankind grid relates to duality consciousness, which is why we tend to judge things as black and white, right or wrong, good or bad. It inflates the ego, and it is our ego that stops us from caring for others and only those close to us, rather than loving everyone as a collective-one-life.

There is one other significant grid, and it is a baby by

matrix standards. It anchored in early 1989. It is called many names, the Unity Consciousness Grid, the Crystal or Crystalline Grid, or Christ Consciousness Grid. This light matrix is a geodesic sphere consisting of triangles and pentagrams that sparkle like a diamond. It is a birth crystal of a new form, the double pentadodecahedron, which has 144 facets. This crystalline grid is spaced across the surface of the planet and created to reverberate a higher frequency for the New Earth.

This network is synthetic. It is *not* natural. Many years ago, in Atlantis, there was a horrible incident involving dimly lit souls who tried to advance their evolution, and it backfired. It brought negative entities and beings from all over this universe and the fourth dimension to the physical reality known as Earth. These presences, for their survival, attached themselves to most Atlanteans. The Atlanteans stopped living from the heart, and this ultimately led to the collapse of Atlantis.

The consequence of the dark entities coming to Earth set the clock ticking back then. There were only approximately thirteen thousand years left to create, anchor, and activate an ascension grid because, without it, the human race will perish at the end of the twenty-six thousand–year cycle, which is happening *soon*.

Before the fall of Atlantis, three higher evolved beings, Thoth, Araragat, and Ra, from higher dimensions knew humanity was heading for a collapse. How did they know? They were part of a tweak to the timeline and permitted to recreate an ascension grid, and this synthetic matrix is essential to humanity's spiritual evolution.

Our two-grid system is changing into a trinity pattern, and our planet's frequency is indeed increasing. Mother Earth is now in a preparation stage to spring into higher aspects.

There is something that many autistic individuals do that is a challenge for me to explain. We can do what is called gridding. The flawless design of the Christ Consciousness Grid is perfect and complete. However, when lifeforms, including people, consciously or unconsciously interact with the grid, the lattice is often pulled into an unnatural state. When this happens, we autists sense something is amiss, and we tune in and fix it.

As I sit here, I become still and tune into the Christ Consciousness Grid. I hear static-like emanations of the grid's distress. At that moment, I know I have work to do. I place my attention on the static-like alarm, and I ooze from one dimension into another, into the heart of the grid's distress. I don't get there directly. I move there through a subset lattice; we call the Chrysalis Gold Grid, which the autistics created. It functions much like a funnel, so that the autistics may bring in the required patterning and technology to upgrade the Christ Consciousness Grid.

There is always an element of uncertainty when jumping into the unknown. To know the beauty of the matrix and to leap into a space that is void of its magnificence is unsettling because we aren't aware of what caused the disturbance in the first place. The opposition, those dimly lit souls are often the source, and we never know what we are tackling.

As I meld into it, though, I sense on all levels the absence of its beauty. There are darkness and sadness and an alarming noise filled with distress. It is unnerving, and I know I am here to restore balance. I also know that I announced my position to the Dark Team. I need to work fast.

In the grid, I have no mask and no autism. My body moves quickly, and I am agile, and with my keen attention, I move the energy so that vortexes form in areas of the grid that remain beautiful. These areas contain consciousness within the network's light and sound. In my mind, I channel the beauty from regions with magnificence into dark areas until there is balance, and restoration within the matrix.

When finished, I have a sense of wholeness and perfection.

I open to messages from the Light Ones. At that moment, brilliant flashes of white light announce the presence of Metatron. His body manifests in a crystalline form and is androgynous. He carries a cube spinning clockwise in his hand. The hexahedron is known to contain all geometric shapes that comprise all creations. Metatron uses it to restore energetic balance and healing. The archangel's presence will protect me from the opposition—no need to worry that my mask is down.

"Shawnami Kaliyuga, your work is Divine," Metatron says.

My palms come together with fingers pointing upwards, and I press my hands to my heart. I lower my eyes in respect. There is nothing I can say to Metatron that he doesn't already know, including how much I love him.

"This matrix is the most meaningful path in the ascension process," Metatron begins. "Your comrades are here, some are helping now, but more will be contributing soon when they remember. Factions of Lightworkers and Earth Keepers are gathering. They will continue to awaken people to their bond with the Living Earth and Universe through love. You will join forces with some of them. These efforts will accelerate the grid's activation.

"The matrix must be fully activated by December 2012; at that time, the New Earth will begin. Of course, this assumes that the Christ Consciousness Grid is more than half operational *soon*. As people choose to serve the Light in the months and years to come, they will visit sacred sites and align themselves with the three grids, and by anchoring to this frequency, their hearts activate. Higher-dimensional doorways at these blessed locations will assist in the person's awakening. Then, these people will return home, all over the planet and help raise the frequency.

"Dark times are coming, though. Some will try to stop you. There will be obstacles and danger. Shawnami, you know better than anyone how important your work is. The ascension grid extends from the fourth dimension through the twelfth. It amplifies the ascending levels of consciousness. If we don't get people to the higher aspect, they will not evolve and remain in three–dimensional destruction.

"Remember, though, as you claim more of what it is like to be human, and embody, bringing your Higher Self in, it will take its toll on your body, and you will risk exposing who you are and undermine your physical health. You may need to transition to a higher vibrational self and assist your comrades from your etheric body. Never forget who you are, the flame of eternal life; it will bring you home.

"I am Metatron, and I share with you these Truths. You are beloved, Shawnami Kaliyuga."

Ami gradually comes back from her gridding experience, finding herself again beneath the cottonwood tree. Leilah is sitting on the ground near her.

"You are back," she says. *"Were you working on the grid?"*

"Yes. I saw Metatron."

"What did he say?"

"We have much work to do!"

"You know I won't be here too much longer. Mom and I will be going to California."

"You must keep in touch. I pray your mother will see the importance of what we are doing. We need you. Never forget how important you are to this, Leilah."

CHAPTER 45:
MITCHELL-HEDGES SKULL ON TOUR

2008

Rebecca sits on her patio, her seasonal sanctuary. She spent the morning shopping for everything she needs to change the covered deck into something new and extraordinary. There is an assortment of clay pots scattered around the veranda. A couple of sizeable potting soil bags along with flats of colorful annuals await her attention. A large carton with a water fountain sits in the corner. This will be her outdoor sanctuary.

By evening, her pots are full of colorful floral arrangements, each with a thriller, spiller, and filler, and the fountain spouts fresh water. A string of patio lights illuminates the ceiling while tiki lamps flicker on the three sides. She cleaned her patio dining set and put away the tools and supplies. Everything is perfect, and now she gets to enjoy the sunset.

As the sun begins to set over the mountains west of her home, she grabs her sweatshirt as the warm May air will quickly cool. She intends to enjoy the peace and solitude of her new sanctuary. Rebecca lights a candle on the table, grabs her well-deserved beer, and sits in a quiet space of gratitude and appreciation for everything in her life. She sips her brew and watches the setting sun behind the mountain range.

Rebecca has always admired her friends' ability to have direction in their life. Many of them know what they are here to do and have set out to do it. The only clear thing to her is that she is Ami's advocate, and while she believes that is enough, there's a part of her that wonders if there is more.

She watches the bright, vibrant orange sky slowly fade. She closes her eyes and meditates. After a bit, she feels a presence. It is an unusual one. She doesn't see it but hears a voice; it sounds like it is coming from within a tunnel.

"You are being prepared to face periods of change and acceleration," the words echo.

Although shaken, she remains still and listens more.

"You do not have the clarity like others who walk with a strong heart on their missions. That will come in time; until then, this will be a faith walk for you. This lack of clarity is necessary. Without it, you could close doors; with it, all possibilities are left open. If you try to control this process of transformation, you will suppress yourself to a more demanding cycle. Bless the mystery and watch with eyes detached from the outcome."

Rebecca sits still, entirely in shock. It is the first time she has heard anything other than voices from this dimension. The sound was different. Higher pitched, slight, yet close. It is hard for her to describe. As she opens her eyes, she looks around to see if someone is there. No one. In the corner of her eye, a flash of quick movement near the fountain. It is something small and fast. It is lit like a firefly yet looks more like a dragonfly. It is there one moment, then gone.

She doesn't know what had just happened. The advice given was to trust what is going on. Trust the journey. The voice suggested the lack of clarity was purposeful, that is enough for her to feel like her adventure is now beginning.

Every evening, except those days she visits Ami, Rebecca finds herself outside on her patio, breathing nature's fresh air, smelling the scent of her flowers, hearing the bubbling of water at her fountain, and feeling the last rays of the sun on her before setting. Each night, she is hopeful for a similar experience. It finally comes one evening in July.

On this warm summer's night, she is meditating when that high-pitched voice says, "Go to your computer and search for Mitchell-Hedges Skull on tour."

'What?' Rebecca comes out of meditation to locate the source of the voice, once again only to see a firefly-like drag-onfly near the water feature before it is gone. She rises, a bit lightheaded from moving too fast and goes into the house. She turns on her computer before she can question what she is about to do. At the Google prompt, she types "Mitchell-Hedges Skull on tour." She clicks a link and learns there is a gathering in Sedona called "Guardians of the Crystal Skulls." A skull called the Mitchell-Hedges Skull will be at the conference.

She clicks on the thumbnail image of a crystal skull, and it enlarges. The picture triggers a vision of her dream she had years earlier. She had forgotten about it. She recalls Ishkamet sacrificing her life to protect a crystal skull. 'What is going on?'

In the morning, compelled to learn more, Rebecca calls the conference center to get more information.

"Wow! I *just* posted that last evening," the woman at the convention center says. "I'm surprised the search engines have even indexed it."

The conference is on the weekend of the fall equinox.

Rebecca looks forward to the convention. When school starts, she requests some personal time for the three-day event. She shares her experiences with Ami, who encourages her to meditate with a crystal skull.

After some reluctance, she ventures to a metaphysical store. Of course, they don't have crystal skulls, but the owner knows where to buy them. A week later, she has three to choose from and selects a small amethyst head; she names it "Precious." She meditates with Precious for about a month and brings her to Sedona.

The evening before the event, while meditating in her

hotel room with Precious, she hears a voice. "To connect with the Mitchell-Hedges Skull, you will need to send it a code." It wasn't the distant, tiny voice she had heard before. This one is much louder, stronger, and more commanding.

The following morning Rebecca excitedly prepares for the conference. After she is dressed and ready to go, she has about thirty minutes to spare. She meditates, and again the commanding voice says, "Your key to connecting with the skull is *holder sequence release valve*."

She comes out of meditation and reaches for her journal, where she jots down the sequence of words, "holder sequence release valve."

Rebecca is in disbelief about all that is happening. She doesn't know what to expect, though admittedly, she is excited to be at the conference and learn more about the ancient skulls. Precious, her stone is safely tucked away in her handbag.

She feels out of place, waiting outside the conference room for the first presentation. A tall man approaches.

"Hi, Rebecca," the man says, glimpsing her name tag. He throws his hand out to her, "I'm Herman."

"Nice to meet you, Herman." If there is such a thing, this man embodies the archetype of a nerd. He is in his late fifties, tall and skinny and wears a plaid shirt, large framed glasses, and sports a bowtie.

"So, where are you from, Rebecca? Sedona?"

"No, Colorado, the Denver area.

"What brings you here?"

"I'm not exactly sure," she admits, not entirely comfortable confiding in the stranger. "What about you?"

"Well, I am a guardian."

"What does that mean?"

"Many years ago, I felt called to understand these crystals. I didn't know what was drawing me to them at the time. I mean, they really are creepy, aren't they?" He smiles.

She smiles, too, nodding in agreement.

He looks around, seeing that no one is eavesdropping. In a hushed tone, he says, "One day it hit me. I was a priest in Atlantis and protector of one of the thirteen skulls!"

She senses that this was a big deal to him, but she hasn't a clue what he is saying. Her initial impression of him is that he has a gentle spirit and is indeed harmless. "I'm new to this," she confides, "What do you mean by the thirteen skulls?"

"I wondered if you were a newbie," he smiles. "In Atlantis, there were thirteen crystal skulls. They were like supercomputers, only much more powerful. They contain consciousness, the knowledge, and wisdom of everything since the beginning of humanity, over two hundred fifty thousand years ago. They hold the spiritual knowledge that can save the planet today and the Divine blueprint of Earth."

It could have been Rebecca's wrinkled nose, and the crease between her eyebrows that tells him she's clueless, encouraging him to keep talking. And he does.

"Twelve skulls hold the knowledge of the twelve tribes from that time. Then there was one master skull, an amethyst skull, that held the knowledge of *all* twelve tribes. Guardians are those who are drawn to the skulls and are willing to work for humanity at this time."

"How do these crystals help?"

"The crystals, even the modern ones, when activated, can channel relevant information. As we draw to them, we awaken. We remember."

"What do you remember?"

"Bits and pieces, enough to know that it's time for all this knowledge to return. The skulls offer a pathway to ascension."

"And, you were a, what did you call yourself, a guardian?"

"Yes, for one of the twelve tribes, I believe."

"You say these 13 skulls hold the Divine blueprint of the planet. What kind of information do they contain?"

"Humanity's origin, our purpose as a collective, our destiny, and the sacred mysteries of the universe!" Herman's eyes are enormous through his large rimmed glasses, which slips on the bridge of his nose a bit.

He pushes the spectacles up his nose. "You see, we're all part of a grand experiment," he continues. "It's a test really, to see if humankind having freewill can maintain a connection to their God-self. We fell and forgot who we are. There was a battle between light and dark, and darkness won, humankind fell; that was in Atlantis. But I believe it was all part of the plan. The grand setup of the battle of light versus darkness was intentional and is part of Earth's divine blueprint."

"I don't understand."

"While we were in Atlantis, we lived at a high frequency. We were much more powerful than we can even imagine today. Psychic does not even begin to explain it. We communicated through telepathy and remembered everything. There was no need for writing. We shared collective consciousness. We vibrated at the eighth and ninth density, some even higher, rather than the third. We carried the codes of unconditional love, compassion, joy, acceptance, and all knowledge. That is who we are. We are that powerful! Only we don't remember."

"What does all this have to do with the skulls?"

"Are you drawn to them?" There is a noticeable twinkle in his eye.

Rebecca thinks about her dream years earlier. She knows she is, but she doesn't understand it. "I believe so."

"Some think that a couple of the skulls have been discovered. I'm not so sure, though. There are indeed skulls from Atlantis here at this exhibit, but I don't believe they are the thirteen. I think they remain hidden. There is a story that the master crystal skull, the thirteenth, was sent to another dimension by a small group of priests and priestesses when the Temple of Light sank."

Rebecca has a flashback of her dream. She remembers Ishkamet and the others performing some ceremony around a crystal skull and how it disappeared as water flooded through the temple's doors.

"I believe the thirteenth Master Crystal was sent to the sixth dimension, to the Halls of Amenti."

This was a lot for her to take in all at once. She wonders who Herman is for a moment, then the conference doors open, and one of the conference staff comes over.

"There you are, Dr. Herman. Here is your name tag," a woman hands him a lanyard with his name tag boasting a ribbon that says, *SPEAKER*.

"Thank you," he says, glancing at his watch. "Oh, my, how time flies!" He smiles at her. "It was so nice to meet you, Rebecca. I hope you enjoy the conference. Perhaps we can chat later?"

Herman ducks into the meeting room, and she watches as he advances to the podium and sets up for his presentation.

The following day, Bill Homann presents the Mitchell-Hedges Skull. He introduces himself as the skull's guardian. From a front-row seat, Rebecca intently listens as he talks about his unique crystal.

"To date, the Mitchell-Hedges Skull is the only ancient skull with a detachable jaw. The head was carved from a single block of crystal, and there are no tool marks from its creation. Many have attempted to recreate skulls in this manner," he shares, "and they've all been unsuccessful."

He talks about the properties of quartz and how it is not only tough to carve, but it is also brittle and can easily shatter with the wrong tool's touch. "We don't have the technology today to create this skull with such precision! The Mitchell-Hedges Skull is a mystery.

"The skull was found by the British explorer F.A.

Mitchell-Hedges, along with his adopted daughter, Anna. They discovered it in the ruins of an ancient Mayan pyramid in 1924. The jaw was found at the same site about twenty-five feet away, three months after the initial discovery. There has been much controversy over the unearthing of the skull. Critics alleged that the explorer was playing a practical joke on his daughter by planting a new crystal head at the Mayan site.

"The head is anatomically correct," Homann continues. "Forensic scientists determined that the skull is representative of a female between twenty-five and twenty-nine years of age and of Mesoamerican descent.

"After F.A. Mitchell-Hedges passed away in 1959, his daughter, Anna, became the guardian of the skull until her passing last year. With her death, I became the new guardian of the crystal skull.

"The Mitchell-Hedges skull has been called the Skull of Doom and is believed to be the inspiration behind the new Indiana Jones movie about the crystal skull." The presenter further hints that his crystal deserves a new name, and one is in the making.

"There are prisms built into the skull that direct light." Homann further explains that when the head sits upon a light source, the sockets function as lenses that transfer the light from below into the upper cranium where there are ribbon prisms and light tunnels.

"Who made the skull? That is the mystery. Skeptics suggest that the Germans made it, others believe that the Atlanteans made it. The Mayans believe that some of the ancient skulls found are rare and sacred gifts by the Grandfathers of the Pleiades. They believe that the crystals contain the consciousness from beyond our galaxy."

After the presentation, Homann continues to field questions from the audience, while attendees inspect the one-of-a-kind skull in front of the room. Rebecca knows this may be her only opportunity to communicate with the crystal. She waits for the perfect opening to approach while the presenter shares stories with fans interested in knowing more about the famous crystal.

When no one else is in line, and no one is at the skull, she approaches. 'It is quite beautiful,' she thinks. The presenter and fans gravitated away from the piece, leaving her an opportunity to be alone with the skull.

Rebecca feels slightly foolish that she is there to communicate a key or code to it. She closes her eyes and tries to center herself. In her mind, she repeats three times, 'Holder sequence release valve.' There, she had imparted it. She is unsure what else to expect. She remains in silence with eyes closed, and it hits her that she has an unexplainable inner knowing about the skull.

From everything she has learned at the conference, and from what is brewing within her soul, she knows that crystal skulls are tools to support our emerging consciousness. She knows they are the holders of high Light and can assist in understanding our true selves. Somehow, she discerns that the new crystals, like Precious, can resonate with the energy of the original skulls of Atlantis. At that moment, Rebecca knows that the crystal skulls hold a template to activate a person's soul growth toward the realization of their authentic Divinity. She understands that keys and codes that will come from these ancient skulls will serve as guideposts toward new and evolving soul growth.

Somehow, Rebecca intuits that the ancient skulls, like the one before her, are highly charged physical *manifestations* of the original Atlantean crystals. She also senses that the Atlantean skulls during the time of Atlantis where physical materializations of consciousness and created before Atlantis, in Lemuria. Those original physical forms contain a blueprint or plan for

Earth; more importantly, they were the ancient people's pathway to the Creator.

As she opens her eyes and sees the age-old skull before her, she understands that it was formed from the etheric body of one of the crystal heads from Atlantis, and in Atlantis, it was created from a skull from Lemuria. 'Was that where it all began?'

She has an inner knowing. 'This skull has the original Earth plan and is a conduit to God.'

She hears someone approach and realizes she has only minutes before the next presentation.

"We're going to move the skull to display in the lobby," a man says.

Rebecca quickly retrieves her camera from her purse. "May I take a picture before you move it?"

Without giving him a chance to respond, she quickly snaps a series of shots. "Thank you," she says aloud.

While directed to the skull, the attendant answers, "You're welcome."

She is exhausted when she returns to her hotel room. She had a compelling experience with *the* skull. She pulls out her camera, turns it on, and views the small pictures of the Mitchell-Hedges Skull. As Rebecca scrolls through the images, she sees how the figures pale to the skull's pure magnificence. Then she comes upon one image that stops her. There is something inside of the crystal. It's gold. Using the magnifier on the camera, she zooms in on the picture. Within the head, there is a clear view of a gold window-like rendering.

Rebecca knows the conference room had no windows. She didn't use a flash. There was nothing that could have caused a reflection. It isn't a reflection—there is something within the skull broadcasting out.

All this is confusing, and she wants to share it with

someone. The exhaustion she had felt was gone. "Who would appreciate this?" She wonders.

Rebecca rummages through her bag from the conference, looking for a card. She knows he would enjoy this and perhaps even be able to explain its significance.

"Here it is!" She pulls the business card from the papers. "Doctor S. Herman, Guardian of the Skull," she whispers.

Chapter 46:
"I Have the Codes."

April 9, 2009

Rebecca leads Ami into her study, which she converted to a meditation room. "Let's see if we can get the codes."

It is the evening of Holy Thursday—the tail end of spring break for Rebecca. She and Ami had been traveling. They just returned home, and she will bring Ami to Cheyenne Village on Easter Sunday. For Rebecca, the Easter weekend always brings back childhood memories of being a preacher's kid. This Easter weekend is different, though.

Tonight, mother and daughter settle in Rebecca's study to meditate. They had returned from Sedona just hours earlier. Both sense something big is about to happen.

While in Arizona that week, codes were entrusted to Ami, but she had not been able to access them. To continue their work, they need to understand the four missing keys.

Rebecca and Ami fall into deep meditation. Both feel swallowed by a high-frequency, a very holy, Divine presence. They feel held by Spirit and in a safe and sacred place.

Gong! The meditation alarm sounds, pulling them from their hour meditation. For Rebecca, she's clueless where the time went.

Ami grunts. Rebecca retrieves the letterboard from the desk.

"I have the codes," Ami grins.

"Wonderful!" She is thrilled.

Rebecca's life today is so different than it had been just six months ago. She had wondered if this day would ever come.

As she shares her excitement with her daughter, she recalls how all this has come to pass.

★★★

Rebecca wanted to reach out to someone who would appreciate the picture she took of the Mitchell-Hedges Skull. There's only one person who came to mind, Dr. Herman.

She called him.

He was delighted that she reached out to him. "Of course, I remember you! I was hoping I'd see you before the conference ends tomorrow."

"I took a picture of one of the skulls, today and I'd like to show it to you."

"If I may be so bold—show me over dinner tomorrow night after the conference wraps up."

That dinner was eventful in so many ways. First, Rebecca shared her story about Ami and their book, which had turned into Ami's book.

"I feel a bit unworthy of contributing to the book. I understand why Ami's writing, as well as the information I am getting from the other autistics, is essential, but—I'm having a hard time seeing that I have anything worthwhile to share."

He listened with interest.

Rebecca, enamored in their conversation, shared how she found the conference. "I was meditating, and I heard a voice say go on Google and search Mitchell-Hedges Skull on tour."

His eyes lit up.

She continued. "Then, in meditation, I was asked to impart a code when I saw the skull. I'm not sure why. I did, though." She pulled out her digital camera, found what she was looking for, and moved to the chair beside him.

He angled his chair closer to her, so they can both could

look at the small camera's display.

"Here!" She revealed the Mitchell-Hedges Skull with the gold distortion.

"What is that?" Herman asked.

"I was hoping you could tell me."

"That is just bizarre! I've seen hundreds of photos of crystal skulls, and in none of them have I seen anything like this!"

"It's almost like a window with panes."

He magnified the picture, "Or...a scroll!"

"A scroll?"

"The skulls contain the knowledge of so much we are ignorant of...they are a path to humankind's evolution to fully realize our divinity as a sacred human. Perhaps it's an invitation to open to it." His eyes were wide with excitement.

Rebecca was wrapped up in it too. Not only about the crystal skull, but she was surprisingly enjoying chatting with this eccentric individual, yet she knew little about him. "Well, how would I open to it?"

"You have a skull, right?"

"Yes, Precious, that's what I call her."

"It's believed that the ancient skulls of Atlantis have keys and codes that'll help humanity ascend to the fifth dimension."

"The fifth dimension?"

"The destination of Mother Earth and humanity's ascension. You know, where the planet is heading. Anyway, the Mitchell-Hedges Skull is a physical manifestation of an Atlantean skull so it would have the keys and codes."

"But I don't have access to the Mitchell-Hedges Skull."

"Sure, you do, through Precious. Based on what you've shared, it's clear that your contemporary skull activated at some point. The meditation this summer—was that your first connection to the crystal skulls?"

Rebecca instantly thought about her dream. Her lips part

and she spoke, "Well, some time ago, I had the oddest dream. I—oh, never mind; it's silly even to bring it up."

"Please share it," he encouraged in a kind voice.

Herman had a way with her that she didn't quite comprehend. Their time together had been rewarding in ways she hadn't acknowledged. Perhaps it was because she missed adult conversations about this metaphysical stuff. Crystal used to be her sounding board, and that had shifted. For a second, she wondered, 'Could it be that I miss the companionship of a man?'

She looked at him differently at that moment, then convinced herself that it is the information on the skulls that beckoned her.

"Well, I did have a dream many years ago." After all the years that passed, she still remembered the details. "I was a high priestess in a temple with six others. It was my job to protect a crystal skull from getting into the wrong hands. We performed a ceremony and teleported the crystal skull to another place. Then, water crashed through the temple's doors, and we all perished."

"I knew it!" He said excitedly. "From the moment I saw you, I knew you were special. You're a guardian too!"

"Well, I'm not sure *special* is the right word." Something within her churned at the word *special*. "I believe that *none* of us are special, or *all* of us are special. No *one* of us is special."

"Spoken like an enlightened master," he smiled.

"There is only one thing that makes me feel 'special.'"

"What's that?"

"That my daughter, Ami, chose me to be her mother."

"You shared earlier that you are unclear of your contribution to your book."

"Yes."

"You should tell your story in the first part. It will open hearts and prepare the readers for your daughter's words."

Something resonated with that advice. "I will give that some thought," she said.

Rebecca left Arizona the following morning, and, surprisingly, she couldn't take her mind off Herman. She had such an enjoyable and entertaining dinner with him, and he oddly felt familiar and comfortable to her. It was hard to explain. It was almost like she knew him, yet she had just met him. She sensed that each of them would always be somewhat connected, and this baffled her, given that they just met. It was as if she found her best friend for life. She couldn't deny that there was an intense, immediate connection with him.

For a moment, Rebecca considered the possibility that he was a guardian of a skull in Atlantis, and she was also. Perhaps they knew each other in a past life. 'Am I crazy to think that?' Maybe that was the reason for her unexplainable feelings of connection to him.

Rebecca and Herman began emailing each other. Then they started telephoning. Their discussions at first were about the skulls; then, they started sharing about themselves. Suddenly, he was heading to Denver for a gem show, and they had a chance to see each other again.

It was during those few days that Herman confessed that his interest in Rebecca went more in-depth than their passion for the skulls. One thing led to another, and soon, they began seeing each other romantically. The best way she could describe him was that he was her compass. She had an expanded awareness of herself when he was around. She felt like a better person in his presence. In some ways, they were very similar and mirrored each other's values. Then, she realized that she could be her authentic self around this man, and that was a first for her.

Spring in Sedona is beautiful. It was spring break, and

Rebecca had the week off. It was time for Ami to meet Herman. Mother and daughter arrived at his home in Oak Creek, just outside of Sedona for lunch.

"Welcome to my abode, Ami," he said. He backed away from the entrance, permitting Ami and Rebecca to enter.

Ami passed through the threshold, uncharacteristically maintaining an eye connection with him.

Rebecca knew this was unusual.

Ami pointed down. She wanted to speak.

It was evident to Rebecca that Ami had something to say. She knew it was best to permit her to type before the urgency was gone.

"Herman, I think Ami wants to say something to you." She pulled the letterboard from her shoulder.

"Of course," he said. "Let's sit in my family room."

"I think we can speak right here. If you don't mind." Rebecca knew that Ami does not need to sit to talk. Unless Ami was in her car, which Ami calls her spaceship, she prefers to stand.

"Of course! What's on your mind, Ami?" Herman asked as if she was an old friend.

Rebecca is there with her keyboard. "You have skull talent in DNA. You were not a guardian of the skull. You were the top scientist in Atlantis."

Herman was surprised. "Is that a fact? How do you know this, Miss Ami?"

"Dream this morning. Watchers told me. You knew that all spiritual advancements would be lost with the fall."

"The fall in Atlantis?" he asked excitedly.

"Y. You knew secrets would be lost. It crushed your heart, and you could not live with that. You developed skull technology to save secrets in the skulls."

"*I* developed skull technology in Atlantis?"

"Y. We need to decode Mitchell-Hedges Skull to gain secrets you hid."

"*I* hid secrets?" Herman tried to take it all in.

"Watchers say there are four missing codes. They will not only help Mom do her destiny work but will help all who will have a significant role during the shift. This is the reason you and Mom met. Need you to use ancient expertise to get codes."

"How? I would love to help you, Ami. I'm just not sure how."

"Your work will be done in the ethers. In dreams."

Herman got so worked up about Ami's new insights that he was unable to sleep that night. He tossed and turned, and in moments of dozing, wheels spun in his head with ones and zeros flashing. The restlessness continued the following evening and into the third night. He was exhausted and didn't know how much more he could take. Then halfway through the third night, the spiraling wheels and binary code suddenly disappeared, and there was a reverberating voice that sounded in Herman's head, *"It is done."*

Herman fell into a deep sleep.

The following morning, when Ami woke at the hotel, she grabbed the keyboard on the nightstand and brought it to Rebecca, who was making coffee.

"What is it, Ami?" Rebecca took the board from Ami and helped her type.

"Coding process is done."

"You have the four missing codes?"

"Downloaded to me. Don't have access yet."

★★★

Rebecca and Ami sit beside each other in Rebecca's study. They had returned from Sedona that day and just finished meditating, Ami wants to type.

"It worked. I have access to the downloaded codes."

"So, what do these codes mean?"

"Will help you get soul ready."

"Just me?"

"Others too. Unclear at this moment of its importance during the shift but will be key for you."

CHAPTER 47:
PRECESSION OF THE EQUINOX

Reflections

Ami

I want to share with you about events that are coming. Remember, though, that it is in flux as it is all choice.

In the years preceding the end of the Mayan calendar, the internet, books, and movies will exploit doomsday conspiracies and fill people's heads. Fear will spread.

The Mayan calendar is indeed ending, but what people don't realize is—it is a cycle, and once it ends, we begin anew. Some call this period the Precession of the Equinox. On December 21, 2012, the sun, earth, and the center of the galaxy will be in a straight line. This event will not happen for another 25,625 years.

At this moment, Earth will begin pointing at the constellation Aquarius, turn toward the light, and begin to awaken. It will initiate the return of the Divine Feminine. Some believe the Divine Feminine will rule, but the truth is the Goddess energy will come back to the planet to restore balance and harmony. There will be rebirth as we shift from duality consciousness to Oneness consciousness. To prepare for this transition, though, we need to move out of our heads and into our hearts.

Have you felt like time is going faster? Human evolution

is speeding up. We are changing on a level that you don't understand.

From 2012 to 2029, there will be chaos. People will act bizarrely, and there will be violence. What exactly happens during this time is ambiguous. Extreme examples of what *may* occur are a pole shift, Earth changes, or the return of Nibiru to Earth. You may have heard of Nibiru as Planet X, more to come on that as our adventures continue. It is more likely, however, that humankind will cause nuclear devastation at its own hands.

What I can say is *if* there is ever an event where you plunge into darkness, and there is no light, remember that the daylight will return. It may take thirty hours or three or four days, but it will return. Be prepared to respond and adapt if your environment or climate changes. Throughout this process, remain in gratitude, do not go into fear, and stay in love. Fear would pull you into more turmoil.

People *may* transition in mass numbers during these years and leave the planet in ways that'll impact humankind. Natural disasters, wars, pandemics, interstellar collisions—if these events occur, help each other, love each other, and mourn for those who choose to go. Those who perish will serve in ways you do not understand now. When people transition in these situations, it is their choice and likely one of their purposes for incarnating. They open hearts, and this is what humanity needs to evolve.

What will happen is unclear as *it is all choice* and remains fluid. The best thing to do is be prepared, don't get pulled into the media, and stay on your evolutionary path to ascension. I am here, along with other autistics, to assist in the shift. This plan has been a long time in the making.

The Ascended Masters are here too. Some of them are autistic. Be suspicious of those in public *claiming* to be the Masters. There are false prophets among you that are

271

deceiving people, and they have many followers who will become codependent on following these dark ones in possible dark times.

Yes, there are indeed spiritual leaders among you with huge followings that are dark. By portraying the role of light, they draw light ones. Those light ones have their essence depleted by the imposters. Be discerning with who you follow, and remember that any real Master will not be making claims of being a Master.

Humankind forgot what happened when it fell in Atlantis. What fell? Humanity fell from grace, a state of high consciousness. It held vast knowledge and lost it because of its actions. That was about thirteen thousand years ago, and humanity fell *nearly* to the bottom.

If natural spiritual evolution were to occur on Earth, it would take hundreds of thousands of years to reach the next level of consciousness. Humanity doesn't have that time to evolve to the next level. It must be achieved during the *end of days* beginning on December 21, 2012, or the Earth will collapse.

Chapter 48:
"You Are Still Reluctant to Accept Who You Are."

November 2009

Levi

Would you believe that our little meditation group Nina started years ago is still active? Yes, we take summer months off, from Labor Day to Memorial Day, then we always meet weekly. Our group has bonded quite nicely.

The years have been kind to me, and my first book is being released later in the year. I have spent a good part of my free time, aside from writing, exploring new levels of spirituality. I have continued with my psychic development.

At first, I ignored what that medium told me years ago, that I was, what did she say? A starseed? 'That couldn't be me,' I told myself. Then the more I thought about it, the more I realized I *was* different from most people. I have a deep need to understand who I am and why I am here. I yearn to know what my purpose is, so I can accomplish it and go home. I have a love for humanity that is unusual and unyielding. Most days, I try to conjure up ideas of how I can help people. I think that rather than writing code for computers, I should put my skills to use by helping solve this world's problems.

It took a little bit, but then I realized I wasn't alone. I learned there were more here like me than I ever suspected. Would you believe that I can tell when I run into another person like me?

★

As I took classes at my church, attended workshops or conferences all over the United States, I ran into many people outside of my work environment, and I found that some just resonated with me. I didn't think much about it at first, then one day a new friend I had made at a conference confided in me. She shared that she is a Pleiadian. At first, I didn't know what that was. I was thinking, 'Perhaps it's a type of magician.' I knew she was into magic. Then she explained that she was from a planet called Erra near a star in the Pleiades constellation.

'Get out of town.' I had thought. That *first contact* blew my mind. Eventually, after a couple of years of friendship, I confided with this friend. I told her what the psychic had told me years earlier, about being a star person.

My friend laughed at me and said, "I was wondering if you were ever going to come out of the closet!"

"You knew?" I asked.

She said, "Of course I knew. Like attracts like energy."

"I can't say that I believe this."

"Really?"

"I believe that I'm different than most. But, to believe I'm an alien incarnated into a human body to help humankind?" I shook my head, "The jury is still out."

"That's okay. It's better to be skeptical than gullible. Where any of us come from is not what's important. What's important is that we're here and that we live authentically. If we do, the planet will be a better place through the ripples we create. Remember, though, you're not alone, and it's always good to connect with others like you."

That's when I began to understand this radar thing. I started to associate different energy with those who claimed to be from other worlds. I realized that some people draw to me, and likewise, I feel drawn to them. Our vibrations complement each other. After being around many people who tend to deplete my energy, these people don't. That is a breath of fresh air. It's like getting a postcard in the mail from a loved one. There is a sense of familiarity with them, even though I don't know them, I have something in common, and no one can take that away.

Aside from the energy thing, I've come to learn that most star people are propelled by a strong feeling that they are here to serve but in different ways. They have optimistic, uplifting attitudes and have little tolerance for discrimination, dishonesty, and violence. They all feel a bit alienated and rarely have successful life relationships. Many of them identify as Lightworkers.

At first, I thought that Lightworker was synonymous with incarnated aliens. Then I realized that isn't the case. While starseeds are indeed Lightworkers, at least the ones I have met, there are some human Lightworkers too. The Lightworker is one who made a pact with its Higher Self to visit Earth to help humans heal from the expressions of fear, or the ego. They have a deep calling to help others and the planet. They are profoundly affected by our social and environmental problems and often become teachers, writers, or counselors. They also feel there is a sense of urgency, as time is of the essence, and there is a strong desire to find and fulfill their life's purpose.

Over the years, I've had people come out to me and identify themselves as incarnated beings from other worlds. They've called themselves Pleiadians, Sirians, Reptilians or Arcturians. Truth be told, there is a part of me that wishes I could distinguish myself as something, anything, but I can't. I do, though, feel comfortable having exchanges with these people.

I know I am a Lightworker, that feels right, and perhaps, maybe I am human. I am holding out on this starseed thing. I mean, after all, if a psychic told you that you were an incarnated alien, would you accept it just like that?

Today I am experimenting with a new meditation tech-
nique Rebecca recommended. She calls it toning. I believe she
and her daughter have been experimenting with this and may
introduce it in the book they are writing.

I am looking forward to meeting Rebecca's daughter,
Ami, one day, and trust it'll happen when the time is right.

I arrive at the threshold of my meditation room, where
I remove my shoes and enter. I close the door, so my dear cat
doesn't interrupt my session. I light candles in the corners
of the room, and then on my altar, I also ignite candles and
incense. I sit on the floor, legs crossed and palms up. When
toning, I use my voice as a tool to influence the energy patterns
in the body. It differs from chanting, which is a rhythmic rep-
etition of a word or words. Instead, I vocalize a sustained note
until I stop to breathe.

The first time I tried toning, it was foreign, and I had a
difficult time with it. Rebecca had presented it in our group
this week. I was self-conscious about my voice and uncomfortable. She explained to us that if we could surrender to it, it
would usher in an altered state. I am all for that, so here I go.

Rebecca had given me an audiotape of her toning. I
press "play" on the cassette player in my stereo system, and the
meditation led by Rebecca begins. After a brief prayer, I start
expressing the sounds of E-O, O-S-V, W-E-S, E-I, and O-M.

I am grateful that my windows are closed because I can't
carry a tune, and my voice cracks before I run out of breath.

I find myself sinking deeper into my meditation, and then
Rebecca whispers an odd phrase, "Holder sequence release
valve."

The black canvas in my head erupts with lightning bolts
and jars me out of meditation. I sink back in, and tone some
more, each time relaxing into the tones, then four more times I

am jolted out of my trance as Rebecca whispers keys or codes, like, "beside the stillness stand," and "find your home here."

The toning wraps up with two other codes, and four "amens" expressed to the different directions, and I am unsatisfied. Forty-five minutes have passed, and I feel like I have gone on a rollercoaster ride. Rather than ending my meditation, I stay put. I enter a deep meditative state, where I feel a presence.

I usually can sense when someone is here, or I hear them speak to me in my head, not my ears. Sometimes I know my thoughts are not my own because they carry different energy. I don't see the presence, but I feel him. Then I hear, *"I see you are still reluctant to accept who you are, dear Levi."*

'You mean the alien thing?' I think.

"There are many incarnated star people here, more than ever. They are here to experience what is going to happen because it has never happened before in this universe. It has failed twice before. Everyone wants to be involved, and all eyes are watching planet Earth. Higher aspects of life have come and continue to come, through birth and even walk-ins. All want this experience, and, of course, to help. Be grateful you are a part of it, for many, many others cannot participate as this planet can only sustain life for so many."

'I am very grateful for being here, and for your presence tonight,' I say in my head.

"The dreamer awakes! I am Metatron, and you are dearly Beloved!"

The presence is gone.

"Metatron? Archangel Metatron?" I whisper aloud, taking myself out of meditation.

I am left to contemplate his message. 'Higher aspects of life?'

CHAPTER 49:
INTO THE CHRYSALIS.

March 27, 2011

Levi

Today, I will meet Ami. I had known I am to meet her, and somehow we are connected since that night so long ago when our meditation group met at Rebecca's Park Hill home. That was almost fifteen years ago. It has been a journey for me since then. First knowing I am to meet her and support her in some unconventional way. Then, the dream with the vision of the butterfly and chrysalis.

After all these years, I am still at Oracle. My book *was finally* published about five years ago. As the psychic told me, in 2001, when Dan Brown came out with *The Da Vinci Code*, it opened doors for publishers to consider similar books. Much of what she had told me seems to be true. My book was not a huge success; apparently, people aren't ready for it yet.

Josh is now a junior in high school, and he is well adjusted and well-liked. He is, in many ways, kind and gentle. It's hard to believe he'll be off to college next year, which saddens me because I know I left my home right after school and never returned. I don't sense that Josh will leave the area, but anything is possible, right?

I am driving to Manitou Springs and meeting Rebecca there at ten o'clock. It is 9:38 when I arrive at the house. There is one car parked in front of the property, and I assume it must be a caregiver's car. I take a swig of cold coffee I brewed before

I left home. Eyeing a picnic table in the backyard, I figure it's the perfect place to wait for her.

I leave the car and make my way toward the picnic table. There I sit with my back to the sun and face a cluster of trees; the aspens have the beginnings of fuzzy catkins indicating their leaves will be coming soon. The Colorado sun warms me. It is a lovely March day, hinting that April is coming soon. I am eager to meet Ami, but a bit nervous. I hope she has insight into how I'm to help her.

As I sit on the bench, I close my eyes and welcome the stillness. Almost immediately, I feel the energy in my hands, face, and torso. I recall the mystical experience I had earlier in the month.

★★★

I am deep in meditation when I enter that perfect place, peace. Suddenly my landscape shifts from stillness to what seems to be a memory. Before me is the butterfly cycle, the one like in the dream I had after the first meditation at Rebecca's home. As if watching a movie, I see the egg hatch, the caterpillar crawl, and the chrysalis. From my previous dream, I know the message is that I am ready to meet Ami.

My landscape morphs from the butterfly life cycle into a scene where there are beings of vibrating light gathering in a circle. I know that I am one of these animations. Across from me is another being, and intuitively I sense that it is Ami, rather Shawnami. Neither one of us speaks to each other with voices. Instead, our minds communicate telepathically.

"We have a great journey ahead of us," I hear. *"It is time that we begin the next phase of our adventure."* The words are coming from Shawnami, the light being across from me.

At that moment, another presence steps into the inner circle from the outer ring. This presence adorns a long white robe. There is light emanating all around this cloaked being with an obscured face. Then he turns toward me, and I see a bearded man with long hair and kind eyes. He radiates wisdom, kindness, and love. It is Melchizedek.

"It is time to begin our journey together in the physical," he says.

I then notice that our inner circle has shrunk as the other beings have moved to an outer ring, leaving myself, a presence who I know to be Ami, Melchizedek, and there is another presence beside me. I don't know who this is. Their light is different than Ami and me.

I am curious who it is, and Melchizedek must have read my mind since he offers. "The only way for humanity to ascend in time to avoid planetary destruction is if we work together, all of us." While his arm raises high and circles to include those in the outer ring, surrounding us, I sense the message is mainly for this tiny inner circle.

"You all have a journey ahead of you that offers hope. It is what one may call a 'long shot.' Without your success, most of humanity will remain in the third dimension and live out their existence in pain, suffering, and struggle for survival. The three of you offer hope that a new life is possible in a place of peace, love, and harmony."

Of course, this can't be possible, can it? How can humanity's hope rely on us three? I know that Ami is a Master. How? I'm not sure; I guess my intuition. Me? I am what? A Lightworker? Who is this other being? It looks very much like Ami and me, a creature of light; only the radiance has a slightly different hue. When I look closer at all the presences here, those circling us, we all look alike, except for an ever so slight variation in the shade of our light.

With my mind, I ask, "Who is this other being here?"

Melchizedek's words fill my head, not my ears. *"It is Jerhesa. The three of you together have had a long history. Each of you is different, yet the same. Each of you exists separately yet is One. The journey of every hero begins with trusting one another and knowing that they need to rely on the One."*

My intellect interrupts the vision. Everything melts away, and I come out of my meditative experience. I find myself sitting on the floor in my meditation room. My skin is warm, and my head a bit foggy. I glance at the clock. It is 11:11 p.m.

★★★

A creak and thud from a car door closing jar me back to the moment. I find myself at a picnic table in Manitou Springs, waiting for Rebecca. I turn toward the sound. She waves at me.

We both move toward each other, and I see she is smiling. It feels a bit odd seeing her outside our small meditation group. We hug.

"It's so great that you are finally here to meet Ami! Why the sudden interest?"

"It's hard to explain, let's just say I'm ready and very excited about it." I look around at the setting. "It is peaceful here. A beautiful place to be."

"It's become home to her. She's been here for fifteen years."

Creaking draws our attention toward the house where a woman holds open a screen door, and Ami steps through the threshold.

The woman waves and yells, "Good morning, Rebecca!"

"Hi, Sarah!" She shouts. To me, "Sarah has been here since Ami's first day."

Sarah assists Ami as she descends the deck stairs, then watches her walk slowly, yet steadily in our direction. Ami is in her mid-thirties and shorter than I had expected. She looks toward us, but not at us. As she approaches, I know we are strangers, yet I feel close to her. It's hard to explain.

She nears, and her eyes meet my own, and I don't expect that. My heart warms with her eye contact. I smile.

"Ami," Rebecca says, "This is a dear friend who wants to meet you."

Ami looks directly at me, her mouth opens, and gibberish sounds come from her. Then, I hear. "Lee—vi."

Rebecca looks at her daughter, mouth ajar, then at me. "Did she say what I think she said?"

I smile and approach her. I want to reach out and hug her, but I know that would not be right. I stop a few feet away from her and smile. "Yes, I am Levi. It is my honor to finally meet you."

Ami walks to me and stops just before hitting me. She brushes lightly up against me, and I carefully place my arms on her shoulders, lean in, and gently embrace her.

I hear Rebecca chatting. "Oh, my God! She spoke. She's been making a lot of noises lately and trying to say things, but she was clear, wasn't she? Levi, how did she know your name?"

I'm not paying attention to Rebecca. I am here, with my arms gently embracing this person who I know is a Master in the flesh. I get this in my heart. Ami has lived many lifetimes, and I wouldn't be surprised if we've known each other before. That is not what is important right now. Ami is the only individual who knows me on a deeper level. I trust that she knows who I am and why the Universe led me to her.

When I sense it is time, I let go and back away. I look at Ami, and she looks directly into my eyes.

"What is going on?" Rebecca's voice pierces the air. "Levi, Ami does not typically respond this way to anyone, never mind a stranger."

I am silent. I am not sure what to say. I want to be present; then, Ami points her finger down, then moves toward the picnic table.

"She wants to talk," Rebecca says. We all move to the

table, where Rebecca places the letterboard that hung from her shoulder. She assists Ami onto the bench.

I sit across from Ami, and Rebecca sits beside her, placing the letterboard in front of her. Rebecca takes Ami's hand and helps her type.

"Ami, how do you know Levi?"

"Comrades, we are," Ami types.

"You've never met her before, though, right?" Rebecca asks.

"We have known each other before. Many times. We have agreed to meet here to work together again."

Rebecca stares at me, then asks, "Does this make sense to you? Do you know Ami?"

I don't know what to say. Finally, I admit, "I have known that Ami is an Ascended Master, and I believe I am to help her. Though, I'm not entirely clear how."

"You told me she was an Ascended Master when we were at my house many years ago. I'm not clear that I understand. What do you mean by this?" Rebecca asks.

"Through many lives, Ami has undergone a series of spiritual transformations. She has regained her union with the I AM."

"Jesus was a Master, right?"

"Yes, Jesus and many others, like Gautama Buddha, Maitreya, Confucius, Mary, the mother of Jesus, Anna, the grandmother of Jesus, and Mary Magdalene, to name a few."

"Mary Magdalene?"

"Yes, Mary of Bethany. Then there are many others, but we don't know who they are. The Masters are returning to the physical realm to help people through the ascension. They typically help as a conduit or a channel to higher consciousness, but like Ami, they are returning to help in the physical."

I stop. I'm not sure how I know what I'm saying. 'Where

is this coming from? Is it my intuition?'

"We are approaching a time when some individuals on earth will ascend," I continue. "But they need help to do so. Many groups are working globally on this process, and Ami is here to help shift the frequency of the planet in a way to help encompass a larger body of people."

"I don't understand," Rebecca says.

Ami raises her hand, implying that she wants to share, and Rebecca assists her typing.

"Here to help MANY ascend. As of right now, only a few will ascend."

"How am I to help you?" I ask.

"Need to reach as many autistics to light them up. Mom helps with that. I need to embody more."

"What does she mean by that?" Rebecca asks.

"Embodiment," I say.

"I still don't understand," Rebecca says.

"Ami lives in the higher subtle realms where the angels and other Ascended Masters live . . . the sixth dimension and beyond. She's tethered there. Currently, there is an infusion of autistics on the planet, and more are still coming. Many of them are spiritual Masters, and they live in higher realms too, overtones of the fourth and fifth dimensions. The physical, denser vibration, the 3D world challenges autistics. There is a difficulty embodying from the higher realms into the 3D world, which saddles autistics with obstacles. In the higher realms, however, they have no obstacles."

"What do you mean by 3D?"

"You and I live in what is known as the third dimension, which is very dense. But there are other dimensions here, and we are not experiencing them. Those dimensions are where Ami lives most of her time. She hasn't been able to embody into the third dimension fully, and because of that, she is unable to communicate well; she can't speak. For similar reasons, other autistics may have trouble with their physiology or biology. They may have physical disabilities; they can't interact well, can't communicate. That's because they haven't fully embodied in the 3D world."

"So, if Ami embodies in the third dimension, she may be able to speak?" Rebecca asks.

"Perhaps, but that's not precisely why she would do this," I glance at Ami. "There is something much larger at play here."

"What?"

"The embodiment of the higher spiritual realms into the third dimension is a service to humanity. When any of us fully embody, we align our higher spiritual truth into the physical, and any of our physical manifestations will change to reflect who we are."

"What do you mean, *who we are?*"

"That we are *all* Divine. We are the ones we have been waiting for. Each of us is a co-creator, a different expression of a God-being connected to the Source. We, through our minds, can create heaven on Earth. If we can get out of our way and identify with our Divinity, all the physical manifestations that we create will reflect our truth. We will spark miracles. We will choose love over fear. We will end the wars. We will show there is no such thing as lack, limitation, or disease. We will show there is only One and that there is enough, and we aren't here to do anything. We are here to be."

At this moment, I am not sure where this information is coming from. I feel like I am downloading it. I look at Ami, and maybe it's in my head, but I think she is smiling at me and encouraging me to go on. *Am I channeling Ami?* I wonder. *Or is it someone else?*

"The thing is," I continue, "it is our ego that challenges us to identify as being Divine. Our egos keep us in separation from God, and because of that, we can't get out of our way.

We live in that illusion of separation. But Ami knows the truth. The more she can embody her true self in the third dimension, her created world will change to reflect her Divinity."

"Is it just me that is so dense? What do you mean by her *created* world?" Rebecca asks.

"Everyone is the creator of their world. We are responsible for the situations in our life through various quantum laws of manifestation and the Divine matrix. We co-create with God, the Universe, or Source. If Ami fully embodies, the tapestry around her will shift."

I stop, close my eyes. I hear words in my head. I know it is the voice of Ami. It is comforting to me, and I smile. I open my eyes and repeat her words.

"She says, 'If a collective of autistics come in and embody more, there would be a dynamic model for humanity to know the Divine in the 3D physical. Through resonance, more and more people will feel the reverberations, move into that frequency, and there would be a global shift in awareness.'"

Rebecca doesn't know what to say. She looks at Ami and takes her hand and Ami types, "Levi, my old friend, who I have known in other worlds, you are here to serve. Would you help me on this journey?"

At this moment, I can't explain what I feel. It goes beyond honor that she has asked this of me. For the first time in my life, I have some clarity on why I am walking this planet. I don't know how I can assist her, but trust it will reveal itself in time. I say, "It is my honor to serve you. I am still unclear how I can do so, Shawnami."

"Who is Shawnami?" Rebecca asks.

Ami raises her finger to type, "You are the observer. When tapping the power of the silent watcher, you enable the divine purpose of the universe to unfold."

I am unclear what Ami is telling me, and she must be

reading my mind.

"You are the witness and scribe, and that brings power."

As Ami finishes typing, I hear her voice in my head, and I speak her words aloud. "You will write our journey and spin it in such a way that it will benefit humankind. Your written words will heal by revealing truths that need to come to light in a non-threatening way, and that will inspire readers. As people are inspired, they change, and the outcome changes, and it must, to avoid the end of days. Love your characters, and that will empower them in this reality, and they will come alive. Write our journey to the New Earth, and it will become a roadmap for those not making the first jump."

All I keep thinking is, 'Hold on. How can I change reality by writing a fairy tale?'

Then I feel something energizing my body; I am tingling all over. I close my eyes and feel a presence. I hear a voice. I know it is Archangel Metatron. *"This is not the reality, dear Levi, this is the illusion. By writing your tale, you will get the attention of your True self who is alive and well, and very powerful, like everyone's True self. By getting your Higher Self's attention, you will have Her support."*

I open my eyes and see this isn't a dream. Ami and Rebecca are here, looking at me. Could this be happening? Could I inspire change?

At this moment, I can't believe this turn. I recall the vision I had in meditation—the circle of beings with Melchizedek. Then the inner circle of three, surrounded by many in an outer ring. "I think there is one other that is part of this journey," I say.

Rebecca knows that Ami wants to respond, and she does, "There are many of us on this voyage, a journey of many lifetimes. You are right, though. One other will play a critical role. Jerhesa."

"Do you know where he or she is?" I ask.

"Sedona. Not ready for us yet. We need to ALL come together."

CHAPTER 50:
I HAVE FEARS TOO!

Ami

I look at Levi. I know she is a bit shaken about how she is to participate in humankind's approaching awakening. She has fears. I do too, and mine creep into my reality. I feel that pit in my stomach, and my insides begin to churn. I know I need to be strong and overcome these feelings and insecurities. I know that I seem cool and calm, but I have fears too. Those terrors can be debilitating at times and make me want to return to my Homeland and sleep this life away.

My greatest fear is that I stay locked in this body with autism. I am here with such a significant role that is unfolding to me every day, and what if I am not resilient enough to escape autism's grip? What if my *only* identity in this life is autism, and I do not fully embody? What if I cannot trigger the events that need to unfold? Then again, if I don't escape this grip, there will be no one to record history.

Another fear is my power and magnificence. My ability is unending when I allow my watery-flow to express the authentic *me*. You may know watery-flow as dynamic stillness, harmonic life, the complete unification with Source. Like you, I have an ego, too. There is a purity of the autist heart, and it must remain pure. What if, as I embody more, I fall into my ego state, and I misuse these powers? What if I fall from grace?

I look at Mom listening to Levi speak about embodiment and the journey we are about to embark. Levi is incredulous. She is unaware of how important her role is, yet all players on this adventure have essential parts. All the players are a cog in a wheel, and if they don't embrace why they're here, the wheel will not spin correctly. Stakes are high, and this journey has been at play for thousands of years.

My third big fear is sharing Mom. Mom is still naïve. She needs to stay that way for some time because she may completely disassociate herself from all this if she knew. I know, though, how significant she is, and if things go as planned, I will need to share her with so many, and she is all I have.

My last fear is regarding my body. My seizures have increased over the years, and while I know that they coincide with downloads of patterning, I need to keep moving forward, yet my body is weakening. I pray every day that this body can withstand the events to come. My journey in this form is not comfortable. It is quite painful. I work through the pain, but what if my body fails before I can lead everyone?

If I fail, only a fraction of the population will ascend, and the rest will experience the end of days. It is no wonder I have ulcers burning the inside of my stomach.

CHAPTER 51:
THE LIGHT SIDE OF AUTISM

November 11, 2011

One in 68 children has autism.

The much-awaited book-launch for *The Light Side of Autism* arrived and is at the Sedona Creative Life Conference Center. The book, by mother and daughter, with contributions from three other nonverbal autistics, including Colin and Holly, was published months earlier. But, they wanted to wait until 11/11/11 to celebrate its release.

Rebecca stacks copies of their book at the table she will use during the signing. She is a bit anxious. She knows George will be there to support Ami. Rebecca had not seen him in years, and they rarely spoke. She had heard that his second marriage hadn't lasted, and he had thrown himself into his work and was now a big shot at Xerox.

When Herman told her that he was going to be out of town for business the evening of the signing, she was a bit relieved that she wouldn't need to deal with that strange dynamics of boyfriend meeting the ex.

Rebecca had sent a special invitation to Crystal, and while she knew it would be a massive undertaking for her and Leilah to be there, she secretly hoped and prayed that they would attend.

★★★

Rebecca did not run their manuscript, *The Light Side of*

Autism, by a traditional publisher, and it was self-published. She anticipated that she'd need to spend every saved dollar toward its production, but George generously funded it.

The mother and daughter trusted that if the book reached parents and caregivers, they might recognize the truth. Rebecca and Crystal couldn't be the only parents that had these supernatural experiences with their autistic children. Rebecca hoped that their book would bring others out to share with the world the autism gifts. Ami hoped that the autistics would be honored and loved so that they light up.

Both Ami and Rebecca had missed Crystal and Leilah. They had moved a bit unexpectedly a few years earlier. For Ami, life at Cheyenne Village had not been the same without Leilah. For Rebecca, she missed her quiet moments and discussions with her friend.

A few years earlier, there had been a shift between Leilah and Crystal. Rebecca wasn't able to put her finger on it, but Leilah stopped typing with Crystal. Every weekend, though, Rebecca and Leilah would find a few minutes of quiet time and have compelling and personal exchanges. Then as she shared some early insights from Ami's entries in their manuscript, Crystal admitted that she was uncomfortable suggesting that the autistics were Ascended Masters incarnated. Crystal didn't want Leilah looked at as the next messiah. After that, she noticed subtle changes in Crystal. First, a new necklace with a cross, then there was a pamphlet at Crystal's home from a Christian ministry. The next thing she knew, Crystal was traveling to California to attend a conference.

Shortly after, Crystal announced that she and Leilah were relocating. She mentioned something about family support on the west coast, but Rebecca always felt there was something else. Rebecca missed their friendship very much. At first, they emailed each other, then the notes came less frequently, and she hadn't heard from her in almost a year.

When Rebecca and Ami considered the target market for their book, they suspected it would appeal to the spiritual community, specifically to those interested in the ascension. Gloom and doom had been all over the internet, suggesting that 12/21/2012 as the end of the Mayan calendar. With the ominous date approaching and their book connected to the phenomena, she planned the book launch celebration in Sedona, because of the large New Age spiritual community.

★★★

Rebecca peeks at her watch. It is 6:45 p.m., and about twenty people have gathered in the Sedona Room at the Creative Life Center. It's a sizeable room with a statue of Sedona Miller Schnebly at the front. More people are coming in and taking their seats. Levi greets people as they enter, while Ami is at the front of the conference room with George.

Ami stands in front of the first row and slowly moves from person to person. From across the conference room, Rebecca watches her. Ami reaches out oddly and touches a woman's face.

'What is she up to?' Rebecca approaches and hears Ami say something to the lady, but she can't make out what Ami noted.

To this day, Ami rarely speaks, so Rebecca moves even closer to observe what is happening. Ami shifts to the next woman in the front row. She stands in front of a lady holding one of their books. Rebecca notices that the book has been well-loved, and there is a bookmark with a picture of children jutting from a page.

The woman smiles at Ami. Ami seems to return the stare, then she raises a hand and gently strokes the lady's cheek. This time she hears Ami say, "Niiiccee." Ami then moves on to another person. George shadows her.

Rebecca knows she must make opening statements soon and introduce Ami. She feels butterflies in her stomach and fears that she may give back her dinner.

More and more people come in, and Rebecca looks at the room set up with forty chairs. The conference facilitator is bringing in a few more chairs. 'That's a good sign,' she tries to calm her nerves.

Some tumultuous activity draws Rebecca's attention to the door, where a tall, thin young man with dark skin barges into the room, past Levi. An Asian man and woman follow him. The young man is undoubtedly autistic. He goes to the back of the conference room where he stands and skillfully rolls a ball in his hand. The older man, who is not very tall, perhaps in his mid–forties, follows the young black man like a shadow. He has a cleanly shaven head, a mustache, and goatee.

She approaches the man and offers her hand. "Hi, I'm Rebecca Griffin."

"Hello, I'm Aaron, and this is my son, Charlie." He steps closer to the young man, and they are now standing side by side. The dark-skinned man stops rolling his ball.

"Nice to meet you," Rebecca says.

"You're the mother–author!" A woman's voice from behind Rebecca broadcasts. Rebecca turns and sees a woman approach. She is dressed somewhat like a gypsy with kind eyes and a warm smile. She extends her hand to Rebecca.

Rebecca shakes, feeling energy exude from the woman's hand. A closer look, she sees a large signet ring with a unique symbol on it.

"I'm Mariam. I've read your book. I found it fascinating."

It is the first time Rebecca meets someone claiming to have read their book. She had given copies to some close friends in Denver, and while she knew they had begun reading it, she hadn't heard a thing about it from them.

"Thank you!" Rebecca eyes the Asian couple and the young man and assumes that Charlie is adopted. "How old is your son?"

"Oh, I am Aaron's sister," she laughs, throwing back her head, revealing an odd birthmark on the bottom of her chin. "Charlie is my nephew!"

"He is seventeen," Aaron answers. "My wife, Sierra, wasn't able to join us, she's working."

"Well, welcome. I'm thrilled you all made it." She glimpses the clock. It's time for her to begin. "If you will excuse me."

Rebecca sees that most have come in and are now seated. There must be about fifty people. The butterflies are back, and she knows it's her turn to get in front of the crowd and introduce herself and Ami.

Moments later, Rebecca stands in front of the audience. Everyone sits except Charlie, who is in the back of the room oddly still. Ami now stands near her, swaying a bit, making that clicking noise with her throat. Rebecca is used to the dolphin-like sound. She has never figured out why Ami does it. Times like this, it's a bit distracting.

"Many, many years ago, Ami, my daughter asked me to write a book with her. At the time, I thought I knew nothing about writing, and it seemed a bit of an uphill battle. Then I thought of the challenges autists like Ami and other autistics, like Charlie in the back, overcome every day, and I thought, how can that stop me?"

Rebecca hesitates a bit, "We know that the messages in our book are, what is the phrase, *out of this world*?" She smiles. "And some will find them hard to believe. For those here with a traditional religious foundation, we welcome you and honor your journey. Our book *will* challenge you—that I am sure.

"We pray that the messages will resonate with some readers and help us bring *The Light Side of Autism* into the world. Now is the time to bring this knowledge to light. This book is our love letter to the world. We hope that it can move each of you in a way that helps you see the truth about autism's role in the spiritual evolution of humankind."

As Rebecca ends her presentation, she notices that Charlie sits down in the back of the room. Oddly, next to Levi.

Rebecca picks up the letterboard on the table and takes Ami's hand to facilitate. Over the years, they had become more proficient with the telepathy and assisted typing, so Ami's message is delivered quickly.

"Ami would like to share some words with you." As Rebecca assists, she voices Ami's message to the group.

"Ami says, 'We, autistics have capabilities and capacities to awaken ourselves and others. When we, the autistics, remember our contract in coming here now, we start to grow into our potential. That potential is not just for us or autism. It is for the whole world to behold and be held and be healed in it.

'We are here to serve God, not ourselves.

'We have a personal role in questioning life. We are not soul ready until we learn our truth. Our truth is that we are evolved beings here to help this planet. Before we were born, we agreed to sit in harsh suits of autism until we are freed to share our purpose for being here.

'We have no agenda except to lose our shell to be God's Light. Our shell is autism. Autism costumes are not to scare you, but to protect who we are from those who do not want the Light to win. Much like a superhero's mask, autism has protected our Light, our identity, from interference and loss.

'It is time to know Autism Truth so that other autistics can awaken. Once autistics are lit, they awaken those around them to their magnificence. Autistics need a reminder of our truth. That comes when honored by our loved ones.

'It is time. Please spread this message.'"

Rebecca stops speaking Ami's words. There is a palpable shift in the audience.

"Honor the autistics in your life," Rebecca finishes, "and they will awaken to their truth, and your life will never be the same, and the rest of the world will be blessed by it in ways we can't see, nor do we understand."

A half-hour after the book signing, Elaine, who sat in the front row, returned home and relieved the babysitter from watching her three children. Her two youngest were in bed, and after checking on them, she returns to her family room where her oldest, Seren, a nine-year-old autistic girl, watches a video that she sees every night, *Free Willy*. There is no audio. She doesn't quite understand how any movie can hold someone's interest so many times, yet she knows there are worse things for her child to watch.

Elaine ponders what the authors of the book *The Light Side of Autism* said that evening. Could our autistic children be here for a role in the spiritual evolution of humanity? Is that why the autistic rate has increased to one in 68 children? Elaine wonders, 'I guess that makes me blessed, having three autistic children.'

She rests the book on top of the coffee table and opens it to the place she had left off. The bookmark displaying a picture of her three angels catches her eye.

"Seren, sweetheart, Mommy would like to share something with you," Elaine says.

The young girl turns and looks at her mother.

Elaine picks up the book, *The Light Side of Autism*, and holds it for her daughter to see. "This book is written by a nonspeaking autistic and her mom. It shares that autistics have an important role at this time."

The young girl rises and moves to her mother while looking at the book. Then, standing before her mom, she reaches for Elaine's face and strokes it softly. Seren smiles, her lips part, and she says, "Niiiccee."

CHAPTER 52:
SHE IS POLLY ON HER TALKER
AND DOES NOT SHUT UP!

November 27, 2011

Levi

It is a snowy Sunday afternoon. The windows to the open space and mountains behind my house have snow crystals clumping on the glass, distorting my view. The gas fireplace is ablaze, and I am curled up in my recliner with a journal in my lap. Josh is over at one of his friends, and I am alone, enjoying the quiet. I sip my hot cocoa, set it on the coffee table, and open my journal.

Earlier this year, when I was with Ami, and she told me about my role in helping her, I was so excited and honored. Really honored. It was a powerful feeling. It was one of those moments you capture in your memory for all times. Yet, that sense of excitement, honor, and determination slowly slipped away.

As the days and weeks passed, those moments of clarity began to cloud. If I think about what Ami said and the things she told me I am capable of, I plummet into disbelief. I mean, really? Me? How could I ever think I have the power to do what Ami is suggesting? This rattled me and still does.

Ami had told me that I am to write the adventure. What exactly did she say? I search my memory. Then turn the pages of my journal back to that event in March. I go to the page where I had met Ami at Cheyenne Village with Rebecca and read what Ami shared. "You are the observer. When tapping the power of the silent watcher, you enable the divine purpose of the universe to unfold—you are the witness and scribe, and that brings power."

I've often frowned upon people who go out of their way to explain how *special* they are to the world. This power, to be able to do what Ami suggests, seems a bit unbelievable, and when I try it on for size, I feel delusional.

On my way back from the Sedona book signing earlier this month, I had a bit of an odd experience while meditating on the plane destined for Denver. I wonder if the experience is related to the autistics.

★★★

The airplane was ascending, and I was meditating, as I usually do after takeoff. Suddenly, the letter "U" emerged in my mind and stood by itself for a few seconds, before an "R" faded-in on the right side of the "U," leaving "U R."

Again, a few seconds passed when a third letter, an "O" emerged to the left of the "U R," leaving "O U R" illuminated on the black canvas of my mind. A second later, a second line appeared, and it was "#1." In my head, I then saw,

O U R

#1

My mind jarred me from the vision, and I considered the timing of each letter emergence, U, R O, #1, decoding it, U=you, R=are.

'You are our number 1.'

'A message?' I sat there on the plane, 'From who?'

As I looked out the airplane's window and saw the white billowing clouds we were skirting, I recalled the book signing the evening before.

I had attended the event to help Rebecca and Ami. While they spoke in front of the conference room, I sat by myself, in the last row, near the door to greet any late newcomers. Shortly after Rebecca began speaking, something odd occurred. An autistic young black man, who had come in with an Asian couple came over to me. I believe his name was Charlie. He sat beside me, remaining quiet for the remainder of the presentation.

As the discussion breaks up, Rebecca, along with the Asian couple, came over to Charlie and me. His father, with his jaw, dropped, stunned by Charlie's stillness.

"If that's not an initiation, I don't know what is," Rebecca said.

★★★

Since returning from the book signing in Sedona, a couple of weeks earlier, I have felt guilty that I don't know how to help them.

The chime from my laptop on the coffee table tells me I have a new email. I welcome the distraction and set my journal aside to grab my computer.

I see that the new email is from Rebecca and open it. She writes,

> *Levi,*
> *I saw Holly yesterday. She asked me to get a message to you. I've attached the file.*
> *Hugs,*
> *Rebecca*

"A message to me?" I say out loud.

I have never met Holly. The only thing I know about her is that Rebecca has worked with Holly for years, and she is one of the autistic contributing writers in *The Light Side of Autism*. I also remember Rebecca sharing a story with me about how she had a spontaneous healing while visiting Holly.

'What would Holly want to share with me? And how would she know I even exist?' I love the marvels and mysteries of these autistic ones.

I click on the attached file, and the document opens in a Word file formatted similarly to Ami's facilitated messages.

Holly's Message to Levi:

> I love Levi, she so much like me on her intelligence. Not see her during my day; see her during my night. She is Polly on her talker with me at night. She does not shut up! At night we travel together to other worlds. She tethered to light far away. She is hardly tied here. She is alien, like us, but not as strange as us. Her identity is tied into the plane where her light comes from. It is a plane of great importance but not known by many. Her intuition is from another lifetime that travels with her. That lifetime is so powerful so that the world here is tiny in her heart. Levi is like us in that way more than other Lightworkers. The beings around her are here as her guardians from that life to light up her truth. We (Holly and Levi) are from the same world; the name does not jump in; we share similar thinking.
>
> Levi, you can ask me to support

you to know your guides, and if you
are quiet, maybe I can help you.
Nothing scary—guides are your truth
grinning back at you. Play with
them as you do at night, and they
will have you know quickly.

All I can think is, 'Holy shit!' I hadn't shared the reading I had years earlier with Rebecca or Ami about the beings that the psychic saw with me. The psychic told me I was from another universe.

Between that first reading years ago, my mystical experience with light beings, the dream of having an alien-like body, the feeling of being different, and now this note from Holly—how can I deny that I am an incarnated alien?

I recall Charlie sitting beside me at the book signing, and the message I deciphered, 'You are our number 1.'

'Was the message from the autistics?'

CHAPTER 53:
PROJECT LAST-DITCH EFFORT

Reflections

Ami

Where did I leave off? I had shared that consciousness fell in Atlantis, and if natural spiritual evolution were to occur on Earth, it would take hundreds of thousands of years to evolve—only Earth doesn't have that time. If planetary ascension doesn't happen during the *end of days* beginning on December 21, 2012, Earth will collapse.

I want to share more about the fall and the Ascended Masters.

Many Ascended Masters have existed since before this universe. About seventy thousand years ago, in Lemuria, one couple learned the secret to immortality and began a school to teach ascension. At some point, Lemuria faced earth changes, and its land began to sink, forcing the Lemurians to leave. At that time, 999 Ascended Masters were walking the planet. Those Masters followed the spiritual energy of Earth to a rising landmass in the Atlantic, called Atlantis. Here, the Masters created energetic vortexes, drawing the highly intuitive Lemurians to settle there, beside Atlanteans. It also attracted two other groups. One group, unfortunately, brought with it a new way of living.

Contrary to the Lemurians' values, what motivated the outside group was their heads, not their hearts. The outsiders were interested in control and causing fear. About sixteen thousand years ago, something happened that changed everything, something horrific—a failed experiment.

As a result, the Lemurians of Atlantis went from being profoundly spiritual interdimensional beings capable of telepathy and living at the heart level, to being stuck in the third dimension and living in fear. All Atlanteans, not only Lemurians, fell in consciousness. That transition occurred over three-to-four thousand years, and eventually, Atlantis sank.

Everyone forgot, except the Ascended Masters, and there were approximately sixteen hundred of them walking the planet at that time.

The Earth fell into a painful loop, a thirteen thousand-year *Groundhog Day*, with each cycle ending in cataclysm. The Masters themselves created this cycle, hoping that humankind would choose differently. It has not.

On your Earth, we executed Project Last-Ditch Effort to Save Earth, which includes a combination of tweaks to various timelines, including Atlantis. Your Earth offers the most significant opportunity for ascension to the New Earth, Earth-616.

Every species has a crystalline matrix, a network surrounding the planet where its consciousness is stored. There are three different matrixes for humankind today. The first is for the indigenous cultures. The second is the duality matrix, which serves the majority of humanity today. Humankind needs to align with a third grid, a synthetic Unity or Christ Consciousness Grid. If they remain on the duality grid, they will not evolve at this time.

That third grid is the vehicle for planetary ascension, and one of the timeline tweaks. Everyone must transfer for the ascent, and those who have already passed will have the chance to resurrect, to Earth 616—the New Earth.

Most everyone I should say. Those wanting to play in the dark will not come to the New Earth. They will have their place, and as odd as this may sound—that is perfect.

How was the Unity Grid created?

Three Ascended Masters infiltrated a couple of hundred years before Atlantis fell. They were Thoth, Araragat, and Ra. Without getting into specifics, they birthed this synthetic grid. These highly evolved beings built pyramids and sacred structures all around the world through various ceremonies and powerful crystals. The grid has grown throughout time-space and completed in the 1980s. It has been tested, improved and tweaked by autistics over the last couple of decades so that it is functional by December 21, 2012.

The Autistic Avatars connect to the matrix through our sub-grid we created, the Chrysalis Gold Grid. Without this Unity Consciousness Grid functional around the planet, humanity will be stuck in the third dimension, will not evolve, and eventually destroy Earth.

I have repeated myself. This message is so important.

Humanity having the free will to choose Light or Dark is an experiment.

It failed on other planets. Do you remember?

On Earth, it failed, over and over—Gaia destroyed. You are in a loop. It is the last chance to win at the polarity game. If this does not work, your consciousness will plummet to the bottom.

There is not much time to turn this around. Mother Gaia is so unhappy. It isn't her time. She is a young planet and has much more life in her. But Gaia is aging quickly because of what humanity has done. She is a living being and will ascend on her time. One concern is what happens to humankind if Gaia shifts before people are ready. Another real concern is the possibility that humanity will destroy the planet before the ascension.

Remember, dear Ones—this is an illusion. Your mind has crystallized this choice into your virtual reality. It is time that you wake up and remember who you are. We need you to do so. You were the ones that set the stakes so high at the universe's creation. It was you who wanted to experience extreme polarities. It is you who must awaken and re-member.

To my group, those beings I am here to connect with, I say, "It is time that we facilitate our purpose for being here. It is time to wake up and work as a group." I set this intent and send out my message, knowing and trusting that those powerful beings who have come here to work on this will join me on December 21, 2012, so we can set the correct course as we enter the *end of days*.

CHAPTER 54:
"THE RIGHT PEOPLE JOIN US."

December 21, 2012

Earlier in the month, Ami shared, "Want to spend 12/21/12 in Sedona."

Perhaps it was because Sedona is close to Herman that Rebecca doesn't press for a reason. She agrees and purchases airline tickets, even tells Herman that they are coming to town. He was thrilled and suggested that they stay at his place in Oak Creek.

The evening before the infamous date, the three gather at Herman's home for dinner.

After dessert, Ami motions to speak. Rebecca gets the letterboard.

"Need to go to the vortex in the morning."

Rebecca knows that getting to any of the vortexes will require some hiking, and Ami is not exactly athletic. She turns to Herman, "Which vortex would be easiest for Ami to get to?"

Herman, familiar with each known vortex, offers, "Bell Rock makes perfect sense. It is the strongest of the vortexes, and she doesn't have to head up any trail to feel it. She will feel it in the parking lot."

This suggestion makes sense to her, then, Ami shows interest in typing, but she falters a bit. She stares into space, clenches her teeth and drools.

"Is she okay?" He asks.

She knows Ami's seizures have been on the incline. No

matter what they have tried, she does not seem to be getting better. Ami was back on medication, had a change in diet, and they had even explored the use of cannabis. Nothing appears to help. She watches Ami closely, assessing the severity of the seizure.

"It is a seizure," she explains and stands by her so that she is there if Ami falls from the chair. A minute later, She wipes Ami's mouth with the bandana around her neck. "I think she's better." Rebecca moves closer to Ami, "Are you okay?"

As if not missing a beat in their conversation, Ami types slowly, "Must be Boynton vortex."

"You are a trooper," She says, turning to Herman, "Is there a Boynton vortex?"

"There is a Boynton Canyon Vortex," he says, "but it isn't the easiest place to get to."

"Is it possible for Ami?"

After seeing Ami's seizure, even though it was small, he isn't sure. "I'll go with you. Besides, I know the way to it. It's not like any of these sites have signs indicating where the vortexes are."

Ami becomes still, and after a pause, she types, "Yes. Herman may come. Need to be at vortex by 11."

It is a beautiful, crisp December morning in the forties. Rebecca, Herman, and Ami set out for the vortex early so that they can be at the site by eleven o'clock to usher in the new cycle. With Ami sandwiched between her mother and Herman, they follow the Boyton Canyon Trail until they reach the Vista Trail. Then they steadily climb until they see an elevated plateau with two rising rock formations.

They hadn't seen any other hikers, but as they approach the last of the incline, there are airy, light, and whispering sounds from a flute. It is lovely and sets the tone for the day. They can't see where the music is coming from, but it gets louder with each step forward.

At 10:07 a.m., they face a challenging ascent leading to a plateau with two tall rock formations, one on each side.

"The rock formation on the left, the taller and thinner one is Kachina Woman," Herman points out. "The one on the right has no name," He says. "I call it the vortex knoll. That's where we need to go!"

The last of the incline is challenging for Ami. Supported between Herman and Rebecca, the trio slowly navigates the red dirt path, maneuvering around large rocks interspersed with cascading pinyon bushes and cacti.

As they slowly climb, Rebecca sees the flutist sitting at the base of the Kachina Woman, facing away. Another person accompanies the flutist and is gently tapping a Native American drum. They appear tiny up against the rising red rock formation. A few other hikers head down from the plateau, passing them on the trail.

Twenty minutes later, at 10:55 a.m., they move up to the plateau flanked between the two mounting outcroppings. Twisted pinon trees and cacti landscape the area between the two rock formations.

Aside from the flutist and drummer, whose backs are to them, they are alone. They gravitate toward the vortex mount, passing a clearing surrounded by stone stacks where other hikers had performed holy rites.

"Wow," Rebecca says as she looks around from their elevated location. She turns 360 degrees overlooking a forest of juniper, ponderosa pine, and sycamore with rising rock formations in the distance. "I feel the energy," she says, a bit light-headed.

"It is always beautiful," he agrees.

"I was expecting to see more people out here today," she says, assisting Ami with sitting on the ground.

"I forgot to tell you! One of my colleagues reminded me

that there is a gathering at Bell Rock," he says. "Some man is threatening to jump off the top of Bell Rock into the portal at some point today. It's a good thing we didn't end up at that circus."

Ami wants to speak, and Rebecca retrieves the letter-board from her daypack.

"We meditate now to center ourselves and set a proper intention."

"What intention are we meditating upon?" she asks.

"The right people join us."

She doesn't understand what Ami means, but she feels the energy from the vortex. Meditation seems appropriate in such a mystical place.

Rebecca and Herman, sit side by side, facing Ami, while Ami looks up at the rising rock formation behind them. They hear the flute and the wind in their ears and feel the sun warm their bodies.

While Rebecca and Ami find stillness and retreat to their quiet places, Herman feels a responsibility to protect the women as they meditate. He sits alert, staying on guard, and watches the surroundings.

He hears the chatter of people coming in the distance and watches two separate groups approach the base of the plateau. There are two women in the first group. They climb to the top and migrate toward the Kachina Woman. Then they turn around and slowly move in their direction. It's a middle-aged and younger woman. The older of the two begins to quicken her pace when seeing Rebecca. 'Could she recognize Rebecca?' He wonders.

The younger woman is expressionless. She also moves swiftly toward them and sits silently beside Ami. Like Ami, she gazes up at the rock formation with eyes wide open.

The older woman smiles at Herman, and he nods. While she clearly wants to say something, she sees Rebecca in meditation. She stands quietly near them.

Herman then sees members of the other group heading toward them. There are four people, two women, one Asian and one Latina, and an Asian man, and a young black man. The young man a bit awkwardly, yet swiftly, quietly, sits. Ami now between the two new arrivals. Like Ami, the young male gazes at a fixed point above him. The other new arrivals form an outer circle with the older woman.

Herman is clueless to what is happening. Ami and the two beside her sit wide-eyed, staring up at the knoll.

Ami begins sounding noises from the back of her throat, reminiscent of dolphin chatter. The other two sitting beside her make similar sounds. The noise brings Rebecca out of her meditation.

Rebecca opens her eyes, stunned. Sitting in front of her, is Ami, with Leilah on one side, while Charlie, the young man from their book signing, anchors the other. Charlie's eyes are almost rolled back in his head, while both Ami and Leilah gawk upwards. Rebecca knows the three autistics are anyplace but here.

She now sees Crystal behind the autistics. She moves swiftly toward her, and whispers, "Oh my God! Crystal!" The two women fall into each other's arms.

"It's so good to see you," Crystal says. "I have missed you so much."

"And I, you," Rebecca says. "How funny, of all places to run into each other."

"It was Leilah's idea. She demanded that we be here to celebrate the winter solstice. What are the chances that we'd both be here?"

The noise rises from the three autistics, now on their feet, swaying and shifting with bodily moves of excitement, getting the group's attention. The three still gazing above the knoll.

Everyone else now looks in the direction the autistics are

watching. Nothing noteworthy.

"Keep watching," Rebecca whispers.

Abruptly, a beam of light streams across the sky, and in an instant, a massive flash of radiance, almost reminiscent of another sun, shines in the center of the light stream, then fades away to nothing.

The autistics awkwardly dance and shriek with excitement. Everyone else stands there with jaws dropped, shooting questioning looks at each other.

CHAPTER 55:
"THE GROUP MUST JOURNEY TO THE NEW EARTH."

The Dawn of the Age of Aquarius

"Oh my God," Rebecca whispers, seeing the flash of light. She recalls the last thing Ami shared, just before their meditation, *"The right people join us."* She turns toward the others standing with them. Across from her is Aaron, Charlie's father, and his aunt Mariam from their book signing, along with a Chicana woman she hasn't met.

'Are these the people Ami needs to connect with?' Rebecca ponders, then turns to Crystal. "Would you excuse me for a minute?"

"Of course."

She moves to Aaron and embraces him. "Aaron, it is so nice to see you again!"

"Fascinating! Meeting you here, of all places." He glances at his watch. "It is 11:11, and it is the beginning of the new cycle," there is a gleam in his eyes.

"It is a bit odd, isn't it?"

"Do you remember my sister, Mariam?"

"Of course!" Rebecca eyes the unusual signet ring on her hand. They hug.

"I want you to meet my wife, Sierra, Charlie's mother." Aaron reaches for the brown-skinned woman.

Sierra had been silently observing the improbable gathering. "It is nice to meet you," She offers her hand to Rebecca.

"Likewise!" Rebecca is curious. "Whose idea was it to be here? Charlie's?"

"No. Sierra's," Aaron says.

"Interesting!" Rebecca looks at Sierra. "Where's my head?" She turns to Herman, then Crystal, and introduces everyone.

"Don't you find it odd," Sierra begins, "Three autistics meeting here at the end of the Mayan calendar?"

Rebecca turns to Ami, who is now very alert and standing with Charlie and Leilah. She grabs the letterboard and migrates beside Ami.

Sierra moves to the other side of her son, noting that Leilah was oddly glaring at her.

The rest of the group forms a circle.

"Ami, what is going on?"

`"It is time for my comrades and me to begin our work."`

"What kind of work?" Rebecca asks.

`"First, we need to rewrite the Master Plan."`

"*The* Master Plan?" Mariam asks.

`"Y."`

Rebecca and Herman glance at each other. "What Master Plan?"

"Our Prime Creator's plan or Golden Age's Master Plan for the planet to ascend to a higher vibration," Mariam says. "The plan to lift the world out of duality and into Love and Light. It's been the plan since the beginning of our universe."

Ami wants to add more, `"Creator's Master Plan needs a grace clause so that those who aren't ready, those stuck on the self, have an opportunity to ascend in future lives. Without such a clause, most will be destroyed and not ever ascend. Need to rewrite the Master Plan before that happens."`

"I don't understand. The Master Blueprint was set in the beginning," Mariam says. "How can we change it?"

"The Record Keeper needs to travel to the past and change it. It was part of a negotiation between the Dark and Light."

All eyes turn to Ami, wondering what she meant.

"Who is the Record Keeper?" Rebecca asks.

Rebecca facilitates the message. Her heart skips a beat when she reads the name; she even hesitates to say it aloud. Then she does. "Ishkamet."

She feels Ami's arm moving toward the board to type more.

"Mom, a higher aspect of you is the holy Record Keeper. You will handle this in a different realm, but I have the downloaded codes Ishkamet needs. Many will be grateful for this service."

Rebecca is thunderstruck. It takes her a beat to press on and continue Ami's message.

"After the clause is written, the group must journey to the NEW Earth."

"The New Earth? What do you mean by that?" Sierra asks.

"You need to find a way to the higher dimensions."

"I don't understand, Ami," Rebecca says. "How does going to another dimension help humanity? Aren't you here so that more people can ascend?"

"By going to the New Earth, then returning, you can teach others the way.

"Each here has a role to play in this mighty mission.

"Each is needed.

"Time is of the essence.

"We are now at the end of days."

Crystal had been quiet. She nervously grasps the large

cross hanging from the chain around her neck. "Does the end of days mean death and destruction?"

Leilah steps closer to Rebecca, who has the keyboard in hand. "Do you want to say something, Leilah?" She takes Leilah's arm to facilitate.

"End of days is a time-period before planetary ascension. Unclear how much time," Leilah says.

"If we somehow rewrite this Master Plan for people who aren't ready to ascend, will they return to Earth?" Aaron asks.

"Likely that life will be on a new planet for those not making the first jump," Leilah types.

"The *New* Earth is a place?" Sierra asks.

Charlie moves to Rebecca as if he wants to say something. Rebecca looks at Aaron, then Sierra, "Does he type?"

"We haven't had much success with it," Sierra voices.

"Let's try," Rebecca says and takes Charlie's almost gyrating hand. It takes a few minutes, then Rebecca feels Charlie is grounded and facilitates, reading aloud his message to the group.

"People need upgrades to get to the New Earth. We, autistics, can assist in this process."

"How do you know this, Charlie? Who are you?" Sierra asks her eighteen-year-old.

"I am the cellular sentry of the Universe. At every moment, I know about the cellular program of the Cosmos. I am the watchman to permit only worthy energetic vibrational patterns into the New Earth." With that expressed, Charlie looks directly into his mother's eyes.

To Sierra, it is the most compelling look she ever received from her son. It hits her that Charlie knows her dark side. She has many questions for him, but this isn't the time nor place.

At that moment, she wonders, 'Is my journey one of Light or Darkness?'

Rebecca continues Charlie's communication. "Opposition does not want us to succeed. As our masks unveil, there will be more threats from those influenced by negative entities and the entities themselves. All of us need safety here. Mom, your role is to provide safety."

As Sierra tries to understand what it means to provide safety, a woman's voice interrupts her thoughts.

"Fancy seeing you all here!"

Everyone turns and sees Levi approach their circle with a flute in hand. Her son, Josh, accompanies her.

A shriek of excitement escapes Charlie's lips when he sees Josh with the drum, and Charlie rocks back and forth.

"I thought you were going to the west coast for the holidays," Rebecca says.

"Me too! I had a feeling at the last minute that I needed to be in Sedona for the solstice.

Mariam is curious and moves closer to Levi. "Who are you?" She asks with a gleam of curiosity. She knows more than she lets on. She senses that the spirit James, who she had been communicating with, knows Levi. She sees him standing beside her in the ethers.

Levi smiles. "I am merely the witness. I am here to write *your* journey," she looks around at everyone, ending at Charlie, "Are you Jerhesa?"

It is Charlie who types, "No, I am Quasar! Mom is Jerhesa."

All eyes are on Sierra. Levi and Ami know how vital Sierra is to their journey's success.

Charlie types one last message, and Rebecca reads it aloud, "It is no accident that all of you are here. This is the holy tribe, and most of the gang is here. ALL have a role to play in the journey ahead. All have chosen to return and help humanity ascend."

While Charlie's message appears directed to those in the physical, he eyes the ring that tethers a djinni to Mariam's signet ring, the greatest djinn of all times. He also sees James, the mystery man who had controlled humanity for thousands of years, lingering in the ethereal plane above Mariam, Sierra, and Levi. Charlie knows James as his brother, Hakathriel, the fallen archangel. He smiles at him—happy to have this former adversary back on the same side.

Charlie knows that James, himself, and others present, are tweaks in the timeline to correct the course of what is to come. He knows there is one other timeline tweak that will not be welcome, but it is necessary, and with the thought, he looks toward Ami. He knows that Ami must assist the Record Keeper in rewriting the Master Plan.

"I hear a voice in my head," Levi says. "I believe it is Ami."

All eyes are on Ami.

"I can hear her, too," Sierra says.

"Ami is saying," Levi begins, "how much she loves you, Rebecca, and how much she will miss being with you in the physical."

Rebecca shoots a questioning look at her daughter, standing silently among them. There is a noticeable halo, a glowing globe of golden energy around her head.

"Ami! You have a halo!" Rebecca says a bit shocked, then Levi's words sink in. "What do you mean that you'll miss me?"

It is Sierra's voice that continues, "She is saying that she needs to go. If she stays any longer, she risks dying in the physical as her Higher Self cannot stay in her poorly formed body."

"But where she goes," Levi continues, "*is* a higher realm."

"And," Sierra continues, "she will be there to welcome us and assist us on our journey to the New Earth through Charlie."

Rebecca is shocked, 'Is this truly happening?'

"More importantly," Levi explains, "Ami will be there to assist our return *from* the New Earth so that we can share the keys to ascension so that others may ascend."

All eyes are now on Ami, and there is a lightness engulfing her tiny body. Then there is a translucence, and everyone can see through her.

Ami knows her ascension will be trouble-free. She solidifies, no longer translucent, yet engulfed in light. She looks at each person in the circle, and has a love exchange, imparting a clear private message to each.

> *'Levi, write the journey.'*
> *'Josh, you are powerful beyond belief.'*
> *'Leilah, thank you. We will continue talking.'*
> *'Crystal, be fuelled with curiosity.'*
> *'Charlie, it's time for you to take the reigns.'*
> *'Sierra, get ready for a rollercoaster ride.'*
> *'Aaron, your love for humanity is a gift.'*
> *'Mariam, don't wait too long to fill them in.'*
> *'Herman, take care of Mom.'*
> *'Mom, I love you.'*

While imparting her message to Rebecca, Ami reminds herself, *'I am Shawnami Kaliyuga, the flame of eternal life.'* With the thought, every molecule in her being vibrates at a higher frequency, and she becomes transparent. Just before she disappears from her mother and friends, two clear words escape her lips.

"Blue ray!"

Ami is gone and nowhere to be seen. Rebecca is down on her knees, sobbing, and Herman gently holds her.

The group silently huddles together for the longest time, surrounding Rebecca and Herman, arm-in-arm with Leilah and Charlie in the wings. Nobody says anything. What's to say? It is December 21, 2012, and while the general public had been expecting doomsday, in their circle, they witnessed a miracle, only the public will never know.

Charlie knows the truth. Ami ascended to a higher realm to provide a safety net to those not ready for ascension so they will have future lives. Without it, those souls, already traumatically injured, would fall in consciousness to the bottom if their plan fails.

Charlie, an Autistic Avatar, can maneuver between dimensions and is not impacted by the veil that obscures humanity from their truth. He is aware of the loop and the many timeline tweaks. He is here as a last-ditch effort to get humankind through this ascension and save the planet.

It is Charlie who will lead this group to the New Earth.

Epilogue

With every light side, there is a dark side. You cannot have one without the other. For humankind to evolve successfully, it must recognize that both the light and darkness need to coexist together. Anything short of this will lead to the destruction of the planet.

The stage is set. Thirty-six Autists walk the planet today, and they are from the twelve Galactic Suns, three from each Sun or Soul. They are here to heal, re-weave, and teach about humanity's Divine Nature and what it means to be a part of ALL THAT IS. Additionally, many Ascended Masters walk among you, some know it, while others are clueless. It is all part of the last-ditch effort to call off Earth's apocalypse and get the planet to ascend.

Unfortunately, I must say that while the Great Dark Brotherhood's leader has teamed up with the Light, for the betterment of both teams, this alliance is not well known to humanity. Many humans still promote agendas that serve the self rather than the whole. This avenue will lead to destruction. Some suggest that the Dark Team didn't get the memo.

Memo: We hope that Earth's occupants soon awaken to their Truth and re-member who they are.

I am Cerian

THE END

Thank you for joining the Blue Ray Alliance on this journey to the New Earth. If you loved the book and have a moment, I would appreciate a short review to help spread the message of awakening, and please know I am grateful for it.

Also, watch for the second book of *A Journey to the New Earth—THE DARK SIDE OF THE LIGHT.*

ACKNOWLEDGMENTS

I must start by thanking my son, Preston, for his friendship, his love, and for being my greatest teacher. Without him, this book would never have emerged. Also, I am grateful to my family for their love and encouragement, Dan, Tracy, Crystal, Tim, and Michael, and Joe and César. For all my relations, my parents, grandparents, aunts, uncles, and cousins, those here, and those transitioned, you're all a part of me.

For those directly and indirectly involved in this project, I can't thank you enough for being part of my awakening and the inspiration for this incredible story. I am forever grateful to the autists and the Autistic Collective, which continue to do the work for the planet. Thank you, Gayle and Lyrica, for asking me to write the journey, and asking again, after I said "no."

Daniel, thank you for repeatedly rocking my world. I am grateful to Adri for showing up in Waterton Canyon and changing the direction of the books. Thank you, Leslie, Austin, Sammie, and the other autistics for the messages, I'll keep listening. I am grateful to all the parents of the autists, Connie, Lee, Kristi, Gayle, Jose, Susan, to name a few; you are real angels.

I am thankful to Shauna, who has shown up big and introduced the lessons of Cerian, the archangels, and the Magdalene voices, of which I am also beholden. She has been my biggest cheerleader, reader, travel companion for grand adventures, and explorations with Team Blue Ray. And to Team Blue Ray, I love all of you and honor that you remain nameless, humble, in the shadows, doing the real work, and demonstrating genuine mastership.

For my friends, Susan, Michelle, Carolyn, Kathy, Sharon, Donna, Sandra, Kris, Madonna, Deb, Lori, Cindy, Linda, Lynne, Katy, you all have been patient with me as I isolated myself all these years to do the work. Thank you. Know that you have never left my heart. For Junia, I'm grateful to you and our Divine Adventures in Peru and France. I am appreciative of the spiritual community of Mile Hi Church, its members, leaders, both past and present. Thank you, Dr. Patty Luckenbach, Cynthia James, and Dr. Roger Teel, for your presence. Carol Anne Liaros and Henry Reed, you are amazing teachers, and to the Wayshowers, I miss our fun times.

And I am appreciative of the readers of the early drafts and marketing materials who provided feedback, Shauna Kalicki, Che, Connie, Sue Gallanter, Susan Bender, Kris Radish, Madonna Metcalf, Michelle McGowan and Joe Marcoux.

For my agent, Lisa Hagan, thank you, I haven't given up. For the editors, Rae Bryant and Laura Smyth, who made me sound good—you rock!

For my professional clients, I thank you for your business. Without you, I would not have the resources to take this journey. We have a great relationship, as I strive to help you live your dreams, you permit me to do the same.

I want to thank my fourth-grade teacher, Sister Clara. She said I was wrong when I said St. Peter was the one who betrayed Jesus. She said, "It was Judas." I told her that Judas was Jesus' best friend and most-loyal disciple. She called me a 'dumb Marcoux,' which fueled me with an inquisitive nature to seek the Truth, and expose it to heal the planet. That passion has never left.

I thank the countless authors, writers, teachers who have directly or indirectly inspired this text. Given this is lifework, there are too many to name, though I am deeply grateful.

Lastly, many wanted to be on Earth at this time to experience what is occurring. There are only so many vacancies, however. I am grateful without end to be here, and I strive to do my part.

APPENDIX

"Release Fear" Light Language Chant

The following Light Language provided by Daniel for humanity to release all fear.

Light Language is an ancient sacred code of Sound and Light. It is a multidimensional language that life forms understand at the soul-level and adjusts to each person's vibrational needs, initiating activation, balancing, clearing, and aligning to a new vibration of Wholeness.

Weassawea   (We Az Ay Wee Ay)
Rawedabefun   (Ray Wee Daw Be Foon)
Feswator   (Fee Sway To Are)
Weassawea   (We Az Ay Wee Ay)
Liesasuroesa   (Lee Say Su Row Ee Sah)
Sawaseaesa   (Saw As Ee Say)
Weassawea   (We Az Ay Wee Ay)
Asducaasa   (As Duke Az Say)
Ifespleeda   (Eye Fee Splee Dah)
Bapoprures   (Bay Po Pru Rez)

Biographies

Cerian

Cerian is a conscious, sentient, collective expression of an energetic field or vibrational pattern of beings from the sixteenth dimension. For more information, see "Who is Cerian" at https://alexmarcoux.com/glossary/cerian/.

Cosmic Christ, Jesus, Yeshua

The Cosmic Christ is an Ascended Master of the Cosmic Council or Great White Brotherhood. In other embodiments and expressions, he is Jesus or Yeshua. He is a member of the Blue Ray Alliance.

Gatekeeper of the Great White Brotherhood (or Cosmic Council)

The Gatekeeper of the Great White Brotherhood (or Cosmic Council) regularly embodies across time and space and reports back to higher levels of consciousness (the Ascended Masters) regarding events on Earth. This gatekeeper is a member of the Blue Ray Alliance.

Hakathriel

Hakathriel is an archangel, a member of the Cosmic Council who, in one incarnation, as an Anunnaki, was Enki and taught ancient secrets to humankind. For this, his brother, Enlil, dubbed him the angel of the bottomless pit, now known as Lucifer, the Devil, or Satan. Alienated from members of the Cosmic Council, he ruled and controlled humanity for eons. Hakathriel is a member of the Blue Ray Alliance.

Melchizedek

Melchizedek is an Ascended Master of the Cosmic Council. Much mystery remains on who Melchizedek is, though some suggest he is the king of righteousness, king of Salem, and the priest of the highest God. Others believe he was either Noah's son or grandson (from the biblical story of Noah and the ark). His energy and priesthood are associated with the Divine Father's energy, and he teaches many disciples.

Archangel Metatron

The prophet Enoch walked Earth for hundreds of years before he ascended, then transitioned to Archangel Metatron. He works with the new generations of children; Crystal Children, Indigo Children, and those seeking esoteric knowledge. Metatron is often associated with Metatron's cube, sacred geometry, and the Merkaba, and he is a member of the Cosmic Council.

Mikael, Archangel Michael

Mikael or Michael is an archangel, a member of the Cosmic Council, and a former opponent of Hakathriel. People often call upon Michael for protection against evil and the devil. He has teamed up with his brother to give humanity another opportunity at ascension.

Mother Ray, Mother Mary

Mother Mary or Mother Ray is an Ascended Master of the Cosmic Council, known in various embodiments, including the Essene known as Mother Mary, the mother of Jesus. She has embodied throughout many timelines to assist humanity in their spiritual evolution. She is a member of the Blue Ray Alliance.

Lady Anna, Anna the Grandmother of Jesus

Lady Anna is an Ascended Master of the Cosmic Council, who was in various embodiments, including the Essene known as the grandmother of Jesus. She lived for more than 600 years and worked with many celestial beings to bring together key players, including Mother Mary, Jesus, and Mary Magdalene, to participate in the events of that timeline. She is a member of the Blue Ray Alliance.

Magdalene, the Divine Feminine

Magdalene is an Ascended Master of the Cosmic Council, who in multiple embodiments including the Essene called Mary Magdalene, the consort of Jesus, as well as a master teacher. She is the Divine Feminine, and Gaia, planet Earth, is an aspect of Magdalene. She is a member of the Blue Ray Alliance.

Thoth, Ningishzidda, Hermes, Hermes Trismegistus

Thoth is a higher dimensional being, known during ancient Egyptian time as a god. He was also known as the Sumerian god, Ningishzidda, the Greek god, Hermes, and Hermes Trismegistus, the author of the Emerald Tablet. They were all the same being, and he was Anunnaki. Before the fall of Atlantis, Thoth worked jointly with Araragat and Ra to birth the synthetic Christ Consciousness Grid and built the pyramids. The three gods also relocated the Ascended Masters to three areas, Egypt, the Himalayas, and Peru, at the fall of Atlantis (the fall in consciousness).

Glossary

36 Righteous Ones

The Lamed-Vav Tzadikim, or 36 Righteous Ones, is a widely-held Jewish belief that in every generation, 36 righteous individuals walk this Earth to greet Shekhinah or the Divine Presence. Many segments in Judaism believe that the 36 Righteous One's role is to justify humankind's purpose to God. The 36 individuals would not be aware of their position, and if they become aware, they would never admit it, and they *must* remain hidden.

Akashic records

The Akashic records are a compilation of all events, thoughts, words, emotions, and intentions to have occurred in all multiverses in the past, present, and future.

Anunnaki

Before the ancient civilizations of Egypt, Rome, and Greece, a group of beings, "those who from heaven came," walked Earth. Humankind called the Anunnaki "gods" in the Sumerian, Akkadian, Assyrian, and Babylonian oral traditions, cuneiforms script, and cave art. Their stories continued in the myths of Egypt, Rome, and Greece, as well as other cultures. To Anunnaki experts, they were Nibiruans, of alien origin and involved in humankind's creation and the manipulation of humanity's DNA.

Autistic Avatars

There is a collective of autistics around the planet who help shift the frequency of Earth to impact a more significant population for spiritual ascension. They are the Awesome Ones.

Thirty-six nonverbal Autistic Avatars lead the autist-collective. Six of these Autistic Avatars are among the 36 Righteous Ones discussed in the Judaism tradition and remain hidden around the planet unknown to humankind. Some believe that 36 beings return to Earth in times of great peril to justify humanity's existence. Unfortunately, the other 30 Righteous Ones have fallen in consciousness and created falsehoods throughout time to suppress and control humanity. The Autistic Avatars are the heroes attempting to dissolve the distortions created by their fallen brothers and sisters. See "Galactic Suns."

Ascended Masters

Ascended Masters are Beings of Light who regained their union with the I AM through other lives and free will, ascending to higher realms. They raised their vibration, mastered the games, themselves, the elements, and re-membered who they were, returning to the One. Some Ascended Masters come from different universes, while others achieved the ascension in this universe. Some Masters have returned to the planet throughout time and space to assist in the spiritual evolution of humanity. See "Great White Brotherhood."

Ascension, The Shift

The ascension is the process of spiritual awakening that moves the individual into a higher level of consciousness and a higher, lighter vibrational frequency—shifting from a denser, egoic state of duality consciousness to more unity and heart-based consciousness. The ascent is moving to the New Earth. It is a conscious choice to engage in the evolution of humanity. It is also called the shift. See "New Earth."

Atlantis

Atlantis was an ancient civilization that existed for over two hundred thousand years in three different phases, beginning as a massive supercontinent and ending as islands in the Atlantic Ocean, destroyed between 10,500 BC and 9500 BC. Atlanteans lived in the higher dimensions and communicated telepathically, sharing a collective consciousness.

Attachments, Entity or Spirit Attachments

An entity attachment occurs when the energy or spirit of a deceased person or entity of a different dimension attaches to a living person. The unwelcome guest(s) usually connects to weaknesses in an individual's human energy field or aura and is typically undetected by the person.

Avyon, Avalon, and Maldek

Avyon, Avalon, and Maldek were three planets in our universe destroyed during a conflict between the Reptilians and Humanoids. Many souls on Earth today were involved in these catastrophes, leaving soul scars. The concern among the Ascended Masters is that, with Earth's destruction in the twenty-first century, many of the involved souls will devolve in consciousness and likely, not recover.

Blue Ray Alliance, The

The Blue Ray Alliance is a subgroup of the Cosmic Council, or Great White Brotherhood, who chose to embody in various timelines, including the twenty-first century, to assist humanity in achieving ascension, and averting the destruction of Earth.

Chakra and Meridian

Chakras are energy centers located in the spiritual bodies of a person. These centers channel the universal life force energy in and out of the physical and spiritual selves. Some refer to the life force energy as Qi/Chi, consciousness, or even the soul. The chakras are considered both transmitters and receivers of the energy and, at times, perceived as vortexes.

Meridians are energy paths in the body through which

consciousness flows. An individual achieves physical, emotional, mental, and spiritual health when the chakras and meridians are balanced. See "Light Body."

Chrysalis Gold Grid

The Chrysalis Gold Grid is a subset lattice of the Christ Consciousness Grid (Unity Grid and Ascension Grid) the autistics created so they can access the grid and perform gridding to upgrade it with the required patterning and technology to assist in the awakening and ascension of humanity. See "Planetary Grids."

Clairsentience

Clairsentience is the psychic ability of clear-feeling, which is more commonly associated with gut feelings and even empathy. It is an ability to tune into another person's physical and mental state and experience their energy also. A person who has clairsentience is clairsentient.

Clairvoyance

Clairvoyance is the psychic ability of clear-seeing, more commonly associated with visions, vivid dreams, daydreams, or seeing auras. A clairvoyant is one who has the psychic ability of clairvoyance.

Cosmic Council

See "Great White Brotherhood."

Crystal Children

See "New Children, The."

Crystal Skull

Crystal skulls are crystals carved into the shape of a head's skeleton. Some form human replicas, others alien. Most are modern, while some are from ancient times and reportedly programmed. The new crystals can be activated when around either ancient skulls or other activated skulls. As crystals, one can program crystal skulls to focus its energy on a specific goal or intention. The ancient heads contain hidden knowledge, offering a path to humankind's evolution to realize its divinity as a sacred human. See "Mitchell-Hedges Skull."

Crystal Skull Guardian

See "Guardian of the Skull."

Dark Team, or Dark Brotherhood

The Dark Brotherhood or Dark Team is a group of beings who are in service to the self, rather than the whole. They seek material wealth and control over others through power, hierarchy, and competition.

Diamond Children, The

See "New Children, The."

Download or Epiphany

An epiphany is a download of information. It is a sudden realization about something's meaning, an intuitive leap of understanding, or communication with Source. To a different degree, given that we are programs, we've made agreements to experience physicality, a download can be an inflow of knowledge, awareness, higher light frequency, or a consciousness update to our programs governing our mental and physical operating system.

Duality

Duality is having positive and negative that conflict; opposing forces that create contrast and potentially chaos. See "Polarity."

Earth–616

Earth–616 is the New Earth. Please note that Earth–616 has no connection with the fictional Earth 616 Marvel Comics multiverse and that any similarity is purely from the stream of consciousness. See "New Earth."

Ego

The ego is the self (lowercase "s"), which keeps the individual in density, in physicality (the illusion), believing that they are separate from the Whole and away from Source, God or the Higher Self.

Embodiment

The embodiment of the Higher Self is the infusion of Light from your Higher Self (I AM Presence, Oversoul) to your third–dimensional being. Humans are multidimensional and live in other domains simultaneously. Any person's embodiment of their Higher Self changes that individual's manifestations. Given that we are Creators, if we embodied our Higher Selves, our creations would be higher frequency manifestations. We would spark miracles and be a service to humanity.

End of Days

The *end of days* is a period preceding the Earth's ascension to a higher realm. It is also called the end times, final days, and others, often associated with a cataclysmic end on Earth. See "Master Blueprint."

Epiphany

See "Download."

Fall of Atlantis

About thirteen thousand years ago, in Atlantis, humankind descended from grace, fell out of a state of high consciousness, and lost awareness. The Atlanteans fell because they made poor choices, choices humanity currently faces. If natural evolution were to have taken place, it would have taken hundreds of thousands of years to reach the next level of consciousness. Humankind did not have that time before the precession of the equinox (12/21/2012). The concern among the Masters is that without evolving, humanity and Earth will perish if they do not reach the next level of consciousness. Master Thoth and friends built the synthetic Christ Consciousness Grid to provide an opportunity for humankind to ascend. The Masters have been working to bring about planetary ascension since the land of Lemuria. See "Planetary Grids."

Gaia

Gaia is the goddess, Mother Earth, and is the Divine Feminine in this universe. She is also the personification of fertility, creation, destruction, motherhood, and nature. She is an aspect of the Ascended Master, Mary Magdalene. See "Magdalene" in Biographies.

Galactic Suns

Suspend any previous teachings on God (Source) and Creation. Go back to before the creation of all universes and galaxies. Go back to the first breath of Source. The Galactic Suns are one of the first Emanations of Source Energy, Source's first exhale. In this first breath, there were/are many lineages of Great Beings that may be considered the first Soul expression, the twelve Galactic Suns, the Council of Twelve, the One. Within the first emanation are twelve languages of Source connected to all manifestations of Creation.

Thirty-six Autistic Avatars walk the planet today, forming twelve triads and twelve Galactic Suns. For each Galactic Sun, three Autistic Avatars form a triad that represents a Sun or Sol (Soul), and the trinity represents one Galactic Sun.

Thousands of autistics around the planet form an autist-collective that works with the twelve triads to heal, re-weave, and teach about humanity's Divine Nature and what it means to be part of ALL THAT IS. See "Autistic Avatars."

Great White Brotherhood (aka Cosmic Council)

The Great White Brotherhood is a group of Ascended Masters, beings who mastered the experiences of the games in other lifetimes and other universes, along with archangels, and unascended disciples (chelas). Many of the Great White Brotherhood and Sisterhood of Light (AKA Cosmic Council) are "game moderators," in the Humanoid Experiment, and were involved in the creation and Master Blueprint of the universe. Many Masters are teachers of humankind and have chosen to assist in humanity's spiritual evolution, though their identity remains hidden. See "Humanoid Experiment, The" and "Master Blueprint."

Gridding

Gridding is an action some autistics perform on the Christ Consciousness Grid. The Dark Team intentionally sabotages the grid to undermine the work of the autistics. When an autist senses that lifeforms consciously or unconsciously interact with the Christ Consciousness Grid and alter its perfection, the autists repair the matrix by gridding. See "Chrysalis Gold Grid" and "Autistic Avatars."

Guardians of the Skulls

A Guardian of the Skull is an individual who has worked with ancient crystal skulls in other timelines (lifetimes). The Mitchell–Hedges skull is an example of an ancient skull. In the current lifetime, a Crystal Skull Guardian would be drawn to crystal skulls and here to work for humanity at this time. See "Mitchell–Hedges Skull."

Higher Self

The Higher Self or Godself is where the collective consciousness begins, the Christ Consciousness exists, and the realm of sacred geometry. It is the True Self and the One. See the "Ego" and "Oneness."

Human Energy Field

Each human body comprises of overlapping energy patterns within the auric layers. The physical body itself is a condensed form of energy that we perceive as density, i.e., the physical body. Seven levels of consciousness extend beyond the physical body and represent the aura. Those layers are the etheric body, emotional body, mental body, astral body, etheric template body, celestial body, and spiritual body. These energy layers are where an individual's characteristics are stored. The energy patterns are unique to each individual. See "Light Body."

Humanoid Experiment, The

The Humanoid Experiment is a game in which every soul chose to participate; only the veil of consciousness obscures the Truth. It is one of the greatest deceptions of all time. Source (God) wanted to experience everything, creating darkness to experience polarity. Obstacles created, and veils to hide the Truth from humankind, make humanity's ascension nearly unachievable. Every soul is equally Divine and here to re-member, awaken itself and realize Itself and Its capabilities (i.e., each is a unique expression of the One). See "Illusion."

Illusion, The

We know that everything is energy. The third dimension (3D) is very dense and is a deception. The truth is that humankind exists in the higher realms, the Spirit realms, and through agreements and veils, it has a physical or "real" experience. What keeps the illusion formidable is the ego, which keeps the human separate from Its Higher Self. Humans are not separate from Source. To think that God is some distant entity that sits in judgment is also an illusion. See "Higher Self."

Indigo Children

See "New Children."

Intuition

Intuition is insight, inner knowing (without having a reason to know it). It is *knowing* from the Higher Self.

Lemuria

About seventy thousand years ago in Lemuria, one couple learned the secret to immortality and began a school, the Naacal Mystery School, to teach the process of ascension. At the time of its destruction, when the Lemurians fled, there were 999 Ascended Masters. Those teachers followed the spiritual energy of Earth to a rising landmass in the Atlantic, called Atlantis. There, the Masters created energetic vortexes, which drew the highly intuitive Lemurians to settle there, alongside Atlanteans. It also called in two other groups; one group, unfortunately, brought with it a new way of living, a way of life driven by their heads, not their hearts, which led to the fall of Atlantis. See "Fall of Atlantis."

Light Body

The Light Body (Lightbody) is the multi-level human energy field or auric body that extends our Consciousness through a holographic-like model or template, creating the illusion of physical manifestations people experience. The multiple-level energy field holds awareness throughout time and maintains a direct connection with the Higher Self, an extension of Source.

The Lightbody is also called the Merkaba Body.

When activated, the Light of the Lightbody reaches the physical body and affects the DNA causing changes on the cellular level. There are twelve levels of Lightbody activation elevating consciousness from the third dimension physical reality to the astral plane (fourth dimension), etheric Plane (fifth Dimension), cosmic plane (sixth–eleventh dimension), and ultimately the Higher Self (Eternal Plane). The Higher Self is also known as the I AM, the Oversoul, the Divine Presence.

See "Chakra and Meridian," "Human Energy Field," and "Merkaba."

Light Language

Light Language is an ancient sacred code of Sound and Light. It is a multidimensional language that all life forms understand at the soul-level and adjusts to each person's vibrational needs, initiating activation, balancing, clearing, and aligning to a new vibration of Wholeness.

Lightworkers

Lightworkers made pacts with their Higher Self. They come to Earth to help humans heal from the expressions of fear, or the ego. They have a deep calling to heal others and the planet. They are profoundly affected by our social and environmental problems and often become teachers, writers, or counselors.

They feel a sense of urgency, as time is of the essence, and a strong desire to find and fulfill their life's purpose. Some light-workers are starseeds. See "Starseeds."

Lucid Dream

A dream is *lucid* when the dreamer is aware that they are dreaming and can control the dream's events. In a lucid dream, the dreamer may ask for the dream's meaning or message.

Master Blueprint

The Master Blueprint is Prime Creator's plan set at the beginning of the universe's creation, also called the Golden Age's Master Plan for the planet to ascend to a higher vibration, to lift the world out of duality into Love and Light.

Medium

A medium is a specific type of psychic who mediates communication between an individual and spirits or other-dimensional entities. They may retain awareness of the events, whereas a *trance* medium generally goes into a trance, and when coming out of the trance, usually is unaware of what happens when the entity communicates.

Merkaba

The Merkaba (Mer Ka Ba or Merkabah) translates to light, spirit, body. It is a higher energy field that surrounds the body beyond the auric field. It is Divine Light (energy) and in everything. The Merkabah symbol is two intersecting tetrahedrons that spin in opposite directions, creating a three-dimensional energy field. The vehicle of light activates with meditation and breathing techniques. The Mer Ka Bah provides protection and transports consciousness to higher dimensions. It represents pure Divine Energy, continually spinning, harmonizing, balancing, flowing, moving, and expanding in all four directions at all times, supporting the individual where they want to go.

The Merkaba is the Light Body through which we travel to higher dimensions, higher planes of existence, to experience our multidimensional self. It is what the Ascended Masters use to reach their higher plane of existence. The Merkaba/Light Body is what transports us to the Higher Self, the I AM Presence, and the eternal plane.

Mitchell–Hedges Skull
The Mitchell–Hedges Skull is the only ancient crystal skull with a detachable jaw. It was carved from a single block of clear quartz, and there are no tool marks from its creation. Many believe that we do not have the technology today to create a skull with such precision. The skull was found in 1924 by F.A. Mitchell–Hedges in the ruins of an ancient Mayan pyramid. The anatomically correct head is representative of a female between twenty-five and twenty–nine years of age and Mesoamerican descent. Skeptics suggest that the Germans made it, others believe that the Atlanteans made it. The Mayans believe that some ancient skulls are rare and sacred gifts to the Mayans from the Grandfathers of the Pleiades. The Mayans believe that the crystals contain the consciousness from beyond our galaxy.

Multidimensional Being
Multidimensional beings are those who have other incarnations, other lives, in different dimensions, at the same time. Humans are multidimensional; only they are not aware of it and don't realize their physical experiences are illusionary. The simultaneous lives are considered different aspects of the person. It is our multidimensionality that explains the meaning of the saying, "we're spiritual beings having a human experience." See the "Humanoid Experiment."

Multiverse

The multiverse is multiple universes, also known as the omniverse, comprising all that exists, all space, time, matter, energy, and the physical laws and constants that define them. Some universes are parallel to each other and referred to as parallel universes, subsets of the multiverse.

Myth

When there are no words to explain profound concepts with complete accuracy, mythology offers a metaphor to convey a fundamental understanding. It does not mean the myth is false; it provides a rudimentary expression of truth.

New Children, The

The New Children are those children, who may now be adults depending on the generation, embodied to assist in humanity's spiritual evolution. The New Children are starseeds. See "Starseeds."

Indigo Children

Indigo Children are first-generation New Children. These people incarnated to bring about a new age of peace. Though not always, they were usually born throughout the late seventies to early nineties. They are typically sensitive and psychic and here to cause a change in society, the environment, and government so that the earth is a place of integrity. Often, they are the ones labeled as the rebels, troublemakers, and even the problem child.

Crystal Children

Crystal Children are second-generation New Children. These children or individuals started coming in during the mid-nineties and are still incarnating. They are here to usher the world into the New

Earth by showing how people can live in peace, kindness, and love. They are full of integrity and truth, and often are telepathic, though at times may be perceived as being slow or even autistic.

Rainbow Children

Rainbow Children are third-generation New Children. These starseeds started arriving around the turn of the century. It is their first *earthly* incarnation, and they are here to generate unconditional love and will play an essential role as they get older. They are higher dimensional beings who express pure love.

Diamond Children

Diamond Children are fourth-generation New Children, and some are first-timers on Earth. There is a small number of Diamond Children already here. Adult New Children must evolve to birth the Diamond Child, which fully embodies Divine Light. The Diamond Children possess the most advanced psychic skills, including telepathic communication, and telekinesis. They are also instant manifesters.

The concepts of anger, hate, fear, greed, and separation are as foreign to Diamond Children as the concept of Oneness is to the majority of the planet at this time. They resonate with Divine Pure Unconditional Love, the highest frequency. They hold the DNA patterning that awakens all those near them who are ready to overcome the illusion. They are walking healers. The Earth's frequency, however, must elevate to accommodate a significant mass of incarnating Diamond People. The Autistic Avatars assist with this work.

New Earth

The New Earth is the Earth in the next evolution or ascension of the planet, which exists in the higher dimensions. See "Ascension, The Shift," and "Earth-616."

Nibiru, or Planet X

Nibiru is the home of the Anunnaki, and while some speculate it to be a planet (Planet X), it is a remnant of a celestial body engineered to serve as a battlestar. Also, consider the possibility that there is more than one battlestar. See "Anunnaki."

Oneness

There is one energy, and that energy is God, and everything is a unique expression of God. Oneness is a state of being at One with Source, where there is no separation between the Self and Source (God) Energy. Unity is a state of re-membering with Source Consciousness, the Higher Self.

Planetary Grids

Spiritual energy grids or planetary grids are etheric crystalline structures of electromagnetic fields, templates, or matrixes that cover the earth and holds consciousness for a species. Each living species, including Mother Gaia, has a grid. There are three different planetary grids for humankind, the primal grid, humanity's existing consciousness grid, and the ascension grid (also known as the ascension grid, or Unity Grid or Christ Consciousness Grid).

Primal Grid

The primal grid is a crystalline matrix consisting of dodecahedrons embedded in the first dimension just below the third dimension and currently thought to be the planet's gravitational field. It holds the consciousness of the original people on Earth, like the Aboriginals, and was the primary consciousness of our Earth until the fall of consciousness in Atlantis. The grid has a relationship closer to Phi or the Golden Mean ratio, which links to patterns in nature.

Humanity's Existing Consciousness Grid

Humanity's existing consciousness grid is a crystalline matrix consisting of chains of icosahedron balls embedded in the lower dimensions from the first and second to just below the fourth dimension, which currently regulates electromagnetic systems such as vortexes and ley lines. It is presently the central consciousness grid for most of humanity, and rather than having a relationship with nature, it has one with duality consciousness, where ego and judgment thrive.

Christ Consciousness Grid, Crystalline Grid, Ascension Grid, or Unity Grid

The Christ Consciousness Grid is a synthetic etheric crystalline structure of double pentadodecahedron electromagnetic fields, a template, or a matrix that covers the earth and holds consciousness for ascended beings. It extends from the fourth through the twelfth dimensions. Ascended Masters, Thoth, Araragat, and Ra birthed the grid just before the fall of Atlantis to offer a path for humanity's ascension, which needs to occur before the end of a twenty-six thousand-year cycle. The Unity Grid was anchored in 1989 and fully activated on December 21, 2012. The ascension grid stretches across the surface of the planet. The matrix was created initially to reverberate a higher frequency for a path to the New Earth.

Many autistic individuals and Autistic Avatars work on this Unity Grid through gridding and make corrections when dark influences impact the structure. See "Gridding" and "Autistic Avatars."

Polarity

Polarity is having positive and negative that attracts each other, complementary forces that work together to create a balance. An example is light and dark. There can't be light without darkness, and Source created Darkness so that It could know Light. Polarities occur so that Source, or God, could experience more of Itself.

Precession of the Equinox

The precession of the equinox occurred on December 21, 2012. At that time, the sun, earth, and the center of the galaxy aligned. With that event, came the close of the Mayan calendar, ending a 25,625-year cycle. What most don't realize is that it is a cycle, and once it ended, we began anew, and Earth began pointing toward Aquarius, turned toward the light, and humanity began to awaken. It initiates the return of the Divine Feminine, where the Goddess energy restores balance and harmony, and humanity experiences a rebirth and shifts from polarity consciousness to Oneness.

Project Last-Ditch Effort to Save Earth
★★★SPOILER ALERT★★★

There was a cataclysmic failure in the early twenty-first century that destroyed Earth. Many of the planet's occupants had not healed from the significant soul scars from other planetary catastrophes on Avyon, Avalon, and Maldek. Rather than humans achieving the anticipated ascension, they once again fall from grace. This failure is a loop; it repeats.

The Cosmic Council (AKA, the Great White Brotherhood) executes a plan to give humanity one last chance for spiritual ascension by introducing timeline glitches. Some of the timeline tweaks include:

- Introducing a grace clause in the Master Blueprint of the universe
- The leader of the Dark Brotherhood returns to the Light
- Members of the Blue Ray Alliance and other Ascended Masters and archangels incarnate in human form in various timelines
- Autistic Avatars walk on the planet incognito, performing miracles to shift the frequency of Earth.

See "Master Blueprint," "Great White Brotherhood," "Dark Team," "Avyon, Avalon, and Maldek."

Sacred Sites

Sacred sites are areas around the world that connect to the Christ Consciousness or Crystalline Grid. One may think of this as where Earth's vortexes or ley lines come together. Lightworkers visit sacred sites around the world so that they will sit in the energy of the three planetary grids (primal, human, and Christ Consciousness Grids), which trigger awakenings. The Lightworkers then return home and serve as a conduit/transducer to help raise the frequency of the planet all over the world. See "Planetary Grids."

Serendipity

Serendipity is an event or situation which unfolds seemingly by accident or chance, which results in unexpected good, something beneficial, or a favorable outcome. It is the Universe's way of getting your attention and sending a sign to journey to the New Earth. Learn more in *Lifesigns: Tapping the Power of Synchronicity, Serendipity and Miracles* by Alex Marcoux.

Starseeds

Starseeds are beings who incarnated in human form from other worlds; in other words, other star systems and referred to as "alien." They walk amongst us as humans. Sometimes they know they are different while other times, they are clueless. Starseeds are often Lightworkers serving in the spiritual evolution of the planet. While there are many beings from other worlds, common ones are the Pleiadians, Sirians, Arcturians, and Reptilians. The New Children are Starseeds. At this time, approximately three percent of Earth's population is alien.

Synchronicity

Synchronicity is a meaningful coincidence orchestrated by the universe to provide guidance, a message, or confirmation that one is on the right path. Each person can work with synchronicity to improve their life and journey to the New Earth. Learn more in *Lifesigns: Tapping the Power of Synchronicity, Serendipity and Miracles* by Alex Marcoux.

Temple of Poseida, Temple of Light

The Temple of Poseida was a place of worship on one of the last standing islands of Atlantis, Poseida. At times it is confused with the Temple of Poseidon in Greece.

Third Dimension

The third dimension is the realm in which humankind lives, which is very dense and has a condensed form of consciousness. Each increasing level of dimension has rising awareness, frequency, and vibration.

Thirteen Skulls

In Atlantis, thirteen crystal skulls contained the consciousness, knowledge, and wisdom of everything since the beginning of humanoid forms on Earth, over two hundred fifty thousand years ago. This information included the Divine Blueprint of humanity, humanity's origin, purpose, destiny, and spiritual knowledge that can save the planet today. Twelve skulls each hold the consciousness of one of the twelve tribes, while the thirteenth skull, a Master Crystal stored the knowledge of all twelve tribes, and was transported to the sixth dimension, the Halls of Amenti during the fall of Atlantis. See "Crystal Skulls," "Fall of Atlantis."

Tiamat

Tiamat is a planet that, in this multiverse, was pulverized during the Anunnaki-Reptilian wars, and half of the planet became fragmented, remaining in the asteroid belt, while the other half exists today as Earth. Given that we live in a multiverse, the Tiamat exists whole in different dimensions where Earth does not exist.

In our universe, Gaia (Mother Earth) is undoubtedly a remnant of Tiamat. Given that Mary Magdalene is an aspect of Gaia, it is not a stretch that Magdalene is also an aspect of the precursor to Earth (Tiamat).

The ancient Babylonian history records that Tiamat was a goddess of the sea who mated with the god of freshwater (Abzû) and produced young gods. These young gods were called monsters (dragons). The myth says she was the dragon-mother who was killed by Marduk, an Anunnaki. Some suggest that Tiamat is a symbol of chaos in creation.

Walk-in

The term walk-in soul or spirit refers to a situation where a person's original soul departs his or her body (walks out), and a new, often more advanced soul replaces it. At times, soul braiding occurs where either a higher aspect of the same soul or an advanced soul walk in, and both souls agree to occupy the same physical body for a higher purpose.

Watchers

Often Watchers are referred to as angels, particularly the arch-angels, who watch over humanity. They are fallen angels and referenced by Watchers in sacred texts, including the Book of Daniel as well as Enoch, where the Watchers observed Eden. There are many parallels between the biblical stories of the Watchers, and the ancient Sumerian text, which predates the sacred writings, suggesting that the Watchers were Anunnaki and the Nephilim were half-human and half-Anunnaki.

About the Author

Alex Marcoux was welcomed into a world few people see, the sacred mysteries and magic of autism. When asked by three nonverbal autists to make known their truth, *The Unsuspected Heroes,* the first book of *A Journey to the New Earth* book series, emerges. Marcoux is the winner of the Living Now Book Awards Silver for *Lifesigns: Tapping the Power of Synchronicity, Serendipity and Miracles.* Regarding her fiction, #1 *New York Times* bestselling author Lisa Gardner says, "Fasten your seatbelt and prepare for a wild ride." She is also a Lambda Literary Award Finalist, a Golden Crown Literary Award Finalist, and recipient of the RMFW Penn Award. Marcoux is the screenwriter and collaborating director for *Back to Salem: The Short* film (2008). Her other novels are *A Matter of Degrees, Back to Salem,* and *Facades* (The Haworth Press and Bella Books). *Lifesigns* (Jenness) is also internationally published (Golden Turtle Press). Learn more about Alex at AlexMarcoux.com.

Made in the USA
Middletown, DE
08 September 2022

72480692R00210